DESIRE'S DAWNING

"Lee-lee, I've got to kiss you," Timothy whispered, cupping her face in his hands. "I've got to kiss you now."

When his lips tenderly met hers, Lee-lee closed her eyes and savored the wonder of his love. Never had she felt anything as beautiful as the delicious warmth now spinning around inside her.

Timothy surrounded her with his strong arms and drew her into his embrace as his kiss grew deeper and more demanding. Unable to stop herself, and unwilling to try, Lee-lee entwined her arms about his neck and returned his kiss with all the passion he had awakened.

Understanding her message of submission, Timothy began to caress Lee-lee's luscious curves, explore her innocent beauty. Lee-lee knew she should stop him, knew she should pull away, but her body cried out for more of Timothy's exquisite torture. Never had she felt so alive as she did at this moment. Now that she was finally able to choose something for herself—if only for one night—she would choose Timothy and the ecstasy he brought her. She longed to learn the secrets of desire, to fill the emptiness in her soul. She wanted it all . . .

THE BEST IN ROMANCE FROM ZEBRA

TENDER TORMENT (1550, $3.95)
by Joyce Myrus

Wide-eyed Caitlin could no more resist the black-haired Quinn than he could ignore her bewitching beauty. Risking danger and defying convention, together they'd steal away to his isolated Canadian castle. There, by the magic of the Northern lights, he would worship her luscious curves until she begged for more tantalizing TENDER TORMENT.

SWEET FIERCE FIRES (1401, $3.95)
by Joyce Myrus

Though handsome Slade had a reputation as an arrogant pirate with the soul of a shark, sensuous Brigida was determined to tame him. Knowing he longed to caress her luscious curves and silken thighs, she'd find a way to make him love her to madness — or he'd never have her at all!

DESIRE'S BLOSSOM (1536, $3.75)
by Cassie Edwards

Lovely and innocent Letitia would never be a proper demure Chinese maiden. From the moment she met the dashing, handsome American Timothy, her wide, honey-brown eyes filled with bold desires. Once she felt his burning kisses she knew she'd gladly sail to the other side of the world to be in his arms!

SAVAGE INNOCENCE (1486, $3.75)
by Cassie Edwards

Only moments before Gray Wolf had saved her life. Now, in the heat of his embrace, as he molded her to his body, she was consumed by wild forbidden ecstasy. She was his heart, his soul, and his woman from that rapturous moment!

PASSION'S WEB (1358, $3.50)
by Cassie Edwards

Natalie's flesh was a treasure chest of endless pleasure. Bryce took the gift of her innocence and made no promise of forever. But once he molded her body to his, he was lost in the depths of her and her soul. . . .

Available wherever paperbacks are sold, or order direct from the Publisher. Send cover price plus 50¢ per copy for mailing and handling to Zebra Books, 475 Park Avenue South, New York, N.Y. 10016. DO NOT SEND CASH.

DESIRE'S BLOSSOM

CASSIE EDWARDS

ZEBRA BOOKS
KENSINGTON PUBLISHING CORP.

ZEBRA BOOKS

are published by

Kensington Publishing Corp.
475 Park Avenue South
New York, N.Y. 10016

First printing: March 1985

Printed in the United States of America

*With much love and warmth
I dedicate Desire's Blossom
to my Uncle Howard and
Aunt Hazel Martin;
Aunt Aggie (Agnes Osborne),
and
Aunt Gert (Gertrude Crist)*

*If you but knew
How all my days seemed filled with dreams of you,
How sometimes in the silent night
Your eyes thrill through me with their tender light,
How oft I hear your voice when others speak,
See you 'mid other forms I seek—
Oh, love more real than though such dreams were true,
If you but knew. . . .*

—Anonymous

Prologue

Only half-conscious, eight-year-old Letitia Taylor felt herself being lifted from the floor of the longboat. Limp from many days of drifting at sea, she welcomed the strong arms about her and laid her cheek against a cool, splendid touch of silk. Beneath this chest of steel she could hear the strong thuds of a heartbeat as her rescuer began running with her, and all around she heard voices speaking some strange sort of language.

Hazily, she remembered that only a few had survived the monstrous crash of waves that had capsized the ship on which she and her family had been traveling. As far as she could gather, her father had handed her over the ship's railing into the arms of another who had been waiting in a longboat.

The rest was just a blur. The fate of her father, mother, and older brother, Richard, was unknown to her. There had been days of just floating beneath the merciless rays

9

of the sun. There had been no food. There had been no drinking water . . . only days upon end of watching for land.

Huddled against this man who smelled strongly of perfume and spices, Letitia licked her parched lips and tried to open her burned, swollen eyelids. But the pain was too great, and she feared that even her eyeballs had been singed for life by the sun.

Her stomach no longer growled from hunger. It felt like an empty, dead crater, only coming to life now as the aroma of fried fish floated through the air toward her.

Mercifully, she fell into a soft doze, only to be awakened suddenly as she was forced to stand on her feet. With weak, trembling knees she stood there, barefoot, feeling a strong hand on her right elbow steadying her. She blinked her eyes, once more trying to see. But still unable to, she just listened without understanding one word of the gibberish being spoken before her.

"Youngest Son, what is this?" Mandarin Heung-Chin Yeung said as he rose from his red velvet chair. "This time you bring a waif from your adventurous play around Port of Foochow?"

"*Ai*, Father," Tak-Ming said humbly, wishing for approval. Being only fifteen and the sixth of six sons, he often felt out of favor with his rich mandarin father. Perhaps this gift . . . this child-woman . . . could win him some badly needed recognition.

Tak-Ming's bold, black eyes followed his father's careful, proud steps, admiring him anew. His father had such a look of authority, clad in his embroidered silks with decorative birds on his gown symbolizing that he

10

was a commissioner, a civil official of the Chinese Empire.

Ai, his father was the Lord of the House of Yeung—a mandarin with a high position in the rich city of Foochow, the walled capital of Fukien Province in China. If his father ordered that a head should roll, the deed would quickly be done!

"Where *did* you find this waif, Youngest Son?" Heung-Chin said, still studying her.

"She was in a longboat with other foreign devils. It drifted to shore."

"And the others? What is their fate?"

"All dead, Father."

Short, stout, strong, and sturdy, Heung-Chin strolled casually around his son and the pitiful excuse of a girl standing beside him. "Hmm," he said, kneading his chin. "And what am I do to with her?" His dark, almond-shaped eyes took in the brilliant red of the young girl's hair. He was unable to see the color of her eyes because her lids were red and swollen partially closed. But he knew to expect a creamy white flesh beneath the burn of her skin. Her clothes were tattered and torn and her smell wasn't pleasant, but Heung-Chin was already envisioning how she could be at possibly age eighteen. . . .

"You ask what you are to do with her, Father?" Tak-Ming said humbly. "Why, anything you *wish*. She is my gift to you. Do you approve?"

"*Ai. Hao*," Heung-Chin said, nodding favorably.

Tak-Ming smiled with pride. "And what *shall* we do with her, Father?" He gave Letitia a half glance. "Shall I take her to be trained as a serving woman?"

11

"*Nay*," Heung-Chin said. He toyed with his curved, gray mustache, then ran a hand over his bald head. "She shall be raised as my daughter in the House of Yeung."

Tak-Ming gasped and took a wide step away from Letitia. "*Puh-kao!*" he exclaimed. "She is a barbarian. She is a foreign devil's child!"

"*Howla, howla!*" Heung-Chin snarled, taking Tak-Ming by his shoulders to shake him. "You doubt your father's intelligence?"

"*Nay*," Tak-Ming murmured, swallowing hard.

"The salvation of my soul has been secured with the blessing of six sons to worship at my ancestral tablet. Now our house needs a daughter," Heung-Chin said. "Perhaps one day she will even be offered as Imperial Concubine to the Son of Heaven, our beloved Emperor Tao Kuang."

"Father, a . . . a . . . concubine?" Tak-Ming asked, only in a whisper.

"*Ai*," Heung-Chin said, nodding. He stepped away from Tak-Ming and lifted Letitia's hair, studying it. "And she will be made to look like a mandarin's true daughter. She will be dressed in the finest silks, her face will be painted, and her hair will be changed from that barbarian red color to that of the Chinese . . . a beautiful color of black."

Heung-Chin's gaze fell upon a glitter of gold at Letitia's neck where her torn dress gaped partially open. His eyebrows rose with interest. He looked more closely and saw that hanging around her neck on a gold chain was a locket in the shape of a heart. He reached for it but was not allowed to touch it as her hand crept upward, blocking his way. . . .

Letitia raised her trembling fingers and bravely covered her locket, never wanting to part with the only thing that she now possessed that had a link to her family. Inside the locket was a lock of her mother's gorgeous red hair. And the necklace had been a special gift given to her by her older brother, Richard, on her seventh birthday— a rare gift from a brother who usually ignored her. His initials, which had been engraved on the back of the locket, were now actually imprinted on her chest like a brand, for the steady, scorching rays of the sun beating down on her those many days had fused the necklace to her skin.

Heung-Chin was alarmed at this young girl's defiance of him. Then he laughed throatily. "So she has spirit," he said. "But, of course, she would. To survive the perils of the sea as she has, one would have to be strong, both in body *and* mind."

He cupped her chin. "And, spirited one, what do you call yourself?" he asked in English, a language with which he had some familiarity because of his dealings with the Americans who traded at the Port of Foochow.

Letitia licked her lips, then softly replied. "My name is Letitia. Letitia . . . Taylor . . ."

Tak-Ming laughed mockingly. "What does she say, Father? She speaks in such a strange way!"

Heung-Chin's dark eyes gleamed. "She says her name is Letitia. But she will be called Lee-lee now that she is of the House of Yeung. . . ."

13

Part One

Foochow, China

Ten Years Later

1849

Chapter One

A lone wick burned in bean oil on the blackwood dressing table which displayed many porcelain cosmetic pots and bottles of various perfumes. The aroma of sandalwood hung heavily in the air.

Lee-lee lowered herself to her knees on a kneeling mat placed before a mirror inlaid with mother-of-pearl and scrubbed her face desperately with a soft cloth. Soon she would have the rice powder and vermilion paint removed and she could once more see her natural skin coloring.

So often she wondered if the complexion on her oval face would ever be truly the same again. She knew that she had changed due to circumstances beyond her control. She could so vividly remember her father bragging about her, saying that her expression was that of one gentle, bright, and intellectual.

She hoped to be able to say that she was still all these things, but there was more to her personality now. There was a daring quality about her, and her tomorrows depended on it. She was fighting for her survival!

Sighing, she stopped to look at her hair. She had

removed the elaborate headdress required of her each day and now her hair hung in thick waves, black and long, across her shoulders and down her back.

Lifting its shiny silkiness, she was remembering its original color of red and hated now, even more than before, the dyes that Mandarin Heung-Chin Yeung had ordered for her hair to make her appear less "the barbarian from the foreign soil of America. . . ."

"*Ai.* By fate I am now of the House of Yeung, a part of the Chinese culture," she whispered. "But for how much longer?"

Her beloved adopted brother, Tak-Ming, had warned her that one day soon she might be sent to Emperor Tao Kuang, possibly to become an Imperial Concubine. If that were done, her free spirit would be stifled . . . forever.

Resuming her face scrubbing, Lee-lee was now even more determined to go with Tak-Ming this night, to share adventures with him on his clipper schooner. If the Fates granted them the chance, they planned to one day soon leave China behind them and seek their freedom together—in America.

But before this could become a reality, many more silver dollars had to be earned, and Tak-Ming had found the quickest, though not the most honorable way to make their fortune. Opium. The illegal trade of opium.

"Lee-lee, open the door."

Lee-lee turned with a start, eying her closed bedroom door. Her heart began to race, having recognized Tak-Ming's voice. Fearing his discovery outside her door by another member of the Yeung family, she hurried and

18

ushered him in. In her graceful, green brocade gown, she clutched Tak-Ming's arm anxiously.

"Well? Is it done? Did your journey prove profitable?" she whispered, her honey-brown eyes brilliant with excitement.

Tak-Ming swung his tall, strong Manchu physique away from her, making it impossible for her to see his smooth, large-featured face with a nose that curved downward and eyes that were black and proud. His hair, black and shining with perfumed oils, lay braided in a man's queue down his back, and he wore a padded tunic, leggings, and straw sandals.

"Tak-Ming," Lee-lee persisted, stepping into his view, "is there a sufficient supply of opium to sell tonight so we might build up our savings for our journey to America?"

Tak-Ming reached a hand to trace the gentle curves of her creamy white face. Most of the cosmetics had been removed. Her eyebrows were still blackened and arched, and the pencil-thin lines at the corners of her eyes were still drawn—all of which contributed to her masklike Chinese appearance.

Though Tak-Ming wished he had time to choose his words more wisely, he knew that one word—time—had just recently become his and Lee-lee's enemy. He dropped his hand to his side as their eyes met and held.

"Before speaking of opium, I must tell you that there is to be a choosing for the Emperor's household much sooner than I had at first thought," he quickly blurted. "A choosing of concubines, Adopted Sister Lee-lee. You do know what this means, do you not?"

Lee-lee paled. Her insides grew cold. "You are saying

that I . . . may . . . soon be sent to the Imperial Palace?"

"*Ai*," Tak-Ming murmured.

"Have I truly fallen out of such favor with my adopted father, Heung-Chin, that he would remove me from the House of Yeung . . . so inhumanely . . . as if I were some sort of . . . animal?"

"It has been his plan to do so since the day I found you almost lifeless in that boat those many years ago," Tak-Ming said.

Lee-lee shook her head mournfully. "Perhaps it would have been best if you had left me to die that day," she sighed.

"If I hadn't taken you from the boat, someone else would have," Tak-Ming said. "You could have ben raised as an *unfortunate*, while in the House of Yeung you have been blessed in many ways. You have been raised as the daughter of the great Mandarin Heung-Chin Yeung. You have been honored with silks and jewels. You could have been sold at an earlier age and used as one even lower than a serving woman."

Lee-lee moved quickly into Tak-Ming's arms. Twenty-five now with muscles rippling beneath his satin flesh, he was a handsome man, but to Lee-lee he was a true substitute brother and as such she couldn't have loved him more.

"Tak-Ming, I will never be able to thank you enough for all that you've done for me," she said softly. She felt the love returned by his strong embrace, and it was now hard to remember how at first he had been resentful of her presence in the House of Yeung. When she had begun teaching him how to speak in English and had

20

shared with him such fascinating, glamorous tales of America, a strong bond had quickly formed between them.

"Do I not speak fluently in English?" Tak-Ming said, looking down into her eyes. He wasn't like his father in size. Tak-Ming was tall and square shouldered. Looking down at Lee-lee, who came to his shoulder, he was proudly reminded of his gift of height.

As he searched Lee-lee's face, now seeing her vibrant, almost heart-stopping features, the child of eight that he had first known could no longer be found. The cheeks which had been sunken with pallor were round, firm, and now rosy from her incessant scrubbings. Her honey-brown eyes, veiled with thick, silken lashes, were provocatively beautiful, and her ruby, smiling lips were still awaiting their first kiss from a man.

Tak-Ming had felt the stirrings of how a man felt toward a woman since Lee-lee's first true buddings into womanhood, but he hadn't dared to touch her. His respect for her was too great as were her feelings for him. He wouldn't risk destroying the warm, comfortable relationship they enjoyed. One day he would find an appropriate maiden—one of his Chinese culture. This was as it should be . . .

"*Ai*, you speak quite fluently in English," she said, smiling. "Do I not speak as well in Chinese?"

Tak-Ming laughed and nodded his head. "*Ai*," he said. "But what I was wanting to say to you is that the time spent in learning *your* ways has been reward enough for what you say I have done for you."

"Soon you will have the opportunity to use your

English in America," Lee-lee said. "I have to ask you again. Did you acquire sufficient opium for selling, Tak-Ming?"

Ten years before, Lee-lee had at first felt a soft pity for this sixth son born into the House of Yeung. All of Heung-Chin's sons, except for Tak-Ming, were scholarly. Yet Tak-Ming was better skilled with his hands. Having learned how to repair derelict sampans and junks for profit, he had made enough money to purchase an old clipper schooner which he also repaired and had put to use for the trade of silk, tea, and the illegal opium.

Tak-Ming's father had humored his son, whom he thought to be a half-wit, and had let him have his ship and journeys at sea, quite unaware of Tak-Ming's opium dealings. And Tak-Ming's brothers, taunting and malicious though they were, had grown happy about Tak-Ming's hobby. With him away so often from the House of Yeung, he was less frequently in competition for their father's good opinion.

"*Ai*," Tak-Ming said proudly. "The most favorable transaction was made at sea. A great ship from Malwa was happy to make the trade for the rich silks and tea I offered. Now I will trade the opium cargo for silver coins. It was told to me that an American ship will be waiting for such a trade on the Min River."

A flush rose to Lee-lee's cheeks. She hurried toward her bed. "Then I must hurry and change my clothes to look like you," she said, breathless with building excitement.

"Why do you see the need to change clothes?" Tak-Ming asked, following along behind her.

22

"Because I am going *with* you," Lee-lee said matter-of-factly.

"*Nay. Puh-kao,*" Tak-Ming said, shaking his head vigorously back and forth. "It is too dangerous!"

A candle glowed in a carved brass ball suspended from the ceiling beside Lee-lee's tall, heavily carved bed. Little drawers with brass handles embellished the lower sides of the bed, and red curtains brightly designed with the shapes of many fabled, graceful phoenixes hung about it.

Lee-lee dropped to her knees and opened a drawer. "Tak-Ming, it is dangerous for me now, is it not, to stay here in my room awaiting my fate?" she asked. She removed a padded tunic, leggings, and straw sandals from the drawer, to match Tak-Ming's chosen night attire. She reached up and placed all these things on her bed, then rose determinedly to her feet.

Going to Tak-Ming, Lee-lee took his hands in hers. "You promised, Tak-Ming," she pleaded. "You are even the one who brought me these special clothes. I shall even hide myself beneath the ugliness of that drab rattan hat that I've also kept hidden for this exciting adventure on your ship."

Tak-Ming tore away from her, his eyes and jaw set boldly. "That was before piracy became so rampant in the East China Sea and now even the Min River," he said, doubling a fist angrily at his side. "These pirate fleets are terrorizing Chinese river towns and coastal villages. Deaths are many. And they seem to be able to sniff out an opium shipment."

"Have you ever known me to be frightened of anything?" Lee-lee scoffed, already loosening the satin sash from around her tiny waist. "Do you forget that it was I who survived the shipwreck those many years ago? As far as I know, I was the *only* one to survive. Doesn't that prove much about my endurance, Tak-Ming?"

"And Father? Are you not even afraid of him?" Tak-Ming asked, showing doubt in the scowl etched on his face.

Lee-lee paused, placing a forefinger to her chin, contemplating this question. Then she grabbed her clothes from the bed, hurried to a fancy folding screen of molded ivory and rich colored lacquer, and stepped behind it. "No," she said flatly. "Not even him, Tak-Ming." She slipped her dress from over her head, then softly murmured, "But I *do* fear his decision to take me to the Imperial Palace."

"*Ai* . . ." Tak-Ming said sadly, turning his back as he saw Lee-lee's dress being tossed aside, onto the bed. "And so you should."

"If I were a true daughter of Heung-Chin Yeung, what I have planned tonight would bring shame to the Yeung family. I would insult my ancestors," Lee-lee said, fussing with the hated breast binder painfully wrapped tightly around her breasts. She hadn't placed this on just for the purpose of her masquerade this night. In truth, she wore it each and every day. No maiden was allowed to protrude in front. She had to appear as flat as a boy according to Chinese custom.

"Well, Tak-Ming," she continued. "I am of no blood relation to your Chinese family, so your ancestors will not be disturbed now or ever by anything I do."

"Instead it is I who shame my ancestors," Tak-Ming

said, shaking his head. "If father should ever find out that it was I who let you accompany me on my illegal adventures. . . ."

His heart could never feel brave when his mind would not forget the wrath of his mandarin father and the power his father possessed in the Chinese community. Should a son shame such a father . . . the punishment would be severe, slow, and agonizing.

Lee-lee quickly slipped into her straw sandals, having already donned her padded tunic and leggings. "If Heung-Chin should ever find out that you are using your ship for anything other than trading silks and tea and spices, your head will roll Tak-Ming," she said. "You know how opium is hated by the Son of Heaven, Emperor Tao Kuang. He does not want it to be a part of the Chinese culture no matter what the British have had to say about it since they won the dreaded 'opium war,' as it was called."

"The British who assaulted and forced trading agreements upon my people think they won, but they did not," Tak-Ming growled. "China and all Chinese ports will always belong to the Chinese. One day the British merchants will see who is the strongest."

Lee-lee, now fully dressed, stepped from behind the screen. She lifted her hair from her shoulders. "Tak-Ming, please braid my hair into a man's queue. I must not look at all female this night."

"*Ai*," Tak-Ming said. He busied his fingers braiding her hair, loving the feel of it. Not coarse like his, hers was the texture of expensive silk. "The streets of Foochow at night are not safe, even for a man."

"But, Tak-Ming, we will not be traveling the streets.

25

We will use the secret passageway, won't we?"

"*Ai*..."

"But even the streets would be welcome," Lee-lee said, squirming in her impatience to be gone. "It is this house that I wish to be away from."

"Your hair is now braided," Tak-Ming said, stepping away from her. "Now we must go. The American ship will not tarry long in the waters of the Min River should my ship not be there to make the trade."

Lee-lee plopped her wide-brimmed, high-peaked, rattan hat on her head. "Then let's go, Tak-Ming," she said eagerly. "You just don't know how long I've waited for this sort of adventure. It takes all my willpower to watch my days idly slip by, embroidering with the rest of the girls my age. A life filled with embroidery and foolish gossip is not my cup of tea!"

Her eyes took on a look of wonder. "And to be so near an American ship, Tak-Ming! Just imagine! If not for our joint plans to travel one day to America together, I might even be tempted to stow away on the American ship."

"*Puh-hao*!" Tak-Ming snarled. "Never! The men who travel those ships *are* foreign devils. Do not ever go near them without me at your side."

Lee-lee laughed nervously. "I was only jesting, Tak-Ming. Do not get so upset so easily."

"It is *buh-hao-eesa* to jest in such a manner," Tak-Ming scolded.

"Oh, Tak-Ming," Lee-lee sighed. As she pulled the brim of her hat far down over her forehead, the blackened, false arch of her eyebrows and the pencil-thin lines at the corners of her eyes helped to make her appear Chinese. But no matter how else they had tried to make her look a man, the soft curve of her face, her lustrous lips, and her creamy-soft complexion would show that she was all female—and American—should someone stop and take a closer look.

It *was* daring to leave the House of Yeung without her face all cosmetic covered! But it had to be that way, for to look the part of a man, all powders and vermilion had to be left behind!

"Adopted Sister Lee-lee, we must leave your room in extreme silence," Tak-Ming encouraged, gripping her right elbow as he slowly opened the door. "Our footsteps must be as light as feathers!"

"Tak-Ming," Lee-lee softly scolded. "How many times do I have to ask you? Please do not address me in such a way. *Ai*! I *am* your adopted sister. But my name is Lee-lee. Please just call me Lee-lee! How will it look once we reach America if you are still calling me Adopted Sister?"

She had grown used to the fact that her name Letitia had been taken from her as if it had never existed. "Lee-lee" had been forced upon her but had become acceptable to her long ago.

"I will try to remember," Tak-Ming said, frowning at her. "But, Lee-lee, calling you Adopted Sister is a way to remember your place in my life. I am a man and you are a woman. So often I find myself lost . . . in your . . . love-liness."

Feeling a blush rising, Lee-lee looked away from him. Then she giggled as her gaze moved back to him. She gently touched his smooth cheek. "You do tease so," she whispered. "And, Tak-Ming, you choose such a crazy moment in which to do your teasing. We should be all serious now as we venture away from the estate of Yeung."

Tak-Ming's bold, black eyes looked momentarily down at her as silence prevailed between them. Then he laughed hoarsely. "*Ai*. You are right," he said. "I am stupid and careless in my timing."

"You are not stupid," Lee-lee quickly defended, knowing how Tak-Ming was sometimes looked upon as being a half-wit because he was not one of the scholarly sons of Mandarin Heung-Chin. "I do not want to hear you downgrade yourself like that. Let's hurry on, Tak-Ming. Let's go to our secret passageway before someone discovers us here, peeking from my door."

"*Ai*," Tak-Ming said, placing an arm about her waist. He began guiding her down a softly lighted corridor with red-stained beams and walls heavily decorated with paintings and beautifully polished gold work. The corridor smelled of incense, and foot long embossed candles in gold holders flickered only occasionally along the walls, producing a mystical sort of atmosphere through which Lee-lee and Tak-Ming made their way.

All was peaceful in the House of Yeung and somewhere behind one of the closed doors someone was passing the evening hours plucking the strings of a lute.

"We must hurry," Tak-Ming once more encouraged as he opened the heavy, red-lacquered door that led out onto the courtyard grounds.

Lee-lee stepped out next to him, glancing quickly about her. The sky was a black satin color speckled by the sequins of stars, and the moon was full with a haze encircling it.

The fragrance of a budding dwarf plum tree pleasantly touched Lee-lee's nose as she watched the courtyard lanterns casting shadows in waving light along the series of buildings which made up the House of Yeung.

"I see no one," Tak-Ming whispered. "Let's move onward."

Lee-lee didn't speak but just nodded her head and followed stealthily along beside him. If she squinted her eyes and looked hard enough she could see the great wall in the distance that protected this Chinese family's rich estate. She knew that Heung-Chin had ordered its construction not only to keep *undesirables* out, but to also keep certain members of his family in as well.

Smiling coyly, she felt smug to know that though the wall was tall and the gate was securely locked for the night, neither would hinder Lee-lee and Tak-Ming. They had found a secret passageway that led beneath the great family wall and on past the heart of the city of Foochow, to the waterfront.

From its decay and stench it seemed the passageway had most surely been there, undetected, for hundreds of years. But Lee-lee had been the one blessed by fate to have found it . . .

It had been on a November day when the wind was blowing falling wisteria pods around like tiny, dancing elves. Lee-lee, only twelve at the time, had been alone in the courtyard, running and collecting these pods, when she had wandered into a thick stand of tall *lanmu* trees. Elbowing her way through the trees, feeling wickedly free to be out of eye range of her serving woman, she didn't see where the ground suddenly gave way to moss-laden steps.

One slip of the foot and she had found herself tumbling through tangled brush, down many steps, landing where a cold rush of damp air blew from a dark, vast tunnel . . .

But that was six years ago. The present was now all that was important to Lee-lee. To get caught? She shuddered at the thought!

Running, panting, casting occasional quick glances over her shoulder, Lee-lee was relieved when once more she was using the tall *lanmu* trees to hide among in her flight to freedom, though again only a short span of time would be allowed her to enjoy it.

But no matter how short, any time spent away from the House of Yeung was a blessing. Each day her fear in being there mounted. . . .

"*Wei*! We are finally within reach of safety," Tak-Ming exclaimed, wiping beads of perspiration from his brow. "At least while we are in the passageway no one will find us."

The wooded area was dark and so dense the light from the courtyard lanterns couldn't penetrate it. Lee-lee grabbed for Tak-Ming's arm and clung to it, fighting her way through the darkness. She stumbled here and there over wild undergrowth and broken, fallen tree limbs. The leaves above her head emitted a sort of swooshing sound, as though water rushed from a fountain. The breeze stroked her face, gently . . . warmly. But once the steps that led down into the passageway were reached, the gentle warmth was quickly changed to that of a whipping, angry, cold gust of air which whistled upward, from around the tunnel's entranceway.

"I was here earlier, before I came to your room," Tak-Ming said, helping Lee-lee down the steps and on inside the tunnel. "Around the bend, I've left a lantern burning. It will help us find our way to the other end of the tunnel without the worry of being bitten by a rat."

"A . . . rat?" Lee-lee gasped. "*Bi-ni-di-zueh*, Tak-Ming," she insisted, laughing as she nudged him playfully in the ribs.

"You think I am jesting?" he said throatily. "If you look closely enough, you will see the glint of many small eyes on all sides of us."

A cold shiver raced up and down Lee-lee's spine. She refused to look around her for fear of seeing such eyes. Instead she clung more fiercely to Tak-Ming's arm, then snuggled into an embrace at his side as his arm stole around her waist.

"Watch your step," Tak-Ming warned and not too soon, for Lee-lee's straw sandals were already slipping and sliding on the slippery mire of the tunnel flooring.

Lee-lee's nose curled up and her eyes burned as an offensive odor invaded her senses. The aroma was that of a dead fish, and the persistent drip-dripping from somewhere in the distance suggested that, though this tunnel had withstood time, it still lay dangerously close to the water table of the East China Sea which bordered the shoreline of Foochow.

"How much farther?" Lee-lee asked, then relaxed when she saw the soft glow of a lantern as she and Tak-Ming followed a slow bend in the tunnel. She got a better look at her surroundings, none of which encouraged her. Water was running in little rivulets, glistening down the walls, cutting its way through deposits of coated mineral and dew-distilling growths.

The whine of the wind was profound and the candle in the lantern flickered ominously. Then a scratching at Lee-lee's feet drew a shriek from her when she saw a

31

flurry of rats scatter and rush toward the darker abyss from where she and Tak-Ming had just come.

"You were forewarned," Tak-Ming said, laughing. He moved toward the lantern; beside it rested a heavy, muzzle-loading gun and a large, curved sword. It was a two-foot-long cutlass with a two-inch blade and crude handle of wood.

Arming himself with both the gun and sword—slipping the sword into a belt at his waist and carrying the gun—he lifted the lantern and watched its soft light glow on Lee-lee's face. "Now we must hurry on," he urged, nodding to her. "You stay close by my side."

Lee-lee shivered, both from the damp chill of the tunnel air and from growing fear of the adventure. Seeing Tak-Ming arm himself with weapons had made her become suddenly aware of the true dangers they were facing. She now wished that she were as armed as he but fully doubted that she could ever shoot a gun or use a sword on another human being. Yet, if her life or Tak-Ming's depended on it . . . ?

Continuing to walk alongside Tak-Ming, Lee-lee could feel her toes squashing together as water penetrated the thin soles of her sandals. Beneath the light of the lantern, she could see that the farther they moved toward Foochow Bay, the deeper the water became in the tunnel. The walls glistened, the dampness clung to her hair, and the sickening odor of dead, rotting fish grew stronger.

The distant sound of water slap-slapping against the pilings along the bay was welcome. Lee-lee was quite aware of now being near the end of the tunnel. How many times had she dared to dream of an adventure like this? The opportunities to be alone, to seek the pleasure of the city, had been few. She had in a sense become a prisoner under the watchful eye of the mandarin whom most people feared, more than not. Heung-Chin Yeung's name was synonymous with power . . .

Tak-Ming suddenly stretched an arm out before Lee-lee and stopped her with the barrel of his gun. "Shh," he whispered, hurriedly blowing out his lantern. "We must now move with much caution. If anyone should see us leave the passageway, it would not only be dangerous for us, but for the House of Yeung as well. All sorts of thieves could use the tunnel to go beneath the great wall which protects our family from *undesirables*."

Lee-lee leaned closer to Tak-Ming, now seeing only a vague outline of him in the dark of the tunnel. "*Ai*. I understand only too well what you say," she whispered back.

"Grab hold of my arm," Tak-Ming said. "And lower the brim of your hat as much as you can and still see where you are going. And keep your head lowered. No one should be allowed to look directly into your face. Without the cosmetics, *ai*, your barbarian features are quite visible."

"Must you use the word 'barbarian' when speaking of Americans?" Lee-lee quietly scolded. "Do I reflect one of barbaric ways? Do I?"

"*Tcha!*" Tak-Ming growled. "You would not. You were raised in the House of Yeung!"

"Not for my first eight years of life," she argued. "It was during *that* time that my true personality was formed, and it was formed by living with my genteel American family. How can you forget? My true name is Letitia Taylor! Not Lee-lee Yeung!"

"Howla! Howla!" Tak-Ming grumbled. "The American ship will leave the Min River if we do not hurry." He leaned down into Lee-lee's face. "And, Adopted Sister Lee-lee, you must not let this American businessman see you," Tak-Ming warned. "While I do business with him from my ship to his, you must stay hidden in the shadows. Do you understand? You do see the dangers, do you not?"

Lee-lee was reminded of the first time she had been near Tak-Ming, with his face so close to hers. His scent of spices and perfume had been the same then as it was now. She smiled up at him, seeing how his bold, black eyes bore down upon her in his way of showing authority as her older brother.

"Ai," she murmured while unable to ignore the strange thrill that surged through her as she imagined being so near a man from America. Trade was heavy at the Port of Foochow, but an American ship was a rarity. Only recently had the American trade increased. From overhearing gossip exchanged between Mandarin Heung-Chin and his five more scholarly sons, Lee-lee knew there were many American ships now moored at the quay, and it hadn't yet been decided if this were good . . . or bad.

Together, Lee-lee and Tak-Ming crept from the tunnel, working their way through tangled brush and roots of trees that hung down from overhead and grew into the ground. Lee-lee spat and fought off the intrusion of buzzing mosquitoes that suddenly appeared from nowhere in a venomous attack. She brushed them from her face and stepped away from the tunnel and the dense growth which hid it from all passersby. Winded from the long walk and the fight to break through the greenery at the tunnel's entrance, Lee-lee stopped to take a deep breath and to look around her.

Behind her were rocks and boulders that eventually gave way to valleys of trees and blowing grasses rising up from the Bay of Foochow. Before her splashed the moonbeam-infested water stretching out into the famous East China Sea. On her left, there was total darkness; but on her right, the sandy beach made a sudden drop and across the glistening expanse of water she could see the Port of Foochow and its many ships, junks, and sampans.

In the harbor, lights winked aboard the assorted water vessels. The scene was strange and pretty with all these crafts lighted by innumerable paper lanterns of many colors. The distance between Lee-lee and this fairy scene lent her a sense of enchantment. . . .

A sudden creaking sound and a flapping of sails caused Lee-lee to spin around on a heel, and she stood awed by the great ship that had seemed to appear from nowhere. But Tak-Ming had told her of these deep, dark coves which could hide even the fiercest of Chinese warships.

"*Ai*, my crew has followed my command and has watched carefully for us to appear here on the beach," Tak-Ming bragged, his chest swelling with pride.

"But . . . how . . . ?" Lee-lee gasped. "I didn't see the ship. How did they see us and won't they know of the tunnel?"

"One of my men was in a longboat just off shore, watching. He knew not of the passageway, only that we traveled from the House of Yeung alone, in the dark. The minute the moon caught our faces in its reflection, he went and alerted the others as he boarded my *Sea Goddess*. They knew to hurry, to get us on board quickly."

"*Sea Goddess* is such a beautiful name for such a beautiful ship," Lee-lee said, now seeing a smaller boat leaving the larger one.

"*Ma-tsoo-poo, Sea Goddess*, was given to my clipper ship because *Ma-tsoo-poo* stands for good luck as you know," Tak-Ming said, reaching for Lee-lee's hand and urging her to run with him into the effervescent foam of the water's edge as the shallow boat came closer.

"*Ai . . .*" Lee-lee said. She climbed into the longboat manned by two short and lowly-dressed Chinamen who spoke so softly and quickly to Tak-Ming that Lee-lee could not understand a word being spoken. But it mattered not. She was seized by tremors of excitement, inhaling the fresh fragrance of the saltwater breeze and welcoming its splash upon her face as a wave crashed against the side of the boat.

Across the black expanse of the restless sea, many adventures awaited Lee-lee. But at this moment, her heart raced with pride for Tak-Ming. The schooner which he had chosen to repair was much more than she had ever anticipated! It was a magnificent work of art which he had so personally, skillfully supervised!

She eyed the *Sea Goddess* as the longboat scooted through the choppy waves of the sea toward it. The ship was a two-masted clipper schooner with fine lines and plenty of canvas in the sail plan, which rose white against the velvet black of night. The ship had to be at least twenty-six feet in length with a teak hull. For the awe-struck girl only one word could describe it—*beautiful*!

Lee-lee proudly boarded . . .

Chapter Two

The coast was unlighted and uncharted. The *New Yorker* was forced to run in along the shoreline, looking for an elusive mixture of land and sea breeze to help it along its way.

Standing watch between the binnacle and the leeward rail, just a few feet from the wheel of this prestigious clipper schooner, was a man just as authoritative in appearance as this ship he owned.

American-born-and-bred Timothy Hendricks stood tall and powerfully built at his age of thirty, with handsome features defined by a long, straight nose and full lips which most women thought to be provocatively sensual. Beneath his silk top hat his hair was dark and hung neatly at a length halfway to his shoulders. His brown eyes were almost haunting with their even darker, thick lashes veiling them. His weather-tanned face was a tribute to his many voyages at sea.

A successful businessman, Timothy was dressed smartly in his impeccable brown wool frock coat, matching tight-fitted trousers, and white silk shirt with a broad, tan velvet cravat on which was displayed a diamond stickpin. He was the owner of a vast line of ships, working in partnership with Calvin Hoots under the title of the *Hendricks-Hoots Line*, operating twenty ships of various types and designs from New York.

Timothy had known that more wealth could be made from commerce with China, so he had journeyed to the Port of Foochow, to work with the China end of their trade, dealing in tea and silk and the best of spices.

But this night Timothy had succumbed to the temptation of rapid profits. He was trying his luck with an illegal purchase of opium . . .

The wind caught Timothy's top hat and threatened to move it from his head, even as it caused sprays of ashes to fly from the cheroot which was clamped between his straight teeth.

Securing his hat in place and taking a puff from his cigar, Timothy frowned. Where was the ship that was going to exchange its opium for his silver? Just how much longer could he be expected to wait?

Beneath the dull light of a whale oil lamp he slid his watch from his frock coat pocket. He drew a deep breath, seeing the late hour and feeling keenly vulnerable in these Chinese waters of the Min River.

"Don't look so good, does it, Timothy?" a deep, scratchy voice said suddenly from behind him.

As Captain Hollister stepped to his side, Timothy slid his watch back inside his pocket and withdrew his cigar from his mouth. "Hollister, how's the crew? Are they becoming edgy?" he asked, letting his eyes roam upriver. He stepped closer to the railing as he caught his first sight of sail in the distance. He studied the approaching ship carefully. Beneath the hazy shadows of the moon, it seemed an apparition with its white canvas shuddering with the movement of the ship. But it was indeed the *Sea Goddess*, just as it had been carefully described to him.

"Aye, they are," Captain Hollister snarled. "And given reason to be edgy, if I was the judge of this whimsical transaction of yours."

"Whimsical?" Timothy said, lifting an eyebrow as his gaze now focused on the short, stocky man who had commanded the *New Yorker* through both stormy and calm seas without ever losing even one sail. It was the captain's cautious approach to all things in life that had convinced Timothy to give him command of Timothy's favorite ship, the *New Yorker*.

And Timothy could understand Hollister's air of apprehension now. Perhaps this *was* an unwise adventure. But Timothy needed the excitement as well as the chance to make a speedy profit once this special cargo was sold in California . . .

"Aye. Whimsical as hell," Captain Hollister growled, spitting across the railing. His beaver hat hid his balding head beneath it, but his carefully trimmed beard and mustache made up for what hair he couldn't grow on his head. A squint of gray eyes showed through gold-framed, thick-lensed spectacles which looked out of place on a man of his chosen profession. He wore a coat of blue broadcloth with flat pearl buttons down its front and at the cuffs of its sleeves. His dove gray pants fit his obese figure much too snugly, and under his arm he held an ebony stick with a gold top.

"You will change your mind once you see the profits," Timothy encouraged, flicking ashes from his cigar.

"Profits to be made from opium taken and sold in California?" Captain Hollister scoffed. "If you even make it as far as California with such a hot cargo, once there you're chancin' many things—"

Timothy interrupted him. "Taking chances is a part of life," he interjected. "Life without risks would be a boring existence, wouldn't you say?"

"Opium bears a reputation of evil power beyond any man's will to conquer," Captain Hollister persisted. "Those who use the stuff become weaklings and fools. I do not look forward to having it aboard a ship I command. And the risk is even greater with the chance of losing the tea trade with China if the Chinese authorities discover this crime you are about to commit."

Timothy tossed his half-smoked cheroot into the river. He laughed smoothly. "Don't you remember who is handing the opium over to us this night?" he said, fitting his hands into his trouser pockets.

"Aye. It is a son of the mandarin who calls himself by the name of Yeung."

"And knowing that, you can't relax with our business dealings with him? There is no way this Chinaman is going to take any chances that his father might discover the illegal trafficking here on the dark waters of the Min River. That alone makes me feel confident about the safety factor of this thing I have set my mind to do."

"Nothing you say will make me want that dreaded drug even near me," Captain Hollister growled.

"It is a product for trade. To me no more or less desirable than anything else brought aboard my ship," Timothy said dryly. "We sail our ships from America in search of the best ways in which to make profits. And, by God, nothing ever stands in the way of my profits!"

Captain Hollister spat into the wind as he watched the Chinese clipper schooner gliding through the water, now only two ship lengths away from the *New Yorker*. He clasped his hands tightly together behind him and began yelling out orders to his crew who were strangely silent in their responses. The sound of scurrying feet, the creak of rope, and the shivering and slapping of the canvas were all that was heard on the ship as the *New Yorker* was brought alongside the *Sea Goddess*.

Timothy's back tensed. He removed his hands from his pockets and leaned against the rail, silently studying the ship and its occupants. It was a surly lot, a mixed breed of nationalities. Then one in particular caught his eye as a tall, quite handsome Chinaman stepped forward with his long braid of hair. The bold, almond-shaped black eyes slowly assessed Timothy . . .

Lee-lee waited in the cabin of Tak Ming's clipper schooner that he had prepared especially for her, for their eventual long voyage to America. She could hear the water splashing against the hull of the ship, a sort of mesmerizing sound if one's mind and body were relaxed to enjoy it.

But neither Lee-lee's body or mind relaxed. The other sounds drifting downward were more pronounced in Lee-

lee's thoughts. She knew that by now the American's crew was surely mingling with Tak-Ming's, transferring the chests of opium from Tak-Ming's schooner to the American's.

Lee-lee hadn't been given the chance to see much of the American's schooner and she most certainly hadn't been given the opportunity to see the American. Once the American's ship had come into view, Tak-Ming had too quickly escorted her to her cabin and warned her of the dangers of leaving.

"To be so close," she stewed, now pacing, resembling a nervous, caged cat. "I want to see the American. It's been so long!"

But trying to force herself to forget chancing a look, she attempted to focus her thoughts on this cabin that was soon to be hers. It didn't appear at all like anything that would be found on a ship. The cabin had red-lacquered floors and satin embroidered hangings on the gilt-trimmed walls. Mosquito net curtains of figured silk were hooked back on both sides of a small, carved, four-poster bed, upon which had been placed a luxurious white satin coverlet. Above the bed was a lone porthole, hidden behind a small bamboo curtain, and colorful lanterns hung from the wall in four places, dispersing soft light from raised wicks fueled by whale oil. A dressing table designed in the shape of a half-moon had been secured to a wall, and in the drawers Lee-lee had found perfumed oils but none of the fancy facial cosmetics which were usually found among a Chinese woman's personal-care items.

Smiling, Lee-lee had understood the absence of the vermilion paints and rice powder. Tak-Ming had known for some time now of her hatred for the things required to mask her face in order that she appear Chinese. Once on her way to America, even her natural red hair coloring would be allowed to grow in . . .

Plopping down on the only chair in the room, a soft velvet in a neutral ivory color, Lee-lee removed her hat from her head. She leaned back in the chair, stretched her legs out before her, and began to spin her hat between her fingers. She sighed resolutely. This wasn't fair! She had waited forever, it seemed, to be able to share this exciting adventure with Tak-Ming, and now only he was participating fully in the adventure!

She placed her hat back on her head and listened intently to the continuing activity on topdeck. Soon the exchange would be completed and her opportunity to see the American would be gone as well!

"I cannot just sit here," she whispered. "How can I let such a chance slip by me? I must see the American. I *must*!"

With her heart pounding nervously, she rose from the chair and went to the door. She placed her ear to it to see if she could detect any voices close by. Hearing none, she crept outside to the dark passageway that led to the companion ladder. She would climb the ladder only part way to the top. One peek was all she required to satisfy her aroused curiosity. And once she had gotten her glimpse of the American, it would surely hold her until she arrived in America and became acquainted with many personally . . .

Remembering her hat, Lee-lee lowered its brim, barely leaving her eyes room to see. Then she inched onward, feeling her way along the wall. The straw of her shoes, which were still wet from the tunnel, squeaked noisily with each step, making her cringe. As each closed door was reached, she took smaller, lighter steps past them, then hurried faster when she was finally clear.

Lee-lee's heart beat even faster when she saw the first reflection of light from a whale oil lamp on topdeck traversing the short flight of steps. Fearing the light could cause her discovery, she stole to the farthest corner of the steps where the way was darkest, and for her, the safest route of travel.

Pressing her back against the wall of the staircase, Lee-lee began her slow ascent, one careful step at a time. The clamor of feet and a sprinkling of voices in all sorts of languages came closer and closer. Yet when she peeked up, over the final step and across the deck, she could see nothing. The men were on the opposite end of the ship and if she was to see, she would have to go farther in her daring escapade. She would have to go on topdeck herself.

Like a phantom of night she left the companion ladder behind her. The breeze caught her face with its heavy dampness as she made a quick turn on the deck to hide behind some stacked kegs of fresh water used for drinking. From this vantage point she could see almost everything. The man at the *Sea Goddess*'s great wheel stood tense, crouched, his forearm muscle locked as he waited to disembark from these dangerous waters. Next to him she recognized Tak-Ming, who stood proudly over his crew.

Tak-Ming's men were a mixture of nationalities, poor souls who had been down on their luck when Tak-Ming had rescued them from whichever blighted town they

44

had been floundering in as Tak-Ming sought a crew for his repaired, quite impressive clipper schooner.

So far only a few of these *unfortunates* hadn't worked out, too lost in their need for a drug—sometimes as deadly as the dreaded opium—to function as proper human beings. Whiskey had not only stolen their power to think rationally but also their souls it seemed.

But none of these things were Lee-lee's prime concern. Her reasons for risking being seen on topdeck only involved her need to see the American businessman. As far as she could gather, and quite disappointing to her, he hadn't boarded the *Sea Goddess* but had instead stayed with his own ship.

She turned her gaze to the powerful ship that stood as a giant beside Tak-Ming's schooner. It was also a clipper schooner, but this ship was made to look larger because it was so well equipped for battle. Long Tom cannons made of brass were positioned amidship and on her forecastledeck, and pivot and swivel guns could also be seen at her bow. Though not a warship, it was prepared to defend itself against thieving pirates and other such scum who so often traveled the high seas.

On the ship's black hull, the name *New Yorker* had been painted in bold, white fancy lettering. The name caused strong memories to surface of Lee-lee's home in New York before the age of eight when she had been catapulted into another, bewildering way of life.

But this was not the time to dwell on the past. This was now and the American businessman had to be somewhere close by.

Slowly Lee-lee began to let her gaze move along the American ship's railing, and when she saw the one better dressed of the men still aboard the *New Yorker*, her heart did a strange sort of flip-flop. Beneath the soft light of a whale oil lamp, he stood tall, powerfully built, and darkly masculine in his handsomeness. Attired in his expensive clothes and fancy top hat, and with his perfectly straight nose and full lips from which extended a lighted cheroot, she thought him to be the personification of a man.

Suddenly Lee-lee's body was a river of strange sensations, none of which were familiar to her. Her heart wouldn't be still . . . there was a weakness in her knees. Fearing these feelings invading her senses, she took a step backward, having the need to flee. She realized the foolishness of letting herself feel anything for this American. They could never become acquainted. She wasn't able to trust anyone but Tak-Ming. The dangers of being sent to the Imperial Palace hung as a dark shroud around her . . .

Still inching backward, Lee-lee suddenly tripped over a coil of rope, causing her to sprawl clumsily across the deck. She fell into the full light of a swaying lantern, and as she hit the deck, her hat tumbled from her head.

"Oh, no . . ." she whispered. She looked quickly about her, relieved to see that no one aboard this ship had witnessed her mishap. She spied her hat, making her pulse race with the fear of being fully seen.

She scooted to her knees and crawled toward the hat. But remembering the American, she swallowed hard and looked toward him just as his head turned her way . . .

Tak-Ming had warned her to stay in the shadows, but she had not. And now Lee-lee was like a moth, being drawn to the flames of a fire. Her body turned into a bizarre sort of liquid as the heat of the American's gaze touched her . . .

A strong arm suddenly around her waist startled Lee-lee out of her moment of enchantment. She jerked her head around and was now looking into the cold and angry eyes of Tak-Ming.

"What do you think you are doing?" he whispered harshly, lifting her to her feet. "You are in full view of the American. Didn't I warn you against that?"

"*Ai*," Lee-lee said, humbly lowering her eyes.

"Then why, Lee-lee?" Tak-Ming scolded, already ushering her down the companion ladder, to personally take her back to her cabin.

"Tak-Ming, did you truly expect me to stay in that cabin while everyone else was a part of this night's adventure?"

"This adventure is dangerous," he growled. He opened the door of the cabin and pulled her inside. "I should never have agreed to let you come. Women! They are all an unpredictable lot! Surely *you* are the most unpredictable of them all!"

Using the way she had learned long ago to get him to forget any anger he might feel toward her, Lee-lee tossed her hat aside then wriggled into his embrace. "*Bi-ni-di-zueh*," she teased.

She hugged him tightly, placing her cheek against his chest, having always found comfort there since the day he had rescued her. "You aren't really angry with me now, are you, Tak-Ming?"

Tak-Ming returned her hug then drew away from her, frustration playing in the dark of his eyes. "*Howla*, Lee-lee. I have things to do. Now will you please stay here, out of mischief?"

Lee-lee placed her fists together before her and bowed from the waist. "*Ai*, my lord," she further teased. Then she lifted her gaze to meet his as a slow smile touched her lips.

Tak-Ming returned her smile then rushed from the cabin with Lee-lee resuming her original nervous pacing. She stewed . . . she listened . . . she sighed. A part of her still felt strangely . . . differently—alive from the exchanged glances with the American. Had he seen her closely enough to see that she wasn't a man *or* Chinese? Had the man's queue down her back or the eye makeup actually fooled him? Had there been enough light for him to have seen . . . ?

"He must have known," she said aloud. "He surely looked at me as a man looks at a woman when he likes what he sees."

Then she had to laugh, looking down at the way she was dressed, and at her flat, bound breasts. "I must be losing my mind," she said. "How could a man look to me as a woman when my breasts are flat and my full figure is hidden beneath such garb as this?"

Her face flushed hot as she realized where her thoughts were taking her. Yet, never even in her fantasies had she seen such a virile, handsome man!

Lee-lee ran to her bed and hopped up on it. The porthole! Why hadn't she thought of looking from it earlier?

Pulling aside the bamboo curtain, she felt an ache swimming around in the pit of her stomach as she watched the American's ship moving away from the *Sea Goddess*, knowing that along with it was being taken a part of her heart.

For a brief moment in her life she had tasted the thrill of how a man could make her feel with a mere touch of his eyes. She now had to wonder about how it would be to *be* with such a man.

"What am I doing?" she cried. She quickly dropped the bamboo curtain in place over the porthole and leaned her back against the wall. Folding her arms over her chest, she thought further of how this American had affected her.

"It surely does not mean a thing," she whispered. "It is because I am so used to only seeing Chinese faces all around me. The American . . . was . . . so different! It is only because a part of me so misses my heritage! And if he did recognize me as American, won't he ask questions of the Chinese at the Port of Foochow that could endanger me?" she cried aloud, now suddenly remembering her original fears of his possibly seeing her.

Tak-Ming burst into the cabin, all smiles and holding up a bag for her to see. He shook it, tinkling the coins together inside it. "We are now *much* richer," he exclaimed. "*Ai*, there are many silver coins to add to our hidden chest of travel money!"

Giggling, Lee-lee rushed to him and took the bag from him. Going to the bed, she shook the coins out onto the white satin coverlet. Beneath the glow of the lanterns, the coins shone invitingly up into her eyes. She fell to her knees beside the bed, swimming her fingers through the coins, loving the cool feel of them against her flesh.

"*Ai*," she quietly sighed. "America doesn't seem so far from me this night . . ."

Chapter Three

Letting the perfumed, hot bath water relax her, Lee-lee sank lower into it. Her raven black hair was coiled tightly above her head and her breasts were free from the dreaded breast binder. Instead they lay only barely beneath the bubble of suds in ripe, voluptuous swells of pink.

Lee-lee had just closed her eyes when footsteps beside her vermilion-lacquered bathtub aroused her from her drifting, lethargic moment of pleasure. Covering her breasts with her hands, she looked toward her serving woman, Soonya.

"I'm not quite finished yet, Soonya," Lee-lee said, then realized how foolish it was to be covering any part of her anatomy from this elderly lady who saw to Lee-lee's every personal need. She lowered her hands and playfully splashed the sandalwood-scented bubbles around her updrawn knees.

Soonya bowed humbly, yet her pale brown eyes never left Lee-lee's face. "It is time to get dressed," she said softly in Chinese. "Too soon you will be expected to be at

50

your place at the table for the evening meal, Young Mistress."

Lee-lee tossed her head angrily. "Soonya, you most surely haven't heard," she said. "I am not allowed to join the family this evening to even *eat* with them. There is to be some important guest here at the House of Yeung. And, Soonya, it seems that the House of Yeung doesn't want this guest to see me, the American foreign devil I am. So they are going to make me eat alone, in the adjoining room, separating me from them by a movable partition. So why should I hurry? No one will miss me should I even decide to stay in my room!"

Soonya reached for a fluffy towel and held it out toward Lee-lee. "It is not Soonya's business to know such private things," she said, blinking her eyes nervously. "It is only Soonya's business to help Young Mistress in her bath and dress this time each evening. It is *buh-hao-eesa* for serving woman to even speak her feelings of why Young Mistress is ordered to do anything in the House of Yeung."

"Yet you order me around also?" Lee-lee questioned, not yet budging from the tub of water. "Soonya, you have been my serving woman since I was eight. Can't you also be my friend?"

Lee-lee studied Soonya, seeing how she had aged so quickly since they had first become acquainted. Soonya's hair was wiry gray and hung in one long braid behind her to her waist, and her back had a slight hump in it, as though a rock had been planted beneath her flesh there. She was short and thin and her dark eyes had lessened in color, with lines on her face resembling the veins on the back of a leaf. Dressed in a floor-length, plain cotton dress and straw sandals, it wasn't hard to set her apart from the family members of the House of Yeung.

A sad, hurtful expression caused Soonya's thin lips to curve downward. "Soonya *is* a friend," she murmured, lowering the towel.

Lee-lee gestured with a hand. "Then leave me to my bath," she said. She closed her eyes and sank farther down into the water, leaning her head back against the mirror that had been set into the wall that bordered the tub. "Go on your way, Soonya. I have just made a decision. I will *not* go and be made to eat alone while the rest of the family enjoys the company of an important guest at their table."

Hearing a low gasp from Soonya, Lee-lee's eyes were drawn quickly open. She looked toward Soonya, seeing a definite look of alarm in the serving woman's eyes. "What *is* it, Soonya?" she asked softly. "Why are you acting so strangely?"

"Young Mistress, you *must* go tonight," Soonya said, nodding her head anxiously.

"What?" Lee-lee gasped, stunned at Soonya's odd behavior.

"Young Mistress, you know that I do not gossip," Soonya whispered, looking across her shoulder, then back to Lee-lee. "Nothing in the House of Yeung is my business but you, my sweet Young Mistress who I do say is my friend as well as mistress. You do know this, don't you, Young Mistress?"

"*Ai* . . ." Lee-lee said, scooting up, straightening her back. She was not concerned that her breasts were fully exposed now and that they had the opalescent glow of moonstones as the soft light from a lantern played and danced in the soap bubbles that clung to them.

"Then when I tell you what the gossip spreaders have said . . . about *whom* the guest is tonight, you will not tell that it was I who has told you?" Soonya whispered even more softly, leaning down into Lee-lee's face.

"I would never do anything that could get you into trouble," Lee-lee said, her honey-brown eyes wide with wonder. "Who *is* the guest to be? Tell me. You are acting . . . so . . . so mysterious about this whole thing, Soonya."

Soonya cupped a hand over her mouth, as though saying the words would, indeed, condemn her. "It is to be an American visitor," she whispered harshly. "An American like you, Young Mistress. Only this American in the House of Yeung is to be a man."

Oh, so vividly remembering the American on board the great ship called the *New Yorker*, something akin to passion rippled sensuously at the pit of Lee-lee's stomach. "An . . . American? An American man will be here tonight?" she asked, feeling a hot flush rise to her cheeks.

"*Ai* . . ." Soonya whispered. "But never tell that I told you. I would be sent far away, Young Mistress, never to serve you again."

Now Lee-lee realized why she couldn't be allowed to be seen this night. If an American saw her—an American— at the House of Yeung, there would be many questions! And with plans for her possibly to be sent to the Imperial Palace, she knew that Heung-Chin would not take a chance of losing her . . .

"My towel, Soonya," she said, rising quickly to her feet. Her heart was racing, yet how foolish it was to even imagine it could be the same American whose eyes had held her momentarily hostage only the previous night. An American dealing in the illegal trafficking of opium most surely wouldn't be foolish enough to drop his anchor at the Port of Foochow, much less have council and a meal with the mandarin who could cause his head to roll because of the opium!

And why was an American a guest of Heung-Chin? His tolerance for any American other than herself was very low!

Soonya wrapped the towel around Lee-lee, all the while dabbing Lee-lee's skin softly with it, absorbing the wetness like a sponge. "Young Mistress, what do you plan to do?" she asked weakly, in a soft sort of whine. "This American. You do not plan to try to talk with him, do you? It would only cause problems, Young Mistress. If you are ordered to eat alone, this is proof enough that you should not see or talk to the American. I shouldn't even have told you."

Lee-lee secured the towel around herself, knotting it where it came together in front. She grabbed Soonya's hands and held onto them tightly. "You did the right thing, Soonya," she encouraged. "And please don't worry. What I do will never reflect on you. Just trust me."

Soonya lowered her eyes and shook her head sadly. "It was right that you know," she said. "If I were in America away from Chinese people and one were to come to the place where I made my residence, I would want to know. If not to talk to . . . to see."

Soonya raised her gaze to meet Lee-lee's. "Your people? You do miss them, *ai*?"

"*Ai* . . ." Lee-lee said then drew Soonya into her arms. She placed her chin on Soonya's head and hugged her tightly. "I do miss my people."

Seeing the American businessman had made Lee-lee even more homesick than ever before for America and the American way of life. But seeing him had accomplished more than that. It had awakened feelings inside her that up to this point in her life had been dormant. She now understood the attraction that could be created so quickly between a woman and a man.

Soonya giggled softly as she drew away from Lee-lee. "You can see the American even if you do not eat at the same table as he does," she said.

Lee-lee resumed drying herself. "How do you mean, Soonya?" she asked, shocked that Soonya was being so open. It was not the way of the Chinese servants. Yet at times, Soonya *had* behaved in a less reserved fashion but only when in the presence of her Young Mistress, as Soonya so fondly called Lee-lee.

Soonya stepped up on tiptoe and loosened the pins from Lee-lee's hair, shaking it loose of its tight coil. "The designs cut through the cypress wood of the movable partition," she replied. "They go all the way through. You can see from room to room, through the cut wood designs. No one would see you looking. They will all be busy entertaining the American with food and drink."

"How wicked you are," Lee-lee teased, watching how

such teasing caused Soonya's head to bow humbly, though her eyes had shown a rare twinkling before she had lowered them from view.

"*Nay*. You are not truly wicked, Soonya," Lee-lee quickly blurted, afraid that Soonya had taken her words much too seriously since she had kept her head bowed much longer than usual. "You are right to suggest that to me. That is the way I shall see this American!"

And if the Fates granted Lee-lee her wish, it would be the American who had occupied her dreams the whole fitful night after having seen him . . .

"Now we must make you beautiful," Soonya said, eyes bright. She was already on her knees before the chests in Lee-lee's bedchamber, where many beautiful dresses and gowns lay for the choosing.

"Surely such a fuss must not be made with my hair or my face," Lee-lee said, now pulling a brush through her hair. "No one will see me. Why should I mask my face to look Chinese?"

She didn't wish to look Chinese just in case she could figure out a way to meet this American face to face. She wanted to be American while with an American.

Yet, what foolishness! She would not be given this opportunity. Heung-Chin would see to that. Her Chinese adopted father was devious in all manner, shape, and form. And when it came to her . . . *wei*! He would not become in the least bit careless!

"*Ai*. It must be done!" Soonya exclaimed. "You cannot be allowed to ever leave your room without being dressed and made up in the Chinese way. It is an order given to me from my first day in the House of Yeung! I

56

must obey!"

Hearing the fear in Soonya's voice and seeing it in the wildness of her eyes, Lee-lee quickly responded. "Do not be so alarmed, Soonya," she said. "I will do what is necessary." She looked toward the bed where her coarse, cotton breast binder lay waiting. "But even the breast binder, Soonya?" she sighed.

"*Ai.* Even the breast binder," Soonya said rising, carrying a long, silk dress. It was peacock blue—the exact shade of a bird's plumage. "No woman should show how her chest fills out—in public." She glanced at Lee-lee's bare breasts and giggled softly. "Especially a woman as gifted as you. Any man who saw you would think his own wife less desirable."

"Oh, Soonya," Lee-lee scoffed, blushing. "You are embarrassing me. Let's get on with the charade of disguise if I must. I'm anxious to take my first peek through the cut designs of the partition." She also giggled. "Wouldn't I be shocked if my eye met an eye staring back at me!"

"That would be *puh-hao*!" Soonya said, visibly shuddering while placing the dress neatly across the bed.

Lee-lee and Soonya became studiously quiet as they began the ordeal of Lee-lee's Chinese dress, coiffed hair, and facial makeup. First the breast binder was wrapped snugly around Lee-lee's breasts, making her groan as it was secured in place. And then she slipped into silk trousers that clung to every crease of her body, followed by a trouser band pulled tight to make her already small waist look even smaller. All of this was then covered by thin, silk underthings.

"Please to sit before the mirror, Young Mistress," Soonya encouraged.

"*Ai . . .*" Lee-lee murmured, settling down on the kneeling mat at her dresser while Soonya dropped to her knees beside her. She watched as though in a trance as she was slowly transformed from American to Chinese, hoping that one day soon she could leave all of this behind her.

Soonya busied her deft fingers, oiling Lee-lee's hair with jasmine oil in which fragrant wood shavings had been dipped. It not only added a pleasing aroma to Lee-lee's hair but also a luster. Her hair was then parted into strands upon which was placed an intricate frame. The strands were drawn through and over the frame until her hair was coiled into a towering edifice.

Soonya smiled back at Lee-lee in the mirror, now busying her fingers with adding into her hair pearl and jade ornaments on gold wire springs and, after the addition of white camellias over each ear, her headdress was complete.

"*Ai*, Young Mistress, your hair is beautiful," Soonya said, sighing as she clasped her hands together before her.

"*Nay*," Lee-lee grumbled. "It is too much to have to wear much less to have to look at, Soonya. It always gives me such a miserable headache to have my hair pulled and drawn in such a crazy way."

She gestured with a hand. "Let's hurry on, though. If my face must also wear the burden of cosmetics, let's get it done and over with. I am anxious to get on with this evening's affairs."

Soonya nodded then busied herself making up Lee-lee's face. First the almond milk was applied to use as a base for the rice powder. Then she dabbed the juice of the ripe pomegranate on the high points of her cheeks, the tip of her nose, the lobes of her ears, her lips and fingernails.

"And for luck I shall place a dot of rouge in the center of your forehead and on the bridge of your nose," Soonya said, giggling.

"I hope I do have good luck tonight," Lee-lee murmured. "I so badly want to see the American."

She couldn't tell Soonya that she would not only *see* the American! If the Fates granted her the chance, she would also *talk* with him. Of late she had become more daring, and this time chancing getting caught would definitely be worth the rewards.

Soonya fussed and painted and then stood back and admired her handiwork, hardly able herself to see Lee-lee's usual facial features beneath the mask of paint and rice powder. And this evening Lee-lee's painted eyes appeared to be even more slanted, which pleased Soonya, who was happy to have once more succeeded at making Lee-lee over to be as beautiful as all Chinese women were!

"A woman's face casts her destiny," Soonya said proudly. "And you, Young Mistress—your future is filled with much happiness!"

Lee-lee's honey-brown eyes misted, and she once more felt the fool as she turned her face from the mirror. "The face you are looking upon to learn my destiny is not mine at all, Soonya," she softly cried. "So you see? My future is not that easily judged by you!"

Rising quickly, she stormed toward the bed. "Enough

time has been wasted," she said, sniffling. She wiped her nose with the back of her hand and cringed when rouge smeared onto it, drawing an annoyed sigh from Soonya.

"Sometimes you are that young girl of eight again," Soonya scolded as she helped Lee-lee get her dress over her head. "Young Mistress, how can you not approve when you are transformed into an enchantress? Even the Imperial Palace cannot brag of having a concubine as beautiful!"

Lee-lee stiffened as her insides splashed cold, once more reminded of her *true* possible fate! Soonya didn't even realize the threat behind such a statement! "Just hurry, Soonya," she said. "Please, just hurry!"

"*Ai*," Soonya said, bowing humbly, frustrated that she could sometimes forget that her place in the world was merely that of a serving woman. But her young mistress always made it so easy for her *to* forget. She was a gentle American . . . nothing like Soonya would ever have suspected a barbarian to be . . .

With loving hands, Soonya fastened Lee-lee's blue silk dress and girdled it at the waist with a length of even darker blue silk. She helped Lee-lee into a lady's coat of pale blue satin embroidered in flower designs, each flower having tiny crystal buttons sewn in its center. The coat touched the tip of her satin, embroidered slippers set high on white soles and center heels.

"And now your jewelry," Soonya said, reaching inside a gold-encrusted case to pull free two heavy, gold bracelets. "A bracelet for each arm. As I have taught you, Young Mistress, jewelry must always be worn in pairs to carry out the fundamental rule of Ying and Yang."

Lee-lee slipped a bracelet on each wrist, her heart thundering against her ribs, so close now to seeing just who the American was! She took one fast, grudging look at the full length of herself in the mirror. She frowned, seeing that Soonya had done her chore quite well. The transformation was complete and a success in her serving woman's eyes. From her head to her toes, Lee-lee was Chinese and no American would ever guess otherwise!

"Oh!" she exclaimed, turning on a heel.

"You do not like?" Soonya asked meekly, holding her hands folded at her waist, hidden inside the wideness of her sleeves.

Knowing the importance of Soonya feeling useful and appreciated, for Lee-lee was now her only responsibility in life, Lee-lee went to her and lifted her hands from inside her sleeves to squeeze them affectionately. "*Ai*," she lied. "I like. You do your duties quite well, Soonya."

Soonya's face lit with a broad smile. "Soonya will wait for your return," she said eagerly. "The satin sheets of your bed will be freshly perfumed. Your *beiwu*—your silk cover—will be folded back."

Lee-lee's smile faded. She released Soonya's hands. If what Lee-lee had planned could be managed, she wouldn't want Soonya in her room waiting for her return. The return just might be delayed by pleasant circumstances, and though Soonya was usually a congenial serving woman always ready to please Lee-lee, Soonya would not understand her Young Mistress's reasons for staying away from her room later at night than most respectable Chinese women were allowed! Only the women on the Chinese fancy flower boats were so bold as to be up at all hours of the night, away from their family's residence.

"*Nay*, Soonya," Lee-lee finally said, fidgeting with one of her bracelets, nervously spinning it round and round on her wrist. "That won't be required of you tonight. You have worked hard. Please retire early to your own quarters."

Soonya gasped. "Young Mistress, that would be unthinkable," she said, taking a step backward. "It is my duty to see to your every need until I see you safely beneath your *beiwu*!"

"Must you argue every time I give you the opportunity to retire early?" Lee-lee scolded.

"You are excusing me much too frequently of late, Young Mistress," Soonya said, bowing. "In the eyes of the master of the House of Yeung, Soonya would be considered lazy."

"No one knows that you retire early but me," Lee-lee said. "I won't tell anyone, Soonya. Please just do as I say."

Lee-lee was afraid that one day soon Soonya would be inquisitive and ask why Lee-lee didn't insist that Soonya assist her in her bedtime preparations. Lee-lee's answers would be vague to say the least! She wasn't sure if Soonya could be totally trusted. Soonya *was* Chinese. Her utmost loyalties first and foremost would surely be to the master . . . the Lord of the House of Yeung, Heung-Chin Yeung.

"*Ai*, Young Mistress," Soonya said, nodding her head favorably. "What you say rules Soonya's movements. I will prepare your bed now, as you leave. It will smell sweetly for you when you return, as though the blossoms of flowers were tucked between the *beiwu* with you."

"All right," Lee-lee laughed. "Do that if it pleases you." She placed a kiss on Soonya's pale, sunken cheek. "But I must leave you now. Already I fear I may have taken too much time. I do not wish a scolding from Heung-Chin."

"Still you cannot call him father?"

"*Nay*. Never," Lee-lee said dryly ."But now is not the time to go into that. My mind is too full of desire to see the American."

Soonya giggled as she looked up into Lee-lee's face. "Do not look so hard at the American that your eyes will ache," she teased.

"*Nay*," Lee-lee said. "I shall not do that, Soonya. He is probably so ugly and fat I will immediately turn up my nose and move my eyes from such a sight."

"*Ai*. Most American men are ugly. They rarely are as handsome as the Chinese."

Lee-lee smiled coyly, knowing that she could argue that point with Soonya, still mesmerized by the American businessman's hauntingly dark eyes and heartstopping facial features. But instead of speaking of it, she continued to store it inside her heart.

Feeling lighthearted and full of spirited eagerness, Lee-lee left her room and began moving down the softly lighted hallways of the palatial mansion. She left a murmur of silk behind her as she traveled along the lacquered floors. Fresh translucent bell flowers and white narcissus were in vases on gilt-trimmed, precious wood tables along the hallway, beneath mirrors of prodigious height, and flanking these were tapered, flickering candles on gold wall sconces.

Hurrying now, not at all like a proper Chinese lady, Lee-lee soon came to the dining quarters of the house. Having been instructed not to enter the main dining room, she angrily stepped into the adjoining room which had been assigned her.

Tensing, Lee-lee heard voices surfacing from the other side of the movable partition of cypress and sandalwood. She could distinguish between Tak-Ming's voice and his five older brothers as they most surely were already sitting at the grand, long table on expensive, red satin-covered high-backed chairs.

Tak-Ming's brothers lived a much different way of life than he, the youngest brother of the six. Each were married and were busy accumulating property and becoming highly educated to attain the top echelon—the scholar-official-administration class of the Chinese. They hadn't married large-footed, hard-working women. Their brides had been lovely, small, and pale, with bound feet, and they seldom left the house.

These five brothers were keeping the Book of Generations filled with the names of new sons, having been taught that a man's life begins with his ancestors and is continued in his descendants. And as they multiplied and held the family in joint ownership, family councils would decide on the careers of the new sons, their alliances to be contracted through marriages, and the buying and selling of land.

Their efforts were focused on living up to the motto: "Five Generations Under One Roof." And what affected the family as a whole was being recorded in the Yeung Family Book of Generations. But neither the brothers and their families nor the Book of Generations was of interest to Lee-lee this night. Her mind was on the American!

Since the dining room led out onto its own courtyard, Lee-lee knew that the American could be expected by that entrance at any time now. Whisking her skirt around, she rushed to a window that looked out onto this same courtyard. She drew back a bamboo curtain and patiently waited, standing back, making sure that she couldn't be seen in her mischief.

The moon was full and high. Such a moon would soon be celebrated by all Chinese with a Moon Festival. In the courtyard garden tamarind trees shone like dark silver, the flowers seemed great, yellow clusters, and the green *kananga* flowers swayed gently in the evening breeze. Brightly colored lanterns hanging on bamboo poles lighted a stone path in and around the garden, which could be a romantic setting if one traveled with the right man . . .

A murmuring of voices drawing near outside the window drew Lee-lee's keen attention from the garden, and she stepped farther back away from the window just in time, for Heung Chin Yeung, dressed in his splendid embroidered silks, stepped into view escorting the American at his side.

Lee-lee's fingers went to her throat when the light from the lanterns shone directly onto the American's face just before he entered the house. With a rapid pulse hammering away at her temples and her blood spinning wildly through her veins, Lee-lee was once more caught up in his handsomeness—he was the same American businessman she had viewed on board the ship *New Yorker*.

Because he was carrying his silk top hat, the American's full facial features could more easily be observed. His midnight black hair waved back from his forehead and hung neatly in place against his neck. His weather-tanned face displayed his long, aristocratic nose, his strong chin, and the sensual fullness of his lips.

But his dark eyes set beneath thick lashes were the most haunting feature about the man. In them—even with only the fast glance Lee-lee had been afforded—she had seen a cool aloofness which represented to her his lack of trust in the Chinaman at his side.

Almost dizzy from excitement, Lee-lee rushed across the room and knelt on the floor beside the movable partition, chose a carved opening in the shape of a lotus blossom, and let her eyes feast upon this man who seemed to have stolen her heart.

Though powerfully built as he was, he still displayed the long, trim torso and narrow hips of a well-proportioned male, set off by muscular thighs and broad shoulders. All of this could be easily seen in the impeccable way his finely-tailored, brown frock coat and trousers fit him.

Arranging herself more comfortably on her knees on the magnificent carpet of green velvet, she continued to watch while listening for any servant who might venture into her assigned room and catch her in the act of spying.

As was the room in which she was to eat her lonely

meal, the dining room was elaborately decorated with furniture of precious wood and expensive satin-embroidered wall hangings. Fancy lanterns adorned with satin fringe hung over the table, lighting the way for the many servants who were now ready to begin serving some thirty courses in solid silver dishes and wine cups.

Slowly Lee-lee let her gaze move from person to person seated around the table. First there was Tak-Ming, who sat taller and much more handsome than his five brothers who were lined up next to him with their wives and children at the table. And then there was Lee-lee's adopted Chinese mother, May-Ling, whose face was as painted and her hair as coiffed as Lee-lee's.

May-Ling, called Lady Yeung by most and who was Heung-Chin's most official wife, had not given Lee-lee much notice during the ten years Lee-lee had been a part of the House of Yeung. She wouldn't feel sad to have to leave this woman behind without even a good-bye, for May-Ling was only interested in seeing that her days were filled with embroidery and idle gossip with other wives of Foochow.

Lee-lee now looked to the head of the table where Heung-Chin reigned over all. And to his left, with his back to Lee-lee, was the American whom Lee-lee most of all had wanted to watch. Now she would not be given the opportunity because the high back of the chair in which he sat hid him quite well behind it.

But she could *hear* him! His voice was velvety and deep and he spoke Chinese quite fluently! And what was it that he and Heung-Chin were discussing? Business! While sharing the best of wine—*shao-shing*—which was known to be well-aged with some of the fiery *by-gar* added to it? This was strange. Business was usually discussed in the privacy of Heung-Chin's private study.

Lee-lee listened hard, becoming more in danger of being caught, yet too full of curiosity to care.

From what she could gather, this special guest was quite a rich American who had only recently arrived in the City of Foochow to spend much of his American silver coins on China's prime pekoe tea, spices, and silk.

Lee-lee watched a slow smile touch Heung-Chin's lips as he leaned toward the American, rubbing his finger and thumb together before the American's eyes, to pantomime the clinking of silver. It was then that Lee-lee realized that, while Heung-Chin despised most American merchants, this one was worth wining and dining because Heung-Chin thought it was best for his city.

If he only knew, Lee-lee laughed to herself.

If Heung-Chin had known that the American's interests lay also in opium, Heung-Chin would not have been so eager to please.

Hearing footsteps outside her door, Lee-lee shuffled to her feet, yet not too late to catch the American's name. He had said it in such a masculine way! Timothy. Timothy Hendricks . . .

Chapter Four

Chicken Velvet, made of the white meat of specially fed chicken and cunningly flavored with ginger, lay hardly touched on Lee-lee's silver plate. She picked at it daintily with her chopsticks made of bamboo, silver, and ivory, understanding fully what was taking the family so long to eat their meal in the adjoining room.

It was the practice of the Chinese to serve hot towels, which had been dipped in boiling water and wrung out by the servants, to cleanse their faces and hands between courses in order to prolong the delights of the meal.

Lee-lee had declined this same courtesy offered her by a servant. She did not want to prolong the wait for what could be the eventual meeting of the American if she kept the courage to follow through with her plan. But she knew that Heung-Chin would encourage his family and the American to follow each custom. It was traditional and Heung-Chin was quite a traditionally trained individual, it having been instilled in him by his family when he was a child.

Pushing her plate away, Lee-lee eyed a tray where

fresh fruit had been laid out before her. Her gaze wandered over the honey oranges, fragrant apples, and slices of *chefoo* pears skewered on toothpicks. And not having the appetite for any of these things, she instead chose a cup of jasmine tea and sipped impatiently from it. Then tiring of it all, especially the waiting, she rose from her chair and went to steal another peep through a fancy hole. Her heart jumped then skipped several beats when she saw that the meal was finally finished in the adjoining room.

Excitement swelled inside her as she saw Timothy Hendricks rise tall from his chair, towering over everyone else in the room except for Tak-Ming, who almost matched Timothy in size.

As Heung-Chin puffed on his silver water-pipe, Timothy was enjoying a fine, slim cheroot. The fragrant aroma of the cigar floated aimlessly toward Lee-lee and through the hole to which her eyes and nose seemed almost glued. When the smoke touched her nose, it didn't repel her but instead gave her a sensual thrill. It was as though the smoke from Timothy's cigar was in a sense Timothy himself touching her, and she closed her eyes and enjoyed the feeling.

But only for a moment. She had to get out into the hallway and no matter how Heung-Chin would reprimand her, she *had* to make contact with Timothy. And then, when she appeared out of nowhere by the great House of Yeung gate, Timothy would not be as totally surprised as he might have been, had he not known of her before the risky meeting that she planned.

Hearing the rustle of Heung-Chin's silk and satin attire

like a cicada's wings rubbing softly together, Lee-lee's eyes flew wildly open, just in time to see Heung-Chin and Timothy step from the room while the rest of the family lingered behind.

Scurrying to her feet and trying to draw courage from her need to meet the American, and possibly to share talk of her homeland with him, Lee-lee rushed from the room, putting the first steps of her plan in motion.

Voices and the aroma of cigar smoke met her approach as she began working her way toward their origin. Lee-lee knew that if she didn't hurry, Heung-Chin and Timothy would reach Heung-Chin's study—which she was sure was their destination—where even more discussion of business affairs would be exchanged in absolute privacy.

Praying that no one else would see her unladylike gait as she half ran, holding her fancy headdress to her head, Lee-lee made a turn in the hallway. To her complete surprise and chagrin, she slammed squarely into the back of Timothy Hendricks. She had made contact all right, but not in the way in which she had hoped!

The sudden jolt sent Lee-lee sprawling on the floor and alongside her fell the camellias from her hair. Stunned momentarily and feeling as if she had been thrown against a stone wall, Lee-lee shook her head and blinked her eyes. Though dazed, she could hear the low, outrageous grumblings surfacing from Heung-Chin. But above this, she heard Timothy's smooth, deep voice.

"I'm so sorry," Timothy said in perfect Chinese. "Here, let me help you."

The touch of his strong hand on her elbow stole Lee-lee's breath away from her and she dared not look up into

71

his face, for her eyes would reveal to him feelings that she didn't yet understand.

Lee-lee had to remember to speak in Chinese. She had to play out the charade before Heung-Chin's close scrutiny and was thankful that Timothy had studied the Chinese language very well and would understand her words.

"Thank you, kind sir," she said in Chinese, humbly keeping her head bowed as she rose to her feet. She so wanted to look up into Timothy's face as she had planned, but she was afraid. Should Heung-Chin guess her game, her days in the House of Yeung would be numbered!

"And I believe you dropped these," Timothy said, rescuing her flowers from the floor.

"Thank you," she said once more, her head still bowed. She reached out a hand, blind. And when it collided with his as he handed her the flowers, the camellias once more fluttered to the floor.

Lee-lee gasped, blushed, and looked quickly up into his eyes, embarrassed from her continuing clumsiness.

There was instant recognition on his part which surprised Lee-lee, for the one time he had seen her only her eyes had been made up to look Chinese. Even *she* had hardly recognized herself this evening beneath all the rice powder and paints. How could he recognize her?

Lee-lee felt the world melting away around her as he gave her an appraising, intense stare from eyes darkening with his discovery. And as his gaze traveled slowly over her, a trail of fire was left by the touch of his eyes.

Then she was startled to an awareness of Heung-Chin's

presence as Heung-Chin began shouting at her, shaming her for being a disobedient concubine.

Lee-lee's eyes widened in disbelief. Heung-Chin was drawing suspicion away from himself by calling her a concubine! An American concubine would be more easily explained than an American daughter!

She glanced hurriedly from Timothy to Heung-Chin, seeing confusion etched on Timothy's handsome face, and then she began to fear the American. If Timothy wanted to truly impress the Chinese mandarin, he could tell how even more disobedient this concubine had been! He could tell that she had also been on a schooner . . . a part of a conspiracy to exchange opium for silver coins! Yet, Lee-lee realized that Timothy couldn't do this. To tell such a truth would also expose his part in a most illegal transaction!

"*Ai*, my lord," she then blurted, bowing toward Heung-Chin. "My behavior is inexcusable. I shall return to my quarters at once."

Heung-Chin gestured fitfully with a hand. "*Wei*! Away with you!"

Still bowing, Lee-lee crept slowly away from him backward. She gave Timothy a quick look then turned and walked in the other direction, forcing herself to take the tiny steps which were expected of a gentle, meek Chinese lady.

Then once out of view, Lee-lee raised the hem of her dress and coat and began running, breathless now with anxieties over the coming adventure. She knew not how long Heung-Chin would hold council with Timothy in his private study. But she did know that she wanted to be at

73

the gate waiting for Timothy when his buggy moved from the House of Yeung's great estate of various courtyards. When he saw her standing there, he most surely would stop for her. And she would worry about Heung-Chin and his punishment later. Even now she doubted there would be any reprimand for her behavior of a moment ago, for she suddenly remembered that of late he had had a tendency toward forgetting. She had begun to suspect that though he outwardly opposed the use of opium, he was possibly enjoying it in the privacy of his quarters.

Smiling mischievously, Lee-lee hurried to her room, panting as she closed the door behind her. The sweet jasmine smell of perfume circled upward into her nose. She looked toward her bed, inviting in its neatness with the lavender satin *beiwu* laid back, awaiting her arrival between it and the matching satin sheet.

She looked slowly around the room, cozy in the soft light of flickering candles. Soonya had done her duties well and had left as she had been instructed. Lee-lee was now gratefully alone, to her *own* choice of toiletries! No makeup was required for what she had in mind, not even around her eyes. She would not have to playact to appear American. She *was* American and she would proudly display her heritage to this American businessman . . . this man who went by the charming name of Timothy Hendricks.

"Timothy Hendricks," Lee-lee whispered, testing the name on the tip of her tongue, enjoying the way it sounded. And not only was his name charming but surely his personality as well. Had he not had the power to attract the attention of the Mandarin Heung-Chin Yeung when no other American had succeeded in doing so?

Tossing her shoes and then her clothes aside as she undressed, Lee-lee was in a half swoon as she remembered the helpless surrender she had felt beneath the hold of Timothy's dark, magnetic eyes.

But she had to force him from her mind. Such foolishness! Her feelings for this American were only because he was the first she had seen up close since the day of the shipwreck. She was most surely fascinated by the fact that he was American, and not because he was a man who had stolen her heart!

"I must hurry," she whispered. "I mustn't let myself get so confused by feelings. I mainly want to talk to him. I want to hear of America! I wonder if he might possibly have known any of my family, since he's from New York."

Unwrapping her breast binder, she sighed with relief when her breasts were set free. She dropped the binder to the floor then rubbed her aching breasts, seeing how their color was returning as they resumed their usual, fully shaped swells.

"I just don't understand the Chinese," she grumbled. "Why do they punish the women so by binding their breasts! Well, tonight I do not have to! Tonight I am American!"

The smell of Timothy's cigar still clung to the perfumed strands of her hair as she began to unwind them from the frame. Again she was caught up in the fantasy of him and this time let herself enjoy it until she was dressed in her padded tunic and leggings. She coiled her hair up into a circle beneath her rattan hat, stepped into her straw sandals, and, after cleansing her face of the Chinese mask, she was ready to proceed with her daring venture.

One sweep of her eyes around the room took in the disarray of her discarded clothes and made her realize how quickly suspicions would become aroused should anyone enter her room while she was gone. And once more she looked toward her bed. Should it even be discovered to be empty . . .

With determination setting her jaw, Lee-lee rushed around the room. She began picking up her clothes, and, devious as it was, she took them and placed them beneath the blankets on her bed. Along with the help of one pillow, she shaped this all to look as if she were there, sound asleep.

Satisfied, she crept around the room, snuffing out candles. And when this was done, she stood as a mere shadow in the opened doorway, pretending she might be an observer looking into her room.

"*Ai*, Lee-lee is peacefully asleep," she whispered, giggling.

She closed the door, pulled the brim of her hat low over her face, and headed for the nearest exit. Once reached, she breathed much more easily then raced across the open courtyards. The pods of a mimosa tree rattling ominously above her, and the dancing glow from the swaying lanterns casting ghost-like figures all around her gave her a momentary start. Suddenly she realized just what it was to be alone. Tak-Ming had almost always been with her when away from the safe confines

76

of the courtyard. Without him she could be in mortal danger. She knew that now.

While in the House of Yeung it had been simple to plan how she would meet the American. But now? She understood just how many things could make her plan go awry.

Foochow was a magnificent city, filled with many lovely things to look at, one of which was its stone Bridge of Ten Thousand Ages that was over one thousand years old. And there were the beautiful pagodas—towers with colorfully bright roofs curving upward at the division of each of several stories. Yet there were many *unfortunate undesirables* who made their residences in the city, most of whom hid in the darkened passageways, living off those they robbed in the black of the night.

Lee-lee stopped to rest against a cherry tree. She breathed hard, more afraid now. Then she looked at the way she had chosen to dress. It was not the attire of an affluent person. There would be no need to knock her mindless, for it was evident that she had no riches to share.

"*Ai*," she whispered. "I am safe enough."

She squinted her eyes and looked into the distance, toward the mansion. The oiled-paper windows glowed with light. And from this angle she was now able to see the horse and buggy waiting for the American, to return him to his ship.

"At least that is in my favor," Lee-lee sighed, repositioning a stray lock of hair back beneath her hat. "Timothy Hendricks hasn't left yet."

She then focused her attention on the main gate only a few yards away from her. Another thing was in her favor. The gate had been left unlocked for the departure of the evening's guest, and of late no armed guards had been required to stand watch there.

No threats had been voiced out loud against Mandarin Heung-Chin Yeung. Most admired and respected him. Yet Lee-lee knew that much of this admiration and respect had grown from fear of him. A beheading to Heung-Chin was like the trees are to the wind—nothing! There was no mercy when his wrath was unleashed, inhuman as the wind that has no feelings in the eye of a vicious, raging storm.

A movement in the corner of her eye caught Lee-lee's attention. Her heart pounded hard and her knees took on a strange, rubbery sensation when she saw Timothy Hendricks boarding his buggy. And when he positioned himself on the padded seat, lifting a whip to the horse's back, Lee-lee began to run fast toward the gate. When safely there, only a few feet outside the gate, she crouched down beside a *lichee* tree and listened as the horse and buggy drew closer and closer.

Now Lee-lee's heartbeats were threatening to suffocate her, for she knew her moment was near. She wiped a bead of perspiration from her brow and swallowed back a sudden dryness that had invaded her throat. Then she rose to her full height, daringly stepped out into the open, and faced the buggy as it rumbled toward her.

There was a pulling sensation in Lee-lee's heart when she saw Timothy raise the whip and this time not to use on his horse. Apparently the night was too dark for him to realize that this was not a lowly, dangerous criminal jumping out to steal from him or, worse yet, trying to kill him.

Lee-lee flinched and screamed at the whip snapping close to her face, catching her on the right hand as its tail whipped by her. When she saw Timothy quickly lift the whip again, she yelled his name, this time speaking in English quite clearly.

"No! Timothy! Stop!" she yelled. She stepped aside, waving her hands wildly above her. "I'm no threat to you! I'm a *woman*! I'm an *American*!"

Hearing the voice . . . hearing his name being spoken in perfect English by someone unknown to him—and by a woman at that, an American woman—Timothy stopped the whip in midair and pulled his horse's reins tightly to stop its further approach toward the sudden intruder in the night.

Fearing this was possibly a trick, he placed his right hand on a hidden pistol belted at his waist and leaned forward with a curious eyebrow lifted. "What is your name and what do you mean by stepping so boldly in front of my buggy as though you don't have any sense?" he snarled.

As Lee-lee stepped closer and came into view, the full moon's glow on the soft features of her face and the magnificent swell of her breasts was evidence enough for Timothy, and his curiosity about this woman was immeasurable! Three times now he had seen her and each time she had taken on a different appearance. She had even pretended to be a man while on the opium-carrying ship! Even though dressed again like a man this night, she at least admitted to being a woman, which she most surely was!

Lee-lee jerked the rattan hat from her head and shook her hair, letting its perfumed, sleek blackness tumble full and free around her shoulders. She lifted her chin boldly.

"My name is Lee-lee," she said, trying to stiffen, to hide her frightful trembles. She wasn't sure yet if the American could be trusted. Should he wheel his horse and buggy around and head back toward the House of Yeung to tell Heung-Chin about her disobedient behavior, she was doomed.

She took another step closer, unnerved by his silence and studious stare as he so nonchalantly lighted a cheroot. It was as if he were now enjoying this game in which she could so easily be the loser.

"Lee-lee is my adopted Chinese name," she said, hating the nervous crack in her voice. "But my true American name is Letitia Taylor. It would please me, sir, if you would allow me to accompany you to your ship for a short, friendly chat. I would like to hear of America. I haven't been there now for ten . . . long . . . years."

Lee-lee tried to ignore the throbbing of the wound on her hand that had been placed there by this man's cruel whip. But she knew that she was lucky, indeed, that the whip hadn't inflicted a wound on her face, which would possibly disfigure her there for life.

"You are of the House of Yeung," Timothy said, flicking ashes from his cigar. "You are the mandarin's concubine. How is it that you are? There is no question in my mind that you are an American. And it was you on the opium ship. How can you be all these different things? Surely the mandarin doesn't realize that you are a person of many disguises."

His gaze once more ventured over her, seeing her

loveliness even in the lowly Chinese garb that she had chosen to wear this night. In his mind's eye he was remembering how strikingly beautiful she had been in the Chinese dress. He had seen the face hidden behind the cosmetics. He had seen the sensual flare of her lips, the haunting honey-brown of her eyes . . .

Feeling much too vulnerable standing near the gate entrance only a stone's throw away from Heung-Chin's private quarters, Lee-lee glanced nervously about her. Then she looked up at Timothy, beseeching him with her eyes, his handsomeness and his virile masculinity almost a threat to her sanity with him so close to her.

"Sir, it is not safe for me to stand here so openly defying my adopted father Heung-Chin's wishes," she quickly blurted.

Timothy absorbed her words and became numbed by them. "Adopted father?" he said, looking over his shoulder at the mansion then back toward Lee-lee.

His eyes took on a confused squint. "The mandarin said that you were his concubine," he murmured. "Did he lie?"

"*Ai*, he did," Lee-lee quickly responded, nodding eagerly. "But that does not matter. What does is that I must leave quickly before I am discovered."

She angrily tossed her head. "Or is it that you don't wish to bother with the likes of me, a woman who dresses Chinese and not American?"

Timothy placed his cigar between his lips and contemplatingly puffed from it. "Is it refuge you want on my ship?" he asked cautiously. "If so, I cannot comply. I cannot afford any mishaps to cause danger to myself or my crew. Should the mandarin . . ."

Rage rose quickly inside Lee-lee. This man was a rogue! He wouldn't help her even if she had asked! What kind of a man was he not to offer help to an American citizen . . . a woman at that . . . so far from her homeland!

Thank God it hadn't been her purpose to ask his services in returning her to America. Thank God for her dear Tak-Ming.

"*Nay*," she said icily. "I do not intend to ask anything of you but conversation, Mr. Hendricks."

She plopped her hat angrily on her head. "But if you fear my presence for even a short length of time, I shall be on my way," she hissed. "But do not expect an apology for my inconvenience to you, because, sir, you are not deserving of such thoughtfulness on my part."

Timothy placed his cigar between a thumb and forefinger and flipped it away from him. He laughed hoarsely as he offered Lee-lee a hand. "You are a spirited one," he said. "I think I will enjoy having you as a guest on my ship, if even for only a little while."

Lee-lee hesitated before accepting his hand. His blunt refusal to offer her any sort of assistance other than agreeing to talk with her had dispelled her earlier amorous fantasies of him. It seemed to her that his charm was a façade, used only when it benefited him.

Realizing this, she trusted him even less and would be very guarded in her words with him. How could she know, even now, that he would not later tell Heung-Chin about her deceit in the House of Yeung?

Shrugging, Lee-lee wanted only to think of now and the opportunity at hand. Oh, how badly she wanted to hear of her beloved America!

Unsmiling, she brushed his hand aside. "I am very capable of boarding your buggy without assistance," she said dryly.

Timothy lifted an eyebrow. "I'm sure you are," he said, chuckling beneath his breath.

His velvet-dark eyes twinkled as she scooted onto the seat beside him. His nose captured the sweet jasmine smell of her and a quiver of sorts disturbed his insides, as he saw now even more closely her flawless beauty.

When her eyes turned to him with anger reflected so openly, causing them almost to dance, Timothy's heart skipped a beat. Not since Cathalina Unser had he been so quickly taken by a lady. He forced his eyes away, realizing the dangers of that. One woman had betrayed his love. That one time was enough to last a lifetime. And he must also remember that this woman at his side belonged to another way of life. She was now most definitely more Chinese than American, no matter how she had happened to become that—

"Sir, what is the delay?" Lee-lee snapped. "If you have changed your mind, just say so." She rubbed her throbbing hand, wincing when she saw him reach for the whip.

Timothy cracked the whip across the horse's back then he lifted the reins and directed the buggy on away from the gate. "No," he said. "I haven't changed my mind."

He gave her a half glance, noting how she was preoccupied with her one hand. Then he remembered her reaching her hand to protect her face when he had used the whip in an attempt to scare her away, having thought at the time that she was a thief. . . .

"Did the whip inflict a measurable wound?" he asked

softly. "You know that I wouldn't have used the whip had I known."

Lee-lee separated her hands and placed them on her lap. "The measure of my wound *or* my pain is truly no concern of yours, sir," she said blandly.

Realizing that he had somehow inflicted a wound not only to her hand but to her pride as well, Timothy wondered how he had come to do this.

But he would not ask. Getting into "feelings" was a sure way to encourage "involvement."

"And, *sir*," she continued, "neither things nor people wound me so easily."

Timothy grimaced at her annoying habit of calling him "sir," even placing special emphasis on the way she spoke it as though purposely wanting to grate away at his nerves.

"My name is Timothy," he said. "Perhaps the name is a hard one to remember?"

Lee-lee's face flamed in added frustrated anger over his insolent behavior. First he denied her help—though she never even asked for it—then he implied that she was ignorant!

Her eyes blazed as she cast him a set stare. "The Chinese have a saying . . ." she said hotly.

Timothy caught her pause in words and had a feeling that she was baiting him, because it was quite obvious that he had once more, somehow, spoken out of turn.

A slow, teasing smile wryly lifted his lips. He would play her game. In fact, he was enjoying it. "Oh?" he said. "And what is that saying . . . uh . . ." He rolled his eyes upward, faking ignorance, then quickly added ". . . Hmm. Seems I forgot *your* name."

Understanding fully what he was up to, Lee-lee was at first annoyed and then amused. She was able to relax her shoulders, feeling more comfortable with him now that she knew that at least he showed signs of having a sense of humor.

"Well, as you surely have heard, most Chinese hate the barbarian, foreign devil American traders," she said, watching his smile fade, to be replaced by a trace of worry wrinkles about his eyes and nose. "The Chinese people say that the barbarians do not know the simplest customs which even a poor coolie knows. They say the barbarians do everything backward."

Timothy's eyebrows forked. He gave Lee-lee a guarded glance. "Oh?" he said. "Like what? What do they mean when they say we do everything backward?"

"Why, Timothy, you do read a book from left to right, do you not?" she teased.

"Do you mean to say . . . ?"

"*Ai*. The Chinese laugh at how Americans read a book backward," Lee-lee giggled.

Her eyes shone in the moonlight and when Timothy looked toward her, her heart skipped a beat. She, for a moment, forgot that he was a rogue . . . someone who had no true feelings for anyone except himself.

"It's good to hear you laugh," he said thickly.

"And why shouldn't I?"

"Your life. I'm sure it leaves much to be desired."

Lee-lee found herself tensing again. She couldn't let herself reveal too much of her personal life to him. It was too risky. "Oh?" she said. "And why do you say that?"

"Later," he said. "We'll discuss it after we get safely aboard my ship. We're drawing near to the heart of the city and I must focus my full attention on any movements in the darkness. I was warned that it was dangerous to be in the city at night."

"You were told right."

Timothy once more glanced her way. "Yet you are here with me, a perfect stranger, nearing the heart of the city," he said. "Don't you know the risks involved?"

"Sometimes risks are necessary and, in the end, worth it."

Snapping his whip against the back of his horse to hurry it along, Timothy began watching all the dark, narrow streets that seemed to trail out in all directions. They were like tentacles on an octopus, bordering shops of all sizes and shapes which were only silhouettes against the black framework of night.

"You are quite a complex lady," he said. "How many personalities rule your life? I have seen suggestions of many."

"Again, that is no concern of yours," Lee-lee said. She was remembering Soonya saying how a woman's face ruled her destiny. Lee-lee knew that Soonya had been referring to how a man might be taken by a certain face, and therefore the man would be the true ruler of the woman's destiny. And what of her? She couldn't allow this to happen. No man would rule her. Especially not Mandarin Heung-Chin Yeung nor Emperor Tao Kuang!

She turned her eyes slowly toward Timothy. He had come the closest to being a threat to her self-preservation. If she let them, the strangest, sweetest sensations could even now swirl around inside her when she let herself look more closely at the man who was only a touch away . . .

"My God, what . . . is . . . that . . . ?" Timothy gasped.

An involuntary shudder raced through Lee-lee as she followed his gaze and she also saw the horrible sight ahead at the side of the road. It was the execution grounds for the city of Foochow. And this night, as the moon was at its fullest, nothing was left to the imagination. Staked naked to the ground with their legs widely spread and arms above their heads, ten men lay waiting to be executed for their various crimes, mostly piracy.

The victims were pathetic, not only because they knew they would soon be decapitated, but also because their bodies had purposely been smeared with syrup, which had attracted a tremendous assortment of flies, gnats, and mosquitoes. Even an occasional rat darted in and out of the darkness to take a quick bite.

The darkness was a blessing, though, for during the day, the fiery hot sun must surely have tortured them horribly. It had been known to drive some men mad before their heads had been separated from their bodies.

"Life is cheap in China," Lee-lee finally managed to say, closing her eyes as the buggy rattled by the men who yelled and cried for mercy.

Timothy blanched, now truly doubting his sanity for having agreed so hastily to Lee-lee's desire to talk in private with him on his ship. It could be him staked naked to the ground if the mandarin ever found out!

Timothy snapped the whip again, feeling nervous perspiration beading his brow. He was not only guilty of illegal trafficking in opium but of being with the mandarin's most private property—Lee-lee.

Chapter Five

Safely inside Timothy's master cabin, Lee-lee wondered about being truly safe. Except for Tak-Ming, this was the first time since she had reached the threshold of womanhood that she was really alone with a man.

With Tak-Ming, she had never worried. He had always treated her with respect as a true brother would. But now? With this American who had already proven himself to be a rogue, she wondered if he would treat her as respectfully?

On a ship with only men, did she appear even to deserve to be treated in such a manner? Surely she wasn't considered a whore for being so bold . . .

Timothy lighted another whale oil lamp which cozily brightened the cabin. "You shouldn't be here," he grumbled. "I was a fool to take such a risk. But now that you are, I will make the best of the situation and see to your return home quite soon."

Lee-lee chose a brown leather-upholstered chair and plopped down into it. "The mistake was mine for having chosen you to have conversation with," she pouted. "Of all the Americans who now drop anchor at the Port of Foochow, why did Heung-Chin decide to wine and dine you? In my estimation, you are the worst of the lot."

Her eyes wavered as she gave him a sideways glance. He was so handsome! And being with him still created such a stir inside her, no matter how little she now thought of his personality. If the truth were known, he had succeeded in stealing her heart away, and she couldn't allow him to keep it. Surely once in America she would find another man who could do the same, and one who could even love her back.

"So I am the worst of the lot, am I?" Timothy said, smiling wryly as he tossed his silk top hat across the room. It landed on a wide bunk on which was a lone pillow and bland-colored blankets crumpled from use.

"You surprise me," he continued, "by saying that. If I am the worst, how is it that you trust me enough to be alone in my cabin with me? A woman can get into all sorts of trouble by behaving so recklessly."

"You wouldn't dare lay a hand on me," Lee-lee hissed, rising angrily to her feet. She was surprised at how quickly she had emitted that outburst, for in truth—though she was silently beginning to loathe the man—she also hungered for him.

She blinked her eyes nervously as Timothy removed his frock coat and cravat, then unbuttoned his shirt halfway to his waist. Crisp, dark, curled fronds of chest hair crept from the front of his shirt, and beneath that, his bare chest shone beautifully in the lamps' subdued glow.

Timothy shrugged. "No, I wouldn't think of laying a

hand on you," he lied. "And why would I? I don't take to making love to a woman in a man's trousers."

Lee-lee's face flamed with embarrassment. "Sir, I don't know why you wish to humiliate me by saying such a thing, but it matters not," she said hotly.

She swept her gaze around the room. The paneling and door frame were made of a rich mahogany, scrolled beautifully for effect. The bunk covered the outside wall, positioned beneath a porthole, and beneath the bunk was a storage drawer. There was a built-in bureau, table, and desk, and several leather-upholstered chairs were anchored to the floor around the room. The floor shone like molasses and was clean enough to eat from if one so desired.

Lee-lee had wanted to spend some time here talking, but now she knew that it was not meant to be.

"No. It matters not to me at all that you enjoy the game of humiliating me," she continued to say. "As I said before, the mistake that was made here was mine and I am quickly going to amend my actions. I am going. And do not bother to see to my return home. I will find my own way."

Lifting her chin haughtily, she spun around and headed for the door. But her breath caught in her throat when he moved quickly, blocking her way, facing her with his smoldering, dark eyes.

"It would be easier for me if you did disappear from my life so quickly," he said hoarsely. He reached for her hat and slowly removed it. "But sometimes the easiest way is not the best way."

"Return my hat to me at once," she stormed, reaching

for it. With him so close, she felt such a sudden onslaught of passion for the man. Should he pull her into his arms, it would be almost impossible for her to refuse him anything he asked of her. Not only was she driven by awakening sensations that were making her heart race out of control, but she also felt the need to test the things shared between a man and a woman, to see how it felt to be kissed . . . to see how it felt to be sensually touched . . .

When Timothy saw the raw wound on the palm of Lee-lee's right hand as it gaped slightly open with blood drying on it, he dropped her hat and gently took her hand in his to study it more closely.

"What do you think you're doing now?" she sighed exasperatedly. "First you take my hat and now my hand? You dropped my hat to the floor. Will you casually discard my hand as well?"

The strange melting was once more torturing her insides as the flesh of his hand warmed against hers. She knew that she should break free from him, but she truly did not want to. These feelings inside her caused by Timothy were too sweet to be denied.

"Come over closer to the light!" he urged. His face had taken on a serious sternness and his eyes showed concern in their depths. "The wound inflicted by the whip is not just a scratch. It is much worse and I believe it needs quick medical attention."

Lee-lee felt both guilt and shame for being disappointed that it was her wound and not herself that he was interested in. "But I would soon be gone if you wouldn't take the time to do that," she said dryly. "Though you

91

stopped my leaving your cabin, you know that is what you want."

Timothy lifted her hand closer to his eyes. "I couldn't let you leave like this," he said. "If you tried to go through the heart of the city alone and were harmed in any way, I would be blamed. Mandarin Heung-Chin would—"

"Again you are only concerned with yourself!" Lee-lee said disgustedly, hoping that her voice had hidden her deep hurt and added humiliation. For a moment or two she had thought his actions had been guided by concern for *her*. Oh, how wrong she had been. He was selfish. He was the most heartless person she had ever met!

"Should I not be concerned for myself?" he said, raising his eyes to meet her hurt-filled gaze. "You saw the prisoners and how they awaited their fate, did you not?"

Lee-lee jerked her hand away, flinching as pain began stabbing away at it. "I assume your concern for my hand is for the same reason?" she said icily. "You are afraid that I will have to reveal to Heung-Chin the source of my wound?"

Timothy walked away from her, torn between feelings of needing her and being wary of his association with her. Yet he could hardly stand this wall of misunderstanding growing between them. And, damn it, he was confused by everything about her. Why was she a part of the House of Yeung? Why had she singled *him* out of all the other American traders? Why had she placed not only herself in danger by doing this thing tonight, but also the entire crew of the *New Yorker*? In this instance, talk certainly wasn't cheap!

Going to his desk, he withdrew a fresh cheroot from his cigar box. He bit off its tip and spat it into an ashtray, all the while watching her. He lifted the cigar, puffed leisurely on it a moment, then withdrew it from his mouth, eying her even more closely. "You are wrong about me," he said thickly.

He sat down on the corner of his desk, needing this distance that he had placed between them. The jasmine smell of her still clung to the hand that had touched her, slowly driving him wild . . .

"And why is that?" she asked, stooping to rescue her hat from the floor. "I am usually not a bad judge of character. And, sir, it's quite obvious why you are concerned for my welfare. Don't try to deny it."

"My name is Timothy. Please refrain from addressing me as 'sir,'" he growled. He balanced his cigar on the edge of an ashtray then rose from his desk.

"As my name is Lee-lee," she said haughtily. "Though I've yet to be addressed so properly by you."

Timothy tossed his head. "Let's do away with this bantering," he said. "Let me see to the wound I am responsible for. I carry all sorts of medical supplies on board my ship."

"All it requires at this moment is a little washing with some fresh water," she said. "I would trust water much more than any medication that you might suggest I use."

Timothy laughed amusedly as he went to his desk and opened a drawer. "I would never confess to being a medical doctor," he said. "But I assure you that I do carry the most up-to-date medications in case of mishaps on board my ship."

"Ah hah," Lee-lee said snappishly. "So there are more dangerous elements on your ship than my presence?"

"Always," Timothy said, chuckling beneath his breath. He did like her spirit! The fire in her eyes made her even more beautiful . . .

He withdrew a metal chest from the drawer and opened it, displaying a various assortment of vials of liquids, packaged bandages, and cotton-tipped swabs.

Lee-lee's hand throbbed unmercifully. She stepped closer to the desk and took an interested look at the ingredients in his medicine chest. "And which of those things are you thinking of using on me?" she asked. She realized that a scar could be left on her hand if it were not treated quickly enough. And there was Heung-Chin to be concerned about. What if he did see the wound and asked about it? A shudder coursed through her at the thought.

"After cleansing the wound I will apply some tincture of iodine to it. It's quite good as an antiseptic," he said thickly. "And it would be best not to bandage your hand. It will heal more quickly without it."

"That is not the true reason you choose not to bandage it, is it?" Lee-lee asked scornfully.

"What other reason would there be?" Timothy asked, pouring fresh water into a round, wooden basin.

"A bandage would draw too much attention to the wound," she scoffed. "Heung-Chin would demand answers. Isn't this what you truly fear?"

"It is common knowledge that such a wound heals much better if left uncovered," Timothy said, sighing, so tiring of her suspicions of him. "And, also, it is best not to cover a wound after doctoring it with iodine."

He gave her a soft smile and offered her his hand. "Now come on over here and sit down on the edge of my bunk and I shall minister to your wound."

Lee-lee eyed the basin of water that he had placed on a table beside the bunk then let her gaze move slowly back to him.

As their eyes met and locked, she knew the true dangers here. This cabin was almost overwhelmed by his darkly masculine presence. She felt every nerve in her body tensing, wondering about the burning ache between her thighs that being near him was causing.

Then her throbbing hand took precedence over all other feelings in her body, urging her to take the steps needed to carry her across the room to the bunk.

"All right," she murmured, sitting stiffly on the very edge of the bunk. "Since you are the only one available at the moment to doctor my wound, then I must accept whatever help you are offering."

She held her hand out before her, trembling. Closing her eyes, she turned her head away. "But please be gentle," she encouraged. "I hate to admit to such a weakness, but I do have a low tolerance for pain."

"Just relax," Timothy said, settling down beside her. He took her hand in his. Its daintiness, with her long, tapered fingers and carefully-manicured nails, made an added ache circle inside his loins. He had been without a woman for much too long now. It tended to eat away at the very soul of a man, this thing called loneliness.

He had learned to guard himself with all women since Cathalina Unser. When she had left Timothy at his age of twenty for another man of more wealth and power, he

95

had not only vowed to become as wealthy and powerful in his own right, but also never to trust a woman again. It had become his practice to use and discard them as one might a paper plaything.

To get his mind off his needs, Timothy began talking—anything to direct his thoughts away from this burning desire to have this particular woman. She wasn't just *any* woman. Somehow she was possessed by the House of Yeung.

He wanted desperately to ask why but felt it best not to wander into a delicate area of conversation which could lead to God knew what! It was best not to know. The sooner she was gone from his ship, the better!

"Did you know that iodine was named for a Greek word meaning 'violet'?" he said, wincing as she let out a loud "ouch" when he lowered her hand into the water.

"No. I did not know," said Lee-lee, still not looking Timothy's way as she felt the water being splashed gently on her wound.

"It was given this name because iodine is made of violet crystals from the ashes of seaweed," he further explained, now lifting her hand from the water. He began softly dabbing it dry with a towel.

"How interesting," Lee-lee sighed mockingly. Then she very softly added, "Are you almost finished? It seems to be taking forever."

"I now have to apply the iodine," he said, feeling her hand tense at his words. "The pain inflicted by the medicine will be brief."

"Just hurry," she cried softly. "This wasn't in my plans when I considered having conversation with you."

"None of this was in my plans for this evening," Timothy said dryly.

Lee-lee's eyes flew open widely. "Is my presence such an undesirable one?" she murmured, now hurt more than angry.

"Your presence here has raised many questions in my mind, most of which I have thought it best to leave unasked because of the circumstances of your residence."

"Ha!" she scoffed. "I, too, have many questions I could ask. You are a tricky one. First you manage to purchase a shipment of opium from Tak-Ming, then you manage to have private council with his mandarin father."

Her face suddenly paled. She hadn't planned to discuss opium or Tak-Ming with the American businessman. She didn't wish to reveal too much to someone whose trust was still in question.

She nodded toward her hand. "I am ready for the iodine, if you are ready to apply it," she said. She once more turned her head away and closed her eyes.

Confused by her sudden change of moods, Timothy resumed rambling on about anything but personal matters. He could not speak openly with someone whose trust was in question.

"The French chemist Bernard Courtois discovered iodine in 1812," Timothy said as he reached for a piece of iodine-soaked cotton. "But it was the French chemist Joseph Louis Gay-Lussac who proved that it was a chemical element and gave it the name of iodine."

"What are you? A scholar?" Lee-lee asked, opening

her eyes to give him a half glance.

"The time spent at sea is quite lengthy," he said. "I read a lot about a lot of things."

He nodded toward her wound, eying her with a cautious air about him. "I am now going to apply the iodine should you once more choose not to watch."

Lee-lee closed her eyes tightly and gritted her teeth. "Just hurry, won't you?" she whispered.

As the cold compound touched her wound, she let out a soft whimper and hated herself when tears rolled down her cheeks. She didn't want him to see the tears and laugh later about the woman who pretended to be strong but who in truth was weak.

Timothy looked quickly toward her turned head, having heard her gasp when he had touched the iodine to her opened flesh. A frown furrowed his brow as he hurriedly tossed the iodine-soaked cotton ball onto his desk. With ease he reached his hand around her and found her chin. He gently cupped it and urged her head around to face him.

The tears were glistening on her cheeks like fallen rain, and it tugged at Timothy's heart to know that he was the cause. If only he had not used the whip on her! But he had, and now he had inflicted even more pain by the application of the medicine.

"I'm sorry," he said hoarsely, becoming enraptured by her wide, honey-brown eyes as she so dolefully looked back at him. "I truly didn't mean to hurt you."

Teardrops clung to her thick lashes like dew. Her lips were ruby red in their sensual fullness and were quivering now as a fresh tear ran from the corner of an eye.

"I didn't mean to be a baby," she said, sniffling. "I rarely ever cry. Why did I have to now, while in *your* presence?"

She wiped her nose with the back of her uninjured hand then felt a delicious shiver of desire as he reached to smooth the tear away from her rosy cheek.

"No one could ever mistake you for a baby," he said huskily, as he now traced the soft line of her jaw with a forefinger. "Lee-lee, you are most undeniably a woman. A beautiful, alluring woman."

His pulse had quickened and the gnawing heat in his loins made him aware of the building dangers of being so near her. But she was so beautiful he would almost chance anything to be wholly with her. Was she capable of making him forget his past?

Lee-lee started to object to his soft, passion-filled words. But when the warmth of his hand once more touched her face, her voice caught in her throat and she was lost completely to her feelings.

She leaned her face gently against his hand and lethargically closed her eyes. Her body was once more a river of sensations, and she knew she hadn't dreamed of this moment only to deny herself of it, so she let the strange euphoria take hold . . .

"Lee-lee . . . ?" Timothy whispered.

Lee-lee could smell the aroma of cigars and expensive cologne which emanated from him, and she could sense that he was leaning closer to her.

"Lee-lee, I've got to kiss you," Timothy whispered, framing her face between his hands. "I've got to kiss you now."

Opening her eyes, Lee-lee watched with a pounding

heart as his lips drew closer. His eyes were closed . . . his face was flushed . . . and the palms of his hands were damp against her cheeks.

Then when his lips tenderly met hers, Lee-lee once more closed her eyes and realized that the moan that she heard in the room was hers. Nothing had ever felt as beautiful as the delicious warmth now spinning around inside her. It was making her feel as if she were floating, and she hoped to never again be brought back to reality.

Timothy surrounded her with his strong arms and drew her into his embrace as his tongue stole gently between her teeth and into the sweet cavern of her mouth.

Feeling the blossoming of rapture ripening inside her body, Lee-lee twined her arms about his neck and returned his kiss with more energy.

Understanding her message of submission, Timothy's blood began to spin hot through his veins. He swept a hand down her spine and then back up again around to where he cautiously began to explore a breast through her coarse, padded tunic.

Feverish with building ecstasy—not fearing the outcome of what she and Timothy were sharing but desiring it fully—Lee-lee withdrew from him and looked into his passion-drugged, dark eyes and slowly began unbuttoning her tunic. Never had she dreamed she could be so brazen. She had never even been kissed by a man before this night and now she was even ready to let him see and touch her breasts!

But she had never felt so alive as she did at this moment. She was tingling with it. And so much had been denied her by her prisonerlike status at the House of Yeung! Now that she was able to choose something for herself—if even for one night—she would choose the continuation of these sensations that the American had aroused in her. She wanted to experience. She wanted it all . . .

She only hoped that in the end she wouldn't respect herself less. She couldn't worry about *his* feelings toward her. That would be foolish. Chances were that they would never meet again.

As though in a drugged trance, Lee-lee freed the last button then opened her tunic and let her breasts fall free. Her breath was shallow as she saw his eyes darken in intensity, and he let his gaze move from her face to rest longingly on her breasts. She was not ashamed of how large she was as most Chinese women were taught to be. She was proud. Yet her face flamed when Timothy reached a hand and gently cupped one fully.

His kiss had sent a wildfire of sorts raging inside her, but the touch of his hand on her breast was making her insides feel scorched with the heated desire flaming there.

She reached a hand and caressed the sculptured lines of his face. She hadn't wanted to worry about what he thought of her, but feeling as she did for him, she had to care.

"What must you think of me?" she whispered, lowering her lashes. "You must think I do this often, when the truth is . . . I never have before."

"I do not dare say that I had suspected this, for to say that would lead you to believe I thought your kiss was one of inexperience," he said, placing a kiss on her lips.

101

"But I wouldn't believe you would freely give yourself to just any man, because in you I see strength and moral character."

"Then why do you think I do this with you?"

"For the same reason I do it with you," Timothy said quietly. "I am no different than you just because I am a man."

"Then . . . *why* . . . ?"

"Because there is a mutual attraction . . . a bond . . . something sensual between us that has drawn us together in such a way."

"The word 'love' is used to describe this sharing between a man and a woman," Lee-lee murmured, quivering inside as his hand dared another touch to her breast. "Is this the mutual attraction we have found in one another?"

Timothy tensed for he feared this word "love," having only spoken it to one other woman in his life, and she had abused it . . .

"Perhaps . . ." he said throatily. "Love is just a word. Feelings are all that are important now between us." His lips moved to her shoulder, then lower, to fasten gently to her breast.

Lee-lee let out a soft gurgle of pleasure. She arched her neck backward, sighing. "*Ai*," she murmured. "Feelings. Ah, if I could but define the feelings you are creating inside me!"

"Remember. Words are not important," Timothy said huskily.

"*Ai*," Lee-lee whispered, watching him now in a haze as he rose from the bunk and began undressing before her.

In his dark pools of eyes she could see the strength of his need for her. As magnets pulling her, these eyes of his seemed to command that she, too, should undress.

Stepping lightly from the bunk, she began to match him, a piece of clothing at a time. And when they both stood naked, facing one another, no words were needed as their eyes traveled over each other.

Lee-lee had never seen a man undressed before and she was finding that looking at Timothy was almost as stimulating as his kiss. As she had known he would be, he was a powerfully built man with thick, corded muscles at his shoulders and quite an expanse of tanned, sleekly muscled chest which displayed an abundance of crisp, black hair tapering down to his waist.

Daring a look lower, Lee-lee saw his narrow hips, and then she saw the male strength of his now swollen manhood and suddenly she was afraid . . .

Timothy's gaze traveled over her, seeing the ripeness of her body in the way her breasts were voluptuously large yet firm, as they swelled perfectly from her chest. The soft pink of her flesh narrowed in at her waist then flared out again at the soft curves of her hips.

Then Timothy's eyes widened in wonder when he saw the triangle of hair at the base of her stomach. It was bright red! Nothing at all like the raven black hair that hung in thick waves down her back. But the color didn't matter. It was the treasure that lay there waiting to be taken!

His gaze shot quickly up when he saw Lee-lee's hands cover herself there and she began to take slow steps backward. He felt a warning shoot through him when he saw the sudden fear in her eyes.

"What is it, Lee-lee?" he asked, taking a step toward her.

"Seeing you . . . well . . . you know . . . has lessened my desire somehow," she murmured, feeling her face flaming with embarrassment.

How had she let this get so out of hand? Why had she let her curiosity get the best of her?

She glanced down at his hugeness, again fearing having it even near her, much less inside her. Yet, she had lied to him. Her fears hadn't lessened her desire. Instead, it had made her want him even more.

Wei! She didn't understand herself at all. Being a woman was much more complicated than being a girl.

"This is your first time to see a man fully unclothed?" Timothy asked.

"*Ai* . . ." she said.

"Not even a brother . . . ?"

Lee-lee's lashes lowered. "In my lifetime I have had one true brother and six adopted brothers, and *nay*, I have seen none in such a way."

"Then, sweet one, it is now time to let yourself," Timothy said huskily as he moved toward her. "If you will just let yourself, you will experience a joy beyond words by relaxing and letting what has begun between us continue."

With him now so close, Lee-lee could no longer see that part of his anatomy which had unnerved her so. But she could feel the heat in its rock hardness as it was now pressed against her flesh.

Timothy coiled his fingers through her hair and drew her face closer to his. "Let me love you," he whispered. "Let me show you the way to paradise."

In a blaze of fury his lips crushed down upon hers, his hands free from her hair and now urgent on her body. He cupped his hands around the curve of her buttocks and pressed her body harder against him in a grip of passion that caused them to melt together, becoming one.

Gently he began to lower her to the bunk, keeping her in bondage against him while all the while kissing her long and demandingly. When he had her on the bunk, only then did he release his hold on her. He leaned away from her and softly touched the fullness of her lips with a finger.

"You're beautiful beyond words," he said, raking his eyes over the soft, pink curves of her body.

"Surely you've said that to many women whose hearts you have stolen," she said, trembling as he lowered his lips to a breast and sensuously circled his tongue around it.

"This is not the time to speak of other women," he said hoarsely. His dark eyes looked into hers, marveling at their honey-brown coloring anew, having never seen such a combination of color before. "As it is not the time to speak of other men." There was a questioning in his tone of voice.

Lee-lee positioned herself more comfortably on the bunk, brushing aside his silk top hat which he had so idly thrown there when they had first arrived. "You can wonder about that after my reaction to seeing you undressed?" she murmured, still being scrutinized by the hold of his eyes.

"In the dark a woman doesn't necessarily have to see a man to enjoy him," he growled. He was thinking of Tak-Ming, the mandarin's handsome son. He was not Lee-lee's true brother and there seemed to be a strange sort of camaraderie between them . . . a bond that surely no one could break.

Lee-lee rose angrily from the bunk. "You are insulting," she hissed. "Oh! Why am I here? What was I thinking to become caught up in what at first seemed such magic between us."

In her anger, she had forgotten her injured hand, and as she began gathering her clothes up from the floor, a white-hot flash of pain went through her. "Ouch!" she cried, dropping the clothes to blow on her throbbing hand.

Timothy hurried to her, took her hand, and softly kissed the wound. "Let me kiss the pain away," he said.

There was more pain in Lee-lee's heart than in her hand, and she knew that his lips could not touch her there, so she pulled away from him. "I must go," she said, bending to once more rescue her clothes from the floor. "I've been gone way too long already."

"We haven't even talked," Timothy said, taking her clothes away from her. He tossed them aside and drew her into his embrace, holding her there and ignoring her squirming in an effort to be set free.

"We haven't yet traveled the complete journey to paradise together," he said, raining kisses across her face and lower, to the hollow of her throat.

Lee-lee was becoming mindless. Fighting her feelings was too hard a thing to do at the moment. The warmth of desire for him was coiling around inside her anew and she gave herself up to the ecstasy. His lips now possessed a breast and his hands traveled down the flatness of her stomach and lower, touching her where no man had ever touched her before.

As his fingers began to slowly caress the spot which now seemed the very center of her being, Lee-lee felt such a rush of heat flame her there, she moaned throatily and opened herself more to him.

Then feeling as though a soft glow had wrapped itself around her, Lee-lee followed him to the bunk. In a flash he was inside her, so quickly the pain of his entrance was now a memory and she only knew a delicious sort of melting as his thrusts were deep and often.

"We're almost there . . ." Timothy said, placing his lips against the softness of her neck, marveling at how she responded so wildly, meeting his thrusts with raised, eager hips. Yet he knew that he was the first with her. Oh, God, he wanted to be the last. But he couldn't let himself get lost in such wants. There was only now . . . now . . . now . . .

"I . . . believe . . . I am there," Lee-lee cried, exploding inside into such exquisite sensations, she trembled violently with the pleasure.

She locked her legs about his waist and clung fiercely to him, too soon losing what had been only a flash of joy. But it had left her feeling strangely at peace inside and she marveled at how he still worked away inside her. He was breathing hard against her neck and he was wet with perspiration.

"I must kiss you," he whispered.

"Please do . . ." she whispered back.

As his lips fell softly against hers and his hands twined through her hair, Lee-lee felt his body convulsing wildly against hers, and somehow she knew that he, too, had finally experienced the same sort of rapture.

Chapter Six

"Who are you?"

Timothy's question was so abrupt and came at such a strange time, Lee-lee pushed herself up on an elbow and stared unbelievingly toward him. "What did you say?" she gasped, still feeling the quivering of sensations between her thighs, though he was no longer inside her, pleasuring her there.

Timothy rose from the bunk and stepped into his trousers. Going to a cabinet positioned above his desk, he opened it and withdrew a crystal decanter of wine. He placed it on his desk then also removed two tall-stemmed wine glasses from the cabinet. But he knew that she had avoided his question long enough. Perhaps he had spoken in haste. She had reason enough to be dismayed by his question.

Turning his gaze to her, he was again taken by her loveliness as she lay so gracefully, so silken, across his bunk. He forced his eyes to meet the hurtful questioning in hers.

"I have a need to know more about you," he said.

"That is all. It is only a natural thing that I would wonder about your presence in the House of Yeung. As you have said more than once to me, the Chinese do consider all foreigners barbarians, yet the Mandarin Heung-Chin houses one beneath his roof?"

"*Ai*, you would wonder," she said, breathing easier. It had filled her full of awe, how he had switched from being a devoted lover to this man now only interested in getting answers to questions.

But, *ai*. She did understand and she, too, had many questions to ask of *him*.

Feeling vulnerable in her nakedness, she let her gaze move about the room in search of something in which to cover herself besides her own clothes.

Then she looked at the foot of the bunk, seeing in its disarray of mussed blankets and sheets and clothing a silk man's robe. She reached for it.

"May I?" she asked, pulling it free from everything else.

"Yes. Go ahead," Timothy said, now pouring wine into the glasses.

The smell of him was on the maroon-colored robe. It smelled of a rich man's cologne and cigars. She inhaled it deeply, savoring it, as she rose to her feet and slipped into it.

She tied it around her slender waist, unable to hide the deep cleavage where the satin of the robe fell sensuously away from her magnificent swell of breasts. She knew that the robe rippled down her body and clung to her, and she felt his eyes as he carried the two glasses of wine toward her.

"Wine for my lovely lady?" Timothy asked, offering a glass.

Lee-lee hesitated. "I don't usually . . ." she said.

"It's good for the soul." He chuckled. "And it's a wine brought from the grapevines of America. Surely knowing that, you can't resist taking at least one tiny sip."

Lee-lee smiled devilishly up at him. "Do you hope that it will weaken my senses, enabling you to seduce me a second time this night?" she teased.

"Now that you've brought it to mind, that wouldn't be a bad idea," he said, lifting an eyebrow as a soft laugh rumbled from deep inside him.

"Do not dwell on it," she said flatly. "Because it won't be permitted to happen again, ever, if I have a say in the matter."

"Oh?" Timothy said, his eyes squinting as he leaned down into her face. "Are you saying that you didn't enjoy it? Wasn't it as pleasurable as you had always dreamed it would be in your wildest fantasies?"

"Fantasies?" she scoffed. "*Nay*. None."

"You didn't answer my most important question."

"And which was that?"

"Did you enjoy our moments together?"

Lee-lee's face flamed. To evade his question she eased a glass of wine from his hand. She balanced it between the fingers of her left hand to avoid aggravating the throbbing soreness of her other.

Taking a slow sip of the wine, she watched his annoyance at her refusal to answer him over the rim of her glass.

Timothy tipped his glass to his lips. "I doubt if I get

any answers out of you," he grumbled.

He settled down on a plush, leather chair behind his desk and propped his bare feet up on it. "But perhaps that's best. The less I know the less the chance of a deeper involvement."

He placed his glass on his desk and lighted a cheroot, following her movements as she went to sit down on the bunk and leaned her back against the outside paneled wall.

"My true name is Letitia Taylor," she said in a rush of words. "I was born in New York City in February of 1831. My father's name was Kenneth; my mother's was Aubrey. Then there was my brother, Richard, who was ten years older than I."

"Damn!" Timothy said, surprised at her sudden openness. He puffed eagerly on his cigar as she once more began talking.

"We were on our way to China on one of my father's new ships," she said as though in a daze. "My father had hoped to interest the Chinese in the types of ships that his company built. He chose his finest and decided to travel to China himself, to show it off personally to them."

Timothy dropped his feet to the floor and leaned forward, absorbing her each and every word. He now held his cigar between the forefinger and thumb of his left hand and took an occasional sip from the wine glass which he held in the other.

"And . . . ?" he prodded.

Lee-lee swallowed hard and her heart began to race. She was even aware of nervous perspiration lacing her brow. To her, talking about that day would be the same as reliving it.

She took a quick sip of wine, coughing as it scorched her throat. She wiped a tear from the corner of an eye then continued with her tale of heartbreak.

"There was a storm at sea," she said softly, in her mind's eye seeing the great waves rushing toward her father's prized ship which he had named *Starblazer*. She could hear the cracking of the masts, the flapping and tearing of the sails. She could feel the blast of the wind as it had tossed her about on the deck before the topsail had crashed only inches away from where she lay. The cries of the crew . . . the shrieks from her mother . . . still tore at her heart, for it was shortly after that that an enormous wave seemed to swallow the ship whole. . . .

"The storm at sea? What then?" Timothy asked, snapping her from her self-induced trance.

"Need I say more?" she murmured, turning her eyes away from him. "I am here. Alive. The other members of my family are not."

"They . . . all . . . perished?" Timothy quietly asked, placing his glass on the desk and then his cigar in an ashtray. He rose and went to sit down beside her.

"As far as I know," she said, clearing her throat nervously when the words seemed to stick there.

"How did you . . . ?"

"All that I can remember is my father handing me over the railing of the ship," she murmured. "There were only two longboats. My brother Richard was in one that left the ship before me. And my mother and father were . . . they were still on the sinking ship when the longboat I was in rowed away from it."

"So you have no doubt that your parents are dead?" Timothy asked, taking her empty glass from between her fingers.

"*Ai* . . ."

"And your brother Richard?"

"Only the longboat I was in was found by Tak-Ming."

"Such a tragedy," Timothy said, taking her left hand and squeezing it affectionately.

"So that is how I came to be of the House of Yeung," she said, sniffling, forcing a smile. "Tak-Ming carried me to Heung-Chin and he decided to raise me as his daughter."

"Such a kindness on his part," Timothy said, closely watching her reaction.

"*Ai*," she said. "I learned the Chinese language quite quickly and their customs. I even taught Tak-Ming how to speak English fluently."

Timothy lowered his eyes. His face became strangely shadowed. "Tak-Ming," he said hoarsely. "You speak so . . . so fondly of him."

Lee-lee's voice became warm and her eyes brightened. "There is no one more special to me than Tak-Ming," she murmured.

Timothy's eyes shot quickly upward. His jaw became set and his pronounced chin became hard. Jealousy raged through him, twisting his gut unmercifully.

"In China, Tak-Ming Yeung would most surely be considered a criminal," he growled. "He illegally transports opium."

Lee-lee's back stiffened. She gave Timothy an icy

stare. "And so do you," she said dryly. "And even I was on Tak-Ming's ship, helping him, as you know. Did that make me less desirable to you?"

"No . . ."

"Then please do not speak of Tak-Ming in such an accusing tone."

Jealousy now tore at Timothy's heart. Lee-lee's feelings for the handsome Chinaman were much too strong to believe she didn't feel more for him than what a sister feels for a brother.

Yet, he hadn't been her lover. There had been proof of that . . .

"Enough about myself," Lee-lee said, rising. She took her wine glass from Timothy and went to refill it, having taken a liking to the red, fiery liquid. Up to now, hot jasmine tea had been the only drink offered her in the House of Yeung.

She twirled around, eyes wide. "Please tell me about America! Please tell me about yourself!"

Timothy, still consumed by jealousy, also went and poured himself another drink. "I must ask you something else before leaving the subject of Letitia Taylor behind," he said. "Are you happy?"

He turned slowly to face her, feeling a strain on her part and a hesitation to answer him. He wondered why.

Lee-lee smiled up into his eyes and gestured with her glass toward him. "Why, *ai*," she said. "Exceedingly! I am spoiled with fine silks, jewels—"

"And a need for dangerous travel on a ship which carries opium cargo," he said, interrupting her. "If you were so exceedingly happy with a life of fine silks and jewels, why on earth would you risk losing it all by traveling, dressed as a lowly coolie, on the dark waters of the Min River? Why did you feel the need to come with me here?"

Lee-lee's pulse raced. She couldn't tell him the truth. She couldn't reveal her need to escape Heung-Chin . . . to go to America. She still couldn't fully trust this man who turned her insides to warm mush.

She stood on tiptoe and spoke firmly into his face. "I told you that I am happy," she said. "That is the answer to your question, and that should be enough." She took one more drink of wine and set her glass down on a table, avoiding his studious stare.

Of course Timothy didn't believe her. The truth was in her voice and in her eyes. Yet he had to pretend to believe her. He wanted no trouble from her or her Chinese family. He could still see the prisoners staked beneath the moonlight.

"All right," he said, shrugging. "So you are happy. Good. I'm glad."

He gave the tip of her nose a quick, affectionate kiss then moved away from her and stretched out on the bunk, leaning against the wall. He crossed his legs at his ankles and leisurely sipped on his wine.

"Well?" Lee-lee said, running to jump on the bunk beside him. She moved to her knees and faced him. "Aren't you going to tell me? I'm so anxious to hear about America."

"And about me?" he teased. His gaze absorbed her nearness, trailing over her, resting on her breasts which were fully visible where the robe fell away from them.

115

"*Ai*. About you!" she said. "You *are* America in my eyes, Timothy."

Timothy laughed hoarsely. "God. What a compliment," he said, almost choking on a sip of wine. He placed his glass on the floor, took her left hand in his, and kissed its soft palm. "Thank you, my sweet. That was a kind thing to say."

"Must I wait forever?" she sighed. "You do have a way of talking around things."

"America?" he said. "You wish to hear about America first?"

"The city of New York," she said. "Have you by chance ever heard of *Taylor Shipbuilders*? My father owned the company before his ill-fated journey at sea."

Timothy kneaded his chin. "No," he said. "Can't say that I have. My partner Calvin Hoots does the purchasing of ships. I am the one who travels the seas. So, no, I would not know of such a company."

Lee-lee sighed heavily. "I doubt if the company has the same name now anyway," she said. "I've so often wondered what became of my father's business and grand estate in Washington Square. When he disappeared at sea—"

Timothy reached a hand to her face and touched her softly on a cheek. "Do not dwell on that," he said. "That was ten years ago. Many things change in ten years."

He paused, then said, "Have you ever wanted to return to America?"

As soon as he asked, he regretted it. He was becoming too involved . . . something he was truly wary of.

Lee-lee wanted to shout "*ai*" over and over again, but

116

she still was too afraid to open up that much to Timothy. Should he by chance meet with Heung-Chin and reveal all her secrets to him . . . *Nay*. She best not. Her future . . . her tomorrows . . . her survival . . . lay in Tak-Ming's hands. He was the only one she could trust without question.

She gave a toss to her head. "*Nay*," she said blandly. "As I told you, I am quite content here in Foochow." Fearing to pursue the talk of America, knowing that her true feelings would show, she grudgingly changed the subject.

"And you? You say that you travel the seas. Does your . . . family miss you terribly when you are gone?" she asked softly. When in his intimate embrace, the thought of his being unfaithful to a wife hadn't even entered her mind. If he now told her that a wife waited for him, Lee-lee realized that the knowing would shatter her.

"My family? No. They do not miss me," he said. "I left them many years ago in Boston. I very rarely travel to visit them. They have their life. I have mine."

Lee-lee blanched. Was he this much of a rogue? Had she been right to think that he was? "You have left your wife and children and you never . . . never go to see them?" she gasped.

Timothy threw his head back, laughing heartily. Then he eyed her warmly. "I didn't mean to lead you to believe that I had left a wife and children behind," he said. "I have neither. It was my parents and one sister of whom I was speaking. I left home when I was fifteen to find my own way in the world."

Lee-lee laughed softly, relieved yet knowing it

shouldn't have made any difference to her one way or the other. Soon he would be gone from her life.

"I see," she said. "And I see that you were quite successful in your venture. You own this great ship and you are quite an affluent, skilled businessman."

"I own many ships in partnership with Calvin," he said with a faraway look in his eyes. "I'm only thirty now but it seems, oh, so long ago when I caught sight of that first ship. The sails were like angel's wings fluttering against the crimson, sunset-splashed evening sky."

"And what did you do then?" Lee-lee asked. She hugged her knees to her chest, eyes wide.

"At the age of fifteen I made my way to New York, to learn about ships. At that age my limbs were more pliable and adaptable to the monkey work of climbing and working aloft," he said. "I then worked as a shipwright and not long after that I was chosen from a muster of nearly a thousand men to become a foreman, assigned to a gang of men. Before long I had saved enough money to make wise investments, one of which was my very first ship."

He placed his hands behind his head and leaned his head against them. "I had learned about fortunes that had been made from woolens, northwest coast beaver, and cotton and lumber," he continued. "Calvin Hoots approached me with his vast sums of money, and together we formed the *Hendricks-Hoots Line* of ships. The rest is history."

He gave Lee-lee a heavy-lashed look. "I'm glad I chose the sea over the land," he said. "I enjoy every hour of sunshine, storm, and rain while on my ship, the

New Yorker."

"And so you then decided to travel to China?" Lee-lee asked, flipping her hair back from her shoulders.

"Yes. It was my idea to travel to China," Timothy said. "I had to believe that a people who had invented the compass, gunpowder, and the abacus, and made a whole industry of silk, could not be the comical heathen Chinese of the jokes in America," he said. "I had to find out for myself and here I am."

"And? Were you right?"

Timothy leaned toward Lee-lee and traced her facial features with a forefinger. "Yes. I was right," he said thickly. "It was a very wise Chinaman who made the decision to take you into his Chinese family and make you one of them."

Then he laughed and dropped his hand to his side. "But you've strayed from the subject you were most interested in," he said. "You boarded my ship to hear of America, not the boring tale of a man you've only just met."

Lee-lee cast a quick glance toward a clock on a far wall. "Perhaps some other time," she murmured. "I truly must return to the House of Yeung. I hadn't planned to stay away this long."

Timothy drew her into his arms, reaching a hand to a breast that had fallen free of the robe as he had pulled her to him. "Are you saying that we can meet again?" he asked, running a thumb and forefinger about the voluptuous, stiffened peak of her breast.

The passion that his hand was once more awakening inside Lee-lee caused her to emit a nervous sigh. She closed her eyes to the building rapture. "*Ai*," she whispered. "We *must* meet again."

"When?" he asked, bending to swirl his tongue around the breast.

Lee-lee twined her fingers through his hair, drowning in the sensations being aroused inside her.

"Soon," she sighed. Then she opened her eyes and searched his face as he drew away from her. "When will you be leaving for America?" she quickly asked.

"Not for a day or two," he said.

"Then tomorrow? Would you like to go into the city with me tomorrow to see how the people celebrate the Moon Festival?" she said, excited.

Then her lower lip curved into a pout. She shook her head slowly back and forth. "But, *nay*, that wouldn't be possible," she murmured. "I would be recognized. Heung-Chin . . ."

"What is a Moon Festival?" he asked, ignoring her sudden downcast mood.

"It is the time of year when the moon attains its great brilliance," she said. "It is when it becomes a perfect circle which is a symbol of unity, a time when lord and wife should be together."

Again her lashes lowered sadly. "But as I said, it is not possible for us to attend the Moon Festival together. I would be recognized."

Timothy rose from the bunk, slowly pacing. Then he turned quickly on a heel and faced her. "You have always dressed as a Chinese in public, have you not?" he asked, a gleam dancing in his eyes. "Hasn't your face always been hidden behind a mask of cosmetics? Haven't you always been dressed as a Chinese lady?"

"*Ai* . . ." she replied, inching her way across the bunk. "But it would not be fitting for me to accompany you, an American, if I am thought to be a Chinese lady. Even the flower boat women do not appear in public with foreigners."

Timothy went to Lee-lee, placed his hands on her shoulders, and urged her up to stand before him. "But an American businessman would go to the city accompanied by his American wife, would he not?" he asked, smiling mischievously down at her.

"Why, yes . . ." she said, not yet understanding what he was getting at.

"Then we will attend the Moon Festival as man and wife," he said, laughing throatily.

Lee-lee's pulse raced. "As man . . . and . . . wife?" she gasped.

Timothy released his hold on her, laughing softly. "Do not act so alarmed by my suggestion," he said, lifting his half-smoked cigar from the ashtray. He relighted it, took a deep drag from it, then sat down on the edge of the desk, coyly eying her.

"It would only be for appearance's sake. No one would know that we were not man and wife," he further stated. "It would be a means of being able to travel together without drawing attention to you, the adopted daughter of Mandarin Heung-Chin."

Lee-lee giggled. She went to him and ran a forefinger down the perfectly straight line of his nose. "And how would we manage that, kind sir?" she asked. "I only have Chinese gowns and dresses in my possession. Or would you prefer my lowly Coolie garb? An American lady dressed in either would most definitely attract much attention to herself."

Timothy leaned toward her and kissed first her lips and then each of her cheeks. "Without the mask of cosmetics and with an American dress on your beautiful body, no one would recognize you, would they?"

Lee-lee's face flushed with rising excitement. "Even Heung-Chin wouldn't recognize me without the cosmetics," she said. "I am never allowed to leave my room without full Chinese makeup and apparel. Soonya, my serving woman, was given those strict instructions upon my first arrival at the House of Yeung."

She lifted her hair from her shoulders. "See my hair?" she asked.

Timothy reached a hand to her hair and ran his fingers through it. "It's as soft as the silk that the Chinese are famous for," he said. "It's as black as the darkest midnights—"

"*Nay.* It is not," Lee-lee quickly said. She made a part in her hair at its crown. She lowered her face. "Look clearly. If you do, you will see that the roots of my hair are red, not black."

"Red . . . ?" Timothy said. He laid his cigar aside, rose from the desk, and guided Lee-lee closer to a lamp. His eyes widened when he was able to see the bright red of her hair against the whiteness of her scalp.

"By God, it *is* red," he said then lifted her chin with a forefinger. "Why, Lee-lee? Why would you cover such beautiful hair with false coloring?"

"It was not my decision to do so," she murmured.

"Heung-Chin . . . ?"

"*Ai . . .*"

Timothy reached for his cigar, placed it between his

teeth, and clamped down on it. "I'm beginning to understand," he growled. "It was just another ploy used to make you look Chinese."

"I would look most barbaric with red hair," she giggled.

Timothy flicked ashes from his cigar into his ashtray. "You don't seem to mind," he said.

"I've had ten years to get used to it," she shrugged. "I've grown used to it all, Timothy. The Chinese clothes . . . the Chinese cosmetics . . . the dyed hair . . ."

Timothy crushed his cigar out and walked to the door. "I'll be back. Just you stay put. I have a surprise for you," he said. "Tomorrow you will most certainly not be dressed in *any* Chinese garb."

Lee-lee rushed to his side. "What do you mean? Where are you going?"

"You'll soon see. I won't be long."

Breathless, Lee-lee watched him leave then anxiously waited, full of wonder. She was quite aware of being alone and she now paid more attention to the night noises of this moored, powerful ship. She could hear the timbers creaking, the splash of water beneath her . . .

"I told you that I wouldn't be long," Timothy said, bursting back into the room.

Lee-lee swung around and her attention was quickly drawn to a large sea chest being carried laboriously by Timothy. She followed him, wordless, to the bunk and watched him flip the lid of the chest widely open. White, frilly lace sewn on the bodice of dresses was quickly recognized by her.

"A chest of dresses?" she said. She gave Timothy a

warm smile. "American dresses. I shall be wearing one of these tomorrow?"

"Exactly," Timothy chuckled. "I have brought several styles to show the Chinese merchants. These dresses are made of the finest cotton from America. I want to show the Chinese that the cotton brought from America is more practical, everyday wear than their usual silk."

"May I see one fully now?" Lee-lee asked, having so missed the American way of dress.

"Yes. Choose the one that you would like to wear tomorrow," he said. "And in another chest I will find you a petticoat with even more lace on it. I may even find a parasol that would be a perfect accessory and would fit in nicely with the occasion we have planned."

With a thumping heart, Lee-lee chose first one dress and then another, liking the first as well as the last. To her, they were all beautiful. She had so tired of the confining layers of Chinese-styled gowns and dresses. In one of these cotton dresses, she would even have spare room for extra breaths!

Then one in particular caught her eye. She shook it free of fold wrinkles and held it up before her, sighing. "This is the most lovely one of them all. I choose this one to wear tomorrow," she said, now wishing that tomorrow were already here. A full night to have to wait! *Wei*! Would she even get one wink of sleep?

This dress that she was still admiring was designed with tiny red rosebuds against a white background, and trimmed with gathers of white lace at its low bodice and at its fully gathered, tiny waist. It had short, puffed sleeves and a long, very full skirt.

To Lee-lee, this was what femininity was all about and she could hardly wait to wear it. But one fast glance at the clock told her that she had no more time, not even enough to try it on, so she gently placed the dress across the bunk.

"Tomorrow," she sighed. "Tomorrow we shall have such fun."

"Will you have trouble leaving your estate grounds?"

"*Nay*. Even the lowliest of coolies will be permitted to leave the estate to go to the city to participate in the Moon Festival," she said. "I will be just a coolie on horseback with a man's queue down my back and my rattan hat's brim pulled low over my face. No one will suspect. At least this one day I will be able to move about freely in my coolie disguise."

"You really believe you will be safe enough?"

"*Ai* . . ."

Timothy reached for her injured hand. "And your hand? How does it feel now?"

She looked down at the wound. "I had almost forgotten about it," she murmured.

She frowned when she saw the brown stain left from the iodine. "The stain. This could draw Heung-Chin's attention to my hand."

Timothy went to his opened chest of medical supplies. "I shall take care of that," he said, lifting one bottle from the many.

Lee-lee's left eyebrow lifted. "What's that?" she asked softly, fearing more pain.

He opened the bottle and poured some colorless liquid onto a cotton ball. "This is spirits of ammonia," he said. "It will remove the brownish stain left by the iodine."

"How clever," Lee-lee said, eying him suspiciously. "But . . . will . . . it . . . hurt?"

"No. Not a bit."

Lee-lee flinched as he applied the liquid around the rawness of her wound then cast him a sour look.

"So it did hurt?" he mumbled.

"I confessed to you my low tolerance for pain," she whispered, lowering her eyes, ashamed of this weakness.

"Again I am sorry for having hurt you," he said. "If only I had not used that whip on you! Now I even have to wonder about the wisdom of using a whip on a horse. I've never thought much about the pain it most surely inflicts upon the poor devils."

"I have also wondered about that," Lee-lee said softly. "Often."

Timothy placed his bottle and cotton aside. "You would, sweet one," he said. "You would."

"I really must go now," she whispered, seeing too much in his eyes as their gazes met and held. Tomorrow would have to be soon enough for their next shared, tender embraces.

"Your hand?" he said thickly. "It will be all right?"

"*Ai* . . ."

"The scar the wound will leave—" he said huskily. "Though I am sorry to have caused it, I did, and now I can say that in a sense I have branded you, making you forever mine . . ."

Lee-lee didn't have time to reply. Timothy drew her roughly into his arms and kissed her with an almost wild desperation.

Chapter Seven

Dressed in her coolie attire and with her hair braided into a heavy, black queue down her back, Lee-lee moved away from the stables on a short-legged, long-barreled Mongolian pony. Her thighs had ached strangely when she had first arisen this morning which had puzzled her until she quickly recalled what she had shared with Timothy the previous evening.

Remembering the heat of his kisses and the intense pleasure she had received when he had positioned the strength of himself between her thighs had made a rush of flame rise to her cheeks. Had she really let him? Was she truly ready to let it happen again? The racing of her pulse and the dizzy sort of feeling inside her head at the mere thought of him were answer enough.

"I will enjoy him . . . before I lose him forever," she sighed aloud.

With a renewed ache in her thighs, now caused by the awkwardness of having her legs spread in the saddle, for shamefully she was riding the pony as a man would, Lee-lee kicked the saddle flaps to hurry the pony along.

The saddle on which she sat was deep seated and covered in black velvet. The horse's bridles, reins, and cruppers were of red felt trimmed with large, red tassels. The saddle flaps were of stiff leather, oiled and painted, and when kicked by Lee-lee, they made a noise annoying to the pony, which made it speed up. Around the pony's neck was a collar of brass bells which jingled while the pony trotted along the gravel drive that wove between the gardens filled with oleanders, orchids, liverleaf, gardenia bushes, and peonies.

The courtyards of the House of Yeung were beehives of activity. The excitement was due to the day of celebration. All servants had been given assurances by the lord of the house that when their duties were completed, they could take time to go into the city to witness the festival day of red lanterns, music, and merrymaking.

In the House of Yeung, the kitchen god would be set out, the house would be cleaned, and meals of steamed cakes, vegetable balls, and wheat flour rolls would be enjoyed by all. It was a day of feasting and merriment for the entire household and everyone would celebrate the Moon Festival in his own way.

Lee-lee had been among the first to take one of the household's finest ponies from the stables. No pony was allowed to leave the estate of the proud mandarin without its tassels and velvet seat, even if it were only being ridden by a coolie. Anything that belonged to the mandarin had to represent the best in taste, especially when viewed by the public.

The incessant jangling of the brass bells about the

pony's neck was an irritation to Lee-lee, fearing this would draw attention to her flight of freedom. She had feigned illness and had left word that Soonya not disturb her the rest of the day and that she suggest to anyone else who might ask of her welfare that she was not to be disturbed.

Lee-lee had clutched at her stomach and had screwed her face up in a pitiful, mournful way when Soonya had mentioned food, telling Soonya not to even speak the word, much less try to force it upon her.

The two who would cause Lee-lee the most problem were Tak-Ming and Heung-Chin, and they both were involved in their own personal obligations for the day. Heung-Chin was traveling the canals of the city, displaying his greatness to the throngs of people in his personal dragon boat with its big, popped eyes on the bow, silk pennants streaming from its sides, and its usual double-decked oars that flashed in perfect cadence.

Tak-Ming was on another thrilling adventure on the East China Sea, once more trading silk, tea, and spices for opium.

"And I am going to meet with Timothy Hendricks," Lee-lee whispered, smiling.

Visions of the cotton, lace-trimmed dress danced through her head. She would walk proudly beside the man she loved, pretending — if only for a short while — that she was indeed his wife!

As Lee-lee left the House of Yeung with its red-lacquered gargoyles behind her, she was relieved to become lost among the flurry of other servants now leaving with her. She mingled with the other ponies and those who traveled by foot, becoming part of the throng, and her fear of discovery was lessened.

Nearing the great red-lacquered gate that opened out to her day of freedom, Lee-lee lowered her head, pulling the brim of the hat down over her eyes. Guardsmen had been placed at the gate this day. With the festival drawing everyone for miles to the city, the danger of bandits was greater than usual.

But the guardsmen were ignoring the outgoing crowd with Lee-lee among them. She held her breath as she passed by the guardsmen, seeing out of the corner of her eye the red gate studded with round brass knobs and the massive Chinamen who stood at each side. Since neither looked her way, Lee-lee kicked the saddle flaps and sent her pony hurrying along its way, thankfully leaving everyone else behind her.

Her heartbeats were almost swallowing her whole as she traveled along the dirt road, knowing that Timothy awaited her arrival on his *New Yorker*. It was a day of celebration all right, but not only for the perfect circle of the moon. She celebrated the joy of being with an American . . . and, *ai, being* an American.

Through the long ten years she had lived in China, Lee-lee had sometimes forgotten that there was another way of life different from that which she had found in the House of Yeung.

Peacefully content, she clung to the pony's reins and lifted her face to the brilliant rays of the sun, absorbing its warmth. It was good to be alive! It was good to be free! Her hand hadn't even throbbed today! She tipped her hat back and began looking all about her, to what was now a familiar setting.

The day was so bright that the landscape appeared to be shimmering. Soft green rice paddies stretched across the plain with sharp hills outlined in hazy blue against the horizon. Chinese laborers waded thigh-deep in the paddies, scrabbling in the fields with hoes or whacking the bony hips of water buffalo. Most wore Lee-lee's own style of high-peaked, rattan hats and padded outfits made of a faded, coarse type of cotton.

"*Ai*, they would welcome Timothy's softer cotton," she whispered. "How much cooler they would be beneath the hot rays of the sun."

Further up the road, a stream of Chinese were making their way toward the city. Women carried small children on their backs and men strode almost bent under the weight of carrying poles, balancing buckets or baskets at each end.

The pony led Lee-lee up a steep hill in the road where from its peak the view never failed to steal her breath away. From this vantage point, she could see for miles and miles—from the surrounding huddled villages, cramped and brown toned, to the brilliant sheen of the East China Sea and the curve of the Min River whose banks were fantastic with their array of color from the orange, lemon, peach, and lichee trees in bloom. The river was clogged with traffic from bank to bank and Foochow Bay was alive with its usual display of junks and sampans.

Tier upon tier of the city's tiled roofs descended toward the harbor, intermingling with gilt and colorfully-painted pagodas rising slender into the sky. All of this was circled by the thick wall which separated the city from the harbor and the turquoise sweep of the sea.

Then Lee-lee's heart thundered wildly against her ribs when her gaze fell upon the great stone Bridge of Ten Thousand Ages which reached to the island in midstream where Timothy's and all other foreign ships were moored, where the true Port of Foochow had been situated to separate its activity from that of the city. The island in the morning sun was streaked in colors of gold and pale oranges, making the ship's sails appear as mystical apparitions.

"But they are as real as Timothy," Lee-lee sighed.

She urged her pony onward until the heart of the city was finally reached, and once more Lee-lee had to lower her head as she became one of the populace. There were the money-changers, artists, brokers, shopkeepers and restaurant-keepers. The streets were filled with the traffic of sedan chairs, camel trains, and the foul-smelling pack mules.

But none of this interested Lee-lee. Her concerns lay only in what the next several hours ahead offered her. She fought the crowd of the city and also that of the Bridge of Ten Thousand Ages, and finally she was alone with Timothy in his master cabin consumed in his eager embrace.

Lee-lee clung to him. "I've brought you something," she whispered, tingling all over as his hot breath swam across her cheek.

"You've brought yourself," Timothy said huskily. "That's all that matters."

Lee-lee laughed softly. "If you squeeze me any harder,

my surprise will be crushed as well as my body," she said, looking up into his eyes as she arched her neck backward.

She would forget that he soon would be gone on his own journey to America. She would forget that beneath his handsome exterior and his façade of gentleness he was a rogue. The moments with him would be savored— something she could keep with her, sealed safely inside her heart forever and ever.

Lowering a kiss to her lips, he chuckled. "All right," he said. "If you insist."

"*Ai*," she said. "I insist. Do you forget? Today all of Foochow celebrates the Moon Festival."

"But the moon won't be out until this evening," Timothy teased, walking away from her to complete the toilette that he had begun before her arrival. He shook some cologne into the palm of a hand then splashed it onto his freshly shaved face. His silk shirt gaped open where it lay, unbuttoned against his chest, his trousers molded to his masculine form, and he had yet to slip into his shoes. A sweep of his fingers combed his hair from his brow, and it hung in a slight wave against his neck.

"The celebration begins early in the morning and runs on into the night, silly," Lee-lee said.

She reached inside her front tunic pockets and pulled from each two round, cooked patties. "And everyone eats moon cakes," she giggled. "Kind sir, will you accept one from the kitchen of the House of Yeung? I sneaked into the kitchen before daybreak, especially to get these for us to share together."

"Moon cakes?" Timothy said, lifting an eyebrow.

"To honor the moon," Lee-lee said. She placed one to

his lips. "Come on. Take a bite."

Timothy took a nibble then Lee-lee took it from his lips and placed it to hers, where he had taken his bite. As she took her own tiny nibble from it, she felt the heat of his eyes devouring her.

She smiled wickedly up at him and tossed both moon cakes aside as she once again fell under his spell. She rushed fiercely into his arms. "Love me," she murmured, running her fingers through his hair. "The nearness of you . . . the passion in your eyes . . . the smell of you. All these things are driving me wild."

She stood on tiptoe and rained kisses across his face, loving even the taste of him.

"The celebration? The moon cakes?" Timothy whispered already releasing her of her bulky tunic.

"We have a full day," Lee-lee sighed, trembling as his deft fingers worked at disrobing her. What would he think when he discovered the breast binder? She had had to wear it as part of her coolie disguise.

Timothy's hands brushed the tunic aside and then began with the buttons of her coarse, faded shirt. He gasped and took a step backward when he reached inside to touch a breast and found something quite different from what his dizzied head had hoped for. He sobered quickly as he ran his fingers over the breast binder, now staring openly at it as Lee-lee went ahead and removed her shirt.

"Did I look enough like a man in my breast binder?" she teased, posing, turning from side to side. Her flesh was pink and smooth as satin above and below the ugly, wrapped fabric, and the taper of her waist showed above the waistband of the padded trousers that hung loosely from her hips.

"God," Timothy gasped, raking his fingers through his hair. "How can you stand that thing? You've succeeded in squashing your breasts completely to your chest. Won't that even cause harm to them?"

"I would certainly hope not," Lee-lee laughed. "All Chinese women wear these terrible things every day. Even I have been forced to beneath my silk dresses and gowns. It is a custom that surely isn't practiced at all by the American women, is it, Timothy?"

"None that I have run across," Timothy said, chuckling.

His face sobered and his eyes darkened as he reached a hand to the breast binder and unfastened it. Slowly he began unwrapping it and when her breasts sprang loose and free, he let the breast binder drop to the floor and cupped both her breasts in his hands.

Lee-lee grew breathless as he lowered his lips to one and then the other. Her insides were ablaze with wanting him. When his teeth sank into one of her stiffened nipples, to tease and torment her to mindlessness, she reached her hands to his face and urged his lips to hers.

Twining her arms about his neck, she kissed him passionately and long. She fit her body into his, wrapping a leg around him to draw him even closer. Through both their layers of clothes she could feel his hard readiness. She moved her breasts sensuously against his chest, feeling the racing of his heart against her flesh.

"You are a she-devil," Timothy said as their lips softly parted. "The way you love. Did you learn this also from

135

the Chinese? Are all women of this culture . . . so . . . so hot-blooded?"

"What I know of love I learned only last night with you," Lee-lee whispered, light-headed in her desire for him.

"Am I such a skilled teacher?" Timothy asked, chuckling as he tossed his shirt aside and lowered his trousers.

"You are a skilled lover," Lee-lee purred, splaying her hands across his chest, flicking her tongue around one of his nipples.

She didn't see his face cloud or see a distant hurt in his eyes. She didn't know that his thoughts had wandered to another time when his skills hadn't been enough to hold another woman's love. Lee-lee was too carried away in her world of rapture.

But she was brought quickly down to earth when he took her by the right hand, to push her away from him. The wound was once more brought to her mind as his hand squeezed tightly before setting it free.

She didn't flinch or let out a cry. She only rubbed it softly, looking quizzically toward him with half downcast eyes. His mood had suddenly changed and she knew not why.

But she wasn't one to give up so easily. She loved him. She needed him. Whatever was bothering him had to be dispelled from his mind. They might never have another opportunity like the present to be together in such a way.

With a flaming face and racing pulse, Lee-lee began unbraiding her hair, wishing Timothy would look her way instead of lighting a cigar with his back to her. She tried to recall what she might possibly have said to offend him. But all that came to mind were her words of love and compliments on his being a skilled lover. And because she was sincere about both, she knew that surely whatever was bothering him would pass.

Timothy chewed angrily on the tip of his cigar and began buttoning his shirt. Without even knowing it, Lee-lee had most definitely brought his senses back in line. He had forgotten to be cautious of his feelings. He had forgotten how Cathalina had used and discarded him. The handsome Chinaman Tak-Ming would reap the harvest of this passion Timothy had unleashed inside Lee-lee. Timothy not only suspected this. He knew this to be true. And he had to keep remembering.

But Timothy had to wonder why Lee-lee was so persistent about being with *him*, when she could be with the Chinaman. Was it because he was American? Was it a game? She didn't appear to be conniving. What type of woman was she? But none of this mattered. He had decided to leave China behind him at the next morning's sunrise.

Lee-lee shook her waves of hair to hang lustrously long across her shoulders and down her back. She crept to Timothy and positioned herself in front of him, unmindful of her uncovered breasts. "What did I say?" she murmured. "Whatever it was, I apologize. Please tell me I am forgiven, Timothy. The time with you is so short. Must it be spent with coolness between us?"

"Why did you choose to celebrate this festival day with me?" Timothy asked in an accusing tone, still wondering why she hadn't chosen to be with Tak-Ming.

137

"A special day should be spent with a special person," she murmured. She reached a hand slowly toward him then reconsidered when she saw him recoil, puzzling her even more.

"Aren't I special to you any more, Timothy?" she asked, no longer able to look up into his cold, aloof eyes.

When he did not answer, she began gathering her clothes in her arms, sadness heavy in her heart. "I shall leave," she said. "Perhaps I can manage to enjoy the festival without you after all. Again I was wrong for having come here."

She turned abruptly on a heel, her eyes suddenly blazing. "But you must know that I think you are the most complicated person I have yet to meet," she stormed, now more angry than hurt. "First you want me. Then you don't. And to think that I risked my life to get to be with you again. I suddenly realize that you are not worth such a risk, Mr. Timothy Hendricks, the famous American businessman who charmed his way into the House of Yeung and in and *out* of my heart!"

Seeing her anger—even feeling it as it tore away at his insides—spurred Timothy into action. He smashed his cigar out in an ashtray, went to Lee-lee, and grabbed the clothes from her arms.

"What do you think you're doing?" she hissed, reaching for them. She watched in silent awe as Timothy threw them across the room and moved boldly toward her.

"What am I doing?" he growled. "Lee-lee, I'm going to quit being such an idiot. I'm going to make love to you."

He drew her roughly into his arms and crushed his lips

down upon hers while one of his hands worked feverishly on a breast, circling it, kneading it.

Lee-lee struggled, pushing against his chest with her one uninjured hand. But the coil of warmth spreading through her insides was beginning to betray any need to be free of his passion-filled embrace.

Slowly she gave in to her feelings, enjoying the delicious sense of being drugged as her head once again began to spin. When his tongue sensuously entered her mouth, a thrill raced up and down her spine. She laced her arms about his neck and returned this type of kiss, letting her tongue meet his in a strange sort of dance as they touched and flicked against each other.

The flames of desire spreading inside Lee-lee caused her to moan and slither closer to him. But she couldn't get enough of him just by being close. She began wandering her left hand across the corded muscles of his shoulders and between their bodies, where she let her hand travel through his springy chest hairs then lower where the waistband of his trousers was a barrier to her further meanderings. She felt a quivering of his flesh as she tried to place her fingers beneath the waistband, feeling his navel, round and sleek.

Understanding her need, Timothy drew his lips from hers and stepped back away from her. His eyelids appeared to be heavy as his thick, dark lashes veiled eyes which were intensely dark with his feelings.

"First you, darling," he said. "Let me undress you, then you can undress me."

"*Ai* . . ." she said throatily. Her eyes felt hot . . . she was seeing him through a lazy haze . . .

139

Timothy placed his hand to the waistband of her padded trousers. He undid them and began lowering them as she kicked her sandals from her feet.

First the gentle flare of her hips was revealed to his feasting eyes . . . then the bright red vee of her hair at her lower abdomen . . . then the silken pink curve of her thighs . . . all of which intoxicated him as if he had been plied with the finest wines.

Lee-lee stepped out of her trousers. Her heart was racing wildly with anticipation . . . her throat was dry with need. She watched, mesmerized by the hungry look in his eyes as he knelt down on a knee before her and framed her vee of red hair with his hands.

As he lowered his lips to her there, Lee-lee's breath was suddenly trapped inside her, watching him kissing her in a place she would have thought taboo for any man's lips.

But as his tongue flicked out and touched her, she felt a strange throbbing there and gasped, melting, oh, so melting from the exquisite sensations his tongue had stirred within her.

Slowly Timothy caressed her there until he heard her moan and tense. He knew that he had lingered too long, having enjoyed the jasmine smell and taste of her almost too much to stop. But now he couldn't even wait to enjoy the slower movements of her undressing him. Their bodies needed release that only their complete union could bring.

Lee-lee's insides ached with a sort of torment she had never imagined possible. In her haze of desire for him she crept to his bunk and draped herself across it. She watched him finish undressing, almost tortured from having to wait. Her face flamed, her heart leapt when she saw his readiness as the last of his clothes dropped to the floor. She held her arms out to welcome him, and he was suddenly there, lowering himself down over her.

Flinching only momentarily from the pain as he entered her, she was relieved when the discomfort drifted into a sweet passion. He nuzzled her neck as he began his slow thrusts. She locked her legs about his waist and lifted her hips to encourage him more deeply inside her.

"I love you," she whispered against his cheek. "Only you, Timothy." She could feel his lips leave her neck and the movements inside her become slower, and she wondered why.

Timothy felt the ache of regret circle his heart, wishing she hadn't said that, not believing her. Yet he was too caught up in the magic of her to turn back now.

"I'm glad . . ." he whispered back.

He lifted her thick, black hair from where it was tangled across her shoulders and spread it out around her head, to resemble a dark, velvet pillow. Lowering his lips to her thick lashes, he kissed her eyes closed. "And I also . . . love . . . you," he added, hating the fact that this was true. She had stolen his heart as surely as day eventually turns to night.

Lee-lee traced his chiseled, handsome facial features with a finger. He caught sight of her wound and, taking her hand, kissed it softly.

"I am a rogue," he murmured. "I didn't ask how your hand is feeling."

"Timothy, this is no time to worry about that," Lee-lee giggled, slowly taking her hand away. "Just make love to me, darling."

Their excitement built as hands explored and kisses melted hotly into each other. Each of his thrusts sent messages of rapture to Lee-lee's heart. And soon their raw passions exploded in unison inside them, leaving them spent, yet still clinging.

"I do love you so," Lee-lee whispered, kissing Timothy softly on the chest.

"Love . . ." Timothy grumbled. "Does anyone really ever know the true meaning?"

"*Ai, I* do," Lee-lee said. "Love is for . . . the losing of self . . . in . . . another."

Chapter Eight

All aglow from the aftermath of lovemaking and from being dressed as a fine American lady, Lee-lee strolled beside Timothy along the busy thoroughfare of Foochow. Her right arm was linked through his, and a lovely, scallop-edged parasol was poised above her head, held leisurely in her left, white-gloved hand.

"I'm not sure this was so wise a thing to do after all," Timothy said, giving her a quick, appraising look.

"What do you mean?" Lee-lee asked, cocking her head to look up into his gorgeous brown eyes which silently spoke love to her.

"You," he said huskily. "You're drawing much attention from the passersby. I should have known that you would, and that dressing as an American would be no true disguise for the lovely lady from the House of Young."

Lee-lee laughed softly. "As I told you before, no one has ever seen me without my mask of Chinese cosmetics and without my breasts being smashed flat beneath my silk dresses and gowns," she scoffed. "There would be no

143

reason to compare me, today, with the person everyone believes me to be. In their eyes, dressed in that fashion, I am Chinese . . . the untouchable daughter of the rich mandarin.''

Timothy leaned his face down closer to hers. "I didn't realize it could be possible, but you *are* lovelier than that daughter of the mandarin who ran into me in the hallway the other night," he said. "You do not need cosmetics to enhance your beauty. Your cheeks are rosy enough and your lips are like the freshly opened petals of an exquisite, ruby-colored rose."

Lee-lee felt a blush rise from her neck upward. She gave Timothy a half smile as her lashes fluttered nervously. "Stop it," she whispered. "People *will* stare if you make my face flame so."

Timothy squeezed her elbow playfully. "All right," he said. "I'll save my compliments till later."

Lee-lee's eyebrows lifted. "Later? What is on your mind besides visiting all these quaint shops of Foochow?"

"Once we're through exploring here, we'll leave this busy crowd of Chinese behind and take the buggy to some secluded spot overlooking the river," he said. "How does that sound? Romantic enough?"

"Ah, so it's romance that's still on your mind, is it?" she teased.

"Always, when I'm with you," Timothy said, leaning to give her a quick kiss on the cheek.

Lee-lee nudged him in the side. "Stop that," she quietly fussed. "What on earth are you trying to do—cause a riot by displaying such affection here in public?"

144

Timothy straightened his back and smiled smugly. "Oh, that's right," he said. "I forgot. The Chinese do not allow it."

He looked down to where her deep cleavage was revealed at the low-swept bodice of her dress. "And, darling, *you* may cause a riot if the Chinamen get hot and bothered by your bosom showing. The Chinese women neglect their men so by refusing them the pleasure of such a sight each and every day. If these neglected husbands look your way, they may be filled with lustful desire and need to be fulfilled right here on the spot, not giving a damn about their poor unfortunate wives at home needing the same but too timid to reveal such a need."

"You must think me anything but timid," Lee-lee said, remembering how being with him had made her such a wanton, mindless thing. There was such power in his passion . . .

"You are a woman with a mind of her own and are not afraid to show it," Timothy said. "I admire that in you. So many women hide behind the fear of revealing their true selves to a man."

"Are you still speaking of the Chinese women, Timothy?"

"No. In America most women are afraid to speak their minds, thinking they would appear less feminine if they did."

"Am I less feminine, Timothy, for speaking and acting so willfully?"

Timothy's gaze swept over her anew. A smile touched his sensuously full lips and crinkled his long, straight nose. "You?" he chuckled. "Anyone who would dare say you were less than feminine would have to be dead inside."

Lee-lee giggled as she kicked at the flutter of layers of lacy petticoats that held the soft-textured cotton dress out away from her. Timothy had not only succeeded in finding her the dress, petticoats, gloves, and parasol, but also white sandals and a fancy straw hat which displayed artificial flowers around its wide brim. A pale red satin bow tied beneath her chin matched the tiny rosebud design of her dress.

"You shouldn't have," she murmured, giving him a sideways glance, smiling coyly.

"Shouldn't have what?" he queried.

"Robbed the sea chests in the hold of your ship," she said. "Timothy, even shoes? Do you even trade women's shoes to the Chinese? You know that won't work. Most Chinese women's feet are bound. This is done to keep the women pure, so I've been told. And the way their toes have been forced back and under their feet so painfully and awkwardly, they would never fit into an American-made shoe!"

"Darling, my travels take me many places," he laughed. "The English and the French are always anxious to see the new styles of shoes and dresses brought to them from New York. These things that you wear this day are left over from my last voyage to both these countries."

"Have you ever traveled to Paris?" Lee-lee asked, suddenly swinging around to face him, stopping his approach.

146

She let her gaze roam over him, admiring his snugly fitted frock coat and trousers of a fine woolen fabric and the silk shirt with his initial "H" monogrammed on the front pocket. This day a wide, colorful tie had been chosen over the usual cravat he wore, and the diamond pin he proudly possessed was now attached to the tie.

He had left his hat behind and the slight breeze was causing his hair to lift and then lay back in layers of dark waves, with one wave hanging boyishly over his brow, resting just above his left eye.

He smelled of cigars and cologne and in his weather-tanned face he wore a serene contentment.

"I've been to Paris many times," Timothy said, taking Lee-lee's elbow to urge her back to his side.

The walk on which they stood was getting busier by the moment and the excitement around them was cause for Timothy to hold Lee-lee closer to him. There were few Americans joining in this Moon Festival celebration, for most foreigners had been urged to stay on board ship.

But today with all the merriment of the city to drown out hate for the Americans, both Lee-lee and Timothy hoped to feel safe enough.

"I would love to go to Paris sometime," Lee-lee sighed. "But I don't see how that could ever be. I'm lucky to be even this far from the House of Young today."

"You've rarely ventured into the city, I gather," Timothy said. "Is that so?"

"*Nay*. Rarely," she murmured.

"Well then, let's see what we can see before the day gets away from us," Timothy said, circling an arm about her waist. "Just follow along beside me. Let me be your

147

guide today, beautiful American lady."

Lee-lee sighed. "I love the sound of that," she said. "American lady. I am, you know."

"Yes. I know," Timothy said thickly, wondering if she had ever considered returning to America. But he doubted that. She had confessed to being content in the House of Yeung with her many treasures showered upon her. His face shadowed, once more remembering Tak-Ming.

He glanced down at Lee-lee, wondering where Tak-Ming was today and why he wasn't with her, since this was a very special day in the eyes of the Chinese. Then he tossed the thought aside, not wanting his suspicions to ruin the day. He let himself get lost in the sights, smells, and sounds of the city.

The shops along the street were resplendently beautiful, decorated with heavily carved exteriors. Most were two-storied with low-hanging balconies. Signs made of heavy cloth were suspended from cross-bars and represented the type of establishment by the drawings on the front.

They noted the fine, large open-fronted places of business. A spicy smell floated from a steaming cook shop where lacquered ducks hung out to tempt the appetite. They passed a tea house where Chinese men and women were at square tables drinking tea. And there were open counters of money changers letting the money scatter through their fingers, mingling their cries with the crash of coins which fell on the counter. Merchants displayed their long yards of gleaming silks, rich furs, embroideries, and silver and jade ornaments.

Along the street, men were pushing wheelbarrows loaded high with their wares. A fruit peddler with a load of persimmons carried his burden balanced on ends of a long pole, and brightly colored sedan chairs pulled by sedan carriers passed by. Vast assortments of street vendors added to the excitement where even now street jugglers were performing. The sounds rose to a clamor. The whir of spinning wheels . . . the hammering of silver . . . the cries of the food vendors.

But above all this was the now persistent sound of firecrackers going off in the distance.

"The Chinese certainly know how to celebrate," Timothy laughed, ducking as a bird flew by, close to his head. He looked over his shoulder, seeing the long row of birds in cages and some free, except for a string attached around one leg, leaving them to hop clumsily about.

"*Ai*, they do," Lee-lee said. She couldn't help but laugh along with him, having seen the loose bird just miss Timothy as it so frantically tried to fly free of the confusion of the crowd.

Timothy brushed some fallen hair back from his eyes. "Birds!" he said. "Suddenly all I see are birds!"

Lee-lee spied something ahead that she had seen only one time before, when she had been traveling behind curtains on a sedan chair. It had left her spellbound then, and it was drawing her into its mystique again.

She eagerly clutched Timothy's arm. "Come on," she said. "Let's go see the retrieving bird. It is quite an amazing thing to watch!"

"I believe I've seen enough birds, Lee-lee," Timothy groaned. "What do you say we buy a bottle of wine and something to snack on and take our ride to the country? I've not only had enough birds for the day, but also noise."

Lee-lee began tugging on him. "I must watch the bird, Timothy," she said. "It will only take a moment."

"Do I sense the child behind the woman?" Timothy teased, now walking with her as she half pulled him along.

"See what you see," she said, shrugging. "I want to watch the lovely, trained bird perform his trick."

"Anything to please the lady," Timothy said, now finding himself standing amidst a crowded audience whose eyes were following the movements of an elderly man and his bird the size of a waxwing.

The man lifted a bamboo peashooter to his mouth and blew a dried pea from it, into the air. The small bird, as though commanded, fluttered off its perch into the brilliant China sky and with a sudden dart he caught and swallowed the pea and returned to his perch to wait for the old man to repeat the same procedure.

"See what I mean?" Lee-lee said, laughing softly. "Isn't the bird not only pretty but smart?"

"Remarkable. Utterly remarkable," Timothy said, kneading his chin.

Then he quickly changed his mood, fitting his hands to Lee-lee's waist to turn her in a different direction. "But I still prefer to be elsewhere," he said. "Let's purchase a rattan basket and fill it with food, a bottle of wine, and be off with us, away from this place."

"All right," Lee-lee sighed. "Let's."

Together, laughing like children, they went from shop

to shop. A basket was purchased and Lee-lee pointed out the foods to place inside it.

"Round and sweet persimmons," she said. "They are a symbol of happiness and unity. Also let's not forget slices of watermelon. Their numerous seeds suggest fertility, their greenness reminds one of youth, and their roundness shows perfection."

There were also olives chosen to symbolize a longer life, lotus seeds for happiness, and apples for peace.

"Anything else?" Timothy asked, feeling the heavy weight of the basket as another shop was left behind.

"You should be happy I am the one with you to advise you what to buy," she said, lifting the skirt of her dress as she stepped from the curb to cross to the wine shop.

"Why?" Timothy inquired, helping her across the street, around and through the rush of people on foot and in various modes of travel. "It all looks the same to me."

"The Chinese say that barbarian foreign devils do not make use of all the things that nature provides," Lee-lee said, giving him a slow smile.

"Like what?"

"Rats, cats, and hairless fat dogs are sold for suckling pigs," she said. "There is also a duck's genitals and the most honorable dish of North China, the rare and exotic bear's paws."

Timothy blanched and felt a queasiness at the pit of his stomach. "And we Americans are called the barbarians?" he gasped.

"Most foreigners who visit China are advised not to inquire what the dishes served them are made from," she laughed. "They are urged to be content that the food is

151

pleasant and wholesome to the taste, though differing considerably from English fare."

"My meal at the House . . . of . . . Yeung?" Timothy tested, remembering how tasty and fulfilling it had been. Had it been duck . . . or . . . dog?

Lee-lee giggled. "All food served in the House of Yeung is of the finest quality," she said. "*Nay*. No substitutes."

"Thank God . . ." Timothy sighed.

Stepping into the wine shop, a pale ale and a rosé wine was chosen. "Now let's get out of here," Timothy said, tucking these new purchases into the basket.

"Only one more stop," Lee-lee said, slipping her arm through the curve of his.

"Oh, no," Timothy groaned. "What next?"

"Moon cakes, Timothy," she said matter-of-factly. "We must have moon cakes. The ones I brought you this morning were too quickly discarded."

"We don't need moon cakes, Lee-lee," he argued.

"*Ai*, we do," she argued back. "The moon cake patties are to honor the moon. Remember? Tonight when the moon is at its greatest brilliance, its perfect circle will be a symbol of unity to all, a time when lord and wife should be together. We—you and I—will pretend to be a lord and wife tonight, will we not?"

"Can you stay that long with me, Lee-lee? Won't you be missed?"

"I have left word for no one to disturb me. My serving woman Soonya is loyal, Timothy. There is nothing to worry about."

Chapter Nine

Tightly grasping the buggy's seat, Lee-lee looked across the tawny swiftness of the river, marveling once again at the profusion of boats that bobbed in the water. Some boats were small traveling farms, carrying chickens and ducks on deck each with one foot attached to ropes alongside. On others, barbers twanged their tweezers to announce their trade, and there were boats that sold flowers. *Tankas*—small, fast ferries—traveled from shore to the boats in a never-ending process from morning to night.

"Do you think this is secluded enough, Lee-lee?" Timothy asked, drawing the buggy to the side of the river.

They had left the great wall, bridges, and roads behind. Timothy had guided the horse and buggy up hilly terrain where in the distance could be seen the terraced slopes where rice and *kina* grew in a haze of ochers, browns, and greens. Beyond these slopes, the streams down the mountainsides were radiant beneath the sun as it dipped lower in the sky.

"It's perfect," Lee-lee said, breathing in the perfumed

aroma of azaleas and rhododendrons that grew beside this section of the turquoise-colored river that was also fringed with feathery bamboo and willow trees.

"Then let's have our own private celebration," Timothy said, climbing from the buggy. He went to the other side and helped Lee-lee down.

Lee-lee's heart fluttered as he drew her momentarily into his arms to gently kiss her. He let his hands travel down the straight line of her back then steal slowly around to cup a breast through the thin fabric of her dress.

"You're so beautiful," he whispered huskily into her left ear. "I'm not sure if I'll be able to keep my hands off you."

"With all that delightful food and wine to tempt your palate?" she whispered back, inhaling the masculine smell of him, savoring it. "Why, darling, surely you're hungry. It's been a long day."

"I'm hungry all right," he said huskily. "For *you*."

The buggy moved and the horse neighed. "You'd best put all thoughts of hunger for me *and* food from your mind until you secure the horse," she softly laughed. "If the horse chose to wander off, it would be quite impossible for you to get back to your ship without drawing attention to yourself. You wouldn't be safe. Not for even a minute, Timothy."

She knew that she could very easily return home without any attention whatsoever drawn to her. She looked over Timothy's shoulder in a different direction, to where the land suddenly dropped off and below it stretched a rocky, sandy beach. Along this beach, hidden behind ground tangle, was the tunnel that she and Tak-Ming had ventured from. It was so close, yet she couldn't tell Timothy about it. It was her and Tak-Ming's secret . . . to be shared with no one.

"If you insist," Timothy grumbled.

"It's up to you," Lee-lee teased. "If you want to take a chance at moving on foot through the city after dark, don't concern yourself with it. I am sure there are only a few fanatical bandits who would murder a *fanqui*—a foreign devil—on sight."

Timothy drew away from her, mumbling beneath his breath. Lee-lee smiled as she watched him secure the horse's reins on a willow tree limb. Then she swirled around, feeling, ah, so deliciously free.

Running to the riverbank, she found a stretch of thick, green moss, so soft and cushiony she felt as if she were standing on a plush, velvet carpet.

"Here, Timothy," she shouted, untying the bow of her hat from beneath her chin. "We shall have our picnic here on the moss." She lifted the hat from her head and shook her hair free and loose. "It's as though we personally commanded the moss to grow for our pleasure," she laughed.

Kicking her shoes off, she curled her toes into the thickness of the small leafy stems growing in clumps. It was not only exquisitely soft to the touch but cool as well. She tossed her hat aside, drew her gloves quickly off, and then ran through the ankle-deep grass to help Timothy, who was taking the rattan picnic basket from the buggy.

"It's been so long since I've had a picnic," she said, excitement showing in the shine of her honey-brown

155

eyes. "As a little girl, our family picnicked often in the various parks in the city of New York. Even Richard seemed to enjoy the outings, though he was stodgy at times and no fun whatsoever to be with."

Timothy took full control of the basket, carrying it to his left side. He placed his other arm about Lee-lee's waist and together they walked toward the blanket of moss.

"You've never spoken much of family," he said. "But when you do, you don't appear to have been all that fond of your brother Richard."

Lee-lee's face shadowed in thought. "He was never a pleasant sort. He was quite selfish. He wanted all of mother's and father's attention. And he would never share anything of his with me."

She then remembered the heart-shaped locket. She knew it had been an exception, but she also understood why he had given it to her. It had been another way of drawing his parents' attention to himself when their attention had been directed too much toward the baby of the family, toward Richard's younger sister, Letitia.

"But you did say that he was older," Timothy said. "Your likes and dislikes would be so different."

"The age didn't make the difference," Lee-lee softly argued. "It was *he*. He would deny me even a piece of candy if he had some. Or if I wanted to borrow a pen to draw pictures with? *Nay*. He was born selfish."

Her voice grew soft and full of despair. "Even during what I imagine were his last moments of life he showed his selfish ways," she murmured. "It was he who made sure to be in a longboat, without even offering to help me, mother, or father."

156

She swallowed hard and blinked a tear from the corner of an eye. "He was a bastard, Timothy," she said. "And I hate to admit this, but I've never thought much about missing him."

"And America?" Timothy said, forgetting his earlier apprehension of encouraging her to talk about it. "Do you miss it terribly?"

He placed the rattan basket on the outside curve of the moss and sank to the ground as Lee-lee had. He began unloading the basket, not looking Lee-lee's way. If he had, he would have seen her guarded expression, a result of his question about America.

"America?" she said in an almost whisper. She still couldn't be sure of Timothy—whether or not he could be trusted. Only Tak-Ming knew of their planned adventure to America. The more who knew, the more the danger.

"Yes. America. Do you ever think of returning some day, should you be given the chance?" Timothy prodded, pouring wine in two glasses which they had also purchased at the wine shop.

"China is now my home," Lee-lee said dryly, finding the ability to lie. Didn't her survival depend on such abilities? Yet, somehow, lies were different with Timothy, now that her love for him was so strong.

"Then shall we drink to China?" Timothy said, offering her a glass, now wondering how on God's earth he could ever bid her farewell!

But he had learned to live without the woman he loved one other time. He could do the same again. And, anyway, such feelings for a woman made a man weak. It would be best . . . to say . . . good-bye.

Lee-lee placed her bare feet beneath the fullness of her skirt and drew her knees up to her chest. She accepted the glass of wine and nodded her head. "*Ai.* Let's drink to China," she said. "And to you, Timothy, and your successful trading ventures with the Chinese people."

They clinked their glasses together and then took sips from them. Timothy was the first to speak again.

"Though you say that you do not wish to travel to America, there are many who do and who are," he said. "The gold fields are the attraction. The whispered word 'gold' is acting on men like a fever."

"Where in America are these gold fields, Timothy?"

"A large-scale gold rush has been in progress since a man by the name of James Wilson Marshall discovered gold at Sutter's Mill in California," he said. "The city of San Francisco is now the destination for all those who cherish this glittering metal called gold. Seems that city grew from a small town to a city of 25,000 in a year's time."

"Have you ever been there?" Lee-lee asked, eyes wide.

"Not yet," he said. "But when I leave Foochow, San Francisco is my next destination. I plan not to only try my luck at panning for gold but also to sell all that I have left in the hold of my ship to those who will need all sorts of supplies after their own long journeys to California."

"I would think you would want to immediately travel to New York," Lee-lee said, eying him closely, wondering if, when she arrived there, he would be there for her to go to him. But that was too much to hope for.

"Later," he said. "But first I have the need to travel on the *New Yorker* as often and as far as I can, to any and all destinations where my ship has not yet been, and that, of course, means San Francisco."

He sighed languidly. "The clipper ship prosperity is just about finished," he said, loosening his tie. He stretched his muscled legs out, crossing them at the ankles, and leaned back on an elbow. "Their days of making voyages to China or any other foreign port are numbered."

"Why is that, Timothy?" Lee-lee asked, reaching into the picnic basket. She began arranging food on delicate, newly purchased Chinaware and placed them on the moss-covered ground.

"With the threat of the Suez Canal becoming a reality, the bottom could soon be gone from the market."

"But I have heard Heung-Chin discussing this canal with other Chinese merchants. They say the Suez Canal is only now being seriously discussed. It will surely be years before it becomes a reality."

"Any time is too soon," Timothy growled. "One hundred and sixty clippers have been built in the last decade. Within a few years, most of them could be rotting in backwater anchorages."

"But Heung-Chin spoke of steamers making the same passages with greater regularity, with much more cargo and decidedly reduced rates."

"Yes, I know. That is why my company is now actively investing in the purchase of steamships."

"Well then? Don't you see? You can still make your voyages to China, Timothy."

"The pleasure will be gone when the clipper schooner is a thing of the past," Timothy said, pouring himself another glass of wine.

Lee-lee placed her glass on the ground and moved to her knees facing Timothy. "But you have a profound love for the sea, Timothy," she said, smiling up at him. "It shouldn't matter on which ship you will be traveling."

"You are not just beautiful," Timothy said, putting his glass on the ground beside hers. "But wise, as well. I like the combination. It is a rare thing in a woman of today."

Lee-lee trembled as he leaned toward her, framing her face between his hands. "You are unusual in many ways," Timothy said thickly, kissing the tip of her nose.

Lee-lee giggled. "I hope I can take that as a compliment," she said.

"Always, darling," he said softly.

As his hands traveled down from her face to her thin, arched neck and then to cup her breasts through her dress, Lee-lee was finding it hard to breathe because of the fires igniting inside her.

"Timothy, what you are doing . . ."

"Yes? And what *am* I doing?"

"You . . . you are once more dizzying my head and you shouldn't. Not here."

"And why not?"

"The world would be our audience," she softly argued.

"Lee-lee, we chose a secluded spot," Timothy said hoarsely, now unfastening her dress from behind. His hand reached inside and traveled around to the exquisitely sensitive nipple of a breast and softly kneaded it. "Whatever we do, there is no chance of being seen. The sky is even losing its brightness since the sun has begun its descent behind the far mountains."

"You are truly a man of no morals," she teased, letting him slip her dress from her shoulders. The breeze was soft against her breasts, a sweet caress.

"None whatsoever," Timothy said, urging her down upon the bed of moss. He lowered his lips to a breast and nipped gently at its budding peak while his hands swept down her stomach. He pushed at the binding waist of her dress until it was low enough for his fingers to search between her thighs for her most delicate pleasure point.

Timothy rained kisses from breast to breast and then along her flesh, down to her flat, quivering stomach.

"Timothy, we shouldn't . . ." Lee-lee said, trying to fight her emotions, feeling too vulnerable out here in the open.

"How can you possibly worry about anything at this moment but the pleasure we can give one another?" he said, scooting her dress and bundle of petticoats down away from her. "All else is of little importance, Lee-lee."

"Our picnic lunch. It soon will be dark and we won't be able to enjoy it."

Timothy laughed hoarsely. "Food is definitely the last thing on my mind," he said.

He removed his tie and everything else, while Lee-lee watched him with passion-filled eyes. Then as he leaned down over her—his silhouette dark against the orange-streaked evening sky—she laced her arms about his neck and let all of her doubts fade slowly away.

"Oh, how I want you," she sighed.

Timothy's lips were quivering as he brushed them lightly against her, kissing her first on her closed eyes, the gentle curve of her cheeks, and the perfumed hollow of her throat. One hand ran freely over her naked body from her breast to a thigh and to the flare of a hip. His lips moved back to hers and bore down upon her in raw passion while his hands positioned themselves beneath her exquisitely soft buttocks and arched them upward to meet his first thrust inside her.

"This is my way of celebrating this day," he whispered into her ear. "But I'm not celebrating a Moon Festival. I'm celebrating my love for you."

Desire washed through Lee-lee, filling her with many pleasurable sensations. She looked up into Timothy's eyes, seeing how they had darkened with mounting passion for her. She reached her hand to his face and caressed a cheek lightly with her fingertips.

"That was beautiful," she murmured. "But do you mean it, Timothy? Do you truly love me?"

She tensed when she saw a sudden coolness enter his eyes, and again wondered why.

"Love has many meanings, Lee-lee," he said hoarsely.

He did love her. He was drowning in his love for her. But he now wished that he hadn't said it. It was a futile thing, this thing called love. But it was an emotion that he couldn't eliminate just by wanting to. Yet such sentiments had caused the downfall of many a man.

"Love has only one meaning," Lee-lee softly argued.

"Why are we talking when we could proceed with making love?" Timothy said, lowering his lips to hers in a rush of need.

Lee-lee groaned and began working with him as he began renewed thrusts inside her. Ecstasy wove its way into her heart. Her head was reeling. She entwined her trembling fingers into his hair and urged his mouth harder against hers. Her body quivered with the intensity of his kisses. The sweet pain between her thighs blended into a massive sort of melting, and as the sensations crashed entirely through her, she moaned with ecastasy.

"Darling . . ." Timothy said huskily. He burrowed his face into the velvet of her breasts and reached his passion's peak in a surge of burning flame in his loins.

Lee-lee clung to him until his quivering subsided and his breathing became less rapid. Then she eased away from him and rose to her feet in her need to be quickly dressed, doing so before Timothy's quizzical stare.

Timothy rose to his feet and drew her into his embrace. "Whoa," he said. "What's the rush?" He kissed her gently on the brow.

"Timothy, what we just shared was absolutely lovely, but I still feel too vulnerable out in the open with no clothes on," she said, looking toward the river and remembering the night Tak-Ming's ship had been moored there in a cove. Now that it was dark, Tak-Ming's ship could return. If Tak-Ming saw her with Timothy . . .

"And I'm hungry," she quickly blurted, eying the waiting food.

"Ah hah," Timothy said, stepping into his trousers. "So making love also whets your appetite as it does mine, does it?"

"I'm hungrier than I've ever been in my life," she giggled. "So maybe what you say is true."

Her face grew suddenly solemn. "I almost forgot," she murmured. "There was another time when I was as hungry . . . even hungrier. When I drifted for days without food after my father's ship sank. I shall never forget the heat of the sun . . . the dryness of my mouth . . . the emptiness of my stomach. I don't see how I lived . . ."

A chill tore through her and a sudden loneliness for her family and America made a sob tear from her throat as tears flowed from her eyes.

Embarrassed, she turned her back to Timothy, not wanting to reveal to him just how strongly she did feel about her American heritage.

"What's this?" Timothy said softly, drawing her gently around to face him.

He framed her face between his hands and as the moon now shone quite bright and high above them, it revealed the shimmering of tears brimming Lee-lee's eyes. "Why are you crying? Surely what I did . . . well . . . it didn't hurt you, did it?"

"*Nay*," she said, sniffling. "You know that it didn't. I told you how lovely it was."

"Then why are you crying?"

"It's nothing, Timothy," she murmured. "Please. Just ignore my tears."

Realizing that pressuring her for answers could possibly reveal more than he had bargained for, and knowing that their involvement could go no further, he moved away from her.

"The moon is at its fullest," he said, nodding toward it. "Should we now share the moon cakes?"

Combing her fingers through her hair, untangling it, Lee-lee was trying to understand why his concern for her had been cut short so quickly. If he had truly wanted to know why she had been crying, nothing would have stood in the way of his questioning her until he had been satisfied with an answer. But this way was best. Perhaps she would have said something she would have been sorry for later.

"*Ai*," she said, laughing softly, yet not looking his way for fear of him seeing the hurt in her eyes beneath the bright rays of the moon. "The moon cakes. I had almost forgotten."

She heard the tinkle of glass and knew that Timothy was pouring the wine. She straightened the lines of her dress and settled down on the moss, looking out across the water where colorful paper lanterns of every conceivable type, color, and shape shimmered aboard the boats in the harbor. It was like gazing through a monstrous kaleidoscope this night, the lanterns were so many.

Somewhere on one of the many fancy flower boats swaying in the water, girls were singing to the accompaniment of the *pi-bah* and a mixture of other musical instruments. It was a lonely sort of sound and Lee-lee was once more overtaken by a surge of tears.

Timothy came and sat down beside her and before he offered her a glass of wine, he saw the sparkle of tears on her cheeks. He set the glasses of wine on the ground and wrapped his arm about her waist, to draw her closer to him.

"I see the tears," he murmured. "Are you sure you don't want to tell me about it?"

"You wouldn't understand," she said, flicking a tear

from the tip of her nose.

It wasn't so much that she thought he wouldn't understand. Perhaps he would understand too much and go and tell her adopted father, though the dangers would be great for him if he did. Heung-Chin would then know that Timothy had been seeing her.

"I'm willing to give it a try," he said, yet fearing this entry into the innermost depths of her thoughts. It was best to leave well enough alone. Yet the tears running down her innocently sweet face twisted his gut unmercifully.

"It is America," she cried softly. "I *have* missed it so. I *do* want to travel there. I *do* want to leave China behind me. On such a ship as yours, Timothy, I could be there in only a matter of a few short months!"

She couldn't reveal how she *was* going to make the journey . . . that this ship like Timothy's was in truth Tak-Ming's . . . that they would fulfill their dreams soon in his ship, the *Sea Goddess*.

Timothy's insides grew suddenly cold. All along, her only need of him had been for . . . his . . . ship? She had been playing games with him—to gain passage on board his ship. Was it, oh, God, happening again? Did all women use men?

"America? But I thought that you said that you've been so happy in the House of Yeung?" he said thickly, slipping his arm from around her. He reached into his frock coat pocket and withdrew a cheroot. He placed it between his teeth and lighted it, glowering.

Lee-lee sensed something was wrong yet didn't quite understand. "I wish Tak-Ming were here to tell you about our shared dreams to travel to America together," she said. "But he is at sea. He wasn't even able to celebrate the Moon Festival today as he had wished."

Timothy's insides grew colder and his shoulder muscles tensed. He was absorbing her each and every word, slowly beginning to switch from loving her to hating her. She had only attended the Moon Festival with him today because Tak-Ming couldn't. And her future—her dreams—only included the handsome Chinaman. The American businessman had only been a diversion—a way to pass time until she could once again be with Tak-Ming. And now that she had been initiated into the world of fleshy desires, Tak-Ming would also be the recipient of her wild passion. Not only that, she even had had the nerve to think that she and Tak-Ming could travel on the *New Yorker* together to go to America, for Tak-Ming's ship surely wasn't strong enough to make such a journey.

But he couldn't let her know that he understood all these things. He would continue playing her little game at least until tomorrow, and then he would be gone.

"Shall we drink to all tomorrows?" he said dryly, flipping his cigar into the river. He lifted both glasses of wine and offered her one.

Lee-lee accepted it, searching his face, wondering about his coolness. "*Ai*," she murmured. "To all tomorrows."

She somehow knew it would be best not to speak of America any more this night. The dangers of doing so seemed many.

Chapter Ten

The sound of the arrival of a carriage at the House of
Yeung had drawn Lee-lee quickly to her bedroom
window. Seeing how withdrawn and strange Timothy had
become after she had spoken of America the previous
night, she had begun to wonder if he had in truth been a
spy working incognito for Heung-Chin, hired to watch
her and draw answers from inside her. Once he had his
answers—those pertaining to Lee-lee's dreams of traveling to America—wouldn't he report bright and early the
next morning to the rich mandarin who most surely had
promised to pay him well to betray his adopted daughter?

"It has to be why Heung-Chin singled this American
out of the many to bring him into the House of Yeung,"
she hissed. Then doubts washed over her. "But, no," she
whispered. "Heung-Chin hid me from the American's
sight that night. Why would he, if the American already
knew of my presence here?"

Slowly drawing her bamboo curtains back, Lee-lee
fussed to herself. The oiled paper used in the window was
a hated thing. It didn't give her the power to see well

enough just who it was stepping from the carriage, moving swiftly toward the front door of the house. All that was afforded her straining eyes was just a blur.

"I've got to find out who it is," Lee-lee said, already slipping her nightgown over her head. "I may get caught snooping but I must do what I must. If Timothy tells Heung-Chin of my wish to go to America, the next thing traveling away from this house could be a sedan chair with me as the passenger. Oh, the journey to the Imperial Palace would be such a sad, torturous one!"

Tears sparkled at the corners of her eyes, for she was already feeling sad and tortured inside. There was no denying her deep love for Timothy Hendricks. She had proven the intensity of her feelings for him by sharing what is usually reserved for marriage.

Yet, no matter how much he had confessed to loving her, he did not. He was the rogue she had at first thought him to be and she wished that she could hate him. But she knew that such feelings could never be. Now that she loved, it would be forever.

Lee-lee dressed hurriedly in a graceful, shell-pink silk dress with plum-colored embroidery swirls across the front. She slipped into buccaneerlike, black velvet boots with white felt soles. She hoped to move soundlessly down the long, endless hallways until she reached Heung-Chin's private study where she knew the conference between Heung-Chin and the unknown visitor would be held. Leaning an ear against the closed door could prove hazardous but not doing so could be even worse. Knowing was more important than the dangers involved.

Taking swift brush strokes through her early morning

tangles, Lee-lee gazed about the room. Should Soonya arrive and find her gone . . .

Again she built a false body beneath the *beiwu* on her bed and drew the bamboo curtains shut at her window. She left only a soft flame burning in bean oil on her dresser and knew that when Soonya looked into the room and saw that her young mistress was asleep, she would leave and return later to see to Lee-lee's morning grooming.

Creeping to her door, Lee-lee slowly opened it, cringing when it squeaked ominously. Thrusting only her head around the corner of the door, she breathlessly looked up one length of the dimly lighted corridor and then the other. At times like this, she missed Tak-Ming, having grown used to depending on his strength and courage. It made her feel much braver and stronger if he was at her side. With his muscled arm about her waist, she could endure any dangers facing her.

They were good for one another and Lee-lee was now worrying about his welfare. Always when he was at sea, she grew anxious for his return. Should the pirates attack, Tak-Ming's ship just couldn't fight them off well enough. That was her only concern when she thought of traveling to America on Tak-Ming's ship. It was not a powerful, sea-going vessel. She only had to think of the one shipwreck in her life to break out in a cold sweat and lose all the strength in her knees.

"I mustn't think of that now," she whispered, stepping out into the hallway. She closed her door and began making her way past all the other closed doors and faintly flickering candles on their fancy gold holders.

A faint aroma of incense touched her nose as did the sound of a woman humming softly beneath her breath followed by the throaty chuckle of a man, and Lee-lee knew that one of her older adopted brothers and his wife were enjoying themselves before the duties of the day began.

Remembering such embraces and kisses with Timothy ate away at her insides. He had only done so with deceit in his heart.

Running her fingers nervously through her hair, drawing it straight back from her forehead, she moved onward. She made several turns down several corridors and finally she was there! She could smell the aroma of tobacco and knew that Heung-Chin's waterpipe had already been lighted. She inched closer to the door, sniffing, ready to smell the scent of cigar should Timothy truly be there ready to reveal Lee-lee's deceits against the powerful Mandarin Heung-Chin Yeung. But no aroma of cigar was there and the other voice was not Timothy's.

Lee-lee closed her eyes, let out a relieved, quaking sigh, and said a soft thank you beneath her breath. Shame engulfed her for having doubted Timothy. He *was* an honest-to-goodness American businessman whose prime reason for being in China was for trading. He wasn't going to endanger her. Perhaps—just perhaps—his cautious air while with her had been because he had not trusted *her*.

"I shall stay and listen since I am already here. It must be something quite important for official business to be tended to so early in the morning," Lee-lee whispered to herself. "Then I shall, somehow, go to Timothy today

171

and tell him of my undying love and trust." And to prove her trust in him, she would even tell him of her and Tak-Ming's plans to travel on the *Sea Goddess* to America. Perhaps after arriving in America, she and Timothy could make plans . . . plans for a future together!

The clear, succinct Chinese being spoken from Heung-Chin's private study—a room of dignity and great peace, well toward the back of the house with its own private, spacious courtyard—prompted Lee-lee to lean closer to the door. She placed thoughts of Timothy momentarily from her mind and listened to Heung-Chin and the voice that was just now recognized by Lee-lee. It was Pu-Kwan Lin, a well-known court grandee, a member of the Imperial Clan and a relative of Emperor Tao Kuang. It was said that he had paid heavily for his appointment and it was supposed to be the most profitable and sought after appointment in China.

"And how is the Emperor faring these days?" Heung-Chin asked in his deep, gravelly voice.

"He grows weary, sire," Pu-Kwan said. "You know that during the Opium War arms were so generally distributed that loose characters of all kinds got possession of them while respect for government waned."

"*Ai*, riots and robber bands, the Banditti of the Triad, that famous secret society whose activities spread over much of southern China, increased so in many parts of our country," Heung-Chin said. "Robbers began to increase on land . . . pirates at sea."

"And as people armed themselves against *banditti*, the less power the government had over our whole land," Pu-

Kwan said.

"Our Emperor has just cause to grow weary," Heung-Chin growled.

"*Ai*. And not only because of his people but also his son," Pu-Kwan said. "It seems his heir, Hsien-Feng is indulging in too much extravagant living."

"Should Hsien-Feng become Emperor, China will surely suffer," Heung-Chin growled. "He is a weakling, incapable of dealing with China's domestic troubles."

"Sire, you should guard your words," warned Pu-Kwan. "Hsien-Feng will be the next Emperor and it could even be tomorrow. No one ever knows. The Son of Heaven, Emperor Tao Kuang, is not well in mind or body."

"*Ai*," Heung-Chin said. "I know all these things."

"And yet you still think it is time to send your adopted daughter Lee-lee to the Imperial Palace?"

"There are many reasons why she should be sent now," Heung-Chin said dryly.

Lee-lee grew quickly numb. She clasped her hands tightly over her mouth for fear of emitting a groan of despair that was building inside her. Tak-Ming had been right all along. She had been raised . . . spoiled . . . nurtured, as one might an animal for selling. Her days of freedom *were* numbered. Possibly even today was the day that she would be hauled away and offered as Heung-Chin's prized gift to the ailing Emperor.

"Where is Tak-Ming?" she worried to herself. "He may return home only to find me gone!"

Lee-lee turned to leave Heung-Chin's door but stopped when she heard Timothy's name being spoken. Turning

173

on a heel, she quickly resumed her silent vigil beside the door and listened, having already missed some vital information exchanged between Heung-Chin and Pu-Kwan and wondering what had been said about Timothy while she had been footsteps away from hearing range.

"So it has been arranged?" Heung-Chin grumbled.

"*Ai*. The word is being spread. Now," Pu-Kwan said throatily, "it is done."

Lee-lee's face flamed with frustration. What had been arranged? The word was being spread about what? She had been away for only a moment, but she had missed the most important information—information that had to do with Timothy, for she had not mistakenly heard his name spoken.

Hoping the words would be repeated, Lee-lee huddled closer to the door, trembling. She feared for herself but now feared even more for Timothy. If he were in danger, she had to find out and somehow find a way to warn him.

"I suppose opium is bought and sold quite openly in Foochow," Heung-Chin said.

Lee-lee heard a light tap-tapping and could envision Heung-Chin emptying tobacco from his silver water pipe.

"I should not try to deceive you or my Emperor by saying that people do not dare to buy and sell opium openly, for we know there is no small quantity being bought and sold secretly."

"It appears to me that in this matter, as it is in most things of life, there must be a flourishing period and a period of decay," Heung-Chin grumbled. "Even if I were to inflict severe punishment, I might punish today and punish again tomorrow and all without benefit. If we wait

174

for two or three years, it will, of course, fall into disuse of itself."

"Certainly, sire," Pu-Kwan readily agreed.

"Yet the American Timothy Hendricks?" Heung-Chin softly questioned.

"He will be dealt with," Pu-Kwan said. "But I question if what you are doing is wise, Sire."

Heung-Chin coughed fitfully then dismissed Pu-Kwan's doubtful words and talked of other things, purposely evading the question at hand.

"Aside from what I have chosen to do today at the Port of Foochow, do you think, Pu-Kwan, from the appearance of things, that the English barbarians or any other people will cause trouble again?" he asked.

Lee-lee clenched her fists to her side, wondering what he meant about Timothy and what Heung-Chin was planning to do at the Port of Foochow this day . . . ? Her heart raced inside her, impatience threatening to drown her. She had no choice but to listen further.

"*Nay*," Pu-Kwan said. "England itself has nothing and when the English barbarians rebelled in 1841, they depended entirely on the power of the other nations who, with a view to open trade, supported them with funds."

"So. It is plain from this that these barbarians always look on trade as their chief occupation and lack the higher goal of territorial acquisitions," Heung-Chin laughed smugly.

"At bottom they belong to the class of dogs and horses," Pu-Kwan said, also laughing. "It is impossible they should have any high purpose."

"Hence in their country they have now a woman, now

175

a man as their prince," Heung-Chin mocked. "It is plain they are not worth attending to. Have they like us, any fixed time for their soldiers' leaders?"

"Some are changed once in two years. Some once in three years," Pu-Kwan said matter-of-factly. "Although it is the Prince of these barbarians who sends them, they are, in reality, recommended by the body of their merchants."

"What goods do the French trade in?" Heung-Chin asked, once more tapping his pipe.

"The wares of those particular barbarians are only camlets, woolen cloth, clocks, watches, cottons, and the like," Pu-Kwan murmured. "All the countries have them. Good or bad."

"What country's goods are dearest?" Heung-Chin questioned emphatically.

"They all have both dear and cheap," Pu-Kwan quickly responded. "There is no great difference in the prices of similar articles, but with respect to the camlets, the French are said to be the best."

"China has no need of foreign barbarians' silk fabrics and cottons," Heung-Chin scoffed. "What necessity is there for using foreign cottons in particular? For instance, garments can be made of yellow, the Imperial color reserved for the Imperial family, a pale yellow for the Palace. Lately the Americans' flowered cottons have come into use which look very odd. Others use foreign cotton for shirts. Now observe me. My shirts and inner garments are all made of Korean cottons. I have never used foreign cottons."

"America's cotton cloth has no substance," Pu-Kwan

said icily. "It is not good for clothing. It is this type of material made into fancy American dresses that this American businessman Timothy Hendricks tried to sell to our merchants."

"*Tcha!*" Heung-Chin shouted. "The American who betrayed me. First he illegally purchased the foreign mud opium, then it was said he had been seen with Lee-lee, who was shamefully dressed in one of his American ladies' garments!"

Lee-lee recoiled as though having been hit in the face. The news had spread to Heung-Chin about her and Timothy, and she knew now that not only were her days numbered, but also her hours . . . her minutes . . . as well!

And if he knew that Timothy had dealt in the trade of opium, did he also know that it was Tak-Ming with whom he had done the trading?

"Good Lord," she whispered to herself. "Even Tak-Ming. . . ."

"You wish to speak of this American Timothy Hendricks now?" Pu-Kwan asked cautiously. "Before, you ignored further mention of him."

"It is because my heart flames with anger toward this foreign devil," Heung-Chin snarled. "I hate to even speak his name!"

"Earlier I tried to warn you of the dangers of what you are planning at the Port of Foochow," Pu-Kwan said humbly. "Sire, though our people are bitterly opposed to the American trade, they are committed to various American firms. There is much profit from trade with them. There would be an immense void in the merchants'

177

lives if the Americans were not allowed to dock at Foochow's port."

"*Ai*," Heung-Chin said, sighing. "But don't you see? It would only be temporary. The mob will run the ships from the Port of Foochow today only. Once you see that Timothy Hendricks's ship has been frightened away, you will arrest the hoodlums who are rioting to make it appear right with the populace."

"But, sire, that *is* a bit underhanded," Pu-Kwan said cautiously. "It was you who gave the orders to encourage the mob to attack the moored American ships. You will have the poor *unfortunates* who obeyed arrested?"

"*Ai*," Heung-Chin growled. "They who would agree to such a thing are ones who would riot against even me if given the chance." There was a silent pause, then Heung-Chin added, "This is the only way not to draw attention to this American's relationship with Lee-lee. Singling out the American Timothy Hendricks and bringing charges against him could eventually bring out the fact that he has been with Lee-lee in a most shameful manner. To rid Foochow of him we must temporarily rid Foochow of all the American ships. Tomorrow we will send apologies to all but Timothy Hendricks."

"*Ai*, sire," Pu-Kwan said humbly. "It is a wise thing that you have done. I see that now."

"Then go and observe. See that Timothy Hendricks's ship is gone."

"And Lee-lee? When shall I take her to the Imperial Palace, sire?"

"Tomorrow, Pu-Kwan. Tomorrow."

Lee-lee's insides froze—her mouth became dry. She

inched away from the door, unable to believe what she had just heard. Her daring ways had not only drawn danger to herself but now also to Timothy. And how could Heung-Chin let her go so easily? There had been true affection shown toward her many times through the past ten years. All along, it had been his plan to cast her aside so coldly.

Torn with feelings, Lee-lee began running. Her eyes were blurred with tears, her heart heavy with a mixture of grief and fear. She was in danger. Timothy was in danger. And she had to suspect that though Tak-Ming's name hadn't been mentioned, he was also among the endangered in the House of Yeung. If Heung-Chin knew of Timothy's dealings with opium, a thorough investigation on Heung-Chin's part would surely uncover the source of the opium.

Running down one long corridor and then another, Lee-lee was fast becoming breathless. But she had much to do. She had to go and warn Timothy! She had to go through the dark passageway to see if she could find Tak-Ming. Perhaps his ship had returned and was now moored in the hidden cove.

"*Ai.* I'll go there first," she whispered. "If he is there I will hurriedly explain about the American and then Tak-Ming will go with me to warn Timothy of the true dangers. Timothy has to know never to return to Foochow. Heung-Chin wouldn't be so easy on him next time."

She then began wondering who had told Heung-Chin about her being in Foochow with Timothy. Dressed as an American, without her cosmetics, no one should have been able to recognize her. She had never left her room to be in the company of others without her mask of Chinese cosmetics. There were only two who ever saw her as her true self. Tak-Ming and . . . Soonya!

Lee-lee stopped, leaning trembling against a wall, eyes wide. "Surely Soonya wouldn't tell," she gasped. "Soonya even encouraged me to look at the American. She talked as though she understood my feelings about America. . . ."

Her insides splashed cold. She had been too open with Soonya, and Soonya, being Chinese in mind, heart, and soul, had done her duty and had surely gone to the master of the house with the information!

"Oh, Soonya, how could you have betrayed me, after all these years of devotion and love?" Lee-lee whispered to herself.

But this wasn't the time to wonder about that. That was trivial compared to everything else that had suddenly gone awry in her life.

The fresh air of early morning was sweet and fragrance filled as Lee-lee rushed from the house and across the courtyard. She listened for any sudden sounds behind her that could mean that she had just been discovered in her flight toward the hidden passageway.

Chapter Eleven

The roar of the mob caught Timothy completely off guard as he was in the hold of his ship, checking to see if everything was secure before moving out to sea. He had tumbled the ship's crew out at the first sign of dawn to make sail, and he could hear their scurrying feet and the commands from Captain Hollister as he was preparing the ship to leave the Port of Foochow.

"Timothy, get up here at once!" Captain Hollister was now yelling into the hold. "Something crazy is happening up here. Seems all of Foochow has suddenly gone stark raving mad!"

Timothy scurried topside. He raked his fingers nervously through his hair and clamped his teeth hard against his cigar, watching rocks and refuse being thrown at the docked American ships.

He watched with disbelief as casks of coal were also being piled up on the wharf close to the ships and upon these were piled tea chests and bulky furniture. All of this was set on fire and torches were lighted and being thrown toward the ships.

Timothy withdrew his cigar and flipped it overboard into the water. "I don't know what's going on here," he grumbled. "But let's get the hell out of here. Give orders to heave the anchor in—and fast—and let's get the sails set and a good stiff breeze behind them. If any of those Chinese discover opium on this ship, I'd hate to describe to you what our fate would be."

"I know. I saw," Captain Hollister growled in his deep, scratchy voice. He pushed his thick-lensed spectacles farther back on his nose and began sending out orders which were quickly obeyed.

Timothy leaned against the ship's rail, his eyebrows forked. The mob which appeared to number way over a hundred was continuing to yell lustily for foreign blood, and now some were trying to climb aboard the ship with cutlasses gleaming orange beneath the rays of the rising sun.

Captain Hollister came back to Timothy in a huff. He took his beaver hat from his head and wiped perspiration from his brow. "Shall I ready the cannons?" he asked, wheezing.

"No!" Timothy shouted angrily. "Just get this ship out to sea. We don't need the wrath of the Chinese warships down our backs while on our way home."

"But those crazed Chinese clambering to board us?" Captain Hollister shouted back.

"Bodily knock them into the water," Timothy said. "But only shoot when shot at."

"Whatever you say," Captain Hollister growled. "It's your ship. I only command it."

"Then, hell, *command* it!" Timothy yelled. "Get her out to sea. Do you hear?"

He was becoming more puzzled by the minute. Of all the ships moored, only the American ships were being attacked. And the shouts from the mob were so filled with rage, it was as if any and all American lives were in danger.

There had been word that a Chinese woman had been raped by an American sailor. Was this the cause of the sudden furor? If so, why wasn't the lone, responsible sailor found and dealt with? Why the entire population of Americans?

Timothy's gut twisted when his thoughts were suddenly filled with Lee-lee. She was American. Was she safe? Then he remembered whose house she dwelled in and knew that, surely, no harm would come to her from the enraged mob. And he only had to think of her deceit to push thoughts of her just as quickly from his mind.

The anchor was short up, hanging dripping at the bow, the sails began to draw, and land and all other ships were flitting by on either side of the *New Yorker*. Timothy lighted a fresh cheroot and stared toward the houses in the distance. He was remembering his time with Heung-Chin and the talk of present and future trade with Heung-Chin's people. While Timothy had been spending time with Lee-lee, Timothy's crew had busied themselves with partially emptying the hold of the *New Yorker* of those things requested by Heung-Chin. Profits had been good but not overly so. It was easy to leave China for that reason, but then, on the other hand, there was Lee-

lee . . . An ache circled Timothy's heart—he was already missing her.

Lee-lee scrambled through the dense ground tangle at the tunnel's end, relieved to finally be out of the winding passageway where rats could be heard scurrying about her feet as she made her way through the dark.

Her knuckles were scraped and bleeding from having fallen against the wall the many times when her feet had slipped and given way beneath her in the slimy muck that covered the tunnel's flooring. Even the palm of her right hand throbbed anew. The scab that had formed on her wound had been knocked aside during one of her clumsy falls and she now blew on it to soothe the fiery burning sensation.

Stepping out into the brightness of the China sky caused Lee-lee's eyes to blink wildly and then to squint as involuntary tears rolled from them. She stumbled over a rock then steadied herself until her eyes grew accustomed to the change in the lighting.

Her pulse raced as she was finally able to focus clearly on everything around her. She held the straight, confining skirt of her dress up above her knees and began running down the beach until she reached the cove. Her heart floundered in her disappointment at not finding Tak-Ming's ship moored there.

But it had been foolish to think that she would. It had only been the anxiety of needing Tak-Ming with her when she went to warn Timothy that had allowed her to hope that somehow she would find him so easily. And now that she had chosen so unwisely to come so far from the heart of the city, she feared that she would be too late to be of any help to Timothy.

She turned and looked in the direction of the Min River. If she looked hard enough she could make out the island where Timothy and all other ships had dropped anchor at the Port of Foochow. Her heart skipped a beat. Billows of black smoke were rising into the sky from the island.

"Oh, no," she cried softly. "It's even worse than I imagined. What if it's Timothy's ship that's burning?"

She turned quickly on a heel and lowered her face into her hands, trembling. "If he is harmed, it is entirely my fault," she murmured.

A part of her was slowly dying, envisioning Timothy's great black-hulled ship slowly sinking into the river. Timothy would not be allowed to be saved. Pu-Kwan would see personally to that!

Wiping her nose with the back of a hand, Lee-lee slowly raised her eyes upward and something drew her gaze far out to sea. It was the magnificent swells of a ship's sails. The morning sunrise had dyed them momentarily a soft orange. It was a sight to see . . . so beautiful and peaceful against the backdrop of the splendid blue sky.

"There's something familiar about that ship," Lee-lee whispered, squinting her eyes, trying desperately to get a better look.

Her eyes began to glow warmly. "It has a black hull such as his . . . it is as magnificent in build . . . and there is bold, white fancy lettering on the ship's hull." A joyous surge of relief flooded her insides when she was able to make out the words "New Yorker" on the hull.

"He is safe!" she screamed, jumping up and down. "Timothy is safely away from the Port of Foochow and it appears that his ship wasn't harmed in the least!"

Her shoulders slumped and she emitted a soft, long sigh. "At least *he* is safe from the wrath of Heung-Chin," she whispered. "Now I must find a way to withstand it as well. I can't be sent to the Imperial City. I just can't."

She took one last, lingering look at Timothy's ship. Though she was happy that he was safe, she felt empty inside for having lost him.

"But it is only temporary," she argued to herself. "Tak-Ming and I will make it to America. We *will*."

She blew a kiss into the wind in the direction of Timothy's ship. "You said that you were going to travel next to a city called San Francisco," she murmured. "So that shall be my destination, Timothy Hendricks."

She turned and headed back to the tunnel, afraid yet not. "If the Fates grant me the chance, I will be with Timothy again," she said.

She then grew silent as she once more began fumbling her way through the passageway, not knowing what awaited her at the other end.

Chapter Twelve

Having made it back safely to her room, Lee-lee was now pacing. There were still no signs of Tak-Ming, and precious time needed for fleeing the House of Yeung was passing much too quickly. The sun had already reached its highest point in the sky and was now moving lower toward the distant mountains. Her last day . . . and it was almost gone.

Seeing shadows deepening in the far corners of her room, Lee-lee thought it best to light a candle. This feeling of being a prisoner was laying more heavily on her mind as each moment passed. If Tak-Ming didn't arrive soon, all would be lost.

A sound at her door drew Lee-lee's attention from the candle and everything else but Tak-Ming. "Tak-Ming . . ." she whispered harshly. She rushed toward the door but stopped in mid-step as it swung widely open and Heung-Chin was suddenly there, standing darkly before her.

"You were expecting someone else?" Heung-Chin

growled, his almond-shaped eyes icy in their accusing stare.

From habit, Lee-lee's eyes humbly lowered, having been taught from age eight that he was a man of greatness and one to whom she should show honor and respect—even more than she might have shown an American father.

Lee-lee had humbly obliged him this courtesy for until only recently she had been grateful for having been raised by him and his close-knit Chinese family.

Though her head was bowed and her fists were held together before her, out of the corner of her eye she could see the boldly embroidered birds on the front of his navy blue silk robe, and she could see a ring of keys that he was switching from hand to hand. She had to wonder about the purpose of the keys. She had never seen him carry them with him before. In fact, he had rarely entered her room! It was he who usually ordered an audience with whomever he wished in the privacy of his private study.

"Has a cat got your tongue this afternoon?" Heung-Chin grumbled, taking a step closer to her to tap her gently on the shoulder. "And your bow has lasted long enough, adopted daughter. Look my way. I wish to look into your eyes which have been neglected today. Why are they not painted? Why did you omit the rice powder from your cheeks and the headdress from your head? No one sent word to me that you were ill. You are, are you not, since you've chosen to remain American in appearance today?"

Lee-lee could hear the mockery in his tone of voice.

She knew that he was now toying with her and was probably enjoying it. A thought flashed inside her brain. Since she already knew his planned fate for her, there was no reason to continue this charade of servitude toward him. She knew how precious she was in his eyes. Because of her, he would gain more power and recognition from the Emperor. Even if she angered him to the point that for most would mean beheading, he wouldn't dare touch her, for surely word had already been sent to the Emperor to soon expect her arrival at his Imperial Palace. Though she was most definitely more a prisoner now than ever before, she felt free enough to say whatever tempted her, to show him that he had raised a willful adopted daughter, not a meek and mild thing who only knew to speak *"ai"* in his overpowering presence.

Smiling almost wickedly, Lee-lee's eyes rose and challenged him in an impudent stare. *"Nay.* I am not ill," she said dryly. "Do I look ill, my lord?"

Lee-lee had changed her dress and now wore a sleek, green lowswept silk that clung to her every curve; a split to the thigh on each side revealed the sensuous taper of her legs. Her raven black hair hung in long waves down her back and her face was void of any false colors. The natural pink of her cheeks and the touch of color to her lips were enough to enhance her innate beauty.

But it was the snapping defiance in her honey-brown eyes that stupefied Heung-Chin. This was not her normal behavior! She was openly defying him! Punishment would be due her, yet he couldn't harm her in any way. Tomorrow she was leaving for the Imperial Palace. She had to be flawless. She would be the most beautiful concubine there, even though she was from the womb of a foreign she-devil.

"You speak so boldly to me, your adopted father?" he snapped, knowing he must show his shock and anger for her disobedience, though his hands were tied against teaching her differently. He had yet to understand her reason for this sudden rash behavior. It was as though she knew his plans for her. But that couldn't be. He had spoken to only a few about this.

"*Ai*," Lee-lee said coldly. "I believe you have forgotten just who my true parents were. Does it not cause you grief to know that I am not yours by blood ties?"

"At this moment you would be a total disgrace to the name of Yeung if you were a true relation," he growled. "But you are not. And what you have done beside this disobedient talk will never be revealed either to the rest of the House of Yeung."

"To what are you referring?" she asked, swallowing hard when she saw his cheek begin to twitch nervously. She knew this was a sign of his building anger. She had witnessed it often enough when he had reprimanded one of his sons. Her eyes widened when he held the ring of keys out before him, singling out one of the many to show her.

"The keys, adopted daughter?" he hissed. "Do you wonder about their purpose?"

Stubbornly, Lee-lee folded her arms across her chest. "*Nay*," she said, shaking her head fitfully back and forth. "A key is just that. A key. Why would I wonder about such a thing?"

Yet she wasn't only wondering—she was worrying! Surely he wouldn't lock her in her room. Tak-Ming wouldn't be able to rescue her once he did return from his voyage at sea.

"A key is used to hold a wild thing at bay," Heung-Chin said, laughing throatily.

"Wild . . . thing?" Lee-lee softly murmured.

"You are that wild thing, so I have been told," Heung-Chin said, lowering the keys to his side. "Is it true that you have been in the city in the company of the American businessman, Timothy Hendricks? Were you even displaying yourself shamefully in an American dress? Has my teaching you of the Chinese culture been worthless?"

Lee-lee shrank back away from him, slowly losing her courage as his face reflected hate and disappointment in its bold, Chinese features. "*Nay*," she lied. "I do not know what you are talking about."

Though she was tempted to brag, Lee-lee couldn't confess her adventures to Heung-Chin. It would only endanger Timothy more. The Chinese warships traveled fast over the East China Sea. Timothy wouldn't be safe no matter how far he traveled from the Port of Foochow. At least now he would be spared these perils.

"Does your serving woman Soonya lie?" Heung-Chin shouted, flailing his arms into the air with the keys jangling over his bald head like many chimes of a church.

Something churned at the pit of Lee-lee's stomach. She had been right to suspect Soonya, yet the knowing cut away at her heart.

191

"Soonya?" she murmured, paling. "Soonya . . . told you such a falsehood?"

Speaking so wrongfully of Soonya, making it appear that she was a liar, made Lee-lee's insides hurt even more, for she knew that she was placing Soonya's life in jeopardy by making her seem a troublemaking, gossipy busybody in the House of Yeung.

But Timothy's life . . . Tak-Ming's life . . . her own life were much more valuable than the woman Lee-lee had grown to respect and love since Lee-lee's first arrival in China—the woman who had betrayed her.

Heung-Chin's almond-shaped eyes darkened in intensity. His forehead creased into a heavy frown. "Do you say that she lies?" he growled. "You do realize Soonya's fate if this is true, do you not? No one lies to the master of his house. No one!"

Lee-lee straightened her back and held her chin proudly high, yet slowly she was dying inside. "I would not lie," she said flatly. "And I am sorry about Soonya, but she has only tried to draw favor in her master's eyes by telling you things that she hoped would make you notice her more."

"That does not make sense," Heung-Chin spat angrily. "And you know this. Soonya would not put her life in jeopardy in such a way. And she has always loved you. She would not make up such a lie. Knowing that harm could come to you by telling such a thing, she would only do so if it were true."

"I am sorry if she has so fooled you with her wily ways," Lee-lee said, meeting his steady stare with the unwavering brown of her eyes. "I am surprised that

192

anyone could succeed at tricking the great Mandarin Heung-Chin Yeung. Soonya has not only tricked you but has also made you look a fool."

A loud, throaty growl reverberated about the room and Lee-lee couldn't step aside quickly enough to stop Heung-Chin's hand from crashing against her face. She closed her eyes as the splat of his hand making contact with her flesh and the snapping of her neck caused her defenses to crumble. The pain made her ears ring and the force of the blow made her tumble backward, where she fell clumsily across her bed.

Her cheek continued to burn. She placed a hand there and slowly turned her eyes to see where Heung-Chin might be, fearing even worse from him before he was finished with her. She had gone too far with her belligerency. It had put visions of the Imperial Palace from his head, it seemed.

"You dare to talk to me in such a way?" Heung-Chin roared. "Even when it is you who are so boldly lying to me? Soonya was accompanied into the city yesterday by a eunuch and made to point you out to him while in the throes of your shameful behavior. She was beaten first, for she did not want to do this thing against her Young Mistress."

"*Nay*, you didn't . . ." Lee-lee softly cried, flinching when he raised another hand in her direction. But this time he just as quickly lowered it and instead stood over her, threateningly large and frighteningly ugly as his face distorted with building anger.

"*Ai*," Heung-Chin snarled. "After she told me that you were not being obedient to the Chinese ways taught you, she immediately recoiled, realizing what she had done, yet being drawn into the telling by her own devotion to me—her Master."

"You . . . beat . . . her?" Lee-lee whispered, now realizing that she hadn't seen Soonya all day. In her overwhelming concern about escape, Lee-lee had somehow overlooked Soonya's lack of attention to her duties through the entire day.

"How . . . is . . . Soonya now?" she dared to ask.

"She has been sent far away from this house," Heung-Chin said dryly. "She will never again disgrace this family."

Lee-lee crept to the edge of the bed, drawing courage from the anger enflaming her insides. "But she had told you what you wanted to hear," she hissed. "Why would you then send her away? Do you ask the impossible of your servants?"

"Soonya should have told me from the beginning when you first began sneaking about like an untrained dog would," Heung-Chin shouted. "How many times have you gone into the city without an escort? How many times did you meet with the barbarian American businessman?"

"Why does it even matter to you now?" she said, scooting to a sitting position, flinging her hair back from her eyes. "I know what you have planned for me. Why should I tell you anything about anything?"

Heung-Chin's face flamed. Red streaks appeared in the whites of his eyes. "You even know this? That you are to be sent to the Imperial Palace?" he stormed. "Does your sneaking about even include snooping outside my door?

Only in that way could you know what I have planned for you. No one would be foolish enough to tell you. A beheading would be quickly ordered for such disobedience."

"Perhaps a beheading would be better for me than having to live the life of a concubine," Lee-lee mournfully said, lowering eyes that were threatening to flood with tears. Her anger had dissolved into a heavy-hearted sadness, pulling her in all directions.

"*Bi-ni-di-zueh!*" Heung-Chin snarled. "You speak like a crazed person."

"But it is true," Lee-lee said, rising to her feet, walking away from him. She was stopped abruptly when she felt the strength of his hand on her wrist. He forced her around to face him. She felt her knees weaken and her insides turn cold as he turned the palm of her right hand upright for his inspection.

"Soonya warned me of this new imperfection to your body," he growled. "You wouldn't tell her how it happened to be there. But you will tell me. Now."

Lee-lee cringed as his fingers dug into her flesh as his hold strengthened. She slowly looked into his eyes, wondering how she could have lived even this long with his overbearing ways. But she hadn't done so by choice, as she didn't even now.

"*Nay*," she said softly. "I shall never tell you. Do with me what you will, but I shall never tell you another thing. It would have been best if Tak-Ming had left me to die at sea. You have only housed me . . . to use me." She let out a small cry when Heung-Chin scraped one of his long fingernails across the newly formed scab of her wound.

He laughed beneath his breath then slowly raised his eyes to meet her tearful gaze. "Do not worry," he said. "That is the only pain I plan to inflict upon you today. Tomorrow you will be gone and out of my thoughts, so why should I bother with you any more today?"

He roughly dropped her hand and began to walk away from her. "The key?" he laughed. He gave her a fast glance across his right shoulder. "It is to stop your further ventures from the House of Yeung, adopted daughter. I plan to lock your door. It will not be unlocked until tomorrow when another more loyal serving woman will be assigned you and will come to your room to prepare you for your long journey to the Imperial Palace."

Lee-lee hugged herself, trembling so that her teeth were loudly chattering. She watched as the door closed and she listened to the key turning in the lock. She was now, indeed, a prisoner! And should Tak-Ming come to her rescue it would be too late.

"Tak-Ming," she whispered, sighing heavily. "At least he is safe. Heung-Chin must not suspect him at all. He didn't mention his name while throwing accusations around."

Barefoot, feeling defeated, Lee-lee went to her bedchamber, settled down on the floor beside the drawers, and slowly opened one. With trembling fingers, she searched through the delicate underclothes until she felt the tiny, satin-lined box in which she would find her precious necklace, which had been hidden there those many years ago after she had first arrived in this house.

She withdrew the box and slowly opened its lid to look

down upon the tiny gold locket in the shape of a heart that was truly her only link with her past. She picked up the locket and chain and, holding these to her chest, she crawled to a dark corner and huddled against the wall there.

She held on to the locket with such a tight grip that her knuckles were white. She was afraid to let go. It was not only her link with her past but perhaps, also, her sanity. The thoughts of what her future held were so fuzzy inside her head she thought that just maybe she was losing her mind.

"But I won't let despair set in," she said, sniffling as tears fought to be set free from her eyes.

The fingers of her right hand crept up to her neck where the necklace had been almost fused to her flesh after she had spent those many days beneath the sweltering, beating rays of the sun. She let herself get caught up in memories of her seventh year . . . when her brother Richard had given her the necklace for her birthday. If Lee-lee felt around on her skin more closely, she knew she would feel the remains of the letter "R" which had, somehow, become branded to her flesh during this time beneath the sun.

"So I have been branded by two men in my life," she whispered, laughing softly. "By my brother . . . and by my lover . . ."

She lowered the necklace and placed it before her eyes and began tracing the heart shape of it, then looked more closely at the chain. She now realized that it was only a cheap imitation of gold. Why else would it now look dull and display a color of pale green along its edges? It resembled how she was feeling inside.

Lee-lee clutched the necklace, watching the waning evening hours turn to night. She didn't bother to light any of her candles. She didn't have any reason to. She was to be alone the rest of the night, awaiting her fateful morning.

Heung-Chin hadn't mentioned food so she knew not to expect any. But she didn't care. Hunger wasn't the cause for the churning and aching of her stomach. It was from a desperate loneliness and growing, gnawing fear.

Trying to block out all of these things from her mind, Lee-lee leaned her back against the wall and began thinking of Timothy. She could envision him on his ship, leaning against the rail. The sea breeze would be blowing his hair gently from his neck and his eyes would be dark and fathomless while they looked out across the vast reaches of the ocean, lost in thoughts . . . of . . . her. . . .

He had had no choice but to leave her. The crazed mob would have destroyed his ship and killed him *and* his crew. There had surely been no time to think of her then. It would be now that he was surely missing her. . . .

A sound outside her door drew Lee-lee from her fantasy and back to the present. She tensed and huddled even more closely to the wall as the sound of the doorknob rattling filled the silent spaces of the room. She feared that Heung-Chin may have decided to return to punish her after all, once he had put more thought into how she had behaved in his presence.

Closing her eyes tightly, Lee-lee was remembering the prisoners that she had seen that one night while with Timothy. She could see the tortured men with their arms and legs outspread beneath the rays of the full moon. She could hear their cries and their groans and moans for mercy. A brisk shiver raced up and down her spine when she also remembered the rats.

Surely Heung-Chin wouldn't have her tortured in such a way! But if he decided against sending her to the Imperial Palace, thinking her unworthy, he could be capable of many things. She had to wonder just how many days she would last, stretched out for the rats to chew on and the sun to beat down upon unmercifully. She had lived through one ordeal without food and water. But could she another?

A key being inserted into the lock made Lee-lee's heart race and her knees become sickeningly weak as she scooted her back up the wall and slowly rose to her feet. She crept warily around the edge of the room, not knowing where she could possibly hide.

She took a deep breath as the door slowly opened, revealing soft light from the hallway. She squinted her eyes, looking toward the shadow standing in the doorway. Then she felt a relief wash through her when she knew that this shadow could not possibly by Heung-Chin's. It was a tall, lean shadow and the voice now being spoken sent hope rushing through her.

"Lee-lee? Are you there in the dark?" Tak-Ming whispered.

In a rush, Lee-lee went to Tak-Ming and fell into his arms. She clung to him with her cheek pressed hard against his chest. She could feel the pounding of his heart and knew that his fear matched her own, for he had now obviously been the most disobedient of the two of them.

He had most surely stolen the key from his father, and such disobedience on the part of a son would never be forgiven.

"Tak-Ming, you have come," she sighed. "Thank God, you have come."

"*Ai,*" Tak-Ming whispered. "But we must hurry. Should father miss the key . . ."

Lee-lee swung away from him and grabbed his hands in hers. "How did you do it, Tak-Ming?" she asked. "Surely he was guarding the ring of keys with his life."

"It is late at night and he is lost in another world of his own making," Tak-Ming growled. "As we had suspected, father enjoys his opium pipe when the rest of the family is soundly asleep."

"He is using opium now? At this very moment?" Lee-lee gasped. "As much as he has spoken against the foreign mud opium . . . he does use it after all?"

"It is good that he does," Tak-Ming said. "If not, there would have been no way I could have taken the key from his key ring. But he will miss it by morning when he awakens with a much clearer head. That will be too late for him, though. By morning, we shall be far out to sea."

"We are leaving? Tonight?" Lee-lee asked, anxiety erasing all her original doubts and fears.

"*Ai,*" Tak-Ming said. "When I returned home earlier in the evening and heard gossip that you were locked away in your room, I knew the time had come to make our big move. Also I heard of the riot in the city today and heard that Pu-Kwan was somehow responsible. And knowing that Pu-Kwan had arrived from the Imperial Palace, I also knew that he was also possibly here for another reason—to take you back with him. *Ai*, father was smart to lock you away. Only by doing so could he be assured that you would be here dutifully waiting to be taken to the Emperor on the morrow."

"You have got your ship and crew ready? Is that what you are about to tell me?" Lee-lee asked, closing the door and locking it from inside. She lit a lone candle and began moving briskly about the room, going through her drawers, pulling from them enough clothes to make her journey as comfortable as could be allowed.

"*Ai*. It is ready and waiting at the cove," Tak-Ming said. "All we have to do is successfully flee this house and courtyards and our life will begin a new chapter, Lee-lee."

Lee-lee locked the necklace about her neck, hoping that it might be a good luck piece, since it had seemed to be the one other time she had worn it at sea. She slipped its satin-lined box inside her valise which she now placed on her bed, alongside her chosen clothes.

"Dress in the coolie clothes once more," Tak-Ming grumbled. "It could be a problem aboard ship should the crew recognize you as a woman. The voyage will be long and without women. Some men find it hard to suppress their urges when the need arises to fulfill the cravings of the flesh."

Lee-lee's face flushed crimson. "All right," she murmured. "Whatever you say, Tak-Ming."

She gathered the ugly tunic, trousers, and shirt together and stepped behind a screen and began changing into them. "Tak-Ming, to save time, begin filling my valise with the clothes I have placed on my bed. And please do not pack any of the Chinese cosmetics," she said. "I never want to see rice powder or vermilion again."

She felt the pressure of the breast binder around her breasts and knew that it would still be required for a while longer if she were to pretend to be a man while aboard the ship. But soon she would throw it away and never be bothered with it again. Fully dressed now, she stepped from behind the screen.

"And dresses? Are you going to take any Chinese-styled dresses with you to America?" Tak-Ming asked, going to the bedchamber drawer, running his long, lean fingers through the clinging silks.

"Why should I?" Lee-lee scoffed. "Once in America I shall have beautifully laced, wonderfully gathered dresses such as those worn today by the American women."

Tak-Ming's brow furrowed. He folded his arms across his chest. "And how would you know what the American women's fashions of today might be?" he grumbled.

Lee-lee paled. Tak-Ming knew nothing of her association with Timothy or the fact that she had even worn one of the American dresses. "Oh, my imagination runs rampant at times," she giggled.

She went to her bedchamber and reconsidered. Perhaps just one dress should be taken to help her remember the happy times, or to show her grandchildren when she could share her experience of having lived in China.

"This one," she said, choosing a brilliant red silk with multicolored embroidered swirls across its front. "I shall take it. It will remind me of many things."

She ignored Tak-Ming's look of wonder. Gently folding the dress and placing it inside her valise, she gave Tak-Ming a half glance.

"Have you decided which city in America to point the *Sea Goddess* toward?" she asked cautiously, having not yet suggested San Francisco to him—not even knowing how she might do it without arousing suspicion on his part. How could she tell him that she preferred San Francisco because she hoped to find Timothy there?

"A city . . . a new city called San Francisco in a brand new state in America called California," Tak-Ming said matter-of-factly. "I've heard that a small portion of this city is called Chinatown because so many Chinese have recently settled there."

Lee-lee swung around, consumed by heartbeats. She smiled coyly at Tak-Ming. "Why, Tak-Ming, how nice," she murmured. "That sounds like a perfect place to go. I, too, am anxious to travel there."

"But this place called New York," Tak-Ming said, lifting an eyebrow. "I thought you would argue to travel there."

"Later." Lee-lee giggled. "We shall go there later, Tak-Ming."

Chapter Thirteen

Night had slipped by much more quickly than had been anticipated and now as the *Sea Goddess* drifted out to sea, Lee-lee and Tak-Ming stood at the ship's rail, watching the China coastline fading behind them.

On the dawn-soft harbor, paper lanterns winked aboard the sampans and junks through gauze veils of fog. The distant mountains appeared purple in color, tipped in copper-reds as the sun rose slowly from behind them.

The topsails of the *Sea Goddess* shivered as the fair and soft wind was captured in their folds. There were shreds of mist in the air, dampening Lee-lee's face with sea water. She licked the salty dampness from her lips and looked toward Tak-Ming. He had never looked as handsome as now, standing so tall and proud in his purple silk robe fluttering in the breeze. It was secured at his waist by a matching silk band and in this was thrust a dangerous-looking curved sword with a gold handle.

His sleek hair was braided down his back and the bold, Chinese features of his face were emphasized by the set of his jaw and the tightening of his lips. It was quite evident to Lee-lee that he was being torn apart by feelings caused by so abruptly leaving his homeland and family, never to see them again.

Lee-lee understood. She had experienced those same feelings ten years ago. Their roles had switched, for now it would be Tak-Ming who would be on foreign soil once America was reached.

Hoping to comfort Tak-Ming, if even in a small way, Lee-lee scooted closer to him and gently touched his smooth face with the fingertips of her left hand. She had kept the scar of her right hand from his sight, not wanting to have to answer awkward questions as to who had inflicted the wound. Only after Timothy was found in America would she tell Tak-Ming about him. Somehow she didn't think that Tak-Ming would understand. He had warned her against the Americans moored at the Port of Foochow, hadn't he? Knowing that she had seen Timothy Hendricks behind his back would be knowing that she had not only disregarded Heung-Chin's teachings but Tak-Ming's warnings as well.

"Tak-Ming, I know how you must be feeling about leaving your family," she murmured, looking up into the dark abyss of his eyes.

Tak-Ming took her hand and kissed its palm, then affectionately held it as he gazed down upon her loveliness. With her hat hiding most of her facial features beneath its wide brim, and dressed so drably in her coolie attire, he still couldn't help but feel an extra beat of his heart because of his intense feelings for her . . . feelings that he would never reveal to her. In her eyes he was a true brother.

"It is shameful to show fear or pain, sorrow or anger," he said thickly. "It is *buh-hao-eese*. I will have to learn to practice more control."

"That's nonsense, Tak-Ming," Lee-lee softly scolded. "Especially now. You are leaving China. You can leave your Chinese ways behind you."

"It is in my blood," he grumbled. "In my heart I shall always be Chinese."

"You're worried about your family, aren't you?"

"*Ai* . . ."

"They will miss you but soon will forget," Lee-lee encouraged. "Remember? They are also Chinese and they cannot show sorrow either."

"They may not show it, but surely they will feel it," Tak-Ming said, stepping away from Lee-lee to clutch the ship's rail. "My mother's heart will be very heavy."

"And Heung-Chin? Your father?" Lee-lee said, moving to his side, looking back toward shore.

"*Wei!*" Tak-Ming laughed. "No doubt his feelings will show. They will be explosive. He will be too angry to be sad."

Lee-lee sighed heavily. "This *Sea Goddess* voyage to America will deprive Heung-Chin of many things," she murmured. "An adopted daughter who was going to bring him recognition and praise from Emperor Tao Kuang, and a son . . . a son of greatness and gentleness."

Tak-Ming gave her a look that Lee-lee couldn't understand, and she was glad when he turned his eyes away from her to take one last look at Foochow with its tall, colorful temples and its rice paddies lacing the hillsides in colorful splotches of green.

Then suddenly it was gone from sight, hidden behind a heavier cloud of fog, as if the city and countryside had never been real—only a dream, a dream that had recently begun to be more like a nightmare to Lee-lee in her fear of being forced to live the life of a concubine.

The ship's masts creaked, the sails bellied against the wind, and the sea rippled and danced. The schooner plunged and rolled her way along, now far out to sea, making its way through white waves heaving high.

Tak-Ming looked behind and then all around him. He then took Lee-lee by the elbow and began guiding her across the deck. He leaned closer to her, whispering just beneath his breath.

"For a while there I had forgotten the dangers," he said. "I shouldn't have shown you any affection while on topdeck. During the bright daylight hours you must stay below in the privacy of your cabin. I have warned you. The crew must never suspect you are a woman. Dressed the way you are, they will believe you are only my boy servant. Nothing more, nothing less."

Lee-lee emitted a soft groan. "All day every day, Tak-Ming?" she sighed. "I'm not sure if I can bear that for the length of time required at sea to reach America. I shall go stark-raving mad! I just know it."

"Lee-lee, I purposely made your private cabin beautiful and luxurious for you with that in mind," he growled, guiding her down the steps and into a low-ceilinged, narrow passageway. "I knew that the voyage would be a monotonous one for you."

"Beautiful tapestried walls and red-lacquered floors are not the same as fresh air and sunlight," she softly argued.

The aroma of tea and spices rose from the direction of the hold of the ship, pleasuring Lee-lee's sense of smell. She had been shown the tea and spice cargo which Tak-Ming hoped to sell upon his first arrival in America. She had thought the chests pretty, covered with a mesh sort of fabric with beautiful designs of latticework.

But while stirring around in the cramped spaces of the ship's cargo deck, Lee-lee had also caught the aroma of opium, a reminder of the illicit shipment that had been negotiated while Tak-Ming sailed the waters of the Min River. This aroma had given Lee-lee a most unfavorable, uneasy feeling, as she remembered the threat of attack from pirate junks now that they were far out to sea. She had heard that these junks were fast and sometimes carried as many as six hundred men and could even be armed with six-pounder cannons.

She knew that the ordnance aboard the *Sea Goddess* was small. There were a few light four-pounder cannons, certainly not enough to fire in defense of the ship, if the need arose.

Lee-lee glanced over at Tak-Ming, praying that nothing would happen to test his skills as the true commander of this ship which he had rebuilt from the bottom to the top. One pirate attack would be one attack too many. It would be more than tragic if pirates—*pilongs* as Tak-Ming called them—stole both Tak-Ming's and Lee-lee's dream from them before it even had a chance to become a reality.

Tak-Ming opened the door that led into Lee-lee's cabin.

"Always bolt lock the door when I leave," he flatly ordered.

After Lee-lee, he stepped into the cabin and screwed the wick up on a whale oil lamp, brightening the room with a false sunlight. He swung around and gestured with the sweep of a hand. "Now it's not all that bad, is it?" he exclaimed, smiling broadly at Lee-lee as she lifted the pitiful excuse of a hat from her head.

"*Nay*, it isn't," she said, tossing the hat aside.

She looked slowly about her, absorbing the Chinese look of the room, even to the figured-silk mosquito-net curtains hooked back on both sides of the small, carved bed. She gave Tak-Ming a warm smile then ran and embraced him, always marveling at his muscled chest and loving the feel of his silks against her cheek. "It's quite lovely, Tak-Ming," she murmured. "Truly. It is. Thank you."

She would never reveal to him that in truth she would have preferred leaving anything that was a reminder of China behind. But to tell him would be to hurt him. So instead she would pretend.

The jasmine scent of her hair and her closeness was pure torture to Tak-Ming, and he wondered how it was that she hadn't discovered the depths of his feelings for her.

Yet with her, he had succeeded at practicing control and hoped to one day find a dainty Chinese maiden in which to lose himself. Only then could he forget these shameful feelings for his younger adopted sister.

Lee-lee could feel the fierce pounding of his heart against her cheek. She had expected him to be excited about their shared journey. But to this extent?

She drew away from him and gazed up into his eyes, giggling. "Tak-Ming, your heart is going wild inside you," she said. "Are you that anxious to get to America?"

Tak-Ming's eyes wavered. He placed a hand on the handle of his cutlass and squeezed it hard. "*Ai*," he said. "And once there I shall go directly to the Chinese community. It is time for Tak-Ming to take a bride."

Lee-lee raised her hands to her cheeks, her eyes wide. "Tak-Ming," she exclaimed. "A bride? What a time to be thinking of women!"

She laughed throatily and once more moved into his embrace, having seen the look of embarrassment mask his handsome face. "I'm sorry," she said. "I shouldn't have said that. Of course you'd want a wife. It is only natural. I would have thought you would have married a long time ago."

"With this voyage my main concern for so long, I haven't had time to think about it," he grumbled.

Lee-lee screwed her face up in wonder then shrugged as she stepped away from him. "It is strange, this timing of yours," she said.

Then she went to the center of the cabin and whirled around in merry circles with her arms stretched high above her head. "We did it, Tak-Ming," she shouted. "We've safely left China behind. We are heading toward America! I can hardly believe it!"

Tak-Ming went to her and grabbed her by the waist and stopped her. "*Puh-hao*," he scolded. "You must be quiet or the crew will recognize your woman's voice. I have explained the dangers in that."

Lee-lee covered her mouth with her hands, drowning out a soft giggle. Then she grabbed onto Tak-Ming's hands. "It is only because I am so happy," she harshly whispered. "We have done what most would say is impossible. We have tricked Heung-Chin!"

"A deed which will haunt me always," Tak-Ming growled.

He tensed, feeling a scabby ridge on the palm of her right hand. He moved her closer to the whale oil lamp and studied the scar. "*Aie-yah*! What is this?" he gasped. "How did such a thing happen to your soft, beautiful hand?"

Lee-lee's joy of achieved freedom was short-lived because now she felt miserably trapped. "My hand?" she said, her eyes innocently wide. "To what are you referring, Tak-Ming?"

"Lee-lee, do not pretend not to know what I am talking about," he softly scolded. He ran a forefinger over the scar and tried to hide the involuntary shiver traversing his body.

Lee-lee eased her hand away from him and hid it behind her back. "Tak-Ming, it's only a scratch," she said dryly. "Do not concern yourself about such a trivial thing. Aren't you needed topside? Shouldn't you see if the ship is on the right course?"

"The helmsman is skilled enough or I wouldn't have brought him on board," he growled. "Now, tell me. What were you up to while I was away on my last voyage?"

Feeling a slow blush coloring her cheeks, Lee-lee walked briskly away from him. She kicked the straw sandals from her feet and jumped up on the bed. She began unbraiding her hair but was stopped when Tak-Ming roughly grabbed her left wrist and drew her up from the bed.

He bent his face into hers. "Tell me," he ordered. "Should I not know everything about you? You know my every move, Lee-lee."

"Perhaps I know your every move," Lee-lee murmured, flinching with the pain. "But I certainly don't know your innermost thoughts. It puzzles me why you are so angry with me now over discovering a blemish on the palm of my hand. Tak-Ming, do not behave as though you possess me just because you rescued me those many years ago. This isn't like you. Not at all! What's got into you?"

"Not only did I rescue you then, but *now*," Tak-Ming stormed. "Do you so easily forget?"

"And I am now to forever be in your service, humble to you because of this?" Lee-lee said, her eyes flashing with building anger. "Do I leave one possessive Chinaman behind only to discover I am in the company of another?"

Tak-Ming's eyes lowered. He then loosened his hold on Lee-lee's wrist and drew her sweetly into his arms. "Can you forgive me my thoughtlessness?" he whispered, placing his face into the curve of her neck.

"*Ai*," Lee-lee whispered. "Always, Tak-Ming. I wasn't truly angry. I just wanted you to realize how you were appearing to me. I love you so, I don't want anything to stand in my way of doing so."

"*Ai*," he said, running his long, lean fingers through

the length of her hair that lay unbraided down her back.

"But I must go see to my duties," he quickly added, unwinding his arms from around her to rush to the door.

He opened the door and gestured with a hand toward the lock. "Remember to lock it. Only open it when you hear my voice on the other side," he flatly ordered.

"*Ai*," Lee-lee said, dazed by what had just been exchanged between them. She was seeing a side to Tak-Ming that she did not recognize . . . or understand.

Chapter Fourteen

Stretching her arms high above her head and yawning, Lee-lee rose from her bed. The wick had been lowered in the whale oil lamp and it cast ghostly shadows along the tapestried walls and low, paneled ceiling.

The timbers of the ship creaking and the splash of the water beneath her were constant reminders that land had most definitely been left behind. One full day and night at sea had passed with many, many more of the same ahead.

"But the hardships will be worth it in the end," she sighed. "First this place which goes by the name of San Francisco and then New York! I have become a world traveler for sure."

Laughing softly, pleased with the way life was changing for her, Lee-lee hurried into her coolie clothes. She couldn't miss the opportunity to go topside before the brightness of daylight forced her to stay in her cabin. Early morning and late evening were the only times that were safe enough for her to move freely about on topdeck.

She had seen the *undesirable unfortunates* who had been hired on as sailors. They were a ghastly lot. But they followed Tak-Ming's orders and that was all that was important. Full cooperation from everyone was needed to make this journey a safe and successful one.

Lee-lee grudgingly braided her hair, though knowing that this was also part of the daily routine that she would have to get used to.

"A boy," she mumbled. "I hate playing the role of a boy. At night my dreams are filled with how a woman should look and feel. Ah, my dreams. I am always with Timothy in them."

A rawness. An itching drew her fingers to her neck. She began to scratch the flesh there when she felt minute, risen welts, and as she touched them, she winced and let out a mournful "ouch."

"What on earth . . . ?" she whispered, now barely running her fingertips along her neck where the chain of her necklace lay and onto her chest where the heart shape of the locket also lay in a bed of sore flesh.

Picking up a gilt-trimmed hand mirror, Lee-lee looked into it in silent horror, seeing red splotches that seemed to outline the complete chain and locket of her necklace. She screwed the wick up on her lamp and looked closer.

"Why, I'm having some sort of bad reaction from the necklace," she murmured, "It has to be. There are no welts anywhere else!"

The soft green coloring which seemed to lace the cheap imitation of gold of the chain of her necklace grabbed Lee-lee's quick attention. She ran her fingers over it. "That must be what's causing the problem," she said. "My skin cannot tolerate having that next to it."

Unlocking the chain, she let it flutter down into the palm of her hand. "I will just have to place it back inside its box," she whispered. "Again it shall be forgotten, sad though that is, since I have only just felt free to wear it again."

An amusing thought shaped her lips into a wry smile as she remembered when Heung-Chin had discovered the necklace hanging from around her neck on her arrival at the House of Yeung. He had surely thought the necklace pure gold, the way he had made over it, while all along it had been only a poor substitute.

"*Ai*, a fool he was, even then," she giggled. "And wouldn't such a gift, cheap as it surely was, be one that Richard would give to me?"

Ai, cheap but yet dear. A lonely feeling washed over her when she looked toward the heart-shaped locket, knowing that sealed away forever inside its tiny chamber was a lock of her mother's gorgeous red hair. If only she could succeed at prying the locket open. How grand it would be to place the silken hair of her mother to her cheek, to pretend that her mother was there with her . . .

A shiver raced across her flesh as she suddenly realized what she was doing. It was ten years too late to think of her mother—there was only now.

Pulling her valise from beneath her bed, Lee-lee opened it and withdrew the tiny, satin-covered box and once more placed the necklace inside it. It would be hidden from her eyes but never from her heart. Her past would always be reflected in the shine of its locket.

She slipped the satin box back inside her valise and as she did this her hand brushed against the soft silk of the one Chinese dress which she had chosen to take with her to America. Strange that even now the dress was already a thing of her past.

Having caught the feel of another chest while stooping to find her valise, Lee-lee had the urge to once more let her fingers swim through the crisp coolness of the silver coins which had been hidden beneath her bed.

With a pounding heart she fell to her knees and felt around beneath the bed. When her hands found the firm square of the wooden chest, she secured her fingers around on each side and slowly drew it toward her.

It had taken many months of Tak-Ming's voyages at sea, filled with the dangers of illicit opium trade, to earn the coins inside this chest. Always in their shine Lee-lee had seen the outline of America! For so long it had only been a fantasy of hers, one to get her from day to day. Only in her wildest dreams had she truly thought to make this voyage a reality.

Releasing a small lock, Lee-lee opened the chest. As always the brilliant glitter of the layers of silver made a low gasp rise from inside her. She dug the fingers of both her hands into the coins and then slowly pulled them free, enjoying the clink from the coins as well as their coolness against her flesh.

She ran her fingers through them over and over again, fully realizing that they were a big part of her survival. Once in America, only the coins could buy her true freedom. Without them . . . ?

A shudder of fear coursed through her, knowing that

even America had devious, evil men who could do worse to her than Heung-Chin.

"But that won't happen," she said, firming her chin and jaw into a stubborn line. "Once in America I will be treated as a true lady and will be respected by all—men and women alike."

The filtering of the early morning sun through the bamboo curtains at the one porthole in her cabin startled her into realizing that full daylight was upon the ship, and she hadn't yet taken her morning stroll. If she didn't do so, and quickly, a full day would pass without fresh air and the ability to loosen up her joints by walking freely about.

Dropping the lid shut on the chest and leaving it where she had dragged it, she grabbed her rattan hat and rushed from the cabin. Slamming the door securely closed behind her, she made her way through the dark passageway. The aromas were enticingly pleasing to the flare of her nostrils. The tea . . . the spices . . . the fresh sea breeze. What a wholesome combination to carry on board this ship with her.

Cautiously, she moved to topdeck and to the ship's rail, feeling only truly safe when her back was to the wondering eyes of the crew. She was already doubting that she would be able to continue fooling them. They surely had to wonder about this "boy servant" who only came briefly topside mornings and evenings.

"But I will worry about that later," she whispered, clinging to the rail.

She looked out over the great expanse of the turquoise-tinted water, admiring it anew. Ah, how it glistened and rippled beneath the morning light. And the sun! As it was rising, it was playing in soft reds, dancing along the horizon where only a few drifting dark clouds remained of what once had been night.

The wind upon the ship made the *Sea Goddess* appear to be alive as she trembled, eagerly pushing her way on through the lacy foam of the water. All her sails were continuing to gracefully draw, and light sprays of seawater clung to the bulwark like a million diamonds sparkling.

Lee-lee sighed, so enjoying this moment of peace. Then a form that had suddenly appeared on the horizon made her tense. She squinted her eyes, shielding them with a cupped hand, as she looked even more closely at the dot on the horizon which was getting larger, too quickly approaching the *Sea Goddess*.

Then Lee-lee's pulse raced when she saw that this dot had changed to take the shape of two Chinese junks. They were quite identifiable now with their bows and sterns broad and high, and with their high poops and overhanging stems. Lee-lee could now count five masts to each junk and could see the orange-colored, bamboo matting lugsails.

"There's a sail to leeward two miles!" Lee-lee heard someone shout. "She's just hauled her wind to cross our course!"

Shouts and a scrambling of feet drew Lee-lee around to watch as the ship's crew jumped into action.

"It's Chinese pirate junks!" another man shouted. "Two of 'em!"

A commanding, deep voice broke through the turmoil.

219

"Ready the cannons!" he firmly yelled.

Lee-lee recognized Tak-Ming's voice and panic grabbed her. The danger was real. It had taken Tak-Ming's voice to shake her from the daze that she had been in after first seeing the intrusion of junks in what had only moments ago been an aura of peace and tranquillity.

Lee-lee was frozen to the spot with fear. She could hear the crack of the masts as the sails bellied against the wind. The beautiful white canvas shone in the morning's perfect light and a light spray of seawater settled on her face.

But the peacefulness of this moment was only a trick being played by nature, for the two junks were now bearing down upon the *Sea Goddess*, so close now the fate of the *Sea Goddess* was most surely in question.

Lee-lee swung around, once more staring toward the approaching pirate junks. Her breath caught in her throat when she saw the stinkpot jars being sent up to their mastheads, rigged on halyards. She had been warned that this was one true way to distinguish a pirate vessel from any other that sailed the seas. And soon the stinkpots could be flung to the deck of the *Sea Goddess*!

"Lee-lee!" Tak-Ming shouted, rushing to her side.

He placed an arm about her waist and began pulling her alongside him, across the deck. "You must get below! Get to your cabin and securely bolt lock the door!"

"*Nay!*" Lee-lee argued, not wanting to be separated from Tak-Ming. If he must die, she would also, while fighting at his side. Her love for him took precedence over her fear.

"*Puh-hao!*" he loudly shouted. "What are you

thinking by refusing to do as I say? Don't you realize the dangers? I cannot let you stay on topdeck to face the scalawag *pilongs*! Why would you even want to?"

Lee-lee struggled away from him. "Give me a sword!" she cried. "I shall fight the lowly *undesirables* alongside you. You know that you need all the help that you can get. There are two pirate junks. Even one would be too many, Tak-Ming."

A cannon shot boomed out from the approaching junk. Lee-lee grabbed for Tak-Ming's arm when the *Sea Goddess* shuddered as the cannonball crashed into her. Lee-lee felt a sick feeling at the pit of her stomach when she heard the splintering of wood.

"Lee-lee, go to your cabin," Tak-Ming again shouted, forcing her on across the deck.

He then stopped and leaned into her face. "Your duty will be to protect our chest of silver," he said in a lower tone of voice. He took the cutlass from his waistband and placed its handle into her trembling hand. "You secure the door to your cabin as best you can, but should the door get broken down, use the sword. Behead the *pilong* if you must. Just do not let anyone near the silver . . . or you."

He drew her roughly into his arms and held her against him, closing his eyes momentarily to the dangers, letting himself absorb the rapture of her. It pained him so to think that he was failing her. And perhaps these might even be their last moments together.

He forced himself to break away from her. "Now go," he flatly ordered. "If the Fates allow, we shall somehow make it through even this ordeal."

Lee-lee touched his cheek. Tears burned at the corners of her eyes. "*Ai,*" she murmured. "If the Fates allow . . ."

The shouts and musket fire on all sides of her made desperation seize Lee-lee. Perhaps this was her last moment with Tak-Ming. She couldn't bear the thought!

Hanging her head, she hurried away from him. And once in her cabin, she leaned heavily against the locked door, breathless. Slowly her gaze moved downward. Her eyes widened and her heart skipped a beat.

"Smoke!" she gasped. "Good Lord, smoke . . ."

Chapter Fifteen

A screen of black smoke over the water ahead caused a flurry of excitement on board the *New Yorker*. Standing tall and straight, attired handsomely in his silk top hat and impeccable frock coat and snug trousers, Timothy placed the sea-glass to his eye and focused it on the trouble spot.

At first, it was impossible to make out anything through the smoke. But as it began to lift slowly in huge billows, Timothy was finally able to see more clearly. And what he saw made his gut begin a slow twisting. There was no mistaking the name on the side of the clipper schooner. It was Tak-Ming's opium-carrying ship, the *Sea Goddess*. It was the source of the smoke.

Timothy then saw the reason. Two pirate junks were attacking Tak-Ming's miserable excuse for a ship! And it was already obvious who was the victor in this battle. And it was not Tak-Ming!

"Shall we go to her rescue?" Captain Hollister snarled as he stepped to Timothy's side. "That schooner ain't got a chance."

Scooting his beaver hat back on his head, idly scratching his forehead, Captain Hollister leaned over the leeward rail to try to get a better look at the schooner, his gray eyes squinting through the thick lenses of his gold-framed spectacles.

"Somethin' mighty familiar about that schooner," he mumbled. "I'm sure I've seen it somewhere before."

Timothy handed him the sea-glass. "Yes, you have," he said. "Take a look."

A part of Timothy wanted to go in quick defense of Tak-Ming and a part of him wanted to ignore the problem. If Tak-Ming were dead, then wouldn't Lee-lee be free in body and soul to love him and be wholly his?

But his mind was full of many doubts. Lee-lee had betrayed Tak-Ming to come to Timothy with only one purpose in mind—to secure transportation to America for both her and Tak-Ming, since it was quite apparent that Tak-Ming's ship could never withstand such a journey.

Love for Timothy had never been on Lee-lee's mind. She had only spoken the words to him to fulfill her role as "lover" and to pull him into her deceit.

Yet Timothy had ordered that his ship be turned around and was now on his way back to the Port of Foochow to rescue Lee-lee from the wrath of the Chinese mob. Guilt had plagued him for having left her there, knowing that the Chinese had suddenly turned venomous toward all Americans in Foochow.

It had been Timothy's plan to rescue Lee-lee, get her to America, then go on his way. With Tak-Ming dead could this plan change?

"It's the opium schooner," Captain Hollister shouted. "I'd know 'er anywhere. The name *Sea Goddess* is one not easily forgotten."

He lowered the sea-glass from his eye and gave Timothy a puzzled look. "You haven't said what we're to do," he said. "Do we? Or don't we? You know we're wastin' time. That ship's soon a goner."

Timothy's eyes darkened and his face shadowed as he gave Captain Hollister an angry look. "Damn it," he growled. "Need you even ask?" He gestured with a hand toward the battle. "Go save the Chinaman Tak-Ming and as much of his crew as possible. Do you think I would ever turn my back on anyone in trouble? I never have . . . and I never will."

Captain Hollister pulled his hat more securely onto his head, studied Timothy for a second or two, puzzling over his strange mood, then thrust Timothy's sea-glass back into his hands as he swung around on a heel and hurried away, shouting out orders.

Timothy wiped a bead of perspiration away from his brow with the back of a hand, feeling almost sick to his stomach for having even for a brief moment considered letting Tak-Ming perish at sea. For that brief moment he had not been himself and it frightened him to realize what the subconscious could do.

Now he had to see to it that the *New Yorker* crew would fight even harder to prove that his intentions were honorable and true. Then he would travel on to Foochow and get Lee-lee, and once more point his ship in the direction of America.

It would be an almost inhumane thing to do to himself,

225

a sort of self-torture, to have the two lovers, Lee-lee and Tak-Ming, on board with him. But he had learned to accept both the ups and downs of life and felt he was a better man for it.

Lifting the tail of his brown frock coat, he placed a hand on the loaded pistol at his waist. It would probably not be necessary for him to fire a shot from such a small weapon. He knew the accuracy of his powerful cannons and he had seen to it that pivot and swivel guns had been placed in the most vulnerable sites of the *New Yorker*.

The range of all these weapons was great and he knew that it would not be required to get that close in order to sink the junks to the bottom of the sea.

He set aside his sea-glass and braced himself against the surge of the wind as the *New Yorker* cut its way through the water. The forecastle and aftercastle groaned, laboring. The masts nodded and swayed. And as the *New Yorker* drew closer to the battle scene, the smoke was so black and intense, it was like moving into the dark of night. But once they were through the more rifted veils of smoke, the pirate junks came into full sight as did the *Sea Goddess*.

"God," Timothy gasped, seeing the inflicted damage to Tak-Ming's smaller ship. A fire was raging in its tarred hemp rigging and the flames had also reached the furled canvas. The topdeck was half blown away, yet the pirates continued to pelt the ailing schooner with their big clay jar stinkpots filled with gunpowder and inflammable oil, dumping these on the *Sea Goddess*'s deck from halyards swung over from the junks.

To Timothy's relief he noticed that the pirates hadn't

226

yet boarded the *Sea Goddess*. They seemed to be first concentrating on inflicting as much damage as possible. And not only were the pirates making good aim with their stinkpots, but they were good marksmen as well. Almost every time one of the surviving crew of the *Sea Goddess* showed himself above the bulwarks, he was hit.

Timothy now doubted he would find Tak-Ming alive. The thought now saddened him. Tak-Ming and his ship were fighting valiantly against great odds. A keen admiration for the handsome Chinaman swept through Timothy, and he was glad that he had decided to at least make an effort to save him.

Black, thick smoke swirled toward the *New Yorker*. It was then that the cannons of Timothy's proud ship began to belch their own smoke as they expelled their cannon balls. The ship shuddered and the crew shouted with each success as the balls crashed into the junks, over and over again.

At this closer range, Timothy could see the pirates. Most were Chinese with a scattering of what might be Portuguese or English. They were sinewy and half-naked and constantly screamed as they ran around on their topdeck, waving creeses with wave-shaped blades and clumsy pistols and muskets. Their faces were shiny with sweat and their eyes wild as their junks were now engulfed in flames and the chance to board the *Sea Goddess* for its treasures a thing of the past.

The *New Yorker* continued its assault in an almost never-ending barrage of cannon balls into the junks until they finally began breaking apart and plunged beneath the water, taking their crews with them.

Shouts of victory rang out aboard the *New Yorker*, but Timothy did not feel the victorious one. The battle had taken longer than he had wanted and he now doubted to find many alive on board the *Sea Goddess*. He wasn't even sure if it was safe to board the ship, to check for survivors, but he had to. If he didn't, he would forever be haunted by the question of why he hadn't.

The *New Yorker* shuddered as it came alongside the *Sea Goddess*. The dangers were great, being so close to the burning hunk of ship with its gaping hole on topdeck around which lay lifeless bodies. If the *Sea Goddess* began to sink, the suction could drag the *New Yorker* right along with it, to forever rest together in a dark, watery grave.

Lee-lee's face kept forming in Timothy's mind's eye, as though trying to warn him about something. This alone spurred his decision to board the *Sea Goddess* himself, no matter the dangers. This wasn't the first time he had met danger head on, and it wouldn't be the last.

"Timothy, lad, you stay behind," Captain Hollister encouraged. "Should the need arise to quickly abandon the search for survivors, you should be on the *New Yorker*. You know the perils of being so close to a weakening ship." He looked at the *Sea Goddess*'s burned sails and leaning masts and at the mass of burned wood on topdeck. "I think it may be unwise for any of us to board it," he growled.

"We will board it," Timothy said stubbornly. "And when I saw 'we' that includes me. I will not just stand by and watch. You should know me better than that."

Captain Hollister shrugged. "It's your neck," he said. "Don't say I never warned you."

Timothy ignored this remark. He tossed his top hat aside then led the way until he and his men were scurrying about on the *Sea Goddess*, checking bodies. There were groans and moans on all sides of Timothy. The smell of burned flesh rose into his nose, making his stomach churn. He went from body to body, kneeling down over them, tensing as he flipped each one over to check the faces. So far, Tak-Ming wasn't among the ones he had looked at.

Then through the haze of low-hanging smoke he saw a movement and when Tak-Ming crawled within eye range, Timothy's heart plunged. He instantly felt shameful for knowing that deep inside where his hopes and fears were formed, he had truly not wished to find Tak-Ming alive.

Hating this weak side of himself and wanting to prove to himself that he was not a devious man at heart, he rushed to Tak-Ming and fell to a knee beside him. Tak-Ming's clothes were scorched and torn and his handsome facial features were hidden behind smears of black.

Timothy searched Tak-Ming's body more slowly now, looking for signs of wounds and finding none.

Tak-Ming pushed himself up on an elbow. "Lee-lee," he said, breathing harshly.

Timothy's mouth went dry. "Lee-lee? What about her?" he said then winced and drew back away from Tak-Ming as Tak-Ming closed his eyes and began coughing fitfully.

Tak-Ming clutched desperately to his chest. Then as his bout of coughing stopped, he once more looked wildly up at Timothy. "My adopted sister Lee-lee," he said, wheezing. "She's below. In her cabin. I've not had a chance to check on her. Go see to her, American."

Timothy didn't wait to ask why Lee-lee was on board the *Sea Goddess* far out to sea. She had told him that Tak-Ming had only taken her with him once on his ship and that had only been in the gentle waters of the Min River the night that Timothy and Lee-lee had seen one another for that very first time. The honey-brown of Lee-lee's eyes haunted him now, as though to warn him . . .

A thought suddenly struck Timothy. Were they—the *Sea Goddess*, Tak-Ming, and Lee-lee—in the East China Sea waters because Tak-Ming had seen the need to carry Lee-lee away from the troubled city of Foochow? Timothy's heart plummeted, thinking that it had been Tak-Ming and not himself who had rescued Lee-lee. She now would forever be in Tak-Ming's debt—even more so than before. Her love for Tak-Ming would be doubled!

"If she is even alive," he softly cried as he now made his way down the dark passageway below deck. The smoke burned his nose and throat. His lungs ached. He coughed, he wheezed, he stumbled on through the dark, opening and closing doors, searching. Then he came to one that was locked.

"Damn it," he mumbled as he tried over and over again to open it. He pushed at it with his shoulder, again coughing as the smoke thickened even worse about him. He didn't have long. He could even feel the shuddering of the ship beneath his feet.

Determined, he stepped back from the door and then made a lunge toward it. With the full strength of his shoulder hitting the door, it crashed suddenly open, causing Timothy to fall awkwardly into the dark cabin which was now filling quite rapidly with smoke.

Squinting his eyes and covering his mouth and nose with a hand, Timothy frantically began to search around the cabin. When he stumbled over something in his way on the floor, he looked quickly down to see what it was. Through the darkness and swirling smoke he discovered Lee-lee lying there, seemingly unconscious, in her coolie outfit.

"No . . ." Timothy gasped, forgetting the painful ache in his lungs from inhaling too much smoke. He dropped to his knees and lowered an ear to her chest, sighing with relief when he discovered her heartbeats still in steady motion there.

He looked down at her, seeing the exquisite beauty of her facial features, never loving her more than at this moment. But this was not the time to get caught up in her loveliness. He had to get her to some fresh air. It was apparent that it was the smoke that had rendered her unconscious, and lungs could stand only so much.

Wheezing, his eyes now fiercely burning, he moved to gather her in his arms but was surprised when he felt sudden blows from her fists pounding against his chest. And when he saw Lee-lee reach for something and then saw the glint of silver from a cutlass at her side, he knocked her hand away. He grasped onto her shoulders and began to shake her.

"Lee-lee," he shouted. "It's me! Timothy!"

He now realized that she had been feigning unconsciousness in a ploy to fool her assailant, not opening her eyes to see who it was for fear the assailant would do her immediate harm if he knew she was alive.

Lee-lee's eyes flew widely open. Her heart became alive with flutterings. "Timothy," she gasped. "How . . . ?"

She placed a hand quickly to her chest as she was thrown into a bout of coughs. Her eyes burned. Her throat ached. But she had been too afraid to leave her cabin to go topside. She had heard the fierceness of the battle. And she had also known the importance of continuing to protect their silver.

"Never mind how," Timothy grumbled, scooping her up into his arms. "I've got to get you out of here."

"Tak-Ming . . . ?" Lee-lee asked, her voice raspy and shallow. "Did you . . . did you happen to see if Tak-Ming was all right?"

Jealousy inflamed Timothy's insides. Again her thoughts were only for the handsome Chinaman. The *Sea Goddess* should have been allowed to burn at the hands of the pirates and along with it Tak-Ming!

Then Timothy reconsidered such a thought. Had the *Sea Goddess* been allowed to sink to its grave at the bottom of the sea, not only Tak-Ming would have perished, but also Lee-lee.

To think that he had almost passed by the *Sea Goddess* made a bitterness rise into Timothy's throat. Lee-lee would have died and he would have been responsible . . .

"Timothy," Lee-lee softly persisted. "Is Tak-Ming all right?"

"Yes. As far as I could tell," Timothy said, hurrying toward the door, too thankful that Lee-lee was alive to think of jealousy any more at the moment.

Lee-lee placed an arm about his neck. "What do you mean . . . ?" she gasped. "*Is* he or *isn't* he all right?"

Timothy rushed out into the dark passageway, holding tightly to Lee-lee. "He's alive," he said. "On topdeck. You shall soon see for yourself."

Lee-lee clung to Timothy, exhausted from her fight for survival as the smoke had slowly filled her cabin. If not for Timothy, she and Tak-Ming would have surely perished. She was full of wonder about his sudden appearance on the *Sea Goddess.* Soon she would know all the answers to her questions. Once more she would be a guest on the *New Yorker*, but this time under much different circumstances.

Filled with a deep sadness over the inevitable loss of the *Sea Goddess*, she closed her eyes tightly and doubled a fist at her side. Then her eyes once more flew widely open, remembering the silver coins and her valise of personal belongings!

"Timothy!" she cried, wriggling quickly from his arms. "I must return to my cabin. I must!"

She stepped down onto the deck barefoot. She felt heat seeping up into the flesh of the soles of her feet and feared that even now everything in the hold of the ship was a raging, fiery inferno. The dangers were increasing by the minute. But she had to rescue the chest of coins and, hopefully, the valise.

Yet she knew their value was beyond that which Timothy would understand, for even now his strong hands were about her wrists, drawing her back toward him.

"What do you think you're doing?" Timothy growled, whirling her around to face him. "We have to get off the ship. Don't you realize that it's near to sinking?"

Lee-lee struggled, trying to get her wrists free. "Let me go," she cried. "Without the chest of coins, my future . . . Tak-Ming's . . . is even more questionable than if you had not arrived on the scene to rescue us."

Her insides did a strange rolling, realizing that she had just spoken openly about the cache of silver to a man that she had at one time not trusted. Could he be trusted even now? The shine of silver had led more than one good, decent man astray.

Then she felt shame for doubting Timothy. He had risked his life . . . his ship . . . his entire crew . . . to save her life! How could she even for one minute doubt him? He had proven to her that he was, indeed, no rogue as she had at first suspected.

The mention of Tak-Ming was just cause for Timothy to release his hands from Lee-lee's wrists. His face took on a sternness as his eyes grew cold and his jaw set. He had been a fool to even for one brief moment consider Lee-lee his just because he had risked his neck to save her. The Chinaman was always there.

"You realize the dangers, yet you still insist on returning to your cabin?" Timothy asked, flinching as a loud crash from topdeck echoed thunderingly all about him in the narrow passageway. It was apparent that another mast had given in to its weakened structure due to the fire or wind. The ship swayed and creaked ominously underfoot.

"*Ai*, I understand all dangers," Lee-lee said from across her shoulder as she raced back to the cabin. Her initial exhaustion had been removed, as she pulled renewed strength from her fear for the future. She would like to wish that it could be with Timothy, but he and his personality were unpredictable, so she still clung to her earlier hopes and desires, only fully trusting and depending on her beloved Tak-Ming.

Breathless, she reached the cabin and stepped across its threshold. Smoke ate away at her eyes and throat, seeping up through the flooring from the hold of the ship. Her feet felt on fire with each step taken as they made contact with the floor's lacquered finish, but nothing would dissuade her from her decision to rescue the chest and even the valise if at all possible.

Groping . . . coughing . . . she fell to her knees, searching around her for the chest. When she found it and tried to lift it, she was rudely reminded of its heavy weight. No matter how hard she struggled with it, she couldn't budge it from the floor.

"Oh, no," she groaned. "What can I do now?"

She winced as her knees grew hotter from their continuing contact with the flooring. She wiped perspiration from her brow and upper lip then swung her head around when Timothy was suddenly there, kneeling beside her.

"Here," he said. "Let me help you."

"I tried," Lee-lee said. "But I just can't lift it. Thank you, Timothy."

She rose to her feet and began another search until she found her valise. She circled the fingers of her left hand around its handle then made her way back toward Timothy.

"This thing weighs a ton," Timothy said, groaning as he carried the chest hurriedly toward the door.

"The silver coins you paid Tak-Ming for the opium are among the many others in the chest," Lee-lee said, panting as she ran alongside Timothy toward the shadows of light ahead which meant they were closer to safety.

Timothy set his lips into a straight, tight line, remembering that night on the Min River. Had fate drawn him there where he would catch his first unforgettable glimpse of Lee-lee to forever haunt his long, sleepless nights?

Though her eyes had been heavily penciled to look Chinese, nothing could have kept Timothy from realizing that he had discovered a lovely, honey-brown-eyed seductress among the lowly Chinese crew aboard the *Sea Goddess*. No ugly clothes or braided hair could fool him either. He had readily recognized her and had even then lost his heart to her.

Loud shouts from overhead drew Timothy's thoughts back to the present. He looked up the just reached companionway and saw Captain Hollister standing there gesturing wildly with his hands.

"Damn it, Timothy, I thought we were going to lose you for sure," he yelled. He met Timothy's approach halfway on the steps and took the chest from him. "Won't be long now. Everything is goin' to go. Get the hell off this trap of a ship."

Timothy placed an arm about Lee-lee's waist and hurried her along after Captain Hollister. Once on topdeck, Lee-lee's eyes traveled desperately around her, seeing the death and total destruction. Her heart ached . . . her stomach churned. It was all lost . . . everything that Tak-Ming had worked so hard for. Gone into the abyss of the East China Sea.

Her free hand stole to her throat. "Tak-Ming . . ." she whispered harshly.

Her eyes searched through the rubble and to each and every lifeless body. She looked beseechingly up into Timothy's eyes. "You said that Tak-Ming was alive," she said. "Where did you see him? Are you certain that it was he?"

"I could never make that sort of mistake," Timothy growled. "I know the Chinaman, Tak-Ming." Yes, he knew Tak-Ming well enough. It was as though the handsome Chinaman's features had become etched upon Timothy's brain as a leaf is fossilized onto stone. How could Timothy be expected to forget the man whom had succeeded at stealing Lee-lee's heart?

"Then where is he, Timothy?" Lee-lee asked. She began running around the deck. She stooped from one body to the next, checking the pale, expressionless faces. When she didn't find Tak-Ming, she didn't know which emotion to feel. Sorrow or grief? If he wasn't among the ones on the ship, had he somehow already been saved and taken to the *New Yorker*? Or had he become a part of the sea . . . swallowed up in its waves, never to be free of a watery grave? The latter threatened to tear her heart to shreds.

"Lee-lee?" Tak-Ming said, suddenly limping across the topdeck toward her. His silk robe was torn and splattered with blood, and his face was black with soot. He clutched at his chest with one hand and reached for her with his other.

Lee-lee dropped her valise and rushed toward Tak-

Ming. She grabbed him by his left arm and steadied him, then framed his face between her hands. With a warmth glowing in her eyes, she searched his face.

"You're truly all right?" she said anxiously.

"*Ai*," Tak-Ming said, breathing hard. He covered his mouth with a hand and emitted a dry cough. "It's only my lungs. They seem to have been damaged by the smoke." His eyes searched her face. "And you?"

"The same," she murmured. "Only the smoke, Tak-Ming. No ruthless pirate was allowed to come near me. If he had, I would have sent his head rolling for sure."

Tak-Ming's gaze lowered and in his eyes Lee-lee could read alarm and she understood why without his even having to tell her. "The coins are safe," she reassured. "They are already safely aboard the *New Yorker*."

She gave Timothy a half glance and a quick smile over her shoulder. "Thanks to Timothy, not only are the coins safe, but you and I as well, Tak-Ming."

"*Ai*," Tak-Ming said in a soft whisper, now wondering about the way Timothy Hendricks was glaring at him as though the American hated him.

And now Tak-Ming realized that the American had even shown undue panic when told that Lee-lee was aboard the *Sea Goddess*. It was as though the American knew Lee-lee and even cared for her, when in truth he should never even have met her.

And hadn't she just familiarly called the American by his given name? The name Timothy had rolled off her tongue as though she was quite practiced in saying it!

All these things were puzzling to Tak-Ming but this was not the time or place to wonder further about it. His beautiful *Sea Goddess* was now taking on too much water and soon would be gone from his sight. It was as though he was a lover losing his beloved.

"She's a sinkin' for sure!" Captain Hollister's voice rang out from his ship. "You've got to get to the *New Yorker* so we can get 'er away from the *Sea Goddess* or she's also a goner!"

Timothy forgot Tak-Ming. He gathered Lee-lee up into his arms and began running across the topdeck of the *Sea Goddess* toward the *New Yorker*.

Lee-lee panicked, seeing Tak-Ming being left behind. She wriggled in Timothy's arms, flailing her arms. "Let me go!" she screamed.

"Not on your life," Timothy grumbled.

"I've got to help Tak-Ming!" Lee-lee shrieked, pushing at Timothy's chest.

"He's capable of fending for himself," Timothy said. "Or is he devoted so much to his ship that he will ride her to the bottom of the sea? If so, I do not intend to let you accompany him on such an ill-fated journey!"

Lee-lee was too weak to continue her fight. She sighed heavily and placed an arm about Timothy's neck then became peaceful inside when Tak-Ming joined them in their escape, carrying her cast-aside valise.

The sails filled and the water sprayed foam across the *New Yorker*'s bow once everyone was safely on board. Timothy grudgingly removed Lee-lee from the safety of his arms. He watched as she ran to Tak-Ming and clung to him while they stood together in silent horror, witnessing the *Sea Goddess* turn on its side and slowly gulp its way beneath the surface of the East China Sea. A strange sort of whirlpool was all that was left of Tak-Ming's prized ship. And when that was also gone, debris from the ship began bobbing to the surface, a crude reminder of what once was, what could have been, and what would never be.

"Oh, Tak-Ming, I'm so sorry," Lee-lee cried, circling her arms about his chest.

Timothy squared his shoulders and stiffened, unable to bear the sight of Lee-lee and Tak-Ming together. He withdrew a cheroot from his inside vest pocket, placed it between his teeth, and strolled angrily away.

Chapter Sixteen

Restless, not understanding why Timothy was avoiding her now that they were safely out to sea with the threat of pirates left far behind them, Lee-lee began pacing the full length of her private cabin.

Wrapped in a loose, flowing silk robe designed in waves of myriad colors, and with her raven-black hair cascading across her shoulders and down her back, she tossed her head in an irritated sigh. It seemed to her that much of her life had been spent not understanding the motives of those who surrounded her. First there had been her brother Richard in those years of growing up with him. He had been as changeable as a chameleon.

Then there was Heung-Chin. He had showered her with exquisite silks and jewelry and all along it hadn't been because of his fondness for her, but because he had wanted her to get used to the beautiful things in life so she could graciously accept being sent to the Imperial Palace where it was said that beauty reigned supreme.

And, ah, her serving woman Soonya. Soonya's motives had been innocent enough. Had she only known the results of her loyalty to Heung-Chin and China, Soonya most surely wouldn't have betrayed Lee-lee!

"And now Timothy," she whispered. "What have I done to cause him to be so cool? I have professed my love for him. What else am I expected to do? And doesn't he love me as well? He was returning to Foochow to carry me away with him, thinking that I was in mortal danger."

Realizing Timothy's first initial fears had been for his ship, crew, and himself that first night she had met and talked with him, Lee-lee had to understand his reasons in facing danger head on to rescue her. He had placed her first in his thoughts and he would only have done so because he had most surely placed her first in his heart as well.

"Then why?" Lee-lee softly cried, circling her fingers into fists at her side. She stopped pacing and looked toward her closed door. She had waited long enough for his knock on that door. She would go to him! She would confront him with questions she would not allow him to ignore! No matter that he had placed her in one of his finest cabins with highly-polished paneled walls and handsomely upholstered furniture. It meant nothing without him.

With a nervous pounding of her heart, she combed her fingers through her hair to smooth it even more than it already was, pinched her cheeks to flame color into them, and softly bit her lips to heighten the color there. She securely tied the silk belt at her waist, ran her hands over the flare of her hips, and threw her shoulders back proudly. The silk of the robe clung sensuously to her voluptuous breasts, and the sharp peaks of the nipples were clearly identified.

She looked down and saw these things, even the deep cleavage where the robe gaped partially open. But she cared not. She was ready to play the role of the seductress if that was what was required to draw Timothy's full attention to her again. And thank God that the welts on her chest had healed and disappeared. That alone could have dissuaded him from touching her if he had not understood how the marks had been inflicted.

Ai. She would go to Timothy. Wasn't there reason to celebrate? She was safe. Tak-Ming was safe. Timothy was safe.

Barefoot, she stepped cautiously out into the dimly lighted passageway. She looked toward the closed door that stood opposite hers. Her heart ached, knowing that Tak-Ming was there, inside his own assigned cabin, already missing China and his family.

His silent brooding had begun after losing his *Sea Goddess* which was quite understandable. He had lost his one and only link to China. And among the large crew of the *New Yorker*, no Chinese could be found. Tak-Ming was the only Chinaman on board and he felt separated from the crew both by looks and customs.

Feeling torn, thinking she should go to Tak-Ming instead of Timothy, Lee-lee closed her door behind her, weighing the importance of her decision.

But it was *her* needs that were the victor here . . . her needs to see and be with Timothy. She would comfort Tak-Ming later. Hopefully by then she would feel more in the mood for consoling. After time spent with Timothy, perhaps she could be more alive . . . more pleasant to be around.

"But only if Timothy welcomes me with open arms and heart," she murmured as she proceeded down the narrow passageway. Timothy's master cabin was at the far end of the ship where portholes were larger, and though she had never remarked over it before to Timothy—always too absorbed in his overpowering masculine presence—she remembered a skylight that emitted vivid splashes of color through stained glass downward onto his plush furnishings.

A sensuous thrill raced through her when she recalled the other times with Timothy in his cabin. She knew not why, but those times seemed ages ago. She only hoped to relive them this bright, crisp morning when the ocean was calm and the breeze serene. When Timothy and she were together, such fiery passion could be created . . . enough to quake the ship as if in the eye of a storm.

Giggling at the thought, she rushed onward. The oak flooring of the ship's deck was cool to the soles of her feet, the sound of the water splashing against the hull of the ship was like a soft lullaby, and Lee-lee's nose twitched as she found herself engulfed by the familiar aroma of Timothy's cigars.

She closed her eyes and inhaled deeply, enjoying being reminded that Timothy was near. On this long voyage to America, he would always be as close as the enticing fragrance of tobacco.

"But I want more than that," she whispered. "I want to touch . . . I want him near me. Without him, I am only half alive."

Shaking her hair down her back, she rushed to

Timothy's door and rapped her knuckles against it. She stiffened when a sudden sweep of nerves invaded her senses. What if he should refuse her . . . ? But why would he . . . ?

Timothy's voice was a low grumble. "Who's there?" he asked, accidentally smearing ink on the page of his ledger as he looked toward the closed door.

Burying himself in paper work hadn't proven engrossing enough to cast the thought of Lee-lee from his mind. With her only footsteps away, in a nearby cabin, it was becoming pure hell for him not to go to her.

But the realization that Tak-Ming was also close by was the force that had kept Timothy apart from the woman he loved.

Having become so temperamental in his agonizing hunger for Lee-lee, Timothy had left strict orders with Hollister that he was not to be disturbed unless the ship had suddenly become endangered for one reason or another.

He slung his pen aside. Apparently Hollister hadn't thought well enough of heeding the warning! And why the hell wasn't he answering by announcing himself instead of standing mute out in the passageway?

He pushed his chair back and rose angrily to his feet and stomped barefoot toward the door.

"Timothy, it's me. Lee-lee," Lee-lee finally said, having momentarily recoiled when she had heard the snappish ring to his voice when he had answered her knock.

She clasped her hands together behind her, aware of the wetness building up on her palms from her anxiety.

Timothy stopped in midstep. It wasn't Captain Hollister disturbing him after all. It was Lee-lee! She had come to him. But for what purpose now? She had won free passage to America on the *New Yorker* for both her and Tak-Ming. No further games were required of her. Once in America, the chest of silver coins would suffice to assure her and her Chinaman lover quite a comfortable life.

Grumbling, unable to pass up the chance to at least be near her again, Timothy yanked the door open and was once more lost in her loveliness. As she looked up at him with her dolefully wide, honey-brown eyes, with her ruby red lips provocatively parted and her hair sleek and shining down the proud, straight line of her back, Timothy couldn't stop the nervous beat of his heart or the dull ache beginning in his loins.

"What brings you to my cabin?" he growled, his eyes lowering to where her breasts lay so perfectly full and curved beneath the cling of the scanty silk robe. The satin pink of them were revealed as they rose and fell with her heavy breathing where the robe gaped temptingly open. And the flare to her hips made Timothy's imagination run wild, as he remembered so vividly the magical valley where her thighs came together in an utter softness.

"Timothy, why have you been avoiding me?" Lee-lee blurted, having already decided to meet this thing head on without any preliminary small talk to get in the way or slow things down. Another moment of not knowing would be one moment too long as far as she was concerned. She loved him. He had said that he loved her.

Well, lovers were meant to be together, not apart as they had been.

A slow flush rose to her cheeks as her gaze lowered and discovered how scantily attired he was. He only wore the silk bottoms of pajamas. Nothing else. Beneath the cling of his pajamas she could see the outline of his sex and this caused a knot of desire to coil inside her.

Timothy turned sideways and gestured with a hand toward his desk. "I've been busy working in my ledgers," he replied, stubbornly refusing to let her know the true reason he had stayed secluded inside his cabin. No matter what, she would never know of his jealousy of Tak-Ming!

"Oh?" Lee-lee said, standing on tiptoe, looking around him and at the desk with its complete disarray of strewn papers and opened ledgers. "So you do see to business other than the voyages of your ships?"

"One must keep ledgers. They contain accounts to which debits and credits are transferred in final form," he said. "Do you expect Calvin Hoots to do this from his desk in New York while not even experiencing it on the spot, day to day, while aboard the *New Yorker*?"

"Calvin? Calvin Hoots?" Lee-lee said, raising an eyebrow questioningly.

Timothy sighed exasperatedly. "My partner. He's my partner," he said. "But I told you this before. Why must I again?"

Lee-lee playfully shrugged then slipped past him and entered the great expanse of his cabin. "I guess my mind has been too preoccupied to think of a Calvin Hoots and what he is to you," she said.

She swung around and faced him, her lower lip

protruding in a pout. "But, Timothy, I have been wondering what *I* am to you. You have been avoiding me. It doesn't take a genius to figure that out. Why, Timothy? Can't you tell me why?"

There was no denying the racing of her pulse as she absorbed his presence, seeing his handsomely sculpted face, the haunting brown of his eyes, and the corded muscles of his wide shoulders. His chest hairs were dark, curled fronds which circled his manly nipples and traveled lower, disappearing beneath the waistband of his beige silk pajama bottoms.

Lee-lee's eyes grew hot with passion, envisioning where else the hair lay and what it so sensually surrounded.

She raised her eyes slowly to his and smiled bashfully back at him, wondering if he had seen the look in her eyes or had successfully read her thoughts.

Timothy closed the door, went to his desk, and leaned over it to thumb through several pages of his ledger. "I haven't been purposely avoiding you," he lied. "My losses are great due to my hasty departure from China. I hadn't yet traded as I had anticipated."

He turned his eyes slowly to hers. "Seems things kept getting in the way," he mumbled.

A hurtful look showed in Lee-lee's downcast expression. "Things, Timothy?" she said softly. "Do you consider me as only a 'thing'?"

He forced a sardonic laugh. "Now aren't you the presumptuous one to assume that I was referring to you," he snarled.

He removed a half-smoked cigar from an ashtray,

relighted it, and settled down into his desk chair, avoiding her still-hurtful stare by pretending to become involved in the figures of his ledger.

Frustration raged inside Lee-lee. She could tell that he was purposely avoiding her. It was as if he were full of regret over having rescued her. Perhaps she would have been better off with the creatures of the sea instead of such a rogue!

She turned and stomped to the door then thought better of her decision to leave. Apparently that would please him too much, and why should she do anything as generous as that? Two could play this game. She would prove to him that he was not the master of such wily ways. She was learning her own share of tricks and life was her teacher. Not Timothy.

Turning on a heel, she strolled casually to his desk and took a cigar from Timothy's cigar case. She twirled it around between a forefinger and thumb, eying Timothy out of the corner of an eye. Dare she go this far to draw him from his self-induced shell of anger?

The thought of having a cigar in her mouth made an involuntary shiver race up and down her spine. Yet if the taste was as pleasant as its smell, what could be the matter with giving it a try? At least it would create attention for herself.

She was remembering her and Timothy's last time alone together. It had been on the banks of the Min River celebrating the Moon Festival. He had been sweet and loving until she had made mention of her wish to go to America. His coolness toward her had begun then and continued even now. She would find out the reason why.

Perhaps he did have a wife awaiting his return and didn't want Lee-lee to confuse his life by also being in America.

Yet he had rescued her . . . he was taking her to America.

But America is a large country, she thought sorrowfully to herself. He will leave me in San Francisco and go on to New York alone, to meet his wife there.

Determined, Lee-lee reached for a match and placed the cigar between her lips. Timothy watched her from the corner of an eye. What the hell did she think she was doing? First a cigar . . . and now . . . a match? Surely she wouldn't. He flinched as she struck the match.

Having never smoked anything before Lee-lee didn't quite know what to do. But she had seen Heung-Chin puffing on his silver water pipe and Timothy his cigar enough times to know that one must first inhale in order to exhale.

She lighted the cigar and immediately gagged. The taste was vile. The smoke became trapped inside her mouth. Some circled upward into her nostrils while some crept to the back of her throat and plummeted downward into her windpipe, choking her. She dropped the cigar into an ashtray and began fitfully choking and coughing, grabbing desperately at her throat.

Timothy lunged from his chair, seeing the scarlet color of her face. "Lee-lee, why?" he asked, patting her on her back. "Why the cigar? You never cease to amaze me."

She continued to cough until tears flowed from her eyes and her throat achingly burned.

"God!" Timothy said, rushing to his liquor cabinet. He poured her a glass of wine and quickly took it to her.

"Here," he urged. "Drink this down with one swallow. It ought to rid your throat of the smoke, but your lungs will have to take care of themselves."

Lee-lee's eyes were wild. She nodded agreeably as she placed her fingers around the tall, thin stem of the glass. She gulped the wine down and then just as quickly regretted doing so, for now her throat burned from both foreign matters. But at least her coughing spell was over.

Frowning, she shoved the glass back into Timothy's hand. "You can keep your wine and cigars," she said raspingly. "Neither seem to agree with me."

Worn out from coughing, she went to settle herself on the edge of Timothy's huge bunk. She breathed hard, still laboring for air.

Timothy crushed both their cigars out in an ashtray, placed the empty wine glass on his desk, then went to stand over her. "Want to tell me what that was all about?" he said dryly, bending to place a forefinger beneath her chin, urging her eyes upward to meet the challenge of his.

Lee-lee swallowed hard and wiped her face dry of the tears caused by the forceful coughing. "You really don't care," she murmured. "Why do you even bother yourself by asking?"

She nodded toward his desk. "Your ledgers are more important to you than me," she softly added. "You've already proven that, Timothy."

She turned her gaze once more to him. "As soon as I get my breath, I shall leave your cabin. I will never bother you again. I believe I know where I belong in your life. Nowhere."

Timothy knew that he should let well enough alone and let her leave. It would be the simplest way for them both. But her words had pierced his heart as though many arrows had been shot into it.

He didn't understand her, but perhaps she had the ability to love two men at once, for she did sound sincere in her feelings toward him. But nothing mattered at this moment other than his need to be with her. And perhaps in time, he would make her forget Tak-Ming!

He reached for her hands and urged her to stand. Then he drew her into his arms. "Lee-lee . . ." he said, speaking softly into her ear. "Don't you know? Haven't I told you enough how I truly feel about you?"

"*Nay*. I do not know how you feel," she said softly, almost swallowed up by her thundering heartbeats. "And, *nay*, you have not told me enough times how you do feel. What are your true feelings, Timothy?"

"I love you," he said huskily, now knowing that these words had to be spoken to win her completely. He would banish thoughts of Cathalina Unser forever from his mind as hopefully Lee-lee would forget Tak-Ming in the days, weeks, months, and years to come. Lee-lee was in his blood as surely as he lived and breathed.

A muted sob tore from the depths of Lee-lee's throat, so happy was she to once more be in his arms, hearing his confessions of love for her. She twined her arms about his neck and clung to him, overpowered by the rush of rapture sweeping through her. Yet she was now more confused than ever, not understanding his sudden change of mood.

She leaned her head back and looked intensely into his

eyes that seemed to be the very heart of his mystique. "You first treat me so coolly—even ignore me—then you say that you love me," she murmured. "How can I ever relax in the type of love you offer me?"

He wanted to question her about her type of love which included two men, not one. But he had vowed never to speak of his jealousy to her and, by God, he wouldn't! A confession of jealousy could make him appear less a man. And while with Lee-lee, he was all man, with manly desires . . . wants . . . needs.

"Darling, I shall show you the depth of my feelings for you in the only way that I know," Timothy said, placing his hands on Lee-lee's shoulders. He curled each of his thumbs beneath the edge of her robe and began to slowly push it aside until it was over her shoulders and fluttering down the full length of her arms.

As her breasts became free, Timothy's hands went to them and softly cupped them. He lowered his lips to one, surrounded a nipple, and drew it inside his mouth to let his tongue curl around it.

Lee-lee wove her fingers through his hair as her insides heated into a burning inferno. She closed her eyes, letting herself get lost in the pleasure. Her robe hung around her waist, over the tied belt, and when Timothy's hands succeeded at freeing her of this, Lee-lee accepted her nudity as the robe settled loosely around her ankles.

"You are exquisitely beautiful," Timothy said, taking a step back to once more admire her. He brushed a hand across her flesh with butterfly touches, from the hollow of her throat downward, outlining a breast, then even lower where her stomach lay flat and smooth.

Lee-lee's eyelids grew heavy as her passion mounted. She licked her lips which seemed to have suddenly gone dry, and she tried to hide the sensuous tremor of her body as his fingers continued to awaken her every nerve with their gentle caresses.

Timothy's blood was spinning hot through his veins. The touch of her . . . the smell of her . . . was causing such a throbbing in his loins, he was experiencing the only sort of pain in life that was truly welcomed. As this pain grew, it always fused into something beautiful and he wanted to delay it, to savor each building moment of pleasure.

"Lee-lee," he said in a husky whisper then drew her roughly into his arms. He crushed his lips to hers and kissed her hotly while his hands moved almost frantically over her, stopping at the utter softness of her buttocks.

He pressed his fingers into her flesh and urged her body closer to his. His swollen sex became imprisoned between their clinging bodies and this made his excitement mount even more.

Lee-lee laced her arms about his neck and feverishly clung to him, feeling the hardness of his need through the silk of his pajamas. Her face became hot . . . her knees strangely weak. In his kiss she was finding a wildness like never before.

Her lips ached from the continuing pressure of his . . . her body quaked with consuming desire. She pressed her breasts harder into his chest . . . she wrapped a leg around him. And when she felt his fingers move to seek the softness between her thighs, she moaned and began a slow, pleasurable melting inside.

As his fingers played, she became as though drugged. And when he stopped to lift her up into his arms, a low sort of sob surfaced from inside her and she welcomed the feel of the bunk as he lowered her onto it. She had never been as happy as now. Everything in life was sweet . . .

No words were spoken between them. Smiles were enough. Timothy let his pajama bottoms drop away from him then knelt down over Lee-lee, kissing her gently as he entered her.

Lee-lee let out a soft moan as she felt him fill her with his throbbing hardness. Her lips quivered against Timothy's, her breasts sensually touching his chest. She clung to him, lifting her hips to meet his eager thrusts. He then molded her closely to him and burrowed his nose into the jasmine scent of her hair. Together they shared a silent explosion of release, then lay, breathing hard, in each other's arms.

Lee-lee brushed some damp, fallen strands of Timothy's hair back from his eyes. "I do love you," she whispered. "Please love me as much."

With his passion-filled, hauntingly dark eyes, he looked down at her. "Darling, the world begins and ends when I am in your arms," he said huskily. "There is only the two of us. What more can I say?"

Lee-lee's lower lip curved into a pout. She began toying with a hair on his chest, refusing to look up at him. "You can say that you love me," she whispered.

Her gaze shot upward. She felt a renewed passion as his eyes burned into her. "I will never hear you say that to me enough times," she added with more determination.

Timothy drew away from her and rose to sit on the edge of the bunk. He raked his fingers through his hair then drew his pajama bottoms back on. Odd that he should once more be filled with doubt when he had just shared such a passionate interlude with her. But he couldn't erase Tak-Ming from his mind no matter how hard he tried.

"Timothy, didn't you hear me?" Lee-lee said, rising to rest on an elbow. Again she felt his coolness, and she had the distinct impression that she had just been used.

Remembering that he had decided to win her away from Tak-Ming, Timothy forced a smile and turned to face her. "Of course I heard you," he said, leaning down to kiss her softly on the tip of her nose.

"Then why don't you answer me?" Lee-lee said. She warmed beneath his kiss and the hands that were once more searching her body, touching her more sensitive pleasure points.

"And what was the question?" Timothy teased, smiling coyly and winking at her.

"Oh, you!" Lee-lee said, doubling a fist, hitting him on his muscled right arm. "You're impossible, Timothy Hendricks."

Placing his hands on her shoulders, Timothy eased Lee-lee back down on the bunk. He crawled over her and straddled her with his knees. "Oh? Is that what I am?" he further teased, showering her face with kisses.

Lee-lee giggled, pushing at his chest. Then as his lips began a descent to circle a breast, her breath caught in her throat. She closed her eyes, relaxed, and enjoyed. His lips stayed at her breast for only a brief moment, then his tongue darted from between his lips and began leaving a trail of fire behind it as it went lower . . . lower . . . and was soon invading that most erogenous area . . . where her heart seemed now to be pounding.

She bit her lower lip as Timothy's fingers opened her more to him and the most exquisite feelings surged through her as his tongue brought her to a quick, almost violent sexual release.

As Timothy stretched out beside her, Lee-lee opened her eyes and looked toward him. She was in a soft daze, yet still tingling from head to toe from the power he displayed in his passion.

She turned to her side and fit her body next to his. "And what other skills do you have, my love?" she purred. "But, *nay*, you'd best not show me now. Surely my body can only take so much in such a short time."

Timothy laughed huskily and placed his arms about her. "My dear, I've many hidden talents," he said. "Just stick with me, kid, and I'll reveal them all to you."

Lee-lee laughed throatily. She began tracing his handsome facial features, leaning up to kiss each spot her fingers strayed from. She looked at Timothy with wonder as he took her hand and turned her right palm to his eyes. He traced her scar with a forefinger than kissed it gently.

"It's all well now, Timothy," she murmured. "Only the scar remains."

"I'm truly sorry about having done that to you, Lee-lee," Timothy said, again kissing it.

Lee-lee blinked her thick lashes up at him, smiling coyly. "I thought that you were pleased with the scar."

"What . . . ?" he said, eying her quizzically.

"The scar. You once said that it was your way of branding me . . . making me wholly yours."

"Oh, yes," Timothy said, placing her hand gently on the bunk beside her. "I do recall saying that."

He rose from the bunk and went to pour himself a glass of wine, avoiding her watchful gaze.

Lee-lee noticed his indifference once more threatening to destroy the peaceful aura that had been created between them. Would she ever understand him!

"Timothy," she said, rising, reaching for her cast-aside robe to slip quickly into it. "Didn't you mean it?"

Timothy emptied the glass of wine in one brisk swallow then casually lighted a cigar. He stiffened as he heard her step behind him and felt her hands at his bare waist trailing around to hug him closely to her. The fullness of her breasts pressed into his back through the silk of her robe, and her lips nibbled at the flesh of his shoulders.

"Timothy, sometimes you pay no attention whatsoever to what I say," she pouted. "Why is that, Timothy?"

"What is is that you want to know?" he asked thickly.

"You had said that the scar was your brand . . . making me wholly yours. Aren't I? Aren't I wholly yours?" She refused to question him about a wife. Surely she was wrong about his having one. He had denied it before, had he not?

Timothy worked himself free of her embrace and turned to look down at her. "You are the only one who can answer that. Are you mine and no one else's?"

Lee-lee paled and took a step away from him. "Who else could there possibly be?" she gasped.

Her confusion became Timothy's confusion. He turned and walked away from her, not wanting to pursue the subject any longer. It strangely drained him.

"Lee-lee, I have something for you," he said, going to his wardrobe to open it. "I should have gotten these to you sooner for your comfort, but I have been occupied with my ledgers."

Lee-lee sighed heavily and shook her head, once more having to adjust to his way of avoiding answering her questions. The thought of a gift from him took precedence over her anger.

Her pulse raced with excitement as she watched him begin to pull beautiful dresses from his wardrobe.

"I've taken these from the sea chests in the hold of the ship," Timothy said, holding several dresses out toward her. "I've noticed that you only wear the coolie attire. Is that all the clothes that you have in your possession?"

"I've only brought one dress with me from China," she said, going to run her fingers through the cool, crisp cotton of those being offered her. Lace lay in abundance at the bodice of each and the skirts were long and fully gathered.

"A beautiful, clinging silk dress, I presume?"

"Ai . . ."

"And when will you model it for me, darling?"

Lee-lee's face creased into a frown. "Timothy, I've just left China behind me. I don't care to be reminded of what I had to wear there so soon."

"Will you promise to wear it one day for me?" he said, smiling as she held a dress before her, flushed with excitement.

"*Ai.* One day I shall. But not now. I want to see how these fit. It will be so pleasant to be able to dress as an American lady again."

"You're beautiful either way, Lee-lee," Timothy said. "As American *or* Chinese."

He watched her pull a dress over her head and into place. He had chosen right. The lowswept bodice displayed the swell of her voluptuous breasts.

"Thank you for your kind words," Lee-lee said. "But I am now and always will be American. Heung-Chin is no longer here to force anything upon me. I am free, Timothy. I am fully free."

Timothy gathered her into his arms. "It's nice to see you so happy," he said. "And I'm glad to have a part in your happiness."

Lee-lee reached a hand to his face and softly stroked his cheek. "Timothy, don't you know? You *are* my happiness."

Timothy's brow furrowed. Once more he doubted her, yet he kissed her anyway . . .

Part Two

San Francisco

Chapter Seventeen

Lee-lee stood lost in thought at the ship's railing. She had adored the vastness of the ocean and sky, the winds, and the magnificent tropic sunsets casting their fiery cascades over the last fluffy clouds of day. But with the voyage to America now nearing its end, she was anxious to set her feet squarely on soil. America's soil.

The sea breeze whipped her dress about her delicate, tapered ankles and her hair was lifted then gently dropped against her shoulders. In its dark waves, traces of red could now be seen, especially at its roots, and she was glad that soon she would be wholly herself again.

Enjoying the cool spray of sea water on her face, she let her thoughts wander to the past several weeks on the *New Yorker*. Tak-Ming had ventured from his cabin only for brief jaunts on topdeck for exercise and fresh air, preferring to spend the rest of his time in the privacy of his cabin. Lee-lee had spent as much time as possible with him, but had found it difficult to divide her time between the two most important men in her life.

Timothy had shown signs of resenting the hours she

spent alone with Tak-Ming in his cabin. At times Lee-lee had even considered accusing Timothy of behaving like a jealous suitor. Then she had thought better of it, realizing that it was ridiculous even to suggest that anyone might mistake her sisterly affection for Tak-Ming.

She had decided that this man she was desperately in love with was a man of many moods, and she had tried to accept him no matter what his disposition might be at any given time.

"Want to take a look?" Timothy asked, suddenly appearing at Lee-lee's side with a sea-glass.

Lee-lee smiled warmly up at Timothy, still glowing deliciously inside from their last full night of love-making, which had ended only a few short hours ago. It had been as if they were trying to recapture every sensual touch and kiss they had experienced together on the long voyage. To her it would be a memory she would lock safely away inside her heart. To him? She truly didn't know. She could only hope that he, too, would cherish their moments together.

"What do you see, Timothy?" she asked, accepting the sea-glass he held out to her. Her gaze swept quickly over him. He was dressed handsomely in an impeccably pressed brown frock coat, matching trousers, and a crisp, white ruffled shirt. He looked quite ready to resume the business side of his life, and Lee-lee couldn't help but wonder if he would soon begin to ignore her. Would she become secondary to all his other interests?

Timothy gestured with a hand toward the distant horizon. "Land," he said thickly. "If you look hard enough, you will get your first glimpse of San Francisco."

"Timothy, truly? Do you truly see it?" Lee-lee squealed, placing the sea-glass to her eye. "Have we, for real, almost completed the voyage? Only in my dreams had I thought it possible."

Timothy chuckled softly. He swung an arm about her waist and drew her next to him, bending forward to be on eye level with her. "It is real enough, all right," he said.

He placed his free hand over his eyes, shielding them from the brighter rays of the sun, and looked where the sea-glass was focused. "Do you see it yet, darling?"

Lee-lee was almost breathless from excitement as she scanned the horizon, peering one-eyed into the glass. She wanted so to see what Timothy had seen.

She scowled. "Nothing," she said. "Timothy, I see nothing. Perhaps you only thought you did."

Then her heart skipped a beat. Her fingers tightened around the sea-glass and her eyes grew wider with anticipation. "Wait," she whispered. "I do see something. It's . . . it's a soft rise in the ocean . . . only a speck . . . barely visible. Timothy, is that what you saw? It's not a mirage after all?"

"No. No mirage." He laughed softly. "This speck you are looking at will grow steadily in size as the ship moves closer. We will soon be there, Lee-lee. We will soon be in San Francisco."

Lee-lee lowered the sea-glass from her eye and shoved it back into Timothy's hand. "Not only San Francisco, but America," she cried, her eyes dancing with excitement.

Lifting the skirt of her dress up into her arms, she began running away from Timothy toward the companionway. "I must go and tell Tak-Ming," she shouted from across her shoulder. "I must tell Tak-Ming that America is near! We've both waited so long for this moment!"

Timothy grew numb inside as he watched her scurry away. And as he absorbed her words, realizing that Tak-Ming was once more foremost in her thoughts, he felt a fool . . . a damn, idiot fool.

Seeing the last of her skirt disappear from his sight down the ladder, Timothy threw the sea-glass to the deck with such force, the glass shattered at his feet.

He kicked at the glass and turned to smash both his hands angrily onto the rail. "I never learn," he growled. "Women! They are all alike. They are users—each and every one of them."

His thoughts darkened . . . his gut ached. "Well, I have done my good deed," he growled to himself. "I have brought her to America. From now on, she can fend for herself."

But he knew better than that. Wasn't there always the handsome Chinaman?

Standing on the waterfront in the shadows of the many moored ships with Tak-Ming beside her, Lee-lee clung to her valise, aghast at what she was seeing. San Francisco was nothing like her recollection of New York. The streets were muck and mire. Houses of all colors, shapes, and sizes lined streets that seemed to climb right into the

266

sky. And along the waterfront and in the city multitudes of people were causing complete chaos and confusion. The dazzling lure of gold had most definitely brought eager goldseekers to San Francisco from all corners of the world. This was evident by the mixture of languages being exchanged amidst the crowd milling around Lee-lee and Tak-Ming.

Tak-Ming, attired in a silk-embroidered robe and with his shiny, black queue hanging neatly down his back, shifted the heavy, wooden chest of silver coins to a more comfortable position in his outstretched arms. "Is this the America that you were so eager to return to?" he fussed. "Lee-lee, it does not resemble anything that you described to me when you spoke so wishfully of being here. *Wei!* This country is *puh-hao!*"

"Tak-Ming, this isn't the America I remember at all," she said, as she sidled closer to him, feeling safer in his tall, handsome shadow. Timothy had become his cool self again and had told her that for a while he would be too busy to be with her . . . to go ahead and get herself settled in a fine hotel . . . that he would see her later.

Tak-Ming screwed his face up into a dreadful frown. "*Tcha!* This is a place of filth," he said scornfully. "Look at the mud of the streets. Look at the poor *unfortunates* wandering about with unruly hair all over their faces, hiding most everything but their eyes and noses from those who look their way!"

Lee-lee placed a hand over her mouth and laughed softly. "That hair that you see is fashionable in America," she said. "Some men enjoy wearing beards. Others feel they are handsomer with only a mustache.

My American father wore both and was quite an affluent American, Tak-Ming."

"In China only the very old men and the noble men such as my father are allowed to wear a beard or mustache," Tak-Ming scoffed.

"But this is America, Tak-Ming. You will have to get used to the customs of the Americans as I had to get used to yours in China."

Tak-Ming raked his eyes over her, his expression dark and almost condemning. He liked her lace-trimmed bonnet well enough, but he despised her dress. "You have left all Chinese customs behind you quickly enough," he snarled.

"You knew that I would," Lee-lee defended, lifting her chin stubbornly.

Tak-Ming's eyes settled on her partially revealed, heaving bosom. A part of him became inflamed with desire for her, and a part of him detested her for showing herself off so brazenly. For a long while he had understood her hatred of the breast binders, but it was hard for him to accept just how free she was without them.

Lee-lee's face colored with embarrassment, fully understanding what it was about her dress that Tak-Ming disapproved of. And it was understandable. She most definitely was not flat as a boy in front, as were the women he was used to in China.

"Tak-Ming, let's move away from the waterfront," she encouraged, hoping to direct his thoughts as well as his eyes elsewhere. "Surely we will find something that we like about San Francisco."

"Is the city named New York which you talked of so often truly very different from what we've found here?" Tak-Ming asked, walking alongside Lee-lee as she began pushing her way through the throngs of people.

"Quite different, Tak-Ming," she said. "I can promise you that once we arrive in New York, you will see the difference and be glad that you are there. It is a city of greatness . . . of wealth . . . of beauty."

"At least in this ugly city there will be Chinese to have council with," Tak-Ming said, stepping up on a board sidewalk that stretched out in front of several different-sized buildings. "I will want to go to the part of the city they have named Chinatown very soon. I miss my people more than I had thought possible."

"We will find it for you, Tak-Ming," Lee-lee encouraged. "*Ai*, soon we will find it for you."

"You will also make residence there, Lee-lee?" Tak-Ming cautiously questioned. He watched her out of the corner of his eye, doubting that she would. She had not eagerly left China behind to be again thrust into any place remotely resembling it. He was trying hard to understand her hatred of his country.

"*Nay*. I shall not," Lee-lee said, then corrected herself by saying, "I mean, *no*, I shall not."

She was in America now. All of her Chinese words would have to be cast aside, for not to do so would cause undue attention and misunderstandings. She could not continue to speak half in English and half in Chinese.

"I'm anxious to mingle with the America populace in every way possible," Lee-lee added. "It's been so long, Tak-Ming."

269

"How can you say that?" Tak-Ming argued. "Were you not in the company of Americans during the voyage from China? You were especially taken by the businessman, Timothy Hendricks."

Lee-lee avoided looking at him, having tried so hard to hide her true feelings about Timothy from Tak-Ming. Hiding away so much in his own cabin, Tak-Ming hadn't noticed her going to Timothy's quarters so often.

"And why shouldn't I have been friendly toward him?" she murmured. "He did rescue us, you know."

Lee-lee wanted to tell Tak-Ming that Timothy would surely hurry through his business affairs and soon be with her. But she knew that Tak-Ming would find out soon enough that she intended to stay with Timothy even now, away from the ship. Tak-Ming would have to understand. One day he would fall in love. . . .

"I can take care of myself well enough, Tak-Ming," she said instead, still too wary of revealing the truth to him. "I will make my residence in the finest hotel. That will assure me of associating with the finest people of San Francisco."

"Perhaps there is such a hotel close to Chinatown," Tak-Ming worried.

"Tak-Ming, please," Lee-lee sighed. "I'm free of China. I want to remain that way."

"Do you also want to be free of me—a Chinaman?" Tak-Ming asked, his hurt thick in his words. "Am I no longer of any use to you?"

Lee-lee stopped and turned quickly to face him. With her free hand she reached up and gently cupped his chin. "Tak-Ming, how can you say such a thing?" she murmured. "You are special. My love for you is sincere. I'm highly devoted to you. Now . . . and . . . always."

"That is spoken from the heart, Lee-lee?"

"*Ai . . .*"

"Then I will try never to doubt you again, adopted sister."

Lee-lee laughed nervously, once more thinking of Timothy and worrying about Tak-Ming's reaction to *that* truth. But she would worry about that later. This was now. She was in America. Oh, how radiantly happy she was!

She glanced down at the heaviness of the chest in Tak-Ming's arms. "Tak-Ming, let's go find me a room, hide the chest of silver inside it, then explore San Francisco," she said excitedly. "We shall even find Chinatown."

Tak-Ming frowned. "The coins. Will they be safe?"

"Behind locked doors? *Ai!*" she heartily exclaimed.

She cringed after using the Chinese word again. It would be such a hard habit to break. But she would. In time . . . she would.

"A key doesn't always dissuade thieves," Tak-Ming grumbled.

"Tak-Ming, we cannot endlessly carry the chest around with us. We must trust that a key will give us full protection."

Tak-Ming shrugged. "*Ai . . .*"

"Then let's go," Lee-lee said, tucking her free arm through the bend of his, urging him quickly along.

The warehouses and trading posts which stood closer to the waterfront were soon left behind, and the street they were now traversing, called Kearney Street, was a

271

lively one lined with one-, two-, and three-storied, false-fronted buildings, some painted, some not. Among these were hovels and saloons, banks, general stores, and an assortment of hotels.

The street itself was busy with travelers in various modes of transportation. Horsedrawn carriages, surreys and black buggies, horses with riders, stagecoaches, and an occasional mule struggled along the muddy mire, and the board sidewalks were beehives of activity. The swelling crowds were even squeezing through the narrow alleyways between store fronts, and miners, hazy with alcohol, weaved in and out of saloons.

Poles and stakes used for hitching posts were placed along the thoroughfare, close to the boardwalks. Flies buzzed around the crowded, reined horses, and their horse dung created a terrible stench.

Lee-lee began watching the women of San Francisco more closely now. Most were dressed in the same types of cotton dresses with matching bonnets that she wore, but some were even more beautifully attired in lowcut, silk and satin dresses with diamonds glittering at their throats and ears. These fancily dressed women displayed faces that were heavily painted, and their hair was piled high atop their heads in extravagant styles. The odor of rich perfume followed along after them and men stopped along the walks to take second looks.

Though these fancier women were beautiful, there was something about them that discouraged Lee-lee from wanting to be like them in appearance. Perhaps it was their painted faces. She had masked her face for too many years in China to want to do it again in America.

The sound of the city was a constant thing—the

tinkling of pianos drifting out from the saloons, the clink of coins from the gambling houses, the clattering of hooves, the squeaking of wheels, the ring of so many voices—and was almost deafening when combined into one loud chorus of chaos.

Lee-lee had a sudden need to flee from this uproar and simultaneously spied a six-storied building at the far end of Kearney Street. She stepped to the edge of the sidewalk and could see the building much more clearly. A smile touched her lips when she read the bold, black letters painted on the brick above the top row of windows.

"Missouri Hotel," she whispered.

Its windows sparkled cleanly beneath the shine of the afternoon sun, and its front door was flung widely aside in an open invitation to all passersby.

"Did you say something, Lee-lee?" Tak-Ming asked, stopping to get his breath. He welcomed the thought of finding a place to deposit the chest. His arms were numb from its weight pressing into them.

Lee-lee nodded toward the hotel. "That's the one," she said. "That's the hotel I choose. Let's hurry, Tak-Ming. Getting settled into a room is the true beginning of my new way of life."

Tak-Ming's gaze moved over the building. He laughed beneath his breath. The Americans lacked imagination. In comparison to the pagodas, palaces, and rich estates of China with their fancy, colorful exteriors, these American establishments were plain and even ugly.

"After the House of Yeung, do you truly think you can be happy living in such a drab dwelling?" Tak-Ming scoffed.

"Tak-Ming, I came to America to be free. To me, everything in America is beautiful. Even this muddy city of San Francisco. Red-lacquered floors and gold-encrusted, scrolled walls are definitely not necessary to ensure my happiness. You must remember, I chose to leave them behind me."

She gave Tak-Ming a searching look. "As you did also, Tak-Ming. Do you regret your decision to accompany me to America?"

Tak-Ming's almond-shaped, dark eyes searched her face imploringly. He would never want to be far from her, though he knew their being wholly together was impossible. "*Nay*," he said hoarsely. "Never."

Lee-lee released her arm from his and reached her hand to her bonnet to push a fallen lock of hair back beneath it. "Then what are we waiting for?" she asked excitedly. "Let's get me that room, and then I want to ride in one of the fancier carriages while exploring the rest of the city."

Rushing onward, Lee-lee tried to ignore those who turned to openly stare at her and then at Tak-Ming. Nowhere else along the walkway could there be found a Chinaman—a Chinaman attired exquisitely in clothes of embroidered silk, looking as if he had traveled directly from the Imperial Palace in China.

A slow smile touched Lee-lee's lips, for she was amused at the people's reactions and proud to have Tak-Ming at her side. He had never looked as handsome with his towering height and bold Chinese facial features. She would never be ashamed to walk at his side, though Timothy had told her that in America most Chinese were subjects of ridicule and off-colored jokes. Well, surely all who looked upon Tak-Ming could tell that he was too great a man to be joked about! Lee-lee thought proudly.

As she stepped in front of the Missouri Hotel, Lee-lee stopped and tilted her head back to gaze upon the immensity of the building. "I want a room at the very top," she sighed. "Surely when one looks from the windows, the entirety of the city can be seen."

"Only birds are supposed to be that far from the ground," Tak Ming grumbled.

Lee-lee gave Tak-Ming an exasperated look. "Will you please be more cheerful, Tak-Ming? Are you trying to spoil my homecoming to America?"

"*Nay* . . ."

"Well, then, please stop grumbling and being so negative about everything," she said, flinching when an outburst of boisterous laughter erupted from a saloon adjacent to the Missouri Hotel.

"You've chosen a hotel wisely," Tak-Ming said sarcastically. "You will be serenaded by men whose minds are warped by whiskey. They could be the ones to spoil your homecoming, Lee-lee, not I. With them so close, you will not be safe."

"I will be safe enough," Lee-lee said, taking her first step inside the hotel.

Tak-Ming leaned down and spoke into her ear. "To be assured of that, one of the first things we will purchase with our silver coins will be a lady's pistol for you to keep with you at all times."

Lee-lee's eyes rolled back as she once more sighed. "Tak-Ming, really. You have become a worrier, for sure," she said. "I wouldn't even know how to shoot a pistol if I were the owner of one."

"You can learn quickly enough. It is required, Lee-lee, or I will never be able to close my eyes at night, for worrying about you."

Lee-lee shrugged. "All right," she said. "Whatever you say. Anything to make you feel better about things."

She walked further into the hotel and became enraptured by its lush interior. It wasn't the same type of plushness that was found in the richer Chinese mansions such as the House of Yeung, but there was a relaxing quality about it. She felt as if she were standing in the middle of a vast, flower-bedecked meadow as she gazed at the sweeping colors of greens and yellows in the velvet-upholstered chairs, divans, and the drapes that hung gracefully at the many long windows. A magnificent glass chandelier with refracted prisms hung from the very center of the room, casting light upon walls which were decorated with many fine, gilt-framed paintings.

A look closer at the paintings and Lee-lee quickly understood how the hotel had acquired its name. The paintings were various landscape scenes of the state of Missouri, and some showed paddlewheelers traveling down the Mississippi River past riverbanks on which stood lovely gowned women with parasols resting on their shoulders. It didn't take much thought to conclude that the owner of this establishment was a native of the state of Missouri. Perhaps he had been one of the first to strike it rich in the San Francisco hills and had quickly invested wisely.

Seeing the familiar scenes of Missouri displayed in the paintings tugged at Lee-lee's heart, bringing forth a memory that caused her both happiness and sadness. It reminded her of a time with her father. She had traveled to Missouri with him only a few short months before his death.

Her father had conferred with a business acquaintance in a city Lee-lee remembered had been called Saint Louis. She would never forget this city stretched out on the muddy banks of the Mississippi River. It had been filled with enterprising traders with vast cargoes of furs, and even some famous explorers had found their way there to begin their own types of adventures.

Saint Louis was the point from which Meriwether Lewis and William Clark had begun their famous expedition to explore the Missouri and Columbia Rivers and the area between them. Even Zebulon Pike, the man who named a fabulous peak after himself, had started his journey from the exciting city of Saint Louis.

But she swept the past from her mind. This was the present, and the excitement of this day still lay ahead of Lee-lee. She hurried to the desk and made arrangements for her room. She was glad she had thought earlier to slip some coins into the pocket of her dress. To have lifted the lid of the chest to pay for the room in the presence of so many would have displayed their wealth too openly.

Happy to have acquired a room on the sixth floor, Lee-lee climbed the stairs, anxiously, too full of anticipation to hear Tak-Ming puffing for wind as the sixth floor landing was finally reached. Swinging the skirt of her dress around, Lee-lee rushed down the narrow hallway, checking the numbers on the closed doors against the key she so proudly possessed. Once she found the corresponding number, she inserted the key, swung the door widely open, and stepped into a room bright with sunshine.

Placing her valise on the hardwood floor, Lee-lee began to dance around the room, laughing, exulting in her freedom. "My own room," she cried. "And I can come and go as I please. There is no one here to tell me what I can or cannot do."

Tak-Ming lowered the chest to the floor and began rubbing first one aching arm and then the other, scowling as he absorbed the decor of the room. "And such a place for you to make residence," he growled. "But you said you didn't need silk tapestries or lacquered floors. Perhaps you can be happy enough in this place of little color."

Lee-lee giggled at his continuing scorn. She hadn't realized it before, but he had become quite spoiled from living in the House of Yeung. But it was surely no wonder with such ancestral riches as his Chinese clan possessed.

She went to Tak-Ming and stood on tiptoe to kiss his cheek. "One day soon you also will learn to relax in your newly found freedom," she said. "My feelings of joy will surely become contagious, Tak-Ming. You will be as happy. I know it."

"I am anxious to find the Chinese people of this city," he said stubbornly. "Perhaps when I do, I'll be able to smile again."

"*Ai . . .*" Lee-lee said, spinning around to take another fast look at the room. A large mahogany bed and matching nightstand seemed to take up the most space in the room. A white eyelet bedspread matched the curtains at the two windows, and the walls were papered in pale stripes of blue. A multicolored, braided rug had been placed on the floor beside the bed, and a chair and a dressing table with a round mirror edged in sculptured mahogany were the only other pieces in the room.

"It is nice," she sighed. "And it has the heavenly clean smell of lemon-oil furniture polish."

Tak-Ming began surveying the room with even closer scrutiny. "And where shall we hide the chest for now?" he asked solemnly.

"In the wardrobe?" Lee-lee suggested, falling to her knees to look beneath the bed. "Or better yet, under the bed, Tak-Ming. We really don't have any choice, do we?"

"*Nay . . .*" Tak-Ming said. He bent and scooped the chest up into his arms, carried it to the bed, and slowly pushed it beneath, while Lee-lee rose to her feet and suddenly became preoccupied at a window.

She leaned against the window sill, looking into the distance. She hadn't been given a room at the front of the building as she had thought but instead at the back. She was glad of the mistake, for not only was she afforded a view of the busy streets, but also she was able to see the wide expanse of the ocean and the moored ships in the bay.

With a pounding heart, her eyes searched from ship to ship until she found the immense black hull with the proud name *New Yorker* painted on it in bold, white lettering. If she only had a sea-glass now. Perhaps she could even see Timothy on board his ship! The thought made a sensual thrill ripple through her . . .

"It is done," Tak-Ming said, moving to stand beside her. "The coins are secured beneath the bed as best they can be. Now let's take our leave, Lee-lee. I am anxious to see this place that is called Chinatown, to see if it has been appropriately named."

Chapter Eighteen

Chinatown had been all that Tak-Ming had hoped for. There were the customs and practices of the Chinese prevailed. Chinatown was quite a large section of town bounded by Kearney, Stockton, California, and Pacific Streets. Colorful paper lanterns of all sizes and shapes had been strung from lamp post to lamp post in front of shops selling wares made by Chinese for Chinese.

Tak-Ming had quickly settled into a daily routine. He had found a vacant room over a restaurant and had even purchased an old clipper schooner, which he planned to repair in order to work the Pacific sea trade and to use eventually for his and Lee-lee's voyage to New York.

Lee-lee had stayed close to her own room after sending word to Timothy by a messenger boy, telling him where she could be found.

"It has been a full week now and not one word from Timothy," Lee-lee said, brooding aloud.

It had just become dusk and she was looking down from her sixth floor window to the lively street below. Candles had been lighted inside the glass street lanterns that lined the busy thoroughfare, and the music filling the air from the various saloons made Lee-lee feel the emptiness of her room.

Squinting her eyes, she looked toward the bay in an attempt to see Timothy's ship. But in the growing darkness, the *New Yorker* blended in with the rest of the ships, as they all formed a huge shadow of night.

Lee-lee hadn't yet succumbed to the urge to go in search of Timothy. Her pride stood in the way. And the thought of mingling with the riffraff who usually inhabited the waterfront had also dissuaded her.

"Why hasn't he come to me?" she whispered harshly, abruptly turning away from the window. "What could I be guilty of to cause him to stop loving me?"

She ran her hands over her newly purchased dress. It was a pale blue taffeta with a darker blue trimming of scalloped velvet ribbon surrounding the hem of its skirt and outlining the bodice, which dipped low to reveal her deep cleavage. The dress was full and worn over an enormous crinoline which made a splendid rustling when she moved.

Lee-lee had managed a beautiful upsweep of her hair, and ringlets of curls hung about her ears and across her forehead. A flower lady's wagon of flowers had been too tempting to ignore, and Lee-lee had purchased a half-dozen bright red roses from which she had chosen two to place in her hair above the tight curls of her left ear.

Going to the mirror inset into the door of her wardrobe, Lee-lee made a slow turn, admiring her American dress. Her hands went to her throat, feeling a void there. But she hadn't wanted to spend any of her silver coins foolishly for jewelry. And perhaps whatever she might have chosen to purchase would have caused her the same sort of rash that her necklace had caused the last time she had tried to wear it.

"Jewelry is not needed," she whispered. "The dress is lovely enough without such adornment."

In the soft light of a kerosene lamp on her nightstand, the reddish tint of her hair became more pronounced. The black dye was quickly fading away. She laughed to herself over her hair's struggle to return to its natural color.

"But even this is hidden satisfactorily enough in the twisted swirls of my hair atop my head," she murmured.

Once more admiring the lines and color of her dress, Lee-lee's face screwed into a troubled frown. "What a shame to waste my lovely dress and fancy hairdo," she sighed. "Only these four walls to see me. Somehow it doesn't seem fair."

Her thoughts returned to Timothy and her heart ached with the remembrance of his lips and the wonderful sensations they could arouse inside her. She closed her eyes, feeling the sweet pain between her thighs, experiencing the sensuality as if Timothy were there kissing her . . . gently fondling first one breast and then another, causing such a sweet passion . . .

Heat flamed into Lee-lee's cheeks as her eyes flew widely open. "My word," she gasped. "What am I doing letting myself think such things?"

The sound of laughter and the music from a piano drifted up from the street to entice Lee-lee even more, for her loneliness was fast becoming overwhelming.

"I can't stay here any longer," she cried to herself. "I must get away—for a little while, at least."

She rushed to a dresser drawer. She opened it and took her purse from inside. It was also new but something that she had noticed most American ladies carried. She had chosen a multicolored beaded purse which easily could be clutched in one hand. And as she carried it with her toward the door, she heard a tinkling from inside it that signified a few silver coins and the key to her room.

Stepping out into the hallway, she looked cautiously from side to side. Perhaps it would be wise if she placed the small pistol Tak-Ming had purchased for her inside the purse, to carry with her for protection.

"But, *nay*," she whispered. "I will be among a crowd of people once I get out of the shadows of this gloomy hallway. Then I will be safe enough." And after carefully locking her door and descending the long, six flights of stairs, she strolled as casually as possible into the bright lights and hum of people in the hotel's lobby. Most moved around in couples, which made Lee-lee miss Timothy even more. With him at her side, oh, what a handsome pair they would make!

Casting her eyes downward, she edged her way toward the front door of the hotel, clutching tightly to her purse. The skirt of her dress rustled voluptuously against her crinoline and the smell of her perfume drifted along behind her. She became aware of many eyes following her.

She had to wonder if it was proper for her to be wandering about, unescorted, this time of evening. But she couldn't stay in her room another minute, and Tak-

Ming had better things to do than to humor her.

And Timothy? His ship was still moored at the bay. Where could he be . . . ?

Stepping out onto the plank sidewalk, Lee-lee looked from left to right, trying to choose which way to turn. Either way she would be passing rowdy establishments such as saloons, gambling halls, and parlour houses, all of which she knew to avoid. Then she remembered the bright lights and lure of a different sort of establishment which had drawn her keen interest as she had stood looking down from her hotel window.

She took a turn around the corner, then let her gaze move across the way to settle on a building which was brightly lighted from kerosene lanterns flanking its red-painted door. A sign over this door swayed gently in the evening breeze and on it was painted in bold letters the words "Dance Emporium."

"I've always wanted to learn to dance," Lee-lee whispered to herself. "Perhaps this dance emporium is where I might be skillfully taught."

Smiling, she lifted the skirt of her dress into her arms and pushed her way through the throngs of people who steadily moved along the walkway. When she reached the street, she studied its nasty condition then spied where boards had been placed for the purpose of crossing and decided that she was not one to step away from such a challenge.

She waited for an appropriate time to cross the street, knowing that at no time would the street be completely free of traffic. As one covered wagon came creaking by her, she read something that had been painted on the canvas of its cover. "California or Bust," she read, smiling to herself.

The lure of gold continued to bring travelers from afar. And this was causing San Francisco to become one of the busiest seaports in the country. Lee-lee had heard talk in the hotel lobby that products from eleven states now moved through San Francisco in ships. There were bonnets and lace from New York, and fruits, grains, and minerals from various other states, along with French wine, and perfumes and silks from China. It was also said that coins from the mint in Philadelphia brought interest of ten percent a month, so bank vaults were crammed with gold and silver. The town clinked with gold and the businesses of San Francisco thrived.

Dodging horsedrawn carriages and men on horseback, Lee-lee stepped out into the street and moved gingerly from board to board. She cringed when she felt the boards sink farther into the mud at her feet, and as she looked down, she could see water bubbling from beneath the boards, threatening to engulf them.

Breathless, she finally reached the other side and once more battled the crowd until she was standing before the closed red door. Stepping back, Lee-lee read the sign again. Then she studied those who were coming and going from the dance emporium. The men were not a surly lot. Most were dressed in fine, black broadcloth suits over white ruffled shirts, with neat, white linen handkerchiefs in their front suit jacket pockets.

But something was missing—the presence of ladies. Surely women had to be taught to dance as did the men! "I know that I do and I shall," she said stubbornly,

285

moving determinedly toward the flashy red door. Before she even had it open she could hear music reverberating through it, and this made her all the more anxious.

Stepping hurriedly on inside, she was met by muted light, yet not so dim that she couldn't see all that was going on about her. She slipped into the darker shadows of the room, behind a potted, tropical plant with wide leaves adorning a thick, tall stem.

Peering from behind the plant, Lee-lee absorbed the red velvet-lined walls and chairs, and the scattered, square oak tables around which sat couples talking over the flickering of candles.

Through a haze of smoke, Lee-lee could see a few men with various types of musical instruments sitting upon a stage, providing the music for the establishment, and close by, a space had been cleared and couples were dancing, clinging, obscenely grinding into each other's bodies.

"So there are women here after all," Lee-lee whispered. Her gaze searched farther around the room and found several other women standing together behind a rail, all without escorts. As those on the dance floor, these women were also scantily attired and their faces were brightly painted.

Lee-lee quickly understood that she had mistaken this place for something that it wasn't. It was no better than a saloon. Even in this place drinks were being shared by men and women at the tables.

Edging her way toward the door, she wasn't aware of a man who had spied her standing there. And just as she reached the door, he blocked her way.

"You can't leave without first dancin' with me, pretty lady," Raymond Benedict said, his pale blue eyes raking slowly over her. "Yes, sir, this place needs a taste of class added to it and I believe you're it."

Lee-lee looked up at a youthful face, thin, yet arresting in its features. His dark blond hair hung to the stiff, black collar of his impeccable suit and his nose was somewhat crooked and very long. His lips were narrow and only widened when he smiled, but it was the glint in his sky blue eyes that made Lee-lee wary of him. If his eyes were reflecting his hidden desires, she knew that he was not one to be trusted, for he had already mentally undressed her.

"Sir, please step aside," Lee-lee said icily. "It is my wish to leave this place. I mistook it for another sort of establishment."

"I shall formally introduce myself to you and hope that by doing so you will change your mind and accept just one dance from one who thinks you are very charming," Raymond said.

He bowed at his waist yet kept his eyes on her, in case she should decide to venture in the other direction. "Raymond Benedict at your service, pretty lady."

Lee-lee was growing more annoyed by the minute. "I do not care what your name is, and I do not wish to dance with you," she hissed. "Step aside or I shall demand to see that you are made to do so by the owner of this establishment."

Raymond straightened his back and laughed softly. "You are lookin' at him," he said. "I'm the proud owner of this place of excitement."

He gestured with an arm toward the dance floor. "Now I must insist that you dance with me. And if you are skilled enough, I'll offer you employment. You happen to be the loveliest lady to show up in San Francisco in many months now. Where did you say that you traveled from?"

"I didn't say," Lee-lee said sourly. "But if the likes of you had been there, Heung-Chin would have chosen to behead you for sure."

Raymond's eyebrows forked. "Heung-Chin?" he said, idly scratching his brow. "Isn't that Chinese?"

"*Ai* . . ." Lee-lee began then felt heat rush to her face, realizing that she had said much too much already. She had even spoken in Chinese.

"I'm becoming more intrigued by the minute," Raymond said, studying her facial features. "Here we have us an American beauty who speaks part Chinese."

He studied her more intensely. "Why is that?" he asked thoughtfully.

"That is no business of yours," Lee-lee said, taking a step forward, daring him.

"I could get you a fancy silk Chinese dress," Raymond mumbled. "You could draw quite a large amount of customers. Yes, I must have you here."

"*Nay* . . ." Lee-lee hissed, pushing at his chest in an effort to move him aside. She flinched when he grabbed her by her wrists and pulled her away from the door once more into the shadows.

"I don't like to use force to get my way," Raymond growled down into her face. "But when I must, I must. Now, pretty lady, you are going to go out on the dance floor and dance with me or do I have to show you the pistol belted at my right hip?"

Lee-lee paled and her knees lost their strength. "A . . . pistol?" she gasped.

"The best way that I've found to persuade a person."

"But, sir, why is it so important to persuade me? This city is alive with women. I'm sure that among them you could find those who are willing to be here."

"But you are the one I have chosen," Raymond growled. "And by God, even if I have to kill to get you, I will."

Lee-lee's immediate thoughts went to Tak-Ming and Timothy. Neither one could rescue her without his life being endangered. She felt trapped—mercilessly trapped!

"Come along," Raymond said, guiding her toward the dance floor by her elbow. "Place a smile on your lips. Those who see you with me must believe you are here because you want to be."

"Is this how you always manage to get girls to work for you in this place?" Lee-lee whispered, giving him a sour glance. "Are they forced to dress as whores and wear that ghastly paint on their faces?"

"Most desire to be under my employ as well as my body," Raymond gloated, guiding her onto the dance floor. "First we will take a few spins around the dance floor and then I will show you my skills at making love."

"You wouldn't!" Lee-lee gasped.

"I would," Raymond said, laughing smoothly.

With a flaming face, Lee-lee followed his lead, feeling the hard steel of his pistol against her body as he drew her into his arms. "Sir, you will soon learn that I don't even know how to dance," she hissed. "Nor will I let you take me to bed. So, you see, I am of no use to you whatsoever. In China . . ."

Raymond looked down upon her face, smiling coyly. "So you *have* traveled from China. One day soon I wish to hear all about it."

Once more Lee-lee had spoken unwisely, so she clamped her lips tightly together and held herself stiffly in his arms as she danced awkwardly with him among the many others on the dance floor.

Raymond fit his body snugly into hers and forced her arm about his neck. "There. You've got it," he said. "Before long you'll be better than the best who've danced here. I'll make the gents pay big to get the chance to dance with you. And then when you take 'em to your room to entertain 'em, we'll double the price."

A fierce knot formed at the pit of Lee-lee's stomach. She pushed at his chest. "You are a vile man," she whispered harshly. "Let me go. Neither you nor anyone else will pay me for either of the unpleasant chores you have planned for me. If I don't shoot you first, then Tak-Ming or Timothy will!"

Raymond held her as though in a vise and guided her from the floor. He held onto a wrist and led her away from the large room, down a dark hallway, then into an office which was mainly occupied by a huge oak desk with a faintly lighted kerosene lamp.

After closing the door behind him, Raymond once more drew Lee-lee into his arms. He crushed his lips down upon hers and savagely kissed her. But when she refused to return the kiss and instead stood cold and

290

lifeless in his arms, he stepped back away from her.

He wiped his mouth with the back of his right hand and glared at her. "You made mention of two men," he growled. "One was Chinese and one was American. What are they to you?"

Lee-lee tilted her chin, stubbornly refusing to answer him.

He jerked her left hand up closer to his eyes, checking for a ring. "You're not married," he further stated. "But, of course, you wouldn't be. Married, respectable women do not enter a dancing establishment unescorted."

Dropping her hand, he reached up and plucked one of Lee-lee's roses from her hair. He sniffed it then twirled its stem around between a thumb and forefinger, studying Lee-lee more intensely. "Whoever you've ventured to San Francisco with, it's easy to see that they are neglectin' you or why would you be alone?" He laughed.

He traced Lee-lee's facial features with a forefinger. "Stick with me and you'll never be alone again," he said thickly. "I may even keep you for myself. You're different from those other whores I've brought in from the streets."

Lee-lee knocked his hand away, her eyes narrow with building rage. "Never!" she hissed. She turned on a heel and grabbed for the doorknob, but he was once more there, blocking her way.

"Now what must I do to persuade you that you're not going anywhere?" he growled, lifting his coat to rest his right hand on the handle of his pistol.

He flipped the rose from between his fingers as a slow, crooked smile turned his lips into a lewd grin. "I'd best reword that," he said. "You're not going anywhere without *me*."

Taking her roughly by a hand, he led her to a door at the back of the room. He opened the door and had to half drag her to get her out into a dark alley. "I'm going to sample you and then decide what I'll use you for," he said. "And should anyone try to stop me . . . well, you'll see."

Lee-lee flinched as he drew her next to him and thrust his pistol into her side. She glanced down and saw that the pistol was hidden beneath his coat so no one could see its threat.

Icy cold with fear, she followed along beside him, down the plank walkway and across the crowded street. And as they entered the lobby of the Missouri Hotel and he began urging her toward the staircase, a ray of hope splashed inside her. He obviously made his residence in this same hotel and just possibly Tak-Ming or Timothy would arrive in time to stop him.

But then she remembered Raymond's threats and hoped that neither of the men she loved would suddenly appear. She feared for them even more than for herself.

Up one flight of stairs, then another and another, and Lee-lee discovered that Raymond's room was not far from her own. And as he opened his door and shoved her inside, she fell awkwardly to the floor, breathless. She scooted back on the oak flooring, wide-eyed as he began to slowly close the door, all the while leering down at her. Then suddenly all hell seemed to break loose as the door crashed open and Timothy was there, trying to wrestle the pistol away from Raymond.

"Oh, God," Lee-lee cried, placing her hands to her mouth. "Timothy!"

She rose slowly to her feet and backed up against the outside wall, watching in horror as Timothy and Raymond continued to struggle with the pistol. They grunted. They cursed. And then a gunfire exploded and both men fell to the floor, seemingly lifeless.

"Timothy!" Lee-lee shrieked, her heart feeling as though it had plummeted to her feet. "Oh, no! Timothy!"

She ran to him and fell to her knees beside him crying. Her hands raced over him, searching for a bleeding wound. Her pulse thumped madly. He was breathing! Thank God he was breathing!

She framed his face between her hands and lowered a soft kiss to his lips. "Timothy, my love," she sobbed, kissing him again. His lips were warm. They even seemed to be trembling!

Lee-lee drew slowly away from him, studying him more closely, and when his eyes flew widely open and he gave her a slow, provocative smile, she gasped and placed her hands to her throat. "Timothy, all along, you—"

"I'm fine," he said, rising up on one elbow.

"Why didn't you—?"

"I was enjoying the attention I was getting," he mused.

"I thought you were—"

"I just about was," he said, rising to a sitting position. He raked his fingers through his hair, straightening it as he looked toward the lifeless figure of Raymond. "Thank God the pistol was pointing in *his* direction when it fired."

"Is . . . he . . . dead, Timothy?"

"Looks it to me."

Timothy crawled over and gingerly inspected Raymond's body, finding the seeping wound in his chest. He checked the pulse at Raymond's throat, then nodded, "Dead as hell," he said.

He gave Lee-lee a heavy-lashed look. "Darling," he said, reaching a hand to her chin to cup it.

He then took her by a hand, drew her to her feet, and wrapped his arms about her.

Lee-lee sighed heavily as she twined her arms about his neck. "Timothy, how did you know?" she murmured, placing a cheek to his strong chest. "A moment later and he would have . . . surely . . . raped—"

Timothy placed a forefinger to her lips, sealing her words. "Shh," he said. "Let's not even think about what might have been."

"But, Timothy, where have you been?" Lee-lee said, sulking.

"Later," he said hoarsely. "We've much to talk about, but later. We've got to get the sheriff and tell him exactly how this shooting came about."

Lee-lee's face flamed with embarrassment. "Must we?" she whispered. "I don't want it to spread that I—"

Once more Timothy sealed her words with his finger. "Shh," he said. "Don't worry about a thing. Your reputation will remain intact. A few silver coins passed into the sheriff's pocket will assure his silence."

"But this man you killed," she argued softly. "Most in town surely know him and will demand to know the details of his death. He owns the dancing emporium across the street from this very hotel. Surely his friends—"

"A man like him has no true friends," Timothy scoffed. "Most will be glad he's dead. I heard gossip that the whores he uses in his establishment are in truth his prisoners, forced to stay with him. But the authorities couldn't prove it."

Lee-lee looked down at Raymond and shivered fitfully. "But he was so young," she whispered. "Surely not much older than twenty. How could he have become so evil so early in life?"

"Gold, my darling, does different things to different people," Timothy growled. "Seems he would've been better off striking it rich in another state, in another way."

Lee-lee shivered again. "Please let's leave this room, Timothy," she murmured. "I don't believe I can bear another moment of being in the same room with his—"

"I'll take you to your room and then go for the sheriff," Timothy said, already guiding her toward the door. They had been so absorbed in each other, they hadn't been aware of the crowd forming in the hallway which had been attracted by the sound of gunfire.

"Oh, no," Lee-lee whispered. She now knew that this fateful night couldn't remain a secret. Most would look down upon her. Now her flight to New York wouldn't come any too soon for her. But till then she would proudly hold her head high. With Timothy once more at her side, all wrongs were made right.

Chapter Nineteen

Timothy walked into Lee-lee's room carrying a bottle of wine and two long-stemmed, crystal glasses. He kicked her door shut with the toe of his shoe, then placed the wine and glasses on her nightstand.

Lee-lee had stripped herself of all the clothes that she had worn while in Raymond's presence and now only wore a thin, white frilly nightgown trimmed with point de Paris lace.

Through its sheerness Timothy could see the silken outline of her body from the swell of her breasts to the gentle curve of her thighs, and he was as intoxicated as if he had already consumed many glasses of wine.

With her hair now combed out and flowing gently down her back, Lee-lee walked barefoot to Timothy and draped her arms about his neck. She gazed rapturously into his hauntingly dark, passion-filled eyes then lifted her lips to kiss him softly.

Timothy placed his hands on Lee-lee's hips and drew her body into his, and she began slow, gyrating movements against him. The touch of her silk-encased body moving seductively over him made a pounding begin in Timothy's temple, which just as quickly traveled to his loins. He groaned and mindlessly moved his hand over her until a breast was found and trapped between his fingers.

Lee-lee drew her lips away from his, sighing lethargically. "It's been so long, Timothy," she murmured. "The days, the nights without you. . . ."

"But I am here now," he said huskily. "Let's talk later about the reasons. I've been almost crazy with missing you."

"The sheriff? Did you find him and tell him?"

"It's all been taken care of. Now you can relax."

"*Ai . . .*"

Timothy laughed softly, noting the Chinese way she still said yes. "It's not so easy to leave everything about China behind you, is it?" he asked.

He was relieved that Tak-Ming was finally out of her life. Earlier—before he had seen Raymond forcing Lee-lee up the stairs with a pistol that was not as well concealed as Raymond had thought—when Timothy first arrived at the hotel, he had checked with the desk clerk to see if a person by the name of Tak-Ming Yeung was registered. And when Timothy had found out that Tak-Ming wasn't, it was then that he realized that Lee-lee had made the separation, was living alone, and perhaps, just perhaps, had managed to put Tak-Ming completely from her mind. She had most surely found that now that she was in America, Tak-Ming was of no further use to her, that he was just another displaced Chinaman—no more, no less.

"I try to remember to speak only in American but it's so easy to forget," she said, brushing her hands through her hair and arching her neck back as Timothy's lips moved to the hollow of her throat.

A sensuous tremor moved in a rush through Lee-lee. And as Timothy began pushing her gown from her shoulders, burning kisses into her flesh the lower his lips moved, following the drifting of her gown, Lee-lee could feel that familiar coil of desire releasing itself inside her.

It was as if the heady sort of feeling were slowly entrapping her, but delightfully so, and she gave herself up to the ecstasy of the moment. She had waited for this. She had silently prayed for Timothy's return. For a while she had thought that his love for her had died, or possibly that he hadn't ever truly loved her at all. But his moods, she reasoned silently. She had forgotten his moods!

"Are you too upset by what just happened down the hall to . . . to make love, darling?" Timothy asked, seeing how she now stood naked in the garden of silk at her feet where her gown had rippled and fallen. Her body was an extension of that silk—all soft looking, creamy white, and lovely. It was hard to practice self-control with her so alluringly close. But he would not fully possess her unless her mind and body were free for the possession.

He averted his eyes from the slow heaving of her breasts with their exquisite pink tips like buds of flowers ready to blossom beneath his lips. Instead he looked into the honey-brown of her eyes and found that he was just as lost in their loveliness.

Lee-lee reached for one of his hands and placed it over her heart. "What do you feel?" she asked, smiling ravishingly up at him.

Timothy's handsome face broke into a slow grin. His eyes were darker with the intensity of the moment. "Your heart," he said. "I do believe it's pounding quite hard."

"And? Do you not know why, Timothy?"

"I would hope it's because of me."

"And, my darling, if I say that it is?"

"I will hurriedly tear my clothes from my body to make love to you."

"Please do," Lee-lee said, slipping away from him, to sink down onto her bed to watch him.

"Why, you sex-starved kitten," Timothy chuckled, already tossing his frock coat aside.

"Do you look at me as wantonly because of my behavior, Timothy?" Lee-lee asked shyly, not able to discourage a blush from rising to her cheeks.

"Never," he said thickly. "You are a woman . . . all woman. And you . . . are . . . mine."

Now completely stripped of clothes and shoes, he knelt over Lee-lee on the bed. He trailed his hands over her flesh, stopping them to absorb the pure heaven of the softness of her breasts. He lowered his lips to one that he was cupping and flicked his tongue over its hardening nipple.

Lee-lee licked her lips and closed her eyes, surrendering herself fully to the wild passion once more embracing her. Her heart pounded fiercely as she felt his skilled lips travel lower until they found the core of her desire where her thighs had gently been parted by a nudge from his knee.

The warmth of his lips . . . the sweet wetness of his tongue . . . made her keenly aware of the flames igniting inside her. She twined her fingers through his hair, pressing his lips even closer, then let out a soft cry of rapture when her peak of passion was reached. The moment of bliss passed quickly, and then she realized what had happened and was embarrassed.

Timothy crept onto the bed beside her. "Now, darling, please get on top," he urged softly. "I want to feel your breasts lowered against my chest. I want you to ride with me to paradise."

She couldn't admit that she had just been there. But she knew that he knew. He was skilled and knowledgeable in all ways of lovemaking. It made a keen jealousy rage through her when she thought of the other women he had had in his life. And suddenly she had an urgent need to please him, as no other woman ever had so she did as he asked and rose to her knees to straddle him.

"Kiss me, darling," Timothy said, reaching to draw her down against him. A soft moan surfaced from his lips when he felt her breasts touch his chest, first softly and then harder as Lee-lee wiggled herself into his full embrace.

Lips . . . breasts . . . stomachs touched. Hands roamed. Tongues probed. Lee-lee felt a renewed spinning inside her head. And as his hardness entered her from below, ecstasy wove its way through her heart.

She lifted her hips and worked with him, experiencing a feeling of power in being above him, feeling strangely the aggressor. She put herself in Timothy's place, remembering how he had performed when being the one in control, and enjoyed this newest way of making love.

Lee-lee pressed her lips against Timothy's throat and softly kissed him there, hearing a moan from deep inside him. He lifted his hands to her breasts, softly cupping them, and Lee-lee felt herself floating as though far out to sea, drifting . . . alone with her desires.

She rose up a fraction and looked down at Timothy, seeing his face a mask of pleasure, his eyes inflamed with passion. Her mouth then bore down upon his in a fiery kiss, all the while working her body with his, quivering with rapturous abandon.

His mouth forced her lips open as his kiss grew more seductively intense. Then his arms tore around her, crushing her hard against him, and together they shook and quaked as their pleasure was finally fully claimed.

Semi-drugged from the aftermath of their lovemaking, Lee-lee moved to Timothy's side and stretched out on her back. He leaned up on an elbow and ran his fingers through her hair as it lay spread out on the bed like a black velvet halo. Brilliant red streaks filtered through it as if she were caught in a tropical sunset. He noticed how her cheeks were flushed and how her lovely brown eyes held a hazy dreaminess.

"You never looked more beautiful," Timothy murmured.

Lee-lee touched his cheek affectionately. "And you never could be as handsome as you are at this very moment," she sighed.

Timothy chuckled. "A man isn't handsome when he hasn't a stitch of clothes on to hide his awkward body," he mused.

She ran her fingers over his body, smiling as his skin

rippled with each added touch. "That shows how little *you* know," she giggled.

"And did you fully enjoy our lovemaking, Lee-lee?"

"Immensely."

"Would you like to make love in a tent?"

Lee-lee rose quickly to a sitting position, her eyes wide with questions. "A tent?" she gasped. "Why on earth would you make mention of a tent?"

Timothy rose from the bed and pulled his trousers on. "Well? Would you?" he persisted. He gave her a half smile and went to pour two glasses of wine. "Would it matter to you where we made love, for, let's say, the next week or so?"

Laughing softly, Lee-lee climbed from the bed and went to her wardrobe to get a robe. She slipped into it, tying its belt in the front. "Timothy, I don't know what you're getting at, but, *ai*, I'd make love to you anywhere . . . any time," she murmured, accepting the glass of wine he brought to her. "But, darling, a tent? And you said something about a full week? Please don't keep me in suspense. Tell me what's on your mind."

"I'm sure you've wondered where I've been this past week," Timothy said, settling down into a chair.

He crossed his legs, sipped on his wine, and watched Lee-lee's delicate movements as she went to settle on the bed, leaning her back comfortably against its headboard.

He had missed her. Hell, how he had missed her. Before he set sail for New York he would ask her to marry him. But first he had to be completely sure of her. He would not be made a fool of again!

"You know that I have," Lee-lee murmured softly. She drew her knees up before her and took a slow, thoughtful sip of wine. Oh, how she had missed him. She didn't want to believe that he couldn't be trusted . . . that he had only used her. At last she would get some answers from him.

"This past week has been a productive one for me," Timothy bragged. "I've traveled to the neighboring mining camps and have been able to sell most of my China wares. And I didn't only sell. I also made quite an interesting trade."

"Tell me about it," Lee-lee said, scooting to the edge of the bed.

"One miner was damned anxious to get his hands on some opium," Timothy chuckled. He rose from the chair and placed his empty glass on the nightstand. He searched inside his frock coat pocket and found a cigar and match.

"Opium?" Lee-lee said softly, her face drawn into a frown. "Good Lord. I had forgotten about the opium. Did you say that you were successful at ridding yourself of that evil drug?"

"All of it," Timothy grumbled, lighting his cigar. "But mind you, don't think that I traded it entirely to this one gent for his claim. Many were interested in trying the opium. I was just lucky I didn't unknowingly offer it to one of the lawmen out there in the hills who are also trying to stake claims."

"Claims? For gold?" Lee-lee asked, placing her empty glass on the nightstand. "Did you actually see some of that gold they're digging out of the hills?"

"Darling, I don't think you've been listening," Timothy said, settling down on the bed beside her. "I now own my own claim. I traded opium for it. I'll be digging out my own gold."

Lee-lee's face flushed with renewed excitement. "You'll be prospecting? Actually prospecting for gold?" she asked, clasping onto his hands.

"With you, hopefully, at my side." He chuckled.

"And that's what you meant about the tent? We'll be living in a tent out there, alone, in the hills?"

"Not alone, darling. The hills are full of prospectors. We'll only have a little corner of the world that we can call ours. How does that sound? Do you think you'd mind sleeping in a tent and cooking outdoors?"

"It sounds very exciting, Timothy. When do we go?"

"Tomorrow."

"Tomorrow?" Lee-lee sighed. "We really can? So soon?"

"Yes. But only for a week or so. My partner, Calvin, is awaiting my return to New York with news of successful trade. I can't keep him waiting forever."

Lee-lee's eyes took on a faraway look. "New York," she whispered. "I wonder just how much it has changed. I wonder what happened to my father's business . . . our beautiful house. . . ."

Not yet ready to discuss her traveling with him to New York, Timothy avoided further mention of it. He went and mashed his cigar out in an ashtray, then went back to Lee-lee and drew her up from the bed and into his arms.

"We've much to do early in the morning before leaving town," he said. "My trade included the old prospector's tent and all supplies except for food. We want to stock up. We don't want to live too much in the rough. Neither of us are used to it."

"*Nay*, we are not," Lee-lee murmured, twining her

arms about his neck. "We both have been terribly spoiled, haven't we?"

Timothy untied her robe and opened it to his searching fingers. "Not enough, darling," he said huskily. "Spoil me some more. Make me stinking, rotten spoiled. Love me, darling. Love me."

Lee-lee's breath came in short gasps as he cupped both her breasts. She leaned away from him, closing her eyes as she felt his lips cover a breast, inhaling its nipple through his teeth. He chewed on it playfully, making it grow harder. A sweet pain rose between Lee-lee's thighs and she felt euphoric as his lips now covered hers. She wriggled out of her robe, feeling a cool rush of air as she became quickly nude.

She let her fingers travel across the corded muscles of his shoulders, down through the crispness of his chest hairs, and then to the waistband of his trousers.

His kiss grew hotly demanding and his body shook in a sensual tremor as Lee-lee unfastened his trousers and began lowering them over his hips. She laughed to herself as he twisted and his trousers crumpled down to the floor.

Lee-lee's fingers trembled as she let them move farther down to where his sex was swollen and ready for her. Boldly circling it with a hand, she became enraptured by its largeness and its smoothness. When she began moving her fingers over it, she heard Timothy emit a soft groan.

Timothy released her lips and looked down into her honey-brown eyes. "What are you doing to me?" he asked thickly. "Don't you know you're driving me wild with wanting you?"

"And do you think I am not fully aware of that?" she replied, giggling.

He urged her hand away. "But, darling, not that way." He sighed. "I can think of a much better way to receive my pleasure with you in my company."

"Oh? And how?" she teased, running a forefinger over his long, straight nose and the seductive fullness of his lips.

"Just get on that bed and I will show you."

"Out in the hills there won't be a bed," she teased further. "What will you do then, Timothy Hendricks?"

"It's not the bed that enhances the pleasure," he chuckled, placing an arm about her waist to guide her to the bed.

"But even if that were true, would you be able to make love in a flimsy tent, Timothy? Won't others see us?"

"When the lamps are blown out at night and a man is lucky enough to have a woman at his side, each tent becomes a lovenest. Ours will be no different."

"I would hope that it would be different," Lee-lee murmured, easing up on the bed, welcoming him at her side. She leaned over him, teasing him as she rubbed her breasts enticingly across his bare chest.

"And just what could we possibly do that would be different?" Timothy asked, placing his hands on the silk of her hips, urging her against his swollen manhood.

"Surely no one makes love like us," Lee-lee said, positioning herself fully over him, trembling as he eagerly entered her.

"Ah, you are like no other woman could be," he said huskily, raising his hips, thrusting.

"I hope you truly mean that," Lee-lee said. She then

rained kisses across his face as she melted inside. Her body was blending into his, as if they were one. She flung her head back sighing. Her hair cascaded down her back like exquisite black satin shimmering with touches of flame.

Timothy reached and circled her breasts with his hands and fondly caressed them. He could feel the passion rising . . . an intense fury raging inside him. He gritted his teeth, closed his eyes, and momentarily stiffened before violently shuddering as he released his burning stream inside her.

Lee-lee felt the delicious hot wetness splash her insides. She felt rapturous shivers encase her as she, too, became lost in her brief moment of heaven.

Timothy welcomed her breasts pressing against his chest as she sighed and slowly collapsed upon him. He could feel the erratic pounding of her heart against his skin, and he could feel the trembling of her lips as she pressed them gently against his neck.

"I love you so," she whispered. She twined her fingers through his hair. "Oh, Timothy, I do love you so."

"And I you," he returned. Then he softly chuckled as he hugged her. "But let's see if you can still say that in a week, after using the ground as a bed and after chasing cockroaches away from our food."

Lee-lee raised her head quickly and searched his face, not laughing. "Cockroaches?" she gasped. "Timothy, tell me you are jesting!"

"We shall see, won't we?" he laughed.

Lee-lee's lips rose into a small smile. "*Ai*, I guess we shall."

Chapter Twenty

Golden poppies carpeted the fields and hillsides, and in the far distance the Santa Cruz Mountains swept upward into the sky in a hazy purple topped by shallow peaks of white. In other directions, there were valleys, then hills, then more valleys. Ponderosa pine, redwood, and spruce trees cast cool shadows upon the land where an occasional great yellow splash of wild mustard bloomed.

But most predominant in this landscape were scattered tents, covered wagons, lean-tos made by tilting logs against flat-sided rocks, smoke from campfires, and the hordes of people who made up these numerous gold-mining camps.

Timothy slapped the reins, urging his sweating, panting horses onward as the covered wagon swayed over land that knew not the carving of a road. The wagon wheels creaked and the canvas covering flapped in the dry breeze.

Glancing beside him on the seat, Timothy saw the redness of Lee-lee's face and the dust that laced her lips. Perhaps he had been wrong to bring her with him. She was used to more genteel ways. Yet, she had seemed eager to accept this newest challenge.

Lee-lee placed her hands to the small of her back and groaned. "How much farther, Timothy?" she asked, squinting as the hot rays of the sun crept beneath the brim of her stiffly starched bonnet. "We've been traveling a full day and night. At this rate, we'll meet ourselves coming and going, since you aren't planning to stay long once we arrive at our destination."

"Our tent and equipment are just over the rise," he said, nodding toward another hill yet to climb. "The old gent who made the trade promised to stay put until I returned. Sure hope to hell he's a man of his word."

"Why would you even want him to, Timothy?"

"Claim jumpers, darling. I wouldn't want to lose my claim before I even got to set foot on it."

"Claim jumpers?" Lee-lee said, wiping a bead of perspiration from beneath her nose.

"Nothing to worry about," Timothy encouraged, patting the holstered pistol at his belt. "I'm here to protect you."

Lee-lee laughed nervously. Her gaze swept over Timothy, seeing how differently he was dressed this day. Instead of his expensive, impeccably tailored clothes, he wore jeans and a blue plaid cotton shirt with a red polka-dotted neckerchief tied about his neck. His head was protected by a wide-brimmed cowboy hat, and he wore fancy leather cowboy boots on his feet.

Seeing him this way made Lee-lee's heart increase in its beats. His dark tan . . . his dark eyes. All she would have to do would be to touch him and she would begin the slow, gentle melting inside.

"Timothy, why did you choose to do this?" she quickly blurted. "It's so different from your normal lifestyle. You are a man of the sea, not of the land."

There was a quiet amusement in his eyes when he looked toward her. She self-consciously straightened the lines of her heavy, dark travel skirt then let her fingers move to the lowswept bodice of her plain white drawstring blouse. She knew that she was less than attractive in such plain garb. But travel in a covered wagon called for anything but a dainty, lace-trimmed dress and fancy petticoats.

She had even purchased heavy flannel nightgowns to wear through the damp, cold nights while sleeping on the ground. Already she was dreading the thought of spending the night in such a way, but if worse came to worse, she would climb into the covered wagon and sleep there.

"Why did I decide to become this sort of adventurer?" Timothy said, lifting an eyebrow toward her. "Because, darling, I just couldn't travel on to New York without first trying my luck at panning for gold."

"You surely don't expect to find enough gold to make you more wealthy than you already are, do you?" she scoffed.

"I was told that if we worked at it, we could take in five to ten ounces of gold dust in a day."

"Is that a lot, Timothy?"

He gave her a slow smile. "That would be enough for me," he said. "Quite enough to please me."

As the wagon traveled up a steep hill, Timothy pointed

toward several bushy evergreens that rose at least thirty feet into the air. "Those gnarled and twisted evergreens are called bristlecone pines," he said. "Those are said to be the oldest living things in the world. Notice the cones. They're thickly covered by scales with chocolate brown tips, and there are long, slender, curving prickles growing on the cones. These give the tree its name."

Lee-lee gave Timothy an awed look. "You never cease to amaze me," she said. "Is there anything that you don't know?"

He chuckled. "Like I said before. I read a lot. The voyages at sea are not only lengthy, but sometimes boring."

Lee-lee scooted over next to him and leaned against his shoulder. "Oh?" she murmured. "And was your last voyage so boring?"

"Interesting," he laughed. "Very interesting. I must say . . . if you were a part of my every voyage, I might gladly toss all of my books into the sea!"

At the peak of the hill, they had a clear view of the next valley. Many tents were set up, scattered near a meandering stream that seemed to originate nowhere.

Timothy shielded his eyes from the sun with the back of a hand and searched for the familiar, small tent. Then he pointed. "Over there," he said. "We have our own, personal bristlecone pine in our square of property. Do you see? It's the tree shadowing that one tent. That tent, darling, is ours."

Scooting to her side of the wagon seat, Lee-lee frowned toward the tent. "Timothy, it is so . . . so . . . small," she uttered faintly.

"I didn't promise you more than that," he grumbled, flicking the reins, urging his horses down the rough, rock-strewn incline. "Don't get picky now, Lee-lee. It's much too late to turn back."

"You don't have to bite my head off," Lee-lee said, sulking. She was hot. She was tired. She was both hungry and thirsty. And she suddenly realized that there wasn't much relief waiting for her, or any of her silent complaints.

But she would make the best of the situation and show Timothy that she could hold up against all odds as well as he. From Mandarin Heung-Chin Yeung's first acquaintance with her, he had noticed her fiery spirit. Timothy Hendricks would know of it as well!

"Sorry, darling," Timothy said, casting her a quick glance. "I guess my anxiety is getting the best of me."

"I'm just as anxious, and I'm not nasty to you," she argued softly.

Timothy sighed exasperatedly. "Lee-lee, I said that I was sorry," he grumbled. "Now let's go and claim what's ours and try our luck at quick wealth."

The horses were drawn to a halt close to the tent that was now Timothy's. Outside its entrance ashes were gray in a cooking place that consisted of a trench dug in the dirt to secure frames made of two forked logs with a crossbar held between them. A branch had been hung from the crossbar and a deep notch had been cut in the lower end to hang a large black kettle. Other cooking utensils were strewn about, and various prospecting equipment such as pickaxes, shovels, and pans lay idle near the tent's entrance.

"Hmm," Timothy said, kneading his chin. "Seems deserted. Guess the old gent gave up waiting for us after all."

"It appears peaceful enough," Lee-lee said, her eyes slowly searching for any signs of danger.

Once more she placed her hands to the small of her back, ready to leave the crude wagon to stretch her legs. The strong aroma of pine was heavy in the air and a breeze blowing from across the nearby creek bed had a quality of coolness about it. But a rumble of thunder high up in the mountains broke the serenity of the setting and posed a real threat in this land of deep valleys and hills.

Timothy climbed from the wagon, secured the horses, then went to Lee-lee and helped her down. "Well? What do you think?" he asked, gesturing with the sweep of a hand. "Our own little gold mine."

Laughing softly, Lee-lee drew the tail of her skirt up into her arms and moved toward the tent. "*Ai*," she said. "You and your vision of quick wealth. Where is this mine of ours?"

Timothy began gently kicking at the shovels and pickaxes. "Darling, I think I've misled you just a mite," he said, giving her a guarded glance.

Lee-lee swung around, facing him. "Oh? How, Timothy?" she asked innocently.

"The claim. It's really nothing—only this tent and equipment."

"What?" Lee-lee gasped. "But you said—"

Timothy went to her and draped his arms about her waist, locking his fingers together behind her. "I know what I said," he murmured. "But, Lee-lee, I had to make

313

it sound alluring enough to get you to come with me."

"But, Timothy, I would have, no matter what you had said."

"You mean that?"

"*Ai.*"

Timothy drew her closer and kissed her softly. "That's what I wanted to hear," he whispered.

Then he swung away from her. "But there *is* gold in the stream, Lee-lee," he added quickly. "Let's have some fun. Let's search leisurely for some gold flakes. If we don't find anything, at least we're together, sharing."

Lee-lee wiped perspiration from her brow and she licked her parched lips. "*Ai,*" she mumbled. "Surely the hardships can be dealt with."

She wandered to the tent, opened its flap, and peered inside. She cringed. Not only was it dirty, but it also smelled of sweat and filth. She gave Timothy a sour glance over her shoulder but saw that he was too busy unloading their supplies to notice.

Falling to her knees, Lee-lee crawled inside the tent and began gathering together soiled clothes and a reeking bedroll and tossed them over her shoulder, outside.

Then she opened the flap at the other end and welcomed the fresh air that began flowing in around her. Perhaps by evening, she might possibly be able to sleep beside Timothy in the tent. The smell, the rough, rocky floor, and the size of the tent were fast spoiling Lee-lee's dreams of intimate, rapturous moments with the man she loved.

*　　*　　*

Settled in, and with two days already behind them, Lee-lee watched Timothy sink a pan into the stream as she tended the coffee warming over the campfire's flames. She eased down onto the grass, placing her feet beneath her, and anxiously regarded him as he scooped the sand and water into the pan and began swirling it with a sharp motion of his wrist.

"What I'm doing is called placer mining," Timothy explained, keeping a watchful eye on the bottom of the pan as the lightweight sand splashed out. "It's a sifting process, panning gold by hand. After swirling the water and gravel from the pan, any gold that might be there is left in the pan, because, although gold is soft, it's heavier than the sand."

Lee-lee leaned up on her knees to take a closer look. "Do you see any yet, Timothy?"

Timothy shook everything from the pan then dipped it back into the sandy stream. "Not one shine of gold," he laughed. "There would be no mistaking its soft, metallic glow."

Lee-lee leaned fully back onto the grassy slope, untied and removed her bonnet, and began fanning herself with it. "I think I'd prefer a bath over even a nugget of gold," she said scornfully. "The sponge baths the last couple of nights just haven't been enough for me, Timothy. How can I take a real bath with so many people around here?"

Timothy chuckled. "When everyone else is asleep, we'll go upstream where the water is deeper, and we'll take a bath together," he said.

"And do other things, I am sure," Lee-lee teased. She tossed her bonnet aside, removed her shoes, and dipped her feet into the coolness of the water.

"Yes, other things," Timothy chuckled.

A low roar of thunder reverberated around them. High in the mountains, streaks of lightning forked from dark, ominous clouds. Lee-lee tensed, watching the play of the heavens.

Timothy ignored the lightning flashes and the ensuing thunder. "Placer deposit particles such as I'm looking for have been washed and carried away from a lode or vein by surface water," he said, seriously resuming his search in the panned sand and gravel bits.

"Placer deposits?" Lee-lee asked, splashing her feet around in the water, watching the sand rising from the bottom, dirtying the water with a brownish-gold coloring.

"Placer deposits are large particles. Some come in the shape of nuggets and some as grains of gold," Timothy said, patiently going through his panning ritual over and over again. "There are two types: eluvial and alluvial. Eluvial deposits are found close to the vein of gold. Alluvials are found farther away, usually in stream beds such as the one I'm working."

A soft metallic glow from where Lee-lee's feet had so fitfully stirred the sand drew her quick attention. She moved to her knees, leaned over the water, and splashed the muddy water on downstream, gasping as the soft, lovely yellow shine from the creek bed proved to be a nugget the size of a hickory nut.

"Timothy," she said, trembling. "I believe . . . I honestly believe that I've found an alluvial placer deposit!"

Timothy dropped the pan into the stream and fell to his

knees beside Lee-lee. "Where?" he shouted.

Lee-lee pointed then placed her hands to her throat as Timothy thrust his hand into the water and plucked the nugget from the bed of sand. "My God!" he gasped, turning it between his fingers. "You did it. You discovered yourself quite a chunk of gold!"

A wanderer with a mule pack trailing along behind him was cause for Timothy to circle his fingers around the newly found treasure, to hide it from roaming, searching eyes. He watched, breathless, as the heavy-shouldered, raggedy-clothed, whiskered man trudged by. It was quite evident to Timothy that this prospector hadn't been as lucky.

Then Timothy grabbed Lee-lee by the hand. "Come on," he encouraged in a whisper. "Let's go inside the tent. No one must know of our discovery. We'd be swallowed alive by the rush of prospectors to this section of the stream."

Lee-lee scrambled alongside him, crying out as sharp rocks pricked the soles of her bare feet. "How much is it worth?" she whispered, clinging to his arm.

"Only the Lord knows," Timothy said, keeping the nugget well hidden inside his fist. "All I know is that no one should know about it, at least until it's safely inside a bank vault."

"Do you think there are more?" Lee-lee anxiously whispered.

"We couldn't be that lucky," Timothy scoffed. "It's just beginner's luck. I'm sure it will stop there."

Looking toward the dipping sun, Lee-lee frowned. "The day is spent," she said. "So we won't even be able to look again until tomorrow."

Timothy chuckled, feeling the smooth coolness of the nugget against the flesh of his hand. "I think this can hold me," he said. "If we never panned for gold again, I'd be satisfied with what we've already found."

"It's ours. The wealth will be shared, won't it, Timothy?"

He wanted to use this moment of headiness to ask for her hand in marriage, yet something held him back. He hoped that their future would be spent in sharing everything, not just a gold nugget.

"Yes," he murmured. "The wealth will be shared. And because we've been so lucky, I'd say a celebration is in order, wouldn't you?"

"A glass of wine for my love?"

"And that promised moonlight swim."

Lee-lee looked toward the mountains, seeing how the dark storm clouds had spread. "If a storm doesn't stand in our way," she said.

"You do worry so," Timothy laughed. "Thunder has been rumbling in those mountains since we arrived here."

He let her enter the tent before him then crept in and sat down beside her on their spread bedroll. He uncupped his fist and placed the gold nugget on the red flannel of the bedroll and let its shine almost hypnotize him.

"It's beautiful," Lee-lee sighed, touching it, turning it from side to side.

"To some, such a discovery is the kiss of death," Timothy growled.

"And why is that, Timothy?"

"Men get too greedy. They kill for gold. They get killed protecting it. I would hope that it doesn't have such an effect on our lives, Lee-lee."

Lee-lee shrugged. "It's a simple gold rock," she said. "Nothing more or less to me."

"A simple gold rock with a lot of shine," Timothy laughed. "A rock to make celebration over. Where's that promised wine, Lee-lee?"

Lee-lee giggled and reached behind her to grab a bottle of La Rosé wine. She had purposely placed it inside the tent out of the heat of the sun. She had later found the crystal glasses beside it, knowing that Timothy had placed them there, hoping to have cause for celebrating. Just being there together was cause enough for Lee-lee.

Handing the bottle to Timothy, she then held the glasses as he poured them full of the sparkling, red liquid. She laughed throatily as she glanced down at the gold nugget, hardly able to believe that she had been the one to discover it. Timothy had worked for the find. She had only been playfully splashing her feet. Somehow she felt he really deserved it.

"To us," Timothy said, clanking his glass against hers. "To all our tomorrows. Darling, may each day shine as the gold we have placed here before us."

"*Ai*," Lee-lee whispered, feeling the magic of the moment intoxicating her. She tilted the glass to her lips, watching Timothy over its brim, seeing his dark, handsome outline in the growing shadows of the tent. Drinking the wine in small sips, tasting its sweet tartness, she watched Timothy remove his neckerchief then his shirt. Her pulse began to race, anticipating the moments ahead.

"Just getting comfortable," Timothy chuckled, tossing his shirt aside. He stretched out, leaning on an elbow, and drank leisurely from his glass.

Disappointment surged through Lee-lee. She had expected to be in his arms by now. Instead, it seemed she would have to wait for the darkness of night to give them the shelter required to be as intimate as they usually were. Her stomach growled and she was reminded of another sort of hunger.

Timothy's hand crept stealthily up Lee-lee's leg, beneath her skirt. "You can get as comfortable," he teased. "Surely that skirt is burdensome and hot. Why not take it off?"

"I hate to disappoint you," Lee-lee laughed, now being the one to tease. "But, Timothy, I'm starved. Let's eat, relax, and cool off, and surely by then it will be dark enough for us to sneak off for a swim or bath or whatever you wish to call it."

Timothy grabbed for her ankle. "I wish to call it making love," he growled teasingly.

Lee-lee fell clumsily against him. "Timothy, I'm all sweaty," she protested softly. Then she twined her arms about his neck as his lips fell gently upon hers.

"Your taste is always the same," he whispered as he drew slightly away from her. "It's as though I've kissed the petal of a fragrant rose, darling."

"Hush," she whispered, moving closer to him, feeling the touch of his chest hairs tickling her nose as she flicked her tongue around one of his nipples. "You've started something. Now you must finish it."

Timothy's fingers went to her drawstring blouse and eased it down from her shoulders. "I thought you were hungry," he said huskily, placing a kiss at the hollow of her throat. His insides ignited as his hands fully encased her breasts. The throbbing in his loins was pure torture.

"My hungers seem to change from moment to moment," she laughed, unfastening his trousers.

"Thank God for that," Timothy chuckled.

"But we're so vulnerable to passersby, Timothy."

"I'll take care of that." He dropped the flaps at both ends of the tent.

The sun had mercifully crept below the horizon and dusk had set in, along with cooler breezes. Lee-lee worked with her skirt and underthings while Timothy slid his trousers off. They laughed softly as their heads collided, then their buttocks, while they awkwardly undressed in the small quarters of the tent. But soon they had succeeded and were touching each other's bodies softly, reverently.

Then Lee-lee's gaze went to the gold nugget. She plucked it up from the bedroll, looking devilishly toward Timothy.

"And what's on that mind of yours now?" he asked, recognizing the mischievous glint in her eyes.

"I will adorn your body with gold," she whispered. She tried to place it into his navel, snickering impishly. But when it wouldn't stay, she just held it there and lowered her lips to it. "I christen thee our love stone."

Timothy threw his head back and roared with laughter

then sobered as her lips moved lower to gently kiss his risen sex.

"As I christen thee my love tool," she murmured, smiling up at Timothy, seeing his eyes glazed with sudden, urgent need of her. She welcomed his hand in hers and let him draw her up next to him. As he shaped his body into hers, Lee-lee giggled, feeling the gold nugget pressed against her stomach.

"Darling," she murmured. "The gold. . . ."

Timothy chuckled and rescued the nugget from between them, placed it beside Lee-lee's head, then swept her into his arms. He kissed her passionately and long, his fingers twined through her hair. He pulled her lips fiercely closer. His insides were on fire. He could wait no longer.

Fitting his sex inside her, he eased his lips from hers and looked down upon her face. He watched her expression become filled with ecstasy as she worked her hips up into him, skilled now in the ways of making love.

Lee-lee's lips were softly parted and her eyes glazed with hungry need. She looked up at Timothy and reached her hands to his face to frame it.

"Darling," she sighed.

She licked her lips; she closed her eyes; she clung to his shoulders. The rapture was rising inside her . . . a flame burning brighter . . . a warmth so deliciously sweet she felt she was swimming in a lake filled with softly scented water lilies.

Timothy's lips were quivering as he kissed Lee-lee. His hands moved lower to mold around her soft, round buttocks, and he held her hard against him as he reached a height of ecstasy he had never before known. He smiled with satisfaction as he heard her soft moans and felt her body shudder in shared passion.

Timothy relaxed against Lee-lee. He hugged her to him, placing a soft kiss into the hollow of her throat then onto the hard peak of one of her breasts. "It's always so good," he whispered huskily. "Darling, I love you so."

Lee-lee was still upon her cloud of rapture. She had never felt so at peace—so content with life—as she did at that very moment.

Running her hands over his muscled shoulders then down the curve of his back to the hardness of his buttocks, she laughed softly. "Is it always this way with love?" she murmured.

"Which way, darling?"

"To touch you—just to touch you makes me heady."

"That is only one of the symptoms of true love, Lee-lee."

"*Ai,*" she sighed. "I know there most surely are many. Timothy, I know that I must have experienced them all with you."

"I hope you never tire of these feelings," he said.

"Why, Timothy, how could I? There is such power in your passion."

Timothy was finally sure of her love for him. He had succeeded at ridding her of thoughts of the handsome Chinaman. He was confident of this and he felt smug. Oh, God, so smug. . . .

His lips possessed hers fiercely and his fingers dug into her flesh. Once more they joined their bodies in the most intimate of embraces. Lee-lee's heart began to beat so rapidly it seemed to be making a crazy sort of echo inside her brain, dizzying her even more. She twined her arms about Timothy's back and clung to him, lifting her hips as his thrusts became long and swift.

Their explosion of pleasure blended into one massive quaking of bodies, leaving them laughingly gasping for breath as they fell away from each other, spread out on their backs.

"I'm not sure if I'm capable of moving from this tent for a moonlight bath and swim," Timothy chuckled.

A growl of thunder and a tremor in the earth beneath them was a reminder of the storm that had been spreading in the heavens.

"If we don't hurry, we may not even get that chance," Lee-lee said, rising to her knees, hurriedly drawing her blouse over her head. "The thunder sounds closer."

"If we wait, we could just stand naked in the rain," Timothy teased, pulling his trousers on. "Now wouldn't that stir up some excitement in this mining camp?"

"Ha!" Lee-lee said, wiggling into her skirt, fastening it around her hips. "That's not the kind of excitement these *unfortunates* are needing, I am sure."

"*Unfortunates?*" Timothy asked, raising an eyebrow.

"They who have so little in life that they have to live here in tents. They are the *unfortunates*," she sighed. "Surely most have nothing. They have probably used all their resources to enable them to get here from the various cities. You know that disappointment is surely the only thing that most have found here."

"We are not *unfortunates*, yet we are here, Lee-lee."

"I'm sure we are an exception," Lee-lee said, leaning

324

over to kiss him softly. "There are more who have not, than have . . ."

"Ah, and don't you sound like the wise one," Timothy chuckled. He reached for his pistol and slipped it into the band of his trousers.

Lee-lee flipped her hair back from her shoulders. She looked at the pistol then up at Timothy, questioning him with her eyes.

"We should never be without it," he explained, having noticed her look of wonder. "The *unfortunates*, as you call the ones who are without luck, are sometimes *desperate unfortunates*."

Lee-lee further watched as Timothy slipped their gold nugget into a trouser pocket. "And there's no sense in taking a chance leaving this in the tent to be stolen," he said. "We'll keep it with us while we take our bath."

The ground trembled violently as another rumble of thunder reverberated through the hills and valleys.

Chapter Twenty-One

Clinging to Timothy's arm, Lee-lee crept stealthily along beside him, hoping that no one would see them. Lamps emitted soft light inside some tents while other tents were pitch black. Fires were burning down into soft glowing embers outside each tent, casting minute, wavering ghostly shadows all about them. Horses neighed and mules brayed nervously as lightning forked in the dark heavens above them, yet everything else seemed ominously quiet except for the increasing crashes of thunder.

"We'd best hurry," Timothy encouraged, looking up at the sky. "I'm afraid our bath will have to be a record-breaking one. That storm has decided to creep down from the mountains after all."

The water on the one side of them glistened beneath a bright flash of lightning, enabling Timothy to see that they had finally arrived at the point where the stream curved into a larger body of water and thick-clustered willows hung lacy limbs over its edges.

Looking cautiously about, Timothy placed his arms

around Lee-lee, stopping her. "This should do it," he said. "It's not only deep enough for a swim but also secluded."

He again looked in all directions. "I don't believe anyone saw us. Let's hurry and get in and out of the water. I'll feel much better about things when I get the gun back on my hip."

Lee-lee's insides quaked. "That's right," she whispered. "I hadn't thought about it, but while we're in the water, we'll be separated from your gun."

"And our gold," Timothy grumbled. He slipped his trousers down and placed them as closely to the water as possible.

Lee-lee undressed and held onto Timothy's hand as they stepped gingerly into the cool wetness. She had to stifle a squeal when Timothy released her hand and gave her a playful shove, causing her to lose her balance and fall headfirst into deeper water.

Timothy chuckled, dove beneath the surface, and found Lee-lee who was now swimming gracefully away from him. He swam up next to her and slid his hand across her body, touching all of her sensitive pleasure points, toying with her.

When she turned and dove more deeply into the water and wrapped herself around him, cupping his risen sex with a hand, a rush of heat traveled through his body.

Timothy placed his feet firmly in sand and drew her head up out of the water to kiss her, but a movement on shore grabbed his full attention and he eased Lee-lee gently away from him.

Sensing something was wrong, Lee-lee's insides grew

cold. "What is it, Timothy?" she whispered, wiping her hair back from her face, trying to focus her eyes while following Timothy's steady, cautious gaze.

"Shh," he encouraged, placing a hand gently to her lips.

Lee-lee's knees grew weak when she suddenly saw two whiskered men at the shoreline. One was carrying a shotgun and one was moving toward Timothy's trousers.

"Damn 'em," Timothy growled beneath his breath.

"Timothy, what should we do?" Lee-lee whispered, fitting her body next to his.

Lightning forked in the sky, momentarily lighting up everything as though it were daylight. The shine of the shotgun barrel caught in Timothy's eyes and his gut twisted, realizing where it was being pointed.

"The shotgun is the ruler here, Lee-lee, and it's pointed directly at us," Timothy grumbled. "And don't move. The men may decide they want more than gold."

"Do you mean—?"

"Yes. I mean *you* . . ."

Lee-lee couldn't stop the trembling of her fingers. Fear laced her heart. She felt so keenly vulnerable in the water, nude.

The anger was rising in splashes inside Timothy, yet he wasn't in any position to do anything about the dilemma they were now in. With Lee-lee's life to protect, he couldn't make any rash decisions. He couldn't do anything to jeopardize her safety, though doing nothing was making him feel less a man.

His lips set in a straight line and his jaw tightened as he saw the one man pick up his trousers and begin searching inside his pockets. He heard the man let out a loud laugh and knew that the gold nugget had been found.

Timothy cringed as he saw the same man pick up his pistol. "Even that," he grumbled.

Lee-lee tensed, seeing the man now lifting her clothes and going through them. She inched closer to Timothy when the man placed her silk underthings to his face to rub them against his nose.

Then she sighed with relief when the other man told him to keep his mind on business, and her clothes were tossed quickly to the ground.

Wide-eyed and barely breathing, Lee-lee watched as the men ran noiselessly away into the darkness. "Timothy, they aren't going to kill us," she said breathlessly. "They've gone."

"And along with them our gold and my pistol," Timothy growled, helping Lee-lee out of the water.

A large drop of rain fell against Lee-lee's cheek. She stooped to pick up her clothes then felt herself being pelted by many more raindrops. The sky then seemed to open up and the rain came down so hard and heavy it was as if someone had overturned a large bucket somewhere high in the sky.

Lightning flashed and thunder boomed. Lee-lee wiped the rain from her face then struggled into her wet, binding clothes as Timothy struggled into his trousers.

"It seems everything is suddenly against us, Timothy," Lee-lee cried, shaking her wet hair to hang down her back. "First those horrible men and now this terrible rain!"

"We'll take one inconvenience at a time and deal with

329

it as it comes," Timothy mumbled, helping her fasten her skirt. He then draped an arm about her waist and began running, half dragging her beside him as they splashed through puddles growing deeper on the sandy ground.

"I'm blinded by the rain," Lee-lee cried, wiping at her eyes, trying to free them of the wetness. "Can you even find your way back to the tent, Timothy?"

"Just stay beside me," he shouted. "I'll get you there."

Lee-lee tried to look about her, hearing the hard splashing of the rain and the crashing of the thunder. When a bright flash of lightning illuminated the landscape, she was able to see the full stretch of the valley, and what she saw caused her insides to freeze. The rain was fast settling into little rivers, filling up around the tents. People were scurrying from their dwellings and loading their wagons. It was evident that no one would be safe staying there. The small rivers being formed by the rain would soon blend in with the stream and become one larger body of water which would swallow up anything and anybody in its destructive path.

Lee-lee pointed. "Timothy, did you see . . . ?" she gasped.

"Yes," he said. "And we're the next to load our wagon, Lee-lee. It seems our prospecting days are over."

"You didn't want it to end like this," she cried. "You were so enjoying yourself."

"Darling, I had my fun. Now it's time to move on," he shouted, helping her down a steep incline, slipping and sliding as they moved on toward their own tent.

"You can leave this behind so easily after having

found that one gold nugget?"

"It was the adventure that I was seeking from the very beginning," he said. "Not gold. I had never thought for one minute that we might find gold."

"But we did . . ."

Timothy shrugged. "So we did," he said matter-of-factly. "And so we also lost it."

"And that doesn't make you sad?"

"It makes me mad as hell," he said. "But only because something was taken from me and I wasn't able to do one damn thing about it." He helped her into the tent, only to find pools of water already splashing around inside it.

"Timothy, everything is ruined," Lee-lee said, finding the water building around her knees as she struggled to back up out of the tent.

"The important thing is for us to save ourselves," Timothy yelled, helping her out and onto the wagon. He busied himself getting his horses attached then boarded the wagon and shouted to them, lifting a whip to each of their backs.

"Hahh!" he cried, feeling the wheels of the wagon spinning, unable to move forward in the thickening mud that was rolling in torrents down from the hills.

Lee-lee clung to the seat, trembling from the wetness, the cold, and the fear that they could be trapped in the valley. "Timothy, hurry!" she screamed. "I'm scared. The water is rising. It's overflowing the banks of the stream. We'll soon be trapped!"

"I'll get us out of here!" Timothy shouted back, blowing rain from his mouth as the heavy downpour continued, now even mixing with minute marbles of hail.

Lee-lee watched as the hail bounced from the horses' bodies and into the water at their feet. Lightning zigzagged across the sky, the thunder rumbled, and the wind began whipping the rain even harder against her face.

She held more tightly onto the seat, coughed and spit, then breathed a sigh of relief as Timothy finally managed to get the wagon rolling. She welcomed the bouncing motion, knowing that at least she was moving away from certain death. Looking about her in the brightness of continuing flashes of lightning, she saw many wagons stuck in the muddy mire and wanted to help rescue the poor *unfortunates*, but she knew that to stop now would mean that she and Timothy might join them in a watery grave.

She closed her eyes to the sadness and made a silent prayer that Timothy could continue to urge the horses onward, though they were showing their own fear in the wildness of their eyes and the constant nervous neighs and jerks of their heads.

Timothy followed the swollen stream to its most shallow spot and urged his horses into it. "Hang on!" he shouted to Lee-lee, tightening his hold on the reins.

He gritted his teeth as the rush of the water lapped at the wagon's wheels. But he silently thanked God for the layer of rocks at the bottom of the stream which enabled the horses to keep their footing and move onward until the other side was reached.

The rain slackened somewhat, and a few stars peeped out from behind the fast rolling clouds. But just as quickly the stars were gone and the rain began again.

"Get back there beneath the cover of the wagon!" Timothy gruffly ordered, nodding toward it. "Now, Lee-lee! Do as you're told."

Lee-lee looked through the rain at Timothy. She could see him shivering and water glistened on his massive chest as if on porcelain. She was worried about his welfare and didn't want to leave him to face the dangers alone.

"No," she said stubbornly. "I won't. I want to stay here with you."

Timothy wrapped the horses' reins around the fingers of his left hand and used his other to grasp Lee-lee's arm. "You do as you're told," he growled, trying to push her from the seat. "You're going to catch a cold. Get in the back and get into some dry things."

"You're as wet as I am," she said, brushing his hand aside. "Even more so. You've no shirt on. You didn't even have time to put your boots on."

"It doesn't matter about me," he argued. "I'm strong as an ox. You're just a woman. It's different for you."

Lee-lee's eyes sparkled with anger. She crossed her arms over her chest. "So I'm just a woman," she said, scowling. "The rain is wetter for me because I'm a woman? It's colder for me because I'm a woman? Why do you men always consider women to be weaklings? I have proven my strength in more ways than one."

"Oh, Lee-lee," Timothy groaned. "This is no time to argue over such nonsense. I'm only trying to get you to do what's best for you."

"I'd prefer to stay here with you," she said, leaning to twist the water from her skirt as the rain slowly subsided.

Timothy shouted at the horses and continued snapping their reins. "You're a stubborn one," he sighed.

A faint outline of the moon broke through the clouds overhead and the wind calmed to a gentle breeze. But the water continued rushing from the hills into the valleys, and it was several more hours before Lee-lee felt reasonably safe. Frogs began croaking, crickets chirped, and only a faint rumble of thunder could now be heard in the distance.

Timothy drew the horses to a halt at the peak of a hill and slouched over, coughing. He raked his fingers through his wet hair to straighten it, and he looked toward Lee-lee. A slow smile transformed his lips when he saw her complete disarray. Her hair was limp and hung across her shoulders in wet strands. Her breasts were clearly defined beneath her wet, clinging blouse, and her skirt hung down between her outspread legs, revealing their sensual, gentle curves.

"You're seductive as hell," he said, laughing throatily.

"What . . . ?" Lee-lee gasped. She looked down at herself and began giggling. "You call me seductive? Timothy, I'm as wet as a drowned church mouse and I know I'm as ugly."

"Marry me. Travel to New York with me," Timothy suddenly blurted.

Lee-lee's mouth opened. Her eyes grew wide and her heart began to race. "What . . . did . . . you say?" she gasped. "Surely I didn't hear right. Perhaps I have water in my ears, making what you said sound as if you . . . you just proposed to me."

Timothy chuckled. He reached and took Lee-lee's right

hand in his. He turned it palm up and traced her scar with his forefinger.

"Do you forget that I have branded you?" he said, now lifting her hand to his lips to place a soft kiss on the scar. "You are mine. It is only right that you should be my wife. Travel with me to New York, Lee-lee."

A slow blush rose to Lee-lee's cheeks. "Then I did hear you right?" she murmured. "You did ask me to marry you?"

"Yes. But first we would travel to New York. We would be married there."

Lee-lee's face shadowed. "Tak-Ming . . ." she blurted, remembering their shared plans to travel to New York together. She had told him so much about the city of New York—its glamour, its larger buildings, and the Chinese section of town that she had recently heard was populated even more heavily than the Chinatown of San Francisco. She knew that he was just as anxious to go there as she was.

Timothy's insides took on a strange numbness. He dropped her hand onto her lap. "Tak-Ming?" he said, trying to control his temper.

"*Ai,*" Lee-lee said innocently. "Tak-Ming and I had always planned to travel to New York together."

Timothy's face grew hot, his shoulder muscles corded tightly, and frustrated anger coiled inside him. He couldn't understand why . . . how Lee-lee could still be thinking of the handsome Chinaman. Timothy had to wonder this after spending so many passion-filled days and nights with her continuously professing her love for him. With a set jaw and racing pulse he flipped the horses' reins and sent them scurrying onward.

Lee-lee saw and heard Timothy's strained silence and didn't understand. "Timothy, what is it?" she asked, clinging to the seat as the wagon crashed in and out of muddy potholes on the ground. "What did I say? You . . . you are suddenly so quiet. Are you angry with me?"

"Poor timing," he mumbled. "I chose the wrong time to ask you."

He wouldn't let her know that she had given him the answer to his question without speaking the words. And he wouldn't let her know just how much her hesitation had told him. As soon as he got her safely to San Francisco, he would immediately board the *New Yorker* and drown the pain of losing her on the high seas.

"Timing?" she murmured. "What do you mean, Timothy?"

"I was a fool to ask you such a question while in such an unromantic setting," he said, casting her a set-featured glance. "There will be a better time . . . a better place."

"But, Timothy, I . . ."

Timothy frowned. "We must first concentrate on getting ourselves back to San Francisco before talking of anywhere else," he said dryly.

He wouldn't tell her that he had no intention of ever asking her that same idiot question again. He wouldn't give her the chance to make him feel the fool again.

"I see," Lee-lee said, studying Timothy in this new, unresponsive mood. Would she ever be able to understand him? First he proposed and then he didn't wish to talk about it. Perhaps he suddenly realized the wealth lost because of the stolen gold nugget. Perhaps that was clouding his thoughts of anything else.

"The gold nugget?" she murmured. "Are you bothered by its loss? Before you said you weren't. Have you had time to think about its value and its having been stolen, and is that why you . . . why you—"

Timothy interrupted her. His thick eyelashes were heavy over eyes dark with hurt pride. Because of this, he refused to look her way but instead kept a watchful eye on the hills and valleys that lay ahead.

"No. I'm not bothered by the loss of the gold," he said thickly. "My life is full of many losses. After a time . . . one gets used to it."

Chapter Twenty-Two

The journey back to San Francisco had been a long and tedious one, for they had not stopped to eat or sleep. Lee-lee hadn't understood why Timothy had been so determined to push the horses so hard. She had hoped that this drive to return to San Francisco so quickly was because he was anxious to bring up the subject of marriage again in a more appropriate setting. Perhaps he needed candles . . . wine.

The wagon creaked and swayed down Kearney Street. Lee-lee could feel eyes following Timothy and her, and she understood why. Both looked completely unkempt with their wrinkled clothes and tangled hair. Timothy was still barefoot, though he had slipped into a shirt.

Lee-lee's face burned from its steady exposure to the sun and her lips were partially cracked. She looked toward Timothy who had rarely spoken a word to her since they had left the raging storm behind them. He had accepted dried fruit when she had offered it to him, but their water supply had been depleted much too soon to counteract the problem of thirst.

"Timothy, I'm so glad we've reached San Francisco," she sighed. "It seemed to take forever."

"I'm sorry that it was less than pleasant for you," he said, casting her a sideways glance.

"It wasn't all that unpleasant. I was with you."

A nervous twitch began at Timothy's temple. He had wanted to believe that her feelings about him were sincere, but her mention of Tak-Ming had proven who was most important in her life.

"I'll take you immediately to your hotel," he said. "I'm sure you'll feel much better after you've bathed and changed into something more comfortable and cool."

"Timothy, maybe you didn't hear me," Lee-lee softly argued. "I said that our journey wasn't all that unpleasant. *Ai*, I am anxious for a bath and a change of clothes, but I'm not anxious to be away from you for even that length of time."

Timothy jerked his head and stared openly at her, confused. She still persisted in appearing to be in love with him. Why?

Then a thought struck him. Had this been her way of acquiring passage—*free* passage—for her and Tak-Ming to New York? First California . . . and now New York? Had this been her sole purpose from the very beginning for being with him? Was Lee-lee a Cathalina Unser all over again? Had he been played for a fool once more? Well, he wouldn't give her a chance to do it again.

Drawing the covered wagon to a halt in front of the Missouri Hotel, Timothy nodded toward it. "Here you are," he said blandly. "I'd walk you to your room, but I don't believe it's wise to leave these horses untended.

They're on the jumpy side from the long journey."

Lee-lee scooted across the seat and kissed Timothy on the cheek. "That's all right," she said. "I understand. I'll hurry on. Will you be long?"

Timothy's face shadowed, understanding her meaning, yet refusing to reveal his true intentions to her. "No. I won't be long," he said dryly.

Not having been able to salvage anything other than what had been left in the wagon, Lee-lee had only her purse and a small bundle of clothes to grab from beneath the seat. And once this was done, she hopped from the wagon and smiled warmly up at Timothy.

"I'll be waiting for you, darling," she said. "Please don't be long. We've much to talk about."

"I'll do the best I can," Timothy grumbled, taking a long look at her, knowing that it would be his last.

Lee-lee swung around and hurried inside the hotel, wanting to get to the privacy of her room as quickly as possible. She was becoming more embarrassed by the minute as her appearance drew distasteful looks from the crowd. She only stopped long enough at the front desk to order a tub of hot, sudsy water for her room.

Finally enjoying her bath, Lee-lee splashed water onto her breasts and shoulders, sighing lethargically. She slipped farther down into the water and rested her head against the wooden tub, staring dreamily into space. Soon Timothy would come to her and their wedding plans would be set. Then she would have the chore of telling Tak-Ming the news.

But it shouldn't be that hard, now that he knew of her infatuation with Timothy. Tak-Ming had found out when she had announced that she was going to be gone with Timothy for several days on an adventurous search for gold.

Lee-lee grimaced even now when she remembered the look on Tak-Ming's face when she had told him. It was a look quite unfamiliar to her, and she doubted if she would ever understand why her plans to travel with Timothy had affected Tak-Ming in such a strange way.

"But I must succeed at talking him into traveling with me to New York," she whispered. "Tak-Ming needs me. He doesn't have the talent to deal with Americans as Americans do. They will take advantage of his honesty . . . his innocence."

Her devotion to Tak-Ming was deep rooted and she would not desert him. He was good with his hands but nothing else. Yet he did have his own ship again. Would he give it up to travel on Timothy's *New Yorker*?

Rising from the tub, Lee-lee grabbed a towel and stepped out onto a braided rug. "How can I manage this?" she murmured. "What if Tak-Ming refuses to travel with me? How can I explain to him the dangers of staying here alone in San Francisco without me?"

Wrapping the towel around her, flipping her damp hair to hang down her back, Lee-lee strolled casually to the window and looked toward the bay. From habit she immediately searched for Timothy's ship, having always been able in the past to single it out within a matter of moments.

Her eyes moved slowly from ship to ship, smiling, knowing Timothy's should be the next in her line of vision. Then a coldness encompassed her as she saw the

341

gaping void where Timothy's ship should be. Frantically, she stepped closer to the window and once more let her gaze move from ship to ship, yet she was unable to find the *New Yorker*.

Her hands went to her throat. Her heart pounded. "Where . . . where is his ship?" she gasped, a slow panic rising inside her. "Why isn't it there?"

Then a splash of white sails farther out at sea grabbed her attention, and she noted the size of the ship and its bold, black hull.

Laughing awkwardly, Lee-lee shook her head slowly back and forth. "I'm being foolish," she said. "That can't be Timothy's ship. Timothy wouldn't be leaving San Francisco. He will be here to see me. And soon."

She forced herself to read the fancy white letters painted on the side of the ship and the name *New Yorker* quickly became blurred as tears fell from her eyes.

"Why, Timothy?" she softly cried. "Why?"

She whirled around, covering her eyes with her hands. Perhaps if she didn't see . . . it would not be true. But she knew that it was true enough and she felt not only betrayed, but empty.

Thoughts of Timothy kissing her and touching her began to plague her every thinking moment. He had seemed sincere enough, yet he was now gone. She had been used again and in the worst way possible—by the man she loved.

Despair suddenly changed to anger. Lee-lee doubled her fists to her sides and once more looked from the window toward Timothy's departing ship. "I don't need you," she said bitterly. "My life will not be altered by the

likes of you. I will do as I planned. I will go to New York.
Tak-Ming will take me on *his* ship."

Determination spurred her next moves. She dressed,
packed her valise, then rushed from the hotel. She was
glad that Tak-Ming had chosen to take their chest of
silver to hide on his ship, for now to have to bother with it
would only slow her down.

Attired in a high-necked, coarse cotton dress only
slightly gathered at the waist, and with her hair hanging
loose and free around her shoulders, Lee-lee shoved and
pushed her way through the crowded city streets.
Carrying her valise, she looked straight ahead, ignoring
all that went on about her. Her thoughts were on Tak-
Ming and his new clipper schooner. What if the ship
wasn't quite ready for sailing? Lee-lee had the desperate
need to leave now. She wanted to leave San Francisco and
her memories behind her and get on with her life.

New York. Soon she would be home. She would see the
fate of her father's shipbuilding firm and the magnificent
mansion in Washington Square.

"But I will only be heartbroken again by this," she
thought sadly to herself. It seemed to her that life had
never been fair to her—first in her childhood and now as
a woman.

The dampness from the bay was in the breeze, and left
a trace of salt water on Lee-lee's lips. She hurried onto a
pier and made her way around coiled ropes and stacks of
shipping crates, paying no attention to the stares from
the men who were laboring there. Her destination was
Tak-Ming's ship, and she wasn't going to let anything or
anybody stop her. She only hoped that Tak-Ming's ship

was in good repair now and was sturdy enough to make the long, hard voyage to New York.

"He's got to understand," she worried aloud. "I must get to New York. I must."

A part of her knew that she wanted to do so in order to follow Timothy, yet a part of her didn't want to believe that she was so weak. But she knew that no matter how hard she tried to hate Timothy, she couldn't. He hadn't only branded her hand, but her heart as well.

Tak-Ming's three-masted clipper schooner finally came into view. It was easy enough to single out from the others. Tak-Ming had painted its hull a cheerful crimson color. Once more he had chosen to use the name the *Sea Goddess*, and its gold, bold letters gleamed back at Lee-lee from the side of the ship.

Feeling dwarfed in the ship's powerful shadow, Lee-lee's confidence in its ability to travel safely to New York grew boundless. No ship as large or as beautiful could fail in its mission. And carrying this thought with her, Lee-lee hurriedly boarded the ship and began her search for Tak-Ming.

The crew was a rowdy bunch, and, not knowing who Lee-lee was, gave her some uncomfortable moments until she rushed down the companion ladder and began tapping on closed doors that led to separate cabins along the dark passageway one deck above the hold of the ship.

"Tak-Ming," she whispered softly as she continued knocking on the doors. "Where are you? I must talk to you at once."

The ship smelled of fresh lumber and paint. Lee-lee now regretted that she hadn't shown enough interest to come and see it earlier. But she had stayed close by her hotel room, waiting for Timothy. She felt guilty that she had let Timothy take precedence over Tak-Ming, when all along Tak-Ming was still the only one she could depend on.

Lee-lee began to feel panicky. So far it seemed that no matter how many doors she knocked on, she still could not find Tak-Ming. And so unruly and nasty mouthed had the sailors been on topdeck that she refused to ask any of them about Tak-Ming's whereabouts. It was his ship. He had to be found somewhere!

At the far end of the passageway, a whale oil lamp offered Lee-lee some relief as she stepped up to the only door left for her to investigate. She raised her hand, but something compelled her to refrain from knocking. So far, that approach had failed her. This time she would just open the door and see for herself what this particular cabin held. Surely it would do no harm. It was probably as uninhabited as the others. Tak-Ming was probably in the hold of his ship, busy at work. Why hadn't she thought of it before?

Lowering her hand, she placed it on the doorknob and slowly began to turn it. And as the door noiselessly opened, Lee-lee's face flamed with color as her gaze settled on the coupling figures on the bed across the cabin from where she stood.

The cabin was brightly lighted by colorful lanterns and with one glance Lee-lee had recognized the man, though all she could see was his back as he skillfully made love to the beautiful Chinese lady beneath him.

It was definitely Tak-Ming, with his hair in its usual

braided queue down his back. But it was his powerful, naked physique that captured Lee-lee's fullest attention, and the strength with which he was thrusting himself inside the moaning lady. Never before had Lee-lee witnessed anything as erotic, and she couldn't help but be totally embarrassed and ashamed at having entered this cabin without first knocking. And who was this beautiful lady in Tak-Ming's arms? He hadn't mentioned becoming involved.

Lee-lee began to creep backward from the doorway, hoping to succeed at leaving without being discovered. Tak-Ming and his lady friend were so carried away in the throes of passion that it seemed nothing or no one could cause their minds to wander from the blissful culmination they appeared to be nearing. But in her desperation to be gone, Lee-lee clumsily tripped over her own feet and fell against the door, banging it noisily back against the wall.

Gasping, Lee-lee covered her mouth with her hands, wanting to die when Tak-Ming jerked his head around and saw her. His almond-shaped eyes wavered. He jerked a *beiwu* quickly over and around him, then rolled away from the Chinese lady and reached for a robe. He slipped it over his shoulders then rose from the bed, holding the robe closed in front as he faced Lee-lee.

"I'm sorry, Tak-Ming," she murmured, trembling. She glanced toward the beautiful, petite lady on the bed, whose eyes showed fear and distrust as she stared back at Lee-lee.

Then Lee-lee again directed her attention at Tak-Ming who still hadn't spoken but whose eyes were accusing and his jaw and lips were set hard with anger.

"Say something, Tak-Ming," Lee-lee said, swallowing hard. "Don't just stand there glaring at me. I said that I was sorry."

Tak-Ming took a step toward her, his arms folded angrily across his chest. He noticed her valise at her side and wondered about it. Had the American disappointed her in his ways of making love? Had Lee-lee discovered that her heart was too full of love for Tak-Ming to deny the fact any longer? It made a gnawing begin in his loins to think of the possibilities.

But even so, if she had decided to come to him to finally profess her love for him, it was too late. Eaten up by jealousy and hurt when Lee-lee had left with the American, Tak-Ming had hurriedly married the beautiful Koo-See to end his lonely nights in bed.

Frustrated and confused, Lee-lee took a step toward Tak-Ming. She reached her free hand toward him. "Tak-Ming, why don't you say something?" she said with a touch of desperation in her voice. "Are you so angry with me that you can't even talk?"

"*Nay*," Tak-Ming quickly grumbled. "I am not angry. But I am full of wonder. Why have you come? And why are you carrying your travel valise? Did you not enjoy being in the company of the American?"

Lee-lee's heart ached, missing Timothy so and wondering why he had left her. But she couldn't let Tak-Ming know that she had been betrayed. Somehow she knew that Tak-Ming would respect her less. Thus far he had looked upon her as a strong, willful woman—one of high spirit. There was no way that she could disclose to him that she had been used and discarded so cruelly.

"*Nay*, I did not enjoy being with the American," she scoffed, jerking her head insolently as she spoke. "In fact, Tak-Ming, I want to leave San Francisco far behind me. I wish now to travel to New York if it is at all possible for your ship to make such a journey at this time. Is it ready for sailing? Could we leave today?"

Her heart pounded, eagerly awaiting his reply. Yet even in her anxious state to be gone from San Francisco, her eyes couldn't stop occasionally straying to the Chinese lady who was still staring back at her from the bed.

Suspicious of Lee-lee's need for a hasty departure from San Francisco, Tak-Ming didn't give her an answer. Instead, he gestured toward Koo-See. "When we begin our journey to New York, we will have company, Lee-lee," he said, turning his eyes to his wife of only a few days.

He didn't yet love Koo-See as a man should his wife, but he would learn. She was not only beautiful but sweet as well.

He smiled warmly toward Koo-See. "My wife, Koo-See, will accompany us to New York," he said, pride thick in his voice. Then he spoke in Chinese to Koo-See. "Koo-See, this is Lee-lee, the adopted sister that I've told you about."

Lee-lee's breath caught in her throat. She was suddenly strangely dizzy, stunned by Tak-Ming's confession. Lee-lee had thought this lady to be a paid companion of which there were many on the streets of San Francisco. But never would she have suspected that she was Tak-Ming's wife!

"Your wife, Tak-Ming?" she finally said, watching as Koo-See pulled the silk *beiwu* around her and rose delicately from the bed to bow humbly toward Lee-lee.

Tak-Ming went to stand beside Koo-See and draped his arm about her waist. "*Ai*, my wife," he said.

Lee-lee looked more slowly at Koo-See. She was typically Chinese with her dark, almond-shaped eyes, delicate facial features, and sleek, black hair which now hung loose over her shoulders.

Ai, Koo-See was the type that Tak-Ming would choose for a wife, Lee-lee thought to herself. She was fragile in appearance, tiny, and seemed to be bashful, since she had yet to speak one word to Lee-lee or Tak-Ming while in Lee-lee's presence.

Lee-lee laughed softly. "I guess congratulations are in order," she said.

She went to Koo-See and bowed before her. "And I'm pleased to make your acquaintance," she said in Chinese, rising to meet Koo-See's steady stare and slow smile.

Then she gave Tak-Ming a long, thoughtful look. "I can't believe you're married, Tak-Ming," she murmured. "It seems so . . . so . . . sudden."

Tak-Ming avoided her eyes. He walked away from her, gathering up his clothes. "Her Chinese family was separated from her on their voyage to America. She had been taken in by an American family and she was being treated badly by them," he growled. He swung around and faced Lee-lee with anger flashing in his eyes. "She was being treated as even less than a serving woman. She was a slave. And the lord of the American house was using her . . . forcing her . . . to . . ."

Once more he placed his back to Lee-lee and hung his head. "I took her away from all of that," he said. "I paid many silver dollars for her. Then I decided it best to marry her since she was already mine anyway."

"How noble," Lee-lee said in a soft whisper. She hurried to Tak-Ming and moved into his embrace, hugging him tightly. She placed her cheek on his chest of steel. "You are a wise and noble Chinaman and I love you so very much, Tak-Ming."

Tak-Ming slowly stole an arm about her. He hadn't lost her, but ironically, she had lost him. He gave her a kiss that only spoke of affection then broke free of her and went to gaze from a porthole. "Your wish to travel soon to New York will be granted," he said hoarsely. "The ship and the crew are ready."

"They are?" Lee-lee asked, stunned.

Tak-Ming watched the sparkle of waves across the bay. "Had you not returned when you did you would have found me already gone," he said, fearing to face Lee-lee and see her response.

"Tak-Ming, you wouldn't have," Lee-lee gasped, paling. "You would have left me behind?"

Turning slowly on a heel, he gave her a pensive stare. "You had chosen to be with the American," he accused. "You didn't need me—a Chinaman—any longer."

Lee-lee was so stunned, she couldn't move. "Tak-Ming, we've been over these feelings before. I've told you many times how much you mean to me. And to think that you could leave me so easily. It was I who was worrying about you . . . never thinking to completely separate myself from you . . ."

Tak-Ming's eyes lowered. "*Ai*, I do remember a similar conversation. And it was then that I told you that I would never doubt you again."

"And still you have, Tak-Ming. You have doubted my devotion to you. I do not understand."

Tak-Ming cast her a hurtful glance. "It is all because of the American," he mumbled. "If not for him . . ."

Lee-lee placed her valise on a chair and went to clasp Tak-Ming's hands. "Shh," she said. "Let's not talk of it any more. We are together. That's all that matters."

"And you will accept Koo-See as a part of us?" Tak-Ming asked, smiling toward his wife.

"*Ai*," Lee-lee said. "And why wouldn't I? If you love her, so shall I."

Tak-Ming laughed gaily and drew away from Lee-lee to once more gather his clothes up into his arms. "We will soon set sail," he said. "I will take you to New York. My newest ship is a great ship and will proudly travel the seas with its lily-white canvases filled to their fullest."

Then a frown creased Tak-Ming's brow. "Even the Cape of Storms will not be a threat to my beautiful *Sea Goddess*," he vowed.

"Cape of Storms?" Lee-lee asked, hearing his voice trying to hide his true feelings behind its sternness.

"*Ai*," Tak-Ming said darkly. "Cape Horn. It lies at the tip of South America. I hear it's a rock fourteen hundred feet high, jutting out of the end of South America to divide the Atlantic and Pacific Oceans."

"But what of it, Tak-Ming?"

"I've been told the winds are violent there, nearly

always blowing from the west, hurling the sea against the ships that try to pass from the Atlantic to the Pacific, or from the Pacific to the Atlantic."

"Is there a real danger in traveling there?" Lee-lee asked, trying not to show the fear that was rising inside her as she recalled her other unlucky voyages at sea.

"*Ai*, the dangers are real enough," Tak-Ming said, visibly shuddering.

"Then go another way, Tak-Ming."

"*Nay*. There is only one way. And it will be the way of the Cape of Storms."

Part Three

New York

Chapter Twenty-Three

Thus far the voyage had been a tame one. By night Lee-lee had slept soundly in the comforts of her private cabin and by day she had spent much time on topdeck, enjoying the perfumed breezes that unfailingly filled the ship's sails. It was on such a day that Lee-lee was strolling casually alongside Koo-See on topdeck, when luck seemed suddenly to reverse itself.

The sky was brilliantly blue and the sun a blessing after the cold hours of the night. Attired in a highly gathered, soft cotton dress of pastel flowers on a white background with puffed sleeves and high collar, Lee-lee felt truly American next to Koo-See with her genuine Chinese attire. Koo-See's red silk dress, gaily embroidered in brighter reds, clung to her every curve, and her feet were adorned in satin slippers.

Koo-See's black hair was fancily designed upon a headdress, and Lee-lee's hair—which had shed its Chinese dye and was now her true color red—blew long and loose in the breeze.

Lee-lee gestured with a hand as she bent to speak into

355

Koo-See's beautiful face. "The word 'sky.' It's easy enough to say in English Say, 'The sky is lovely today.'"

Lee-lee had enjoyed having something to do to help pass the days more quickly. Teaching Koo-See how to speak in English had been a saving grace for her, enabling her at least for a while to place Timothy from her mind.

In a quiet, chirping sort of voice, Koo-See attempted to follow Lee-lee's instruction. "Sky," she said almost too softly. "The . . . sky . . . is . . . is . . ."

She frowned up at Lee-lee, sad that she wasn't an apt enough student for her newest, dearest friend, Lee-lee. But the word "lovely" was a difficult one to say! Her tongue seemed endlessly to get in the way!

"L-o-v-e-l-y," Lee-lee repeated, mouthing the word very slowly as she spoke it. "It should be easy enough for you to say, Koo-See, because it describes you."

Koo-See blushed and humbly lowered her eyes, knowing that a compliment had, indeed, just been paid her. And this made her more determined than ever to speak like an American.

She lifted her chin and straightened her back proudly. Licking her lips, she prepared herself to try once more to please Lee-lee, which in turn would please Tak-Ming. These two were strangely close. Koo-See was trying hard not to let jealousy enter her heart.

"The sky . . . is . . . l-o-v-e-l-y," she said, breathless as she awaited Lee-lee's response.

Lee-lee threw her head back and laughed heartily, jubilant over Koo-See's success at finally saying the one word that had seemed to be the hardest of all they had attempted at this point in her lessons.

She sobered and took both of Koo-See's hands to squeeze them affectionately. "You see? You can do it, Koo-See. It just takes a strong will and much practice. Soon you will be speaking as clearly as I."

Again Koo-See blushed. "*Nay*," she murmured. "*Nay. Nay.*"

Tak-Ming, in his embroidered silks, came and positioned himself between Lee-lee and Koo-See. He placed an arm about each of their waists and gazed out to sea. "The Cape draws near," he said.

He looked from Koo-See to Lee-lee. "And when it does, I want you both below deck. You stay together in one cabin and if the waves get strong, tie yourselves to something to keep yourselves from being tossed about too severely."

"You fear it so much, Tak-Ming?" Lee-lee asked, having heard it in his voice.

"I do not wish to, but one must be realistic about these things, and the Cape of Storms gives reasons to be plagued by fear."

"But your ship is strong."

"Even strong ships have been known to be beaten by the Cape of Storms," Tak-Ming grumbled. He looked around and toward the crew. "Look into the crew's eyes. Look upon their faces. They have heard many tales of ships lost at sea. And they know that the Cape of Storms never lets a ship pass without a fight. That's what they all have been talking about these last few days. It never leaves their minds."

Even as Tak-Ming talked, the sky began to change its

colors. Piles of rolling altocumulus clouds were forming on the horizon and the sky overhead was fast changing to a peculiar yellow color.

Lee-lee tensed as her breathing became shallow, quite aware of the changes about her. The wind had abandoned the sails, leaving them lifeless, and everything—even the crew—had become eerily, mutely quiet.

"Just as I feared," Tak-Ming said, shielding his eyes with the back of a hand as he followed the clouds now blowing overhead. They had darkened the sky, making the day appear as night. There were vivid flashes of lightning which danced from cloud to cloud and such crashes of thunder as seemed capable of bursting creation.

The winds once more were with them, howling. A great rush of rain began to fall, turning the ocean white with spume. The forecastle and aftercastle of the *Sea Goddess* began to groan, laboring, and the masts nodded and swayed and bent, and Tak-Ming began to doubt that the clumsy rope cordage of the shrouds were sufficient for the strain.

He gave Lee-lee and Koo-See a gentle shove. "Hurry below!" he shouted. "And remember to do as you were told. Secure yourselves tightly with ropes!"

Paling from fear, Lee-lee grabbed Koo-See by the hand and together they fled down the companion ladder, already being tossed about as the *Sea Goddess* tumbled beneath the awful shock of the waves swelling around it and beating incessantly against the bulwarks.

Lee-lee flinched when she heard Tak-Ming shouting at his crew, like the roar of the storm himself. She glanced quickly upward and saw the sails large and spread out as the tempest raged with ever increasing fury. Lurid lightning flashes lit up the sky and sea, and wild shouts sounded from the deck.

Unable to stop her nervous tremors, Lee-lee guided Koo-See down the ladder, and when Lee-lee's cabin was reached, she half dragged Koo-See inside.

Lee-lee looked frantically about, wondering what rope she could use to secure her and Koo-See from the furious tossing of the ship.

Then she stopped to think of the foolishness of being tied up should the ship begin to sink. If they were tied up, they might possibly sink to the bottom of the sea along with the *Sea Goddess*. She remembered the two other times that she had been on board a sinking ship and knew to stay alert and be ready . . . to . . . run!

"If I get out of this alive, I will never travel by sea again," she vowed softly, gathering together her clothes and the satin-covered box in which lay her necklace. Hurriedly, she placed these inside her valise and chose a wall to huddle against.

"Koo-See, come with me," she ordered, pulling the terrified Chinese beauty down beside her. "We will be all right. Come on. We shall sit here and wait until the storm passes."

Lee-lee placed one arm about Koo-See's shoulder and with the other clung to her valise. It was all that she had, all that she could call her own. She tucked it under an arm and held tightly to it, hearing Koo-See's whimpers as the Chinese girl softly wept into her hands.

Then Lee-lee became more aware of the crash of water

and the creak of ropes as the ship lurched, heaved, and pitched. The wind shrieked. In huge right-to-left blows it hit the ship. And as the swells grew higher, Lee-lee could tell that the ship was threatening to roll over, for she was thrown away from Koo-See to the opposite side of the cabin. When she landed, her head hit the wall with a bang and everything began to spin crazily, until suddenly she saw nothing . . . felt nothing . . . heard nothing.

Timothy stood on the pier looking up at the black hull of his ship. Cape Horn had almost won this time. The storms had been the fiercest of all the times the *New Yorker* had ventured around it. The carpenters were now busy stuffing caulking by the handfuls into opened seams. This was the first time that the *New Yorker* would have to stay moored for a questionable length of time for repairs. Timothy already felt restless, and he had only been in New York for one day.

Seeing another ship edging its way between the *New Yorker* and another ship, Timothy recognized it as one of his company's other ships, the *Bronze Lady*. It had also been moored at San Francisco's busy seaport with its delivery of tobacco.

Frowning, Timothy lifted his silk top hat and raked his fingers nervously through his hair. From the look of the *Bronze Lady*'s torn sails, it had had its own bout of bad luck on the voyage home. He began walking toward the *Bronze Lady* after its anchor was dropped and the gangplank spread out to the pier. He quickly boarded it then froze in his steps when he saw a familiar figure just stepping up on deck from the companion ladder.

"Tak-Ming . . ." he gasped to himself. "Tak-Ming and . . . his chest of silver."

Timothy stepped out of sight behind the mainmast, hoping Tak-Ming hadn't seen him. Breathless, he watched as Lee-lee followed along behind Tak-Ming, and then came many others unfamiliar to Timothy.

With an ache swelling inside him, Timothy watched further as Lee-lee, carrying her valise, left the ship with Tak-Ming and the others.

"So they managed to ride one of my ships after all," Timothy grumbled.

He went to the ship's railing and leaned over it, seeing that Lee-lee's hair was now the color of fiery flames. Her cotton dress clung to her voluptuous curves as the sea breeze whipped it snugly against her. Then Timothy noticed something else which numbed his insides with a trace of fear. Lee-lee's walk wasn't steady and her steps were uncoordinated.

"Got a glimpse of our passengers, eh?" Captain Wilson said as he moved to Timothy's side.

Lee-lee was now out of Timothy's sight, a part of the crowded pier. He glanced over at Captain Wilson, seeing exhaustion in his pale gray eyes and deeply-lined face. "How is it that you agreed to bring those people to New York on the *Bronze Lady*?" he asked, trying not to reveal his anxieties about Lee-lee, and why she hadn't appeared to be her normal, healthy self.

"Didn't have much choice, Timothy."

"No choice?" Timothy asked, raising an eyebrow quizzically. "Since when do you not have a say as to which passengers do or do not travel on the *Bronze Lady*?"

"When the passengers board the ship in mid-ocean," Captain Wilson growled.

"Mid-ocean . . . ?"

"Aye. I rescued this bunch at sea, right past the Cape."

Timothy turned on a heel and stared disbelievingly at Captain Wilson, whose navy blue suit was wrinkled and whose ruddy complexion was even less desirable, with a fresh growth of whiskers blackening his face. "My God," he gasped. "What are you saying?"

"We found two longboat loads of 'em floating aimlessly about, right past the stormy waters of the Cape."

"How did they get there?"

"I didn't get many answers. But I did find out that it was a ship named the *Sea Goddess* that sank."

"*Sea Goddess*?"

"Aye. That was the name, all right. But that's about all I know. They weren't a talkative lot. So I gave them space in the hold. Seemed that was the best place for 'em."

Timothy paled, knowing the conditions of the hold of any ship—even his own.

He turned his head away from the captain, envisioning Lee-lee hidden away in the dark, smelly confines of the hold, crowded together with what appeared to have been at least a dozen other survivors of the ill-fated ship. And *Sea Goddess*? Why on earth had Tak-Ming named his next ship the same as the one that had sunk in the East China Sea? Surely that had cast a spell of doom over it from the first.

Yes. This ship that had also sunk must have been the ship that Tak-Ming had purchased and had been in the process of repairing in San Francisco. Fool that he was, he had thought himself skilled enough to rebuild a ship and make it strong enough to round the Cape.

But fool or not, Tak-Ming was the one who solely possessed Lee-lee. An ache circled his heart. Lee-lee. He had to know what had caused Lee-lee not to appear at all well.

"I would've given a day's pay to have had the redhead with me for even an hour in my bunk, but she wouldn't separate herself from the Chinaman. I guess she saves it for him, eh, Timothy?" Captain Wilson said, chuckling.

Timothy circled his hands into tight fists at his side, angry at the captain's desire for Lee-lee and at Lee-lee's continued show of feelings for the handsome Chinaman.

"But maybe it was her injury that caused her to be so stand-offish," Captain Wilson said, shrugging. "I guess she must've had a king-sized headache."

"Injury? Headache?"

"She was suffering from a head injury. Seems she hit her head durin' the storm. But she wasn't unconscious when we found her in the longboat."

Timothy gritted his teeth from anger, and his eyes darkened. "And knowing she was unwell, you still placed her in the hold?" he growled.

"Aye, I did. She seemed well enough. She clung to that damn travel bag of hers like it was made of gold, so I knew she had not been hurt bad enough to be unable to think right," Captain Wilson said, kneading his whiskers. "And why is it any concern of yours? You act as though you know her. Do you?"

"Yes. I know her," Timothy said, turning to once more circle his fingers around the ship's rail. His gaze swept over the throngs of people, searching for the blaze of her hair. Though she had chosen Tak-Ming over him, Timothy couldn't bear to think of her searching for a place to live and possibly having to live with riffraff.

"You know her?" Captain Wilson gasped.

"Yes. And, Wilson, see to it that someone gets out there on that pier, finds her, and gives quick assistance to her—guides her to a desirable hotel."

"But, Timothy—"

Timothy glowered toward the captain. "Do as you are told," he flatly ordered.

"What you don't know is that the Chinaman said something about Chinatown," Captain Wilson grumbled. "Now, do you still want me to send someone after her? She's with the Chinaman. That's very obvious, or don't you know her well enough to know that?"

Timothy's heart sank. He avoided the captain's eyes and strolled quickly away from him.

"Do I or don't I send someone after her?" Captain Wilson shouted after Timothy.

"Hell, no!" Timothy shouted back.

Then he stopped and turned slowly back to face Captain Wilson. "But make sure that she's followed to see that she's all right," he said, reconsidering, knowing that he wouldn't be able to live with himself if he didn't know that she was being taken care of properly.

He lowered his eyes as he slowly turned once more to walk away from the captain. "Then report back to me," he said from across his shoulder.

He hung his head, almost doubled over with the pain of missing Lee-lee, yet hating her for the agony she was causing him.

Chapter Twenty=Four

With eager fingers, Lee-lee positioned her new flower-bedecked hat onto her upswept coil of hair, feeling scornful eyes on her as she dressed to go in search of a hotel in which to make her residence. Swinging around, causing her many layers of fine silk petticoats to rustle luxuriously beneath her long-sleeved, green satin dress, Lee-lee gave Tak-Ming a small, nervous smile.

"You still don't understand, do you, Tak-Ming?"

Tak-Ming deliberately turned his back to her and lifted a yellowed lace curtain at a drably dirty second story window. "Nay," he growled. "This city is too large for you to decide to live alone in it, away from my protection."

"But, Tak-Ming, I didn't travel all the way from China just to place myself in the same sort of environment," she argued softly, smoothing her gloves on, a finger at a time. "This section of city—New York's Chinatown—is too much a reminder of my years in Foochow. I want to live totally as an American. And I can only do so by finding myself a place of residence elsewhere."

Her gaze swept the shabby, one-room apartment. Only black-lacquered screens divided the sleeping areas from the eating area. Not only had it unnerved Lee-lee to hear the sensual moans at night being exchanged between Koo-See and Tak-Ming in the throes of passion, but it had embarrassed her as well.

This one drab room had been the only space available in Chinatown on the day they arrived in New York. It was a room with only one window, which meant that darkness prevailed both day and night. The walls were covered with peeling, faded wallpaper, and the furnishings were odds and ends of pieces of upholstered chairs and wobbly, chipped tables. There was only one kerosene lamp which emitted a horrible odor along with its pale, faded light.

"Is it this place that you run from or do you leave today in search of more than a place of residence for yourself? Do you intend to find the American businessman, Timothy Hendricks?" Tak-Ming growled, turning on a heel to face Lee-lee.

His gaze roamed disapprovingly over her, seeing her newly purchased, low-bodiced dress with its touch of velvet twisted decoratively at the fully-gathered waist and at the cuff of her sleeves. He hadn't begrudged her the money to buy appropriate attire for the streets of this fancy city, but he didn't wish to think that she had purchased such lovely dresses with only the American businessman in mind.

Upon leaving the *Bronze Lady*, Tak-Ming had seen the *New Yorker* moored at the quay. Lee-lee hadn't mentioned seeing it, but surely she had and was this day going in search of the man who she professed to loathe, not love.

Lee-lee heard the bitterness in Tak-Ming's voice, which also seemed to carry a trace of jealousy, and this she did not understand.

She glanced over at Koo-See just as she stepped from behind a screen, a vision of petite loveliness in her high-necked, embroidered silk dress the color of lilacs. Her petiteness was only marred by the obvious swell of her abdomen, where she now proudly carried her and Tak-Ming's first child.

Had Koo-See also heard the jealousy in Tak-Ming's voice? Had this drawn her from her own private corner of the room?

As of late, Lee-lee had felt the complete awkwardness of the three of them being so close in the small quarters of the room.

"*Nay*," she finally said, lifting her chin in defense of Tak-Ming's accusations. "Timothy Hendricks is not on my mind. It is as I have told you. I want to go in search of a hotel in which to make residence."

She now knew that Tak-Ming had also seen the *New Yorker* that first day in New York. Strange that he hadn't mentioned it earlier. It would have been so easy for him to accuse her of wanting to travel to New York to follow its owner.

Lee-lee lowered her eyes to Koo-See, who was now clinging possessively to Tak-Ming's arm. "You and your wife need privacy," she quickly added. "And soon you will need the extra space for your first-born."

Her gaze lifted and she looked warmly into Tak-Ming's bold, dark, almond-shaped eyes. He was so handsome in his pale green embroidered robe with its full sleeves and high neck. "And, Tak-Ming, I've come to New York to be near my past," she said. "I must go today to see where my father's shipbuilding empire began, and I also want to see my . . . my . . . childhood home."

"Your headaches? They are gone, Lee-lee? You feel like traveling alone?"

She laughed lightly. "*Ai*. The wound to my head was only a minor one. You know that nothing keeps me down for long. You, above anyone else, should know my strengths and weaknesses."

"You will feel safe enough while traveling unescorted on the streets of New York?"

"This is not Foochow, Tak-Ming, as you saw while escorting me shopping the other day. Many women travel alone safely."

"I still wish that you would reconsider leaving us to make residence elsewhere," he grumbled. "Soon I will find a more spacious dwelling. I am even now talking business with a new Chinese acquaintance of mine who is willing to sell me his restaurant. Above the restaurant there are many rooms. I will make them as lovely in decor as the House of Yeung, Lee-lee. And my Chinese restaurant will be the best in the whole city of New York. Surely you want to be a part of all these plans."

Lee-lee's face flushed darkly in her frustration. "Tak-Ming, still you don't understand," she sighed. She went to him and framed his face between her hands. "I'm going to live as an American now that I am free to do so. But I will return to visit you and Koo-See. Often."

Tak-Ming brushed her hands aside. "I should have left my newest *Sea Goddess* moored at the San Francisco seaport," he grumbled. "Now that I didn't, I have not only lost it but you as well."

"Oh, Tak-Ming," Lee-lee sighed heavily. "You haven't lost me. I'll return."

"We shall see," Tak-Ming said thickly.

"Please, Tak-Ming," Lee-lee argued softly, dropping her hands to her side. "Please resign yourself to the fact that I must do what I must."

"Lee-lee, there will be no third *Sea Goddess*. We are in New York to stay. So I guess I will have to learn to accept the bad as well as the good in my life."

"We are lucky to be alive, Tak-Ming," Lee-lee said, picking up her velvet purse which matched the trim of her dress. "You were saved twice from the cruelties of the sea, while I have been rescued three times. I doubt, Tak-Ming, that I shall ever venture on board any ships in the future. It seems that tragedies at sea follow me wherever I go."

Tak-Ming's eyes wavered. "I feel a fool for failing you twice, Lee-lee, while I was in command of a ship. My skills are lacking, it seems, in most everything I try. Perhaps my father and five brothers were right for calling me half-wit behind my back."

Lee-lee's heart ached for Tak-Ming, and she would have eased herself into his arms to console him, but she knew that for now such embraces should be avoided. And she smiled to herself when Koo-See took her place, hugging Tak-Ming while speaking in Chinese to him, softly scolding him for doubting his worth.

Backing up toward the door, Lee-lee was consumed by a strange loneliness when she saw Tak-Ming bend his head to kiss Koo-See's words away. Lee-lee felt the void as an empty ache in the pit of her stomach, for she starved for such sweet embraces and kisses from the man she loved. Did Timothy ever think or dream about her and their passionate moments together? She couldn't believe that he could have put her from his mind so easily. It hadn't been that easy for her, though so often she had tried to will herself to hate him.

Fleeing down the one flight of stairs to the street, Lee-lee was swept up into a world of Chinese, and had she not known where she was, she would have thought she had been unknowingly transported back to Foochow.

It was a cool day in late September. Street vendors with their open-ended food shops displaying their China-made wares, poultry, and fish were scattered along the walks. Beautifully-colored lanterns swayed on ropes that had been strung from street lamp to street lamp, and a pagoda stood elegantly tall with its many, colorfully bright roofs curving upward, and it glistened beneath the soft rays of the mid-morning sun.

Hearing Chinese gibberish on all sides of her, Lee-lee was reminded of the day she had first arrived at the Port of Foochow. She hadn't been able to see because of her swollen, burned eyelids, but she had been able to hear. It was only a short while later that she had realized that the chest draped in cool silk on which she had rested her cheek was, indeed, that of a Chinese gentleman who was more boy than man at his age of fifteen.

Feeling the need to place these thoughts from her mind and to leave this Chinese section behind her with its clamoring crowded walks occupied solely by Chinese dressed in Chinese attire, Lee-lee set her sights toward Fulton Street which was only a short walk south. There she would board a fine buggy to pretend this was the first day of her life and hope that it would be a much happier one for her.

"If only Timothy . . ." she whispered, then clamped her lips tightly closed and shook her head. It would be hard to remember that he would be no part of her future and she would try her hardest not to subconsciously look for his place of business, which most surely would be near the waterfront, where she planned to venture this day.

"But he has surely returned to his travels at sea," she scoffed to herself. "He admitted to me that he rarely stayed at his New York place of business and that his partner worked the New York end of the trade."

Having left Chinatown behind her and now walking among people of her own nationality, Lee-lee soon found a vacant buggy. She paid the fare, instructed the coachman where to take her, and sat back to enjoy the sights of the city.

The grooved Belgian blocks of the streets were being traversed by many stately carriages and smaller buggies which clopped over the cobbles, transporting various wealthy-looking people. Almost everyone she looked at wore a hat, the men in silk top hats and the women in various showcase velveteen, satin, or fancy straw bonnets with attractive decorations adorning them.

Tall buildings cast their shadows lengthwise across Fulton Street where Lee-lee was now traveling in awe toward Schermerhorn Row, where her father's ship-building empire had been born. The open buggy in which she was a passenger gave Lee-lee a full view of the blocks of buildings that spread out as far as the eye could see, and the city of New York proved to be much more breathtaking than she had remembered it, even at the age of eight.

The sidewalks were crowded by shoppers frequenting ladies' dress shops, millineries, and tobacconists, and with workers pulling racks of clothes in and out of buildings. Newsboys in battered caps shouted the names of their papers, men with trays of oysters were bawling, "Rockaways, Rockaways! Strictly fresh," and again there was the incessant rattling of carriages and wagons.

Turning onto South Street, the buggy now carried Lee-lee into a part of the city where markets and trading sites were the centers for commerce and business, and whose influence extended far beyond the relatively few blocks they encompassed.

Lee-lee's heart began to race, recognizing and remembering, oh, so much—the seafood restaurants, the bakeries filled with mouth-watering sweets, and the fish markets with their food halls exhibiting and selling any type of fish the mind could conjure up.

And now in view of the many moored ships which lined the waterfront, Lee-lee was totally caught up in her memories. When the site was reached where tea auctions were held, she was sadly reminded of the times she had attended these auctions with her father, purely for the excitement they offered.

It was there that tea cargoes brought the highest prices in the port. Chests of tea had been carried halfway around the world and Lee-lee could remember that the names of the teas had been fascinating. Now that she had been a part of the Chinese culture, the names of the teas were easily remembered. There had been Tuckking Imperial, Lumking, Young Hyson, and even Quichne

Young Hyson . . .

Suddenly out of the corner of her eye, Lee-lee caught sight of the bold black of a ship's hull. With a jerk of her head, she looked toward it and was quickly engulfed by nervous, erratic heartbeats when she read the name written on its side.

"The *New Yorker*. Timothy," she gasped. "He's here . . . he's still in New York."

Moving eagerly to the edge of the seat, Lee-lee let her eyes move over the ship's deck, hoping to get a glimpse of Timothy.

Then she tore her gaze away, angry at herself for being this anxious to see a man who had deserted her. He was no more than a rogue, and she couldn't want to see him. He wasn't worth one moment of her thoughts. She would not waste her time with further curiosity about him. Yet her heart ached, realizing that he was so close, yet so far away.

Focusing her eyes straight ahead, she eased back into the full comfort of the seat, nervously straightening her hat. Oh, what loneliness she was feeling at this moment. There was such a gnawing emptiness invading her whole body and she felt as though she would never feel normal again. If she just . . . hadn't . . . seen his ship.

The buggy traveled onward and finally Lee-lee saw her father's building as it came sharply into view. She was instantly torn by different types of grief. The building represented her father in many ways. It had been built tall and strong like its owner, Kenneth Taylor. Always when seeing it in the past, Lee-lee had in a sense also seen her father, since he alone had supervised every inch of its construction.

Standing six stories, overlooking the bay and its busy port, to Lee-lee the brick building would always represent the Taylor Family, even if the sea had claimed them all but her.

As the buggy came to a halt before the building, Lee-lee's breath caught in her throat. The sign above the door was the same sign that her father had placed there those many years ago! She read it over and over again—Taylor Shipbuilders.

"Why would the new owner retain the original name of the company?" she wondered to herself, curiosity building inside her in leaps and bounds.

She hadn't planned to enter the building. She had just wanted to see it one more time, for memory's sake. But now that she had seen it, she was compelled to go inside, to walk the same paths that she had walked when she had been old enough to take her first steps.

The coachman, in his stiff black attire and top hat, assisted Lee-lee down from the buggy. "Please wait for me," she said softly, still unable to take her eyes from the building. The color of the aging bricks was muted by an encrusted glaze of grime, yet the many windows gracing the front were sparkling clean and reflected the shine of the blue sky and the refracted rays of the sun.

Swallowing hard, Lee-lee lifted the skirt of her dress and walked slowly to the door, accompanied by memories of her father walking beside her, holding her hand with pride deep in his shadowy-brown eyes.

Blinking back tears, missing her father so, Lee-lee stepped inside where closed doors reached out on each side of her all the way to the back of the building.

Clutching tightly to her purse, Lee-lee listened to the

drone of voices from those busy at work behind the closed doors. There was a mixture of men's and women's voices, intermingled with occasional laughter.

The muffled sound of paper rattling and footsteps from people moving about made her keenly aware that business continued as it had when everyone had been under the employ of kind-hearted, ambitious Kenneth Taylor.

Ten years had passed, yet it appeared that nothing had truly changed in this shipbuilding empire which still boasted the Taylor name as it had from its inception.

A staircase at the far end of the hallway became Lee-lee's prime interest. Should she? As a child she had run up and down those stairs, laughing, happy, free . . .

"I will," she whispered. "I must."

With determination in her steps, Lee-lee went to the staircase—her cheeks almost as flaming red as her hair in her great excitement—and she began her ascent.

She reached the first landing, the second, third, and up to the sixth, where she stopped, breathless, seeing the difference in this top floor from the other floors she had left behind her.

Lee-lee stepped into a small foyer where she found a secretary sitting primly behind a desk, her loveliness not hidden behind the gold-framed eyeglasses on her tiny, tilted nose. White lace graced her long, thin neck from a delicate, long-sleeved white blouse. Her fingers were folded together where her hands rested on the desk.

"May I help you?" the secretary asked, now trying to appear busy as she began searching through papers strewn across her desk.

Lee-lee suddenly felt trapped, not knowing how to

explain her presence there on the floor which had once been occupied by the owner of this pretigious company. She smiled blandly toward the secretary and just as she was about to speak, the door that led into the maze of private offices was flung widely open.

Paling and feeling faint, Lee-lee steadied herself against a chair as she watched this quite tall, thin man step up to the secretary's desk to give her some instructions.

"Richard!" Lee-lee said in a low gasp. Though ten years had passed and he would now be thirty-five, he hadn't changed all that much. He hardly seemed any older in appearance. He was alive! Somehow he had survived the tragedy at sea! She knew that it was he. He had the same ruddy complexion and burnt-orange hair coloring and she saw that his hair was carefully styled and hung neatly against his neck to his shirt collar. The only difference in his appearance was a carefully trimmed mustache. Wearing his dignified manner well, he was attired in a dark suit and a ruffled shirt, and he displayed a large diamond ring on the ring finger of his left hand.

Richard turned slowly on a heel and met her questioning gaze with a cold, distant stare. "Yes? Did you want to see me?" he asked icily. He frowned upon anyone disturbing him at any time of the day without a set appointment. Yet, wasn't she a lovely one? Maybe he could make an exception for her.

His gaze lowered, admiring the exquisite swell of her bosom, yet he was astounded by the quick pulse beat at her throat. Either she was frightened to death of being near him, or she was overly anxious to be alone with him.

Either way, he was finding this quite amusing. It seemed that women followed him around no matter where he might be at any moment of the day. Yes, he had been wise to stay unattached. And if he married, wouldn't he have to share his wealth? That was the last thing he desired.

Needing to touch him . . . to feel him . . . to make sure that he was real, Lee-lee reached a hand to his cheek. "Richard, is it . . . really you?" she murmured, then flinched when he grabbed her hand and lowered it to her side, leaving it hanging awkwardly there.

Suddenly Richard was no longer amused, but instead, annoyed. His golden brown eyes became even colder than before. "What do you think you're doing?" he said dryly. "Who are you? Why are you acting so strangely? I don't have time for games. Now will you please leave? I have work to do."

Lee-lee's mouth dropped open as he hurried away from her and slammed the door shut behind him. He wasn't even going to give her the chance to explain who she was. It was understandable enough that he wouldn't recognize her after all these years, since she had only been a child of eight when he had last seen her. But surely he had to wonder about her reaction to seeing him. It was not the reaction of someone just walking in from the street. And how had he survived? She had never dreamed it possible.

"He hasn't changed," she murmured, wiping a tear from the corner of an eye. "Not . . . at . . . all."

"Did you say something, miss?" the secretary asked, rising from behind her desk to go to Lee-lee.

Lee-lee cleared her throat nervously, still staring at the closed door and realizing that she had to go after Richard

377

to get some answers, if not love, from him. "No. Not a word," she said, taking a step toward the door.

A firm hand on her arm made her stop and swing around to face the secretary. "Please remove your hand," she ordered softly, giving the secretary an icy stare.

"You can't go in there."

"Oh, yes, I can."

"It is my duty to keep Richard from being disturbed. You cannot go in there, miss."

Lee-lee very politely lifted the secretary's hand from her arm. "Yes, I can," she said dryly. "And, yes, I will."

Boldly stepping between Lee-lee and the door, the secretary blocked Lee-lee's way. "You don't seem to understand," she hissed. "I won't let you or anyone cause trouble for my boss."

Lee-lee's heart raced with her growing anger, and her eyes flashed. She lifted her chin haughtily. "It is you who is the ignorant one here," she fumed. "You see, I am not just anyone. I am Letitia Taylor, Richard's sister."

It was strange saying those words, realizing that Richard was, indeed, alive and that she was here, so close to being with him again. But her joy in such a discovery was being marred first by Richard's callous behavior toward her, and now by his secretary. Lee-lee tried to remember that he wasn't aware of who she was, this woman he had treated so unkindly.

The secretary's face took on an ashen color. She removed her eyeglasses and peered toward Lee-lee in disbelief. "You are . . . did you say that you are . . ." she stammered.

"*Ai.* I am Richard's sister. Now step aside. I have a few

things to discuss with my brother." She cringed, realizing that she had just spoken partially in Chinese again. It was such a hard habit to break.

The secretary didn't budge. She lifted the tail of her black serge skirt and began idly cleaning the lens of her eyeglasses with it, still closely scrutinizing Lee-lee. "No. It cannot be," she argued. "You are an imposter. Richard's sister, Letitia, was lost at sea ten years ago, along with Richard's mother and father."

"Richard thought I was lost at sea, just as I thought he was," Lee-lee tried to explain. "But it's plain to see that we were both wrong. And because of this, we have much to celebrate. Now step aside. I must go and speak further with my brother."

"If you are his sister, why has it taken you so long to come to see Richard?"

"Because I have been in China. I only arrived in New York a few days ago. Had I known that Richard was alive, I would have been here sooner."

Placing her eyeglasses back on, the secretary continued her stubborn vigil at the door. "I still don't believe you," she scoffed. "Anyone could make up such a story."

"Why would anyone do such a thing as that?"

"For the Taylor fortune."

"The Taylor . . . fortune?" Lee-lee whispered, her honey-brown eyes wide. Her insides became filled with a strange sort of mushiness. She hadn't thought of anything beyond the joy of finding her brother. But she now realized that she *was* entitled to half of the family fortune! She hadn't even been thinking about the money involved. She had just automatically thought that once the news had reached New York of the deaths of the entire Taylor family, the estate would have been dealt with by the lawyers, and once liquidated, have been given to charity as stated in her father's will. Never, had she thought to be able to claim any of it now as her own.

Recognition by her brother had been utmost in her mind when she first discovered him to be alive. She knew not to have expected him to draw her into his arms and show any affection toward her. He hadn't all those years ago. He wouldn't now. But he could at least show pleasure in knowing that she was alive!

"I do not plan to stand here and bicker with you all day," Lee-lee suddenly blurted, having decided just what had to be done. "Now if you don't step aside, I will be forced to make you."

Gasping, the secretary backed up closer to the door. "You just try," she warned.

Sighing, Lee-lee gave her a gentle shove, and once the path was clear, she opened the door and rushed inside another foyer which led to various other rooms. With a thundering heart and mouth dry from excitement, Lee-lee knew just which door to open next. There was one very special room which had been her father's favorite, and she knew Richard's personality well enough to know that he, too, would choose the best as his own private office.

Without knocking, Lee-lee opened the door and stepped inside a room bright with sunshine exhibiting a full view of the bay in its gleaming blue luster. One whole wall displayed a wide range of books, and crystal glasses and decanters of wine sparkled from a large liquor cabinet on the opposite wall. In the middle of the room, a large oak desk was prominent and Richard was there, sitting tall in a thickly upholstered leather chair, with shock registered in his widely staring eyes.

"What is the meaning of this?" he barked, throwing a pen down on his desk. He pushed his desk chair back and rose abruptly from it. "What do you mean by barging in here as if you owned the place?"

Lee-lee started to tell him that she did own it, at least as much as he did, but she didn't get the chance. His secretary burst into the room. She went to Richard, stood on tiptoe, and whispered into his ear, then turned and let her gaze travel over Lee-lee, smiling smugly toward her.

Lee-lee watched Richard's face screw up into a dark frown. He began thoughtfully kneading his chin as he made a slow circle around Lee-lee, eying her closely. "Hmm," he said. "This is a first for me. I've never had a woman use this technique before. My sister, huh? Clever. Yes, clever."

He stopped and leaned his face down into Lee-lee's. "But it won't work, sweetie. Now why don't you just leave? It could save us a lot of time and trouble."

Lee-lee's insides knotted, feeling so many things at this moment: her brother's presence; the warmth this room radiated around her, with so many memories of a father so near and dear to her heart; but also alienation because of her brother's refusal to recognize and accept her.

"Richard, I *am* your sister Letitia," Lee-lee finally blurted. "Aren't you . . . aren't you even in the least bit glad to know that I'm alive? I'm dying to give you a big hug, Richard. You just don't know how happy it makes me to know that you are alive and well. How is it that you are? Who rescued you?"

Richard flung his hands up in the air. "Enough!" he shouted. "This is ridiculous. You aren't Letitia, so stop trying to play me for a fool by continuing with this charade of yours."

Frustrated, angry, and humiliated, Lee-lee went to Richard and looked up into his face. "Look at me," she said firmly. "Study my face. I haven't changed all that much, Richard."

She gestured with a hand. "See my eyes? You always said that you had never seen such a combination of colors before."

She took a hatpin from her hat and removed the hat from her head. Then she busied herself with taking all the pins from her hair and shook her hair loose to hang long and lustrously red down her back.

"My hair, Richard," she continued. "You always teased me about it being so red, though yours was red also."

"Stop this!" Richard shouted, walking away from her. "Get out! Do you hear? Get out!"

His heart was pounding furiously and his gut was twisting painfully for he had recognized her and wanted desperately to admit it. But to do so would mean to lose half his riches to her. He wasn't prepared to do that. He had thought her dead for ten years. It would be so easy to still pretend that she was. He was too used to having it all, to have any less. And, by God, he wouldn't have less. She had survived quite well these past ten years without him, and he without her. So she could just go back to where she had been.

His eyes wavered as he gave her a half glance, wondering where she had been and who had rescued her.

But he could never ask.

Lee-lee sadly shook her head. "You always were cold-hearted and hard to understand," she murmured. "But I would never have suspected anything like this of you. Why, Richard. Why?"

She slammed her hat back onto her head and ran from the room, sobbing. Broken-hearted, she ran blindly down the six flights of stairs and climbed into the waiting buggy. Wiping her eyes, she said, "Take me to one of New York's finest hotels. And please hurry, sir."

She settled back against the seat, watching everything passing by her through a blur of tears. Then her eyes focused as she wiped them dry, and found herself staring at the black hull of the *New Yorker*. Suddenly she had a strong need to see Timothy. Perhaps he could help her persuade Richard to accept who she was. Surely Timothy was smart about the ways of scheming, corporate minds such as Richard's, because Lee-lee had to believe that money and Richard's fear of losing his wealth were behind his refusal to recognize her and to accept her back into his life.

"*Ai*, I shall find Timothy and ask him to help me," she whispered. "But first I will get settled in my own private residence and it will be the best the city has to offer. I will claim my half of the Taylor wealth! I *will*!"

A slow smile touched her lips. She was glad to have a reason to seek out Timothy's whereabouts. It would not look as if she were going to beg him to notice her again.

Chapter Twenty-Five

Reaching for the bronze knocker in the shape of a wolf's head, Lee-lee hesitated. Was this truly a wise thing to do? Wouldn't seeing him just begin her heartache all over again?

"I have no other choice," she whispered. "Besides Tak-Ming, Timothy is the only person I know in New York. And Tak-Ming can't help me this time. Surely Timothy can."

Still hesitating, she looked at the row of handsome houses stretched out on each side of her, flanking Timothy's. All were stately mansions owned by men who also owned the ships that came in and out of New York. They had been built close to the harbor for convenience, and now, as dusk was falling around her, Lee-lee could hear the distinct sounds of foghorns and ships' whistles rising from the busy port.

"This is ridiculous," she murmured. "Why am I afraid to knock?"

Glancing down at herself, she felt that she looked presentable enough. After acquiring a plush hotel suite, she had gone to Tak-Ming's for her belongings. It had been another awkward, tension-filled farewell, but she had finally returned to her new place of residence, settled in, changed clothes, and rented a horse and buggy to go in search of Timothy.

She had succeeded in finding Timothy's place of business, only to learn that he wasn't there. But his partner, Calvin Hoots, very kindly had given her directions to Timothy's house, where he thought Timothy had gone.

"*Ai*, this dress should do," she mused, taking one last quick glance. It was a pale green smooth velveteen and was held out from her waist by stiff crinolines. Its sleeves were long and tapered to the wrists and its bodice was cut low, displaying the exquisite whiteness of her shoulders and the topmost swells of her breasts. Darker green satin ribbons had been sewn beneath delicate lace across the full bodice, and Lee-lee wore a stylishly matching straw bonnet which displayed the exact lace and satin ribbon design that was on her dress.

Without further thought she raised the knocker and then banged it noisily against the door. She winced. In the still of the evening the sound seemed to travel from house to house, echoing through the fog beginning to settle in around them, looking as soft as cotton and almost as white.

With her face flushed and her heart racing out of control, Lee-lee began to back away from the door. She felt too vulnerable standing there alone. She had been foolish not to wait until full daylight to travel this far from her hotel suite alone. But she had been anxious to see Timothy again. There was no denying just how anxious.

Turning to flee, already taking her first step down the marble stairs, she tensed when she heard the door open behind her. She waited for his voice, already melting inside from such sensual recollections of it, but was surprised when the voice that spoke was not his.

"Ma'am, did you knock?" a voice thick with a southern drawl said from behind her.

With a sweep of the skirt of her dress, Lee-lee swirled around and looked up into a dark face with even darker eyes. The male negro servant was dressed in all black, except for a trace of a white collar at his throat.

Ai, Timothy would have many servants for such a grand, three-storied house as this, she thought to herself, smiling.

"*Ai*, it was I who knocked," Lee-lee finally murmured softly. "I've come to see Timothy Hendricks."

"Mr. Timothy is in his study. Would you step right this way, ma'am?"

Lee-lee's knees weakened, realizing that she was so close to finally seeing Timothy. She proceeded to follow the servant inside the house, immediately awed by its grandeur. She had known that Timothy was a man of wealth, but to own such an elaborate showcase of a house and not . . . even . . . be married?

Clutching tightly to her purse and breathing softly, she followed behind the servant along a fully carpeted floor, seeing massive rooms that led from this hallway, which were plushly furnished with imported pieces. In each room a fire was blazing, and in one she noted a fireplace of black marble and then another of fancy maroon tile. But the thing of magnificence that stole Lee-lee's breath away was a staircase that spiraled to the third floor, where a breathtaking crystal chandelier hung from the cupola, lighting everything in reach with its dancing prisms reflecting light fueled by gas.

The servant stopped at a closed massive oak door. "Please wait here, ma'am, while I announce you," he said. "And who may I say is calling?"

Feeling light-headed from anxiety, Lee-lee only murmured softly. "Lee-lee."

The servant lifted a thick, gray eyebrow. "Lee-lee?" he questioned.

Then his chin lifted and his jaw became set. "Your full name, ma'am. Please state what your full name is so I can properly announce you to Mr. Timothy."

"Lee-lee is all that is required, sir," Lee-lee said dryly. Then seeing his displeasure growing in intensity, and tired of waiting, she swept on past him and placed her hand on the doorknob.

"I shall announce myself since you seem to be having difficulty in doing so," she said then hurriedly turned the knob, ignoring the gasp emitted behind her.

The strong aroma of cigar met Lee-lee's entrance into this grandiose room of books and ceiling that reached beyond the first floor. In fact, the room encompassed all three floors that the house possessed, with steps leading to a balcony at each level, giving easy access to even more rows of books that lined the walls there.

Fancy gas wall fixtures brightly lighted the room along with flashes of light from a roaring fire in a white marble fireplace before which were set many high-backed velveteen chairs and a long, beige-colored divan.

Seeing smoke spiraling upward from behind one of these taller chairs, Lee-lee's pulse began to race. She quietly closed the door behind her and walked toward the chair, suddenly dry mouthed. What would he say? Would he order her from his house? San Francisco seemed years away. Had they truly celebrated finding the gold nugget? Or had that been one of the many fantasies that she had lost herself in while lonely and missing him?

Stepping lightly over the plushly carpeted floor, she didn't make a sound except for her nervous breathing. And when she reached the chair where the smoke was still spiraling lazily, she stopped behind it to take a deeper breath and to draw more courage into herself before facing Timothy.

Then boldly, quickly, she took the few steps required and watched Timothy's hauntingly dark eyes widen in disbelief as he suddenly found her standing there, looking down at him.

Timothy jerked his cigar from between his lips. "What the—" he said, almost choking on his words. He rose slowly from his chair. "Lee-lee, how the—?"

"You aren't a hard person to find, Timothy, even in this large city of New York," Lee-lee said. She swallowed hard as he now towered over her, his lashes heavy over his eyes and his darkly-tanned, sculpted features soft in wonder. She thought him so handsome dressed in a maroon satin monogrammed smoking jacket.

Timothy tossed his cigar into the fireplace and drew Lee-lee roughly into his arms, searching and finding her lips seductively open and ready to accept him. He crushed her chest against him, holding her as though in a vise, and kissed her long and hard.

Then just as quickly he released her, turned on a heel, and walked to the fireplace to rest an arm on the mantel. His insides were in agony, torn by feelings as he suddenly remembered the handsome Chinaman and Lee-lee's love for him.

With a spinning head and her body aglow from his kiss, Lee-lee placed her fingers to her lips, still tasting him. His passion was still as fierce and his moods as puzzling. He had kissed her as if he had missed her, but now he was being strangely withdrawn and quiet, not even recognizing that she had responded willingly—joyfully—to his kiss and embrace. Perhaps he had a wife who would enter at any moment now. That would explain many things.

"Timothy, I'm sure my being here comes as quite a surprise to you," Lee-lee finally said, going to stand beside him, wishing that he would look her way. "Perhaps once I explain. . . ."

Timothy turned to her, his face shadowed by frustrated doubts. "Explanations are not your forte, Lee-lee," he grumbled. "I'm not sure if I even want to hear any."

Hurt, Lee-lee's eyes lowered. "You are surprised that I am in New York, aren't you, Timothy?"

"Should I be? New York was your destination from the very beginning, wasn't it?"

"*Ai.* But you last saw me in San Francisco."

"That I did," Timothy said, once more turning his

eyes from her, feeling too threatened by her loveliness and her soft, sweet voice which still held so much innocence.

"Then don't you want to know the circumstances surrounding my now being in New York, Timothy?"

He didn't want to reveal to her that he had known all along. She would then be full of questions as to why he hadn't seen about her or where she happened to make her residence. It would be hard to tell her that he had known all along. He wasn't sure how she would react to having been watched from the very beginning, from her very first day in New York. Only less than an hour ago he had found out that she had finally left the Chinaman's dwelling and now resided alone in a hotel of high quality. Had she and Tak-Ming quarreled? No. He couldn't reveal any of this to her. To do so could make him look the fool all over again.

"Why are you here, now, in my house?" he blurted, going to a liquor cabinet to pour himself a shot of whiskey. "That is the only thing I'm interested in at this moment, Lee-lee. To come to the privacy of my house? Surely it's something of great importance for you to go to such trouble to find me."

"It's a lovely house," Lee-lee murmured, placing her purse on a table, looking around her slowly. "It's so large, Timothy." She eyed him warily. "Do you . . . do you live here alone, Timothy, in a house of so many rooms?"

"If you are asking if I have a wife, I've already answered that. Long ago."

Lee-lee's face flushed deeply. "Then you haven't taken

390

a wife . . . since . . . I last saw you?"

Timothy drank the whiskey in one fast gulp, eying her while doing it, then slammed the glass down on a table. "If I had a wife, I wouldn't be in this study," he said thickly. "This house possesses many bedrooms. That's where I would be, Lee-lee. In a bedroom."

"I thought you would be on your *New Yorker*," Lee-lee said quickly, ignoring his reference to a bedroom, fearing she would reveal her overwhelming desire for him.

"The *New Yorker* has a few required repairs," Timothy grumbled. He gestured toward the divan. "Pardon me for being rude. Please sit down. And may I offer you something to drink? Perhaps some wine?"

"I require neither," Lee-lee said, standing her ground.

"Then please get on with it. Tell me your purpose for being here." He bit the tip from a fresh cigar, spat it into the flames of the fire, then struck a match to the cigar and slowly inhaled.

"It's about my brother, Richard," Lee-lee said, deciding to sit down after all. She eased into a chair, sitting stiffly on its edge.

Timothy settled down opposite her and crossed his legs. One eyebrow tilted quizzically. "Your brother? What about him?"

"Timothy, Richard is alive!"

"I know."

"You . . . know?"

"Yes."

"How is it that you do? Before, you said that you knew nothing of him."

"With time on my hands while my ship is being

readied for my next voyage, I did some investigating. I found that your brother is alive and is still the owner of Taylor Shipbuilders.''

"My word," Lee-lee gasped, placing a hand to her throat. "I had no idea that you cared enough to do this."

Timothy wasn't about to admit to this "caring." There were too many dangers where his pride was concerned. He couldn't let her, or any other woman, hurt him again. He had to place himself above such humiliation, though deep in his heart, his love for her crowded out all his other feelings.

"Like I said," he mumbled, "I was bored."

Lee-lee lowered her eyes as her heart plunged. "Oh, I see," she whispered.

"And what does your brother have to do with me?" Timothy asked, letting smoke roll and coil upward from the corners of his mouth as he took the cigar from between his lips.

Feeling his aloof coolness and lack of concern, Lee-lee rose from the chair. She grabbed her purse and headed toward the door. "It was a mistake for me to come here," she said from across her shoulder. "My problems are just that—mine. And I shan't bother you further with them. Good-bye, Timothy."

She felt almost destroyed inside, having expected too much from this man who at one time had even asked her to marry him. It had taken all of her willpower not to ask him why he had left San Francisco without a word of explanation to her. That was one humiliation she would forever do without. She would never ask him why. Never! And now she would probably never even see him again. She would try not to care.

Placing her hand on the doorknob, she hurriedly turned it then felt the strong grip of his hand on her wrist.

"Lee-lee . . ." he said huskily, urging her around to face him. "Don't go. Damn it, don't go."

"But, Timothy . . ." she murmured, weakening in her defenses.

"Those bedrooms of mine," he said, brushing his lips gently over her eyelashes, nose, and then her mouth. "There are so many of them from which to choose. Shall we . . . ?"

Choking on a sob of rapture, Lee-lee slowly shook her head. "*Nay*, Timothy," she whispered. "*Nay*."

"Your way of saying no—it doesn't carry enough strength of truth in it for me to believe that you mean it." His lips went to the hollow of her throat and kissed her softly there.

"Timothy, please don't," Lee-lee said, trying to push him away from her, afraid of being used and discarded again. Yet her body was screaming to be taken. She had never experienced such a sweet pain between her thighs before, and her breasts had never felt so hot and swollen.

Ai, her body was betraying her again and the lethargic giddiness inside her head proved that her brain was a part of this betrayal as well.

Timothy scooped her up and into his arms so abruptly that Lee-lee's breath was momentarily stolen away from her and her bonnet slipped sideways on her head. "What are you doing?" she gasped, reaching to reposition her bonnet.

393

"Hush," he murmured, opening the door to step from the study into the hallway.

"The servants . . ." Lee-lee argued softly, looking from side to side as Timothy headed for the spiral staircase.

Timothy chuckled. "Yes, what we are doing will give them reason to gossip amongst themselves," he said, now climbing the stairs, securely holding on to her. "You see, I do not make such things a habit."

Lee-lee's face was flaming hot. "I would certainly hope not," she giggled.

Timothy bent his head and gave her a swift, soft kiss on the lips. "I've never been tempted to before," he said huskily. "Only you have the power to make me lose my senses."

And so she did, he realized inwardly. But he wouldn't think about anything now except her and what they would soon be sharing. Without her, there had been such a void in his life. He was only truly alive in her presence. He would take her . . . while he had her.

In a state of pure bliss, forgetting all yesterdays, not fretting over any tomorrows, Lee-lee twined an arm about Timothy's neck and lay her cheek against the sleek satin of his smoking jacket. She was reminded of the time she was eight when another man's chest had offered her silk to lay against.

But she just as quickly forget Tak-Ming when Timothy's fingers slipped around her left breast and began stroking it through her dress. A shiver of ecstasy raced across her flesh, and she was glad when Timothy moved from the staircase and on to a bedroom where a magnificent, carved oak bed awaited them.

Too drugged with passion to see anything else in the dimly lighted room but Timothy, she watched him disrobe. Then she rose from the bed and did the same, caught up in the magic of him and his manly physique as he stood tall and tautly muscled and quite naked before her feasting eyes.

Tossing her bonnet aside, she seductively slipped out of her dress and underthings and kicked her shoes aside. Then slowly, one by one, she removed the pins from her hair until it was hanging long down her back.

Against the velvet white of her skin, her hair appeared even a more brilliant red, and the nipples of her breasts were a deep, dark brown as they stiffened in building anticipation.

"Lee-lee . . ." Timothy said hoarsely, going to her to frame her face between his hands. He lowered his lips to hers and kissed her, easily parting her lips to slip his tongue inside the sweetness of her mouth. Feeling the heat rising in his loins, he moved his hands from her face and instead cupped both her breasts, circling the nipples of each with his thumbs.

Lee-lee was being carried away on a cloud of ecstasy, her senses wildly awakened by his kiss . . . his touch.

With her arms about his neck, she drew him closer to her and when she felt the heat and strength of his risen sex against her flesh, she emitted a soft moan and rubbed her body suggestively against it.

"I need you," she whispered as he set her mouth free. "Oh, Timothy, I've missed you so."

She rained kisses across his face and lower, flicking her

tongue around one of his nipples. He lowered his hands and sank his fingers deeply into her buttocks and drew her even closer to him, senseless now, hungering to have her completely.

Slowly, as he held her against him, he led her downward onto the bed. And once there, he thought best to postpone the ecstasy, knowing that the longer he waited, the greater it would be. Instead he began to explore her exquisitely gentle curves with his lips.

Squirming, having never before been so tormented by her needs, Lee-lee savored his each and every kiss. She twined her fingers through his hair and guided him to where she wanted to be kissed. She trembled as he sucked first one nipple between his lips and then the other. He placed his hands on her hips and lifted her closer to his lips as she encouraged his head to move lower. She remembered the forbidden thrill of his lips between her thighs, and now, lost in her throes of passion, she wanted to experience it again.

Timothy questioned her with his eyes and when she licked her lips seductively and nodded her approval, he took his first taste of her since he had done so, oh, those many months ago in San Francisco.

His tongue . . . his lips . . . fed from her spring of jasmine scents, while she spread herself open to him and enjoyed the warm wetness of his caresses. Her senses were reeling. And when it became too much for her, she urged him to enter her and joined him in his eagerness to reach the pinnacle they both were seeking.

Clinging, wrapping her legs about his waist, enjoying his lips against hers, Lee-lee's passion for him fully blossomed as her mind became filled with a sudden burst of beautiful colors. She screamed out her joy against his quivering lips and felt his own pleasure exploding as his body convulsed rapidly against hers.

Sighing . . . breathless . . . still feeling the sweet throbbing of release between her thighs, Lee-lee burrowed her face against the corded muscles of Timothy's shoulders. His body was wet with perspiration and she could feel the rapid beat of his heart against her breast.

"It was beautiful, Timothy," she whispered, coiling a finger through his chest hairs. "Why can't it last forever?"

"If it did, my heart couldn't stand it," Timothy laughed, rising to look down into her eyes.

"Don't you feel cheated when it is over?"

"Why would I?"

"The moment of bliss is too short-lived."

"It just makes one more anxious for the next time."

"And will there be a next time, Timothy?"

Not yet knowing her true purpose for being there and still not fully able to trust her, he rolled away from her, onto his back. He wiped a bead of perspiration from his brow. "I guess that all depends," he said, avoiding her eyes.

"Depends on what?"

He slowly turned his gaze toward her. "On you, darling," he said thickly. "Always on you."

She could argue that point! He had left *her* in San Francisco, not she him. But she still refused to bring up that argument. It was in the past. This was now. And now was all that was important.

"If we depended on me, we would never be separated," she whispered softly.

She rose to a sitting position and pulled her knees to her chest, not caring that she was still undressed and very vulnerable to his rekindling desire. She would welcome it. Over and over again. And knowing this, she wondered if she might be some kind of wanton, depending so much on the sins of the flesh even before signing papers of marriage. But there had only been Timothy. What could be so wrong in that?

Timothy wasn't ready to travel down the path that she had entered, a path which could once again lead to talk of marriage. He had fallen into that trap once. The next time he had to be sure of everything.

"Your reason for coming here this evening," he said. "It wasn't to make love, was it?"

Lee-lee blushed and lowered her eyes. "Do you truly expect me to be brazen enough to confess such a thing to you?"

"No. I suppose not," he said, reaching to trace the curve of her left thigh. "But I would hope that it was the reason, Lee-lee."

"*Ai*, it is truly a part of it," she blurted, now looking eagerly toward him. She flipped her hair back from her shoulders. "But there is more, Timothy."

"More?"

"*Ai*."

Timothy tensed and rose from the bed, drawing on his smoking jacket and tying it in front. "And this something else," he said guardedly. "What is it?"

He combed his fingers nervously through his hair,

waiting. Had her purpose been to use him again? Damn her if it were true!

Lee-lee climbed from the bed and went to Timothy, to slip her naked body next to him. "I need your help," she said, eyes wide.

Timothy blanched. "Help? What sort of help?" If it involved Tak-Ming, he would surely never trust her again!

"My brother, Richard," she said. "He refuses to accept me as his sister. He . . . he . . . has turned his back on me, as though I am truly dead, Timothy, and my heart breaks from the rejection."

"He what?" Timothy said, loosening the muscles of his neck, relieved to know that Tak-Ming was not involved in Lee-lee's latest problem. "What do you mean? Have you gone to him? Did you tell him who you were?"

"*Ai.*"

"Tell me all about it, Lee-lee. Maybe I *can* help."

Lee-lee spoke fast, yet clearly, explaining her one visit with Richard, and how she now was ready to fight for her half of the Taylor fortune.

"Can it be done, Timothy? Am I due my half?"

"Yes. And I will help you." He raised her right hand and ran a finger over her scar. "My brand. It is still there," he said hoarsely.

"*Ai*, it is," Lee-lee said before letting his arms and lips fully consume her once more.

Chapter Twenty-Six

"What is the meaning of this?" Richard shouted as he rose quickly from his desk chair.

Lee-lee clung to Timothy's arm, tight lipped and unaffected by her brother's outburst. She knew to expect it after barging into his office unannounced. But the full night spent with Timothy had given her the courage she needed to face her brother again.

Smiling devilishly, she watched Richard's secretary rush into the room, fidgeting nervously with her eyeglasses which she held in her hand.

"I apologize, Richard," she said, casting first Lee-lee and then Timothy an ugly glance. "They didn't even stop to ask. They . . . they just took it upon themselves to rudely pass me by."

"Don't fret over it so," Richard grumbled. "I hired you to be my secretary, not my bodyguard." He gestured with a hand. "Just leave us be. I can handle it."

"Well, if you say so," his secretary said, inching past Lee-lee and Timothy to hurry from the room with the bang of the door evidence of her departure.

Looking serenely confident of himself in his dark suit and white ruffled shirt, Richard clasped his hands tightly together behind him and smiled sardonically toward Timothy. "And so you are the pimp who is behind this charade," he laughed. "You plan to get half of what this street whore tries to squeeze out of me?"

He hoped that he wouldn't burn in hell for all eternity for what he was doing, but yet he really wasn't certain that it was truly Letitia, was he? Perhaps . . . just perhaps, it wasn't. Then he would be able to live with himself. This past night he had been haunted by dreams of her, remembering her as she had been as a small child, playing with her dolls.

Then the dream had quickly changed to that day of the storm and how he had taken the first longboat, and he remembered Letitia's honey-brown eyes accusing him from the sinking ship. He looked into such honey-brown eyes now, seeing so much of Letitia in this lovely face staring disbelievingly at him with her lips slightly parted in a quiet gasp.

"What . . . did you say?" she asked, paling.

Timothy gently eased away from Lee-lee and stepped toward Richard, glowering. His fists were doubled at his sides and his face was scarlet with rage. "I don't believe you will make the mistake of saying that again," he growled. "I believe you know that you could find yourself plastered against the floor if you did."

Richard backed away from Timothy, turning his sardonic smile into a frown. "I must remind you whose place of business you are in," he said icily. "I can see that you both are arrested."

401

"Just you try it," Timothy snarled, stepping closer to Richard, meeting him face to face, eye to eye.

"What's your game, mister?" Richard asked, turning on a heel and walking to a liquor cabinet to pour himself a glass of wine.

"My game?" Timothy asked. "This is no game that I play, you bastard."

"Then why are you here?"

"First, before we get into that, you owe this lady an apology," Timothy said, gesturing with a hand toward Lee-lee.

Richard tilted the glass to his lips and took a quick swallow. He slammed the glass down on his desk and laughed throatily. "And why should I?" he said.

"Because you called her a whore."

Richard shrugged. "A whore is what she is. She should be called nothing else."

Timothy took one large step toward Richard and slammed his right fist into his jaw. And as Richard's body jerked and he fell backward, awkwardly falling over his desk chair, he let out a loud yelp of pain.

Lee-lee's hands went to her throat and her heart skipped a beat. She stood trembling, wondering what might happen next. She didn't wish to see Timothy and Richard fighting. She had wanted to settle this thing peacefully. Why, oh why was Richard behaving so irrationally? Surely he knew that she was who she professed to be. Never had she thought he would continue with this farce. She had imagined that when he had had a full night to think it over, he would have decided that, yes, he would recognize her as his sister—

his only living relative.

Richard rose slowly to his feet, rubbing his jaw. "I will have you arrested," he shouted.

"I don't believe you would want the attention which that would bring," Timothy growled, rubbing his sore knuckles. "How would it look in the newspapers when the truth of how you are treating your sister is disclosed?"

"She's not my sister. She is only someone you have found that looks like her. How did you know to do this? How did you find out about my family?"

Timothy shook his head, disgusted. "Lee-lee was right," he said thickly. "You are one cold-hearted bastard. You know damn well that this is your sister. How could you treat her this way? Aren't you even glad to see her after all these years that you thought she was dead? And how is it that *you* are alive? How did you get rescued at sea? It's for sure the Chinaman didn't rescue you along with Lee-lee."

Richard smoothed his hair back in place, his eyes narrowing into two slits as he looked toward Letitia. "Lee-lee? Who is this Lee-lee you are now speaking of?" he asked hoarsely.

Lee-lee took a step forward, her chin haughtily lifted. "I am Lee-lee," she said dryly. "I was named this by Heung-Chin Yeung on the day his son, my adoptive brother, Tak-Ming, rescued me from the sea. If not for them I would be dead, Richard. Don't you truly care? What would Father and Mother think if they knew of your callous behavior? They would disown you for sure."

Richard turned his face from Lee-lee, swallowing hard. He felt a tearing of his heart, yet he still couldn't confess to her that he believed what she said. His future would be questionable if he took her into his heart and home. And now there was even this stranger who she had brought with her to be concerned about. Somehow he seemed more a threat than Letitia.

He slowly moved his eyes to Timothy. "If you're not a pimp, who the hell are you?" he growled. "Why are you in on this thing with this . . . this person who goes by two names?"

"You don't know?"

"And should I?"

"My company has bought many of your ships in the past," Timothy said, reaching into a pocket, pulling a cigar from inside it. "The Hendricks-Hoots Line? Ever heard of it, Richard? My partner, Calvin Hoots, told me only today that much of your profits come from us. We sail only your ships. Now what might happen to your profits if we decide to go somewhere else?"

"Blackmail!" Richard hissed. "Are you now planning to blackmail me into confessing something that I do not wish to confess?"

"I would hope that wouldn't be necessary," Timothy said, lighting his cigar with a match. He then purposely flipped the burned out match on the hardwood floor at his feet, crushing it into the beautiful oak finish.

Richard glowered from Timothy back to Lee-lee. "I need honest-to-God proof that you are who you say you are," he said bitterly. "Only then can I accept that you are my sister. Bring me proof and then I shall say nothing else."

"Richard, oh, Richard," Lee-lee sighed, sadly shaking her head. "I can't believe this is you behaving so . . . so poorly. What did Mother and Father do to raise such . . . such an unpleasant person? You are no better than . . . than the devil!"

Richard strolled to a window, looking across the peaceful waters of the bay, wishing that he was just as peaceful inside. A part of him wanted to reach out to Letitia, yet a part of him refused him the feelings required to do so. "Proof," he said tightly. "Bring me proof."

Lee-lee's eyes became moist with tears. She grabbed Timothy by the arm. "I've got to get out of here, Timothy," she blurted. "I cannot bear to be near my brother another minute."

"But, Lee-lee," Timothy softly argued. "We can't quit now. Surely—"

Lee-lee stood up on tiptoe and spoke into Timothy's face. "Please, Timothy," she whispered. "I do not wish for this brother of mine to have the satisfaction of seeing . . . seeing me weep. We shall settle this later. Please?"

Filled with frustrated anger and a deep sense of sadness for Lee-lee, Timothy placed an arm about her waist and began guiding her toward the door. "All right," he said. "But only because you have asked that we leave."

He looked across his shoulder toward Richard. "But we'll be back," he said. "You haven't won, Richard. You shall not win. If proof is what you need, proof is what you will have."

Sobbing into her gloved hand, Lee-lee was swept along beside Timothy as he guided her down the six flights of stairs and into his waiting carriage. He instructed Ralph, his personal coachman, to return him to his residence, then, settling himself beside Lee-lee, he drew her next to him, trying his best to comfort her.

"It'll be all right, darling," he crooned, smoothing a forefinger along her cheek, absorbing her tears into his own flesh.

"I am usually a much stronger person," Lee-lee said, sniffling noisily. "But, Timothy, I am almost swallowed up whole with pity for my brother who . . . who doesn't seem to have even a soul. What has happened to him? Why is he such a bitter person?"

"It is only normal that you are upset, Lee-lee," Timothy murmured. "You have come face to face with your past and have not been able to reconcile anything from it."

"*Ai*, you are right," she sighed. "But I just wish I could understand why, Timothy."

"Greed. Money," Timothy growled, his face shadowing with remembrances of his own past. Cathalina Unser. She had denied him love because of her own greed, her own wish to have money . . . wealth . . . power.

"But he has so much," Lee-lee said. "Surely I am not that much of a threat to him."

"Anyone who speaks of sharing his wealth with him becomes a threat to such a man. Is he married? I would bet that he isn't. Why, he wouldn't even want to share his wealth with a wife. And then there would be children to think of."

He straightened his cravat, feeling guilty that he, too, might be that tiniest bit greedy himself, since he hadn't yet taken a wife, or shared in the happiness of seeing a child born to him by such a union. But it was more than greed that had dissuaded him from these things in life. It had been his lack of trust in women— any woman.

Wiping her eyes of the last of her tears, Lee-lee straightened her back. "I haven't yet driven past my childhood home," she said. "Timothy, do you think it possible that you and I could do this now, before we do anything else? I have this sudden need to feel the comforts of my childhood memories, being coddled by both a mother and father."

"I certainly can see to it that you are taken there," Timothy said. "Where is this place, your childhood home?"

"It is a mansion similar to yours located in Washington Square."

Impressed, Timothy smiled. "The wealth of the Taylor family is much more than I would have imagined, it seems," he said. "Mansions in Washington Square are looked upon as the best in the city and owned only by the richest businessmen and their families."

"*Ai*. That has been said of my father's residence," she murmured.

"Perhaps one day it will be yours, Lee-lee."

"I do not see how that is possible," she sighed.

Timothy began to drum the fingers of his left hand on

the seat beside him. "Proof," he said. "Hmm. Proof is what that bastard needs. Proof is what we shall come up with. Any ideas, Lee-lee?"

Lee-lee thought hard and long. "At this moment I can think of nothing," she said. "But there are too many memories and feelings crowding my brain. In time, I shall come up with something."

After Timothy instructed the coachman, the carriage ride down Fifth Avenue to Washington Square was made in silence. Lee-lee leaned against Timothy's shoulder, trying to take comfort in being with him. Besides Tak-Ming, he was all that she truly had. Richard, her brother, her only true brother, was not one she could think of in loving terms. To her, he was still the same as dead.

Closing her eyes tightly, trying to blot out such a thought, Lee-lee moved even more into Timothy's embrace, feeling the strength of his arm as he hugged her for reassurance.

"In time you will look back on this day in your life and laugh," he said thickly. "You'll see. Everything will work out. Richard will come to his senses."

"Even if he does, I don't know if that is what is best," Lee-lee sighed. "I could never feel anything for him now. Not after what he has done to me."

"That's understandable."

Lee-lee shook her head slowly back and forth. "I just cannot come up with any proof that I am his sister," she murmured. "It's been ten years. It was so long ago, Timothy. So much has happened. Oh, if only Mother and Father were alive!"

"But they aren't, darling. And don't torture yourself

now with thoughts of their tragic deaths. You must clear your head to be able to win against that damn brother of yours."

A row of stately mansions came into view outside the carriage window. Lee-lee's heart began to pound against her ribs and remembrances began to flood her, as if it were only yesterday that she had traveled along this street. The only difference was in the size of the trees. Ten years of added growth had made them tower above the roofs of most of the houses, though some of these residences were three stories high.

Scooting closer to the window, Lee-lee began watching for the Taylor mansion, recognizing all those that she was now observing. She could even remember the names of some of the families—Johnson, DuBois, Rockefeller . . .

Then she saw the slight rise of the street as its cobblestones formed a hill. "We're almost there," she said in a whisper. "Only a little way to go. . . ."

"Shall I direct the coachman to stop once we arrive there?"

"*Nay*. Seeing it will be enough. Later I will return and enter. After Richard and I come to some sort of an agreement, I will also claim this house as partly mine. The family portraits, the furnishings chosen by my mother while abroad, all these things I hunger to see. But, *ai*, later."

Her breath caught in her throat as she saw the terraced lawn and the house upon the hill which was an adaptation of the French Third Empire style with its measured roof, dormers, and cupola with sixteen windows. A horseshoe-shaped drive led to and away from the house, and towering pines separated the house from those on either side of it.

"So that's it?" Timothy asked, leaning over to also look from the window.

"*Ai.* Home. Home, Timothy. It is beautiful, isn't it?"

"Yes. Quite. Are you sure that you . . . you don't want to stop?"

"*Nay*," she murmured, lowering her eyes. "Please instruct the coachman to return me to my hotel, Timothy. I believe I need to be alone."

"That would be the worst thing for you at this time," Timothy argued. "I don't like the way you are taking this. Your fiery spirit seems to have been stripped away. And seeing you in such a state of mind, I won't leave you alone. I'll instruct Ralph to take you to your hotel, but I am going to accompany you, darling."

"Timothy, I truly don't think—"

"I won't take no for an answer," he said, kissing her softly on the cheek.

Lee-lee looked adoringly up into his hauntingly dark eyes and melted inside from feelings of love for him. "All right," she whispered. "Whatever you say, Timothy. But please don't expect me to be . . . to be receptive to all that you suggest when we arrive there."

"I want just to be there with you. That's all."

"*Ai.* And I do believe that you are right. I do need someone with me. And, Timothy, I can think of no one else who could brighten my mood at this time but you."

Timothy drew her into his arms and together they leaned back against the cushion, he with his sudden thoughts of Tak-Ming and she with her own memories about Tak-Ming. She felt guilty for not having brought him into her confidence about all that was happening in her life.

Timothy felt the familiar surge of jealousy when he thought of the handsome Chinaman and what he had always meant before to Lee-lee. Had she forgotten about him?

Has she placed me before Tak-Ming? he wondered silently to himself, praying that this could be so. Soon . . . soon he hoped to be able to once more ask Lee-lee to be his wife. But the time had to be right. She had to be at peace with herself before being faced with the proposal of marriage. Nothing could be allowed to go wrong this time. Her answer had to be a definite "yes" — a joyful "yes!"

Chapter Twenty-Seven

Comfortably relaxed before a fire in the fireplace, Lee-lee accepted a glass of wine from Timothy. She had changed into a silk lounging gown of muted blue with the design of many wild irises on the background. Lowcut and with lace at the bodice, it displayed the swell of her bosom, and its full looseness was gathered to lay splendidly across her legs which she had drawn up next to her on the plush velveteen sofa.

Having removed his suit jacket and cravat, Timothy set his glass of wine on a table and loosened his shirt at his throat. Watching Lee-lee and worrying about her, he settled down beside her, once more drawn into her exquisite loveliness. Even when pouting, she was beautiful. The blush of her cheeks matched the red of her hair and made her look even more ravishing. But in her honey-brown eyes, there was a keen sadness.

Slipping his arm around her shoulder, drawing her close to him, Timothy burrowed his nose into the depths of her jasmine-scented hair. "Surely I can do something to help you with your sad thoughts," he murmured.

"Just your being here with me helps, Timothy."

He glanced around the room, seeing its expensive furnishings of rosewood tables and upholstered velvets and satins. The floors were fully carpeted and the drapes at the windows were an eye-catching damask fabric, all lighted perfectly by hurricane lamps.

"Your hotel suite is grand," he said, reaching for his glass of wine and taking a small sip from it.

"It is nothing compared to what should be mine at Washington Square," she sulked. "It's not fair, Timothy. I should be there. Not here."

"One day you shall," he said, watching the shadows from the fire playing on her face, making her appear spellbound, yet if so, it was not a spell of her liking for still she did not smile.

She looked quickly toward him. "But how, Timothy?" she softly cried. "I feel as though I have lost everything all over again, yet only yesterday I did not suspect that I had anything to lose. What am I to do now that I know better?"

Timothy rose from the sofa and went to get the wine decanter from the liquor cabinet. He sat back down beside Lee-lee and refilled her glass. "Drink some more wine," he encouraged. "It will relax you. Maybe you will be able to think more clearly. Surely you can think of something to use as proof to please that damn brother of yours."

Twirling the wine glass around between her fingers, Lee-lee looked down into the red liquid sparkling from inside it. "*Ai*," she whispered. "I must think. Surely there is some way."

She slowly lifted the glass to her lips and accepted the wet tartness on her tongue and down her throat. And when the glass was empty she didn't argue when Timothy poured her another and then another and another. The wine was affecting her in a most delightful way, and she suddenly felt a strong urge to giggle, which she did.

Raising an eyebrow, Timothy smiled toward her. "Feeling better, I see," he teased.

"Much, much better, Timothy," Lee-lee said, loosely giggling again.

She emptied the wine from the glass and leaned toward the end table to place the glass there. But when she couldn't focus accurately enough, she misjudged where the table was. She flinched as the glass tumbled to the carpet and bounced against the brick that made up the hearth of the fireplace, breaking into many slivers of crystal.

Lightheaded, Lee-lee covered her mouth with a hand. "Oh, see what I did?" she giggled. "Letitia Taylor is a bad girl. Now she'll get a spanking for sure."

Scooting to the edge of the sofa, she leaned over to gape at the broken glass. "I'd best clean it up," she said, once more giggling.

Timothy grabbed her by the hand. "No. You're in no condition to pick up that broken glass," he said. "You'd cut yourself for sure."

"But Timothy, it's such a mess."

"It can wait," he argued softly. "What I think you need now is to go right to bed and sleep all of this off."

"But I feel so good," Lee-lee argued. "I don't have a care in the world."

"That's good. That was the idea behind my encouraging you to drink freely of the wine. Now let's go put you to bed and maybe after you wake up in the morning you'll be able to think more clearly and we can come up with a way to get what is rightfully yours."

Lee-lee's face clouded. Her lower lip curled under. "I don't wish to be reminded of him," she said sourly. "He says I'm not his sister. Well, I don't even want him to be my brother. He's a very unlikable person, Timothy."

"Yes, that he is," Timothy agreed, rising from the sofa and avoiding the broken glass. He bent over, placed his arms beneath Lee-lee, and gently scooped her up into his arms. "But no more thoughts of Richard. I'm taking you to bed."

Lee-lee teasingly traced a forefinger over his highly tanned facial features. "Are you going to tuck me in like my daddy used to do?" she asked in a soft purr.

An ache began in Timothy's loins, a burning fire that holding her so close always caused him. His lashes became heavy over his darkened, lustful eyes as he placed a hand against the soft swell of her breast. "Is that what you'd like for me to do, darling?" he asked, huskiness revealing his need.

Wetting the tip of a forefinger, Lee-lee placed it inside one of his ears and giggled as she felt a tremor erupt through him. "What else is there to do?" she asked, giving him a provocative look with one eyebrow lifted and her lips sensually parted. "I thought that you were stressing the importance of sleep."

Timothy chuckled. "Well, maybe just a bit later," he said, using the toe of his shoe to open the door that led into the bedroom.

"Then you are going to do something to keep me awake?"

"Something like that."

"Something like what, Timothy?"

As they reached the bed with its ornately carved headboard and ivory-colored, velveteen canopy draped over it, Timothy eased Lee-lee to her feet. "Like this," he murmured, slipping her gown from her shoulders to let it flutter like a butterfly's wings to the floor. He cupped both her breasts, squeezing each nipple between his thumb and forefinger, while he placed a kiss at the hollow of her throat.

Feeling passion rising like a raging river swelling over its banks, Lee-lee closed her eyes, arched her neck, and let out a soft moan. She wove her fingers through her hair and lifted it from her shoulders and back, quivering with ecstasy as she felt the flick of Timothy's tongue teasing first one breast and then the other and then lower to circle her navel, while his hands moved over her body leaving a trail of fire behind them.

Then as she felt him once more lift her up and into his arms, she opened her eyes and watched as he placed her gently on the bed and quickly shed his clothes. Her heart pounded madly as she saw his swollen sex in its readiness to pleasure her.

Spreading her arms out to him, she motioned with her fingers for him to come to her. "Darling, please kiss me," she whispered. "Never have I felt . . . so . . . so in need of you. Perhaps it is the wine?"

Lowering himself to the bed, Timothy knelt down over

her. "I would hope that the real reason would be me, not the wine," he murmured, letting his gaze move over her, seeing the gentle, silken curves of her body, the invitation in her honey-brown eyes.

"Kiss me, Timothy," Lee-lee sighed, placing her arms about his neck, urging his lips toward hers. "It matters not why I need you, does it? Only that I do is important." She brushed her lips teasingly against his. "Kiss me. Love me. Fill me fully with the strength of you, darling."

His lips quivered against hers in a soft kiss. He placed his arms about her and drew her to him, loving the feel of her breasts against his chest as he molded her body into his. With fiery passion, he kissed her harder, working himself into a mindless frenzy, and then he spread her thighs and entered her.

Clinging to him, melting inside, and then feeling as though they were blending into one another, Lee-lee let the sweet pain of ecstasy engulf her. When his lips moved to a breast and locked themselves over a nipple, sucking, stirring even more magical feelings inside her, Lee-lee placed her teeth to his shoulder and gently bore down upon him until she heard him let out a soft groan of pain.

Smiling softly up at him as his eyes questioned her, she locked her legs about him and urged his thrusts to continue, eagerly meeting them with quick movements of her hips.

"I love you," she whispered, smoothing some fallen locks of his hair back from his face. She then twined her fingers through his hair and pulled his lips to hers, kissing him sensuously and long until she felt her rapture mounting, leading to an explosion of intense love which washed through her in one fiery splash of pleasure.

Breathless, Lee-lee still clung to Timothy and then smiled to herself as she felt him receive his own moment of wondrous release. And after he rolled away from her, yet still holding one of her hands, Lee-lee looked toward him, adoring him, loving him.

"Stay with me the full night," she asked, leaning up on an elbow, looking down upon his sculpted, handsomely dark face. "I would like to feel you next to me throughout the entire night."

"You know there are dangers in that," Timothy teased. "You do remember last night, don't you?"

"*Ai*." Lee-lee giggled.

"As was the case last night, you wouldn't get one wink of sleep tonight."

"*Nay*. I would not."

"But you must have a clear head to think about what must be done tomorrow."

Lee-lee's eyes lowered. "Again you remind me of my sad affairs of the heart," she murmured.

"Only because I must, Lee-lee, for you to get what is yours."

"*Ai*, I know," she sighed.

Her gaze rose and her thick lashes blinked nervously. "But for now, let's only fill our minds with thoughts of one another, Timothy. Tomorrow will come soon enough."

He drew her right hand to his lips and kissed its open palm. "If that's what you want, your wish is my command."

When his lips brushed against the scar on her hand,

his brow creased with a frown, feeling renewed guilt at having been the one to inflict such a wound on her delicate flesh. He kissed it fervently again then looked up to find her eyes on him.

"You know that I wish that I'd never raised that whip to you that night, don't you?" he asked hoarsely.

"*Ai*," she murmured. "You've told me. Many times before."

Then she laughed softly. "But if you hadn't used the whip, I wouldn't have been branded by you, would I?"

"You can laugh about it. That's good."

"*Ai*, it's something of you that I will carry with me the rest of my life." She shrugged. "Now that can't be all that bad, can it?"

"I will be the only one to give you such a gift, I'm sure." Timothy laughed, kissing the scar again. "One branding in a lifetime is surely enough for one woman."

Lee-lee suddenly paled. She rose quickly to a sitting position, easing her hand from Timothy's. Slowly she moved it to her throat, where she remembered having been branded another time. The necklace! The initials on the necklace . . . her brother Richard's initials . . . had been fused to her flesh in the sweltering heat from her many days of aimlessly floating about beneath the rays of the sun in the longboat, before she had been rescued by Tak-Ming.

"The necklace," she whispered softly.

Then she jumped from the bed, shouting. "The necklace! Why didn't I think of it before now!"

Timothy rose to a sitting position, watching her exuberance as she bounced across the floor and riffled through an opened dresser drawer. "Lee-lee, what the devil are you doing?" he asked, eyes wide.

Lee-lee's heart raced as her hand made contact with the small, satin-covered box. She circled her fingers about it, pulled it free from beneath her silk underthings, and held it out before her eyes, seeing a brighter future for her and Tak-Ming. Perhaps she could help him financially in establishing his Chinese restaurant! She would prove to him that she hadn't forgotten him though she had neglected him of late.

Going to the bed, settling down beside Timothy, Lee-lee slowly opened the box and looked down at her locket. "This is the proof we need, Timothy," she said, gathering the necklace up into her hand, feeling its coolness against her flesh.

But it hadn't always been this cool. When the sun beat down upon it as she had drifted at sea, it had felt as if a heated iron scorched her. But she hadn't dared remove it for fear of losing it in the treacherous sea.

A slow smile touched Timothy's lips. "Ah, now I remember," he said. "It's the necklace given to you by your brother, Richard."

"Exactly," Lee-lee said, turning the locket over, running her fingers across Richard's engraved initials. At one time they had been imprinted on her skin—another brand of sorts. Why hadn't she remembered earlier?

She handed the necklace to Timothy. "Turn the locket over and see what is written there," she said, excitement bright in her eyes. "Do you remember? The initials. Richard's initials!"

Timothy took the necklace and studied the initials,

laughing throatily. "Little did Richard know when he gave this to you that it was going to cost him much more than the few dollars he originally paid for it."

"*Ai*," Lee-lee giggled, clasping her hands together, pleased.

Timothy gave the necklace back to Lee-lee, scowling. "But we must not fool ourselves," he grumbled. "It won't be all that simple, Lee-lee."

Lee-lee gingerly replaced the necklace inside its box. "But why not, Timothy? Richard surely will recognize the necklace. It's only one of a kind with his engraved initials—initials that he paid to have placed on the locket."

"Yes, he did. And even if he admits to having given you the necklace, that won't guarantee anything."

Lee-lee placed the closed box on the nightstand, then scooted over next to Timothy. "What do you mean? What sort of guarantee are you talking about?"

"His word is surely not worth a damn, Lee-lee."

"His word?"

"We will take papers for him to sign, to state in writing that you are who you are."

A sad feeling circled Lee-lee's heart. "Surely that won't be necessary," she murmured. "It just doesn't seem right . . . making . . . making him sign a paper such as that."

"To assure you getting your half of the Taylor fortune, this is the way you must approach Richard."

Shaking her head, Lee-lee said, "My own brother. How can he do this to me?"

"For him, it's easy," Timothy grumbled.

421

"Well, tomorrow we will show him, won't we?"

"Yes, tomorrow," Timothy said, gathering her into his arms. "But what about now? I'd love to be shown a thing or two myself."

"*Ai . . . ?*" Lee-lee giggled, twining her arms about his neck.

"How do you feel, Lee-lee?"

"I feel fine," she laughed. "In fact, I feel better than fine. I'm immensely happy. Why do you ask?"

"The wine. Has its effect worn off?"

"In which way?"

"Are you still in a, well . . . what would you say . . . a romantic mood?"

"With you? Always, Timothy."

Timothy framed her face between his hands and kissed her lashes closed. "You are gorgeous, you know," he said, placing a soft kiss on the tip of her nose.

"Am I?" she giggled.

Timothy's lips brushed against hers, tasting her sweetness. "The most gorgeous woman in the world. My own little Chinese-American doll," he murmured.

His hands lifted her hair from her shoulders. "Your hair is the color of late summer roses and smells as perfumed," he said, lowering his nose into its depths.

"Do you like me better with red or black hair?"

"If it were my choice, you would have red hair one day and black the next." He chuckled. "You must remember . . . I fell in love with you when it was black, when you were dressed in that lovely Chinese dress. Ah, what a picture of sensuality you made!"

"Without the Chinese dress, do you think me as

beautiful?" she pouted.

"Do you mean are you as beautiful now—this moment?"

"*Ai.*"

Timothy's gaze traveled over her, absorbing her gorgeous, satin sheen and the exquisite swells of her breasts with their hardened, sensitive nipples. "You have to be jesting," he chuckled. "You could never be as beautiful as at this moment."

Lee-lee curled up into his arms and snuggled her cheek against the soft cushion of hair on his chest. "Timothy, you do say the nicest things," she purred. "You make me so happy. Do I make you as happy, darling?"

"Yes. Quite," he said, wrapping a leg about her, drawing her beneath him. "And about a Chinese dress. Did you by chance bring one with you from China?"

"*Ai*, I did," she said, heating up from his touches as his hands probed her most sensitive pleasure points. "But only what you might call a souvenir of my other way of life."

"Do me a favor?"

"*Ai?*"

"Wear the dress for me one day soon? Model it for me?"

Lee-lee cringed with the thought of having to wear such a dress again, bitter memories of her days in China still so vividly etched on her brain. "I don't know, Timothy," she said. "It would not be a thing I would enjoy doing."

"You hated China so much?"

"Not so much China as the feeling of being a prisoner

423

while there. The dread of being sent to the Imperial Palace lay heavy on my mind as well as in my heart for so long."

"I'm sorry, darling. It's just that you were so lovely that evening," he said. "I will always remember our first meeting, brief though it was."

"Would it mean so much to you to have me wear the dress, Timothy?"

"Only if you wouldn't mind."

"After we get things straightened out with Richard, then I promise that I will wear the dress for you. But for only a brief moment."

"It will be my reward for having helped you?"

Lee-lee giggled. "*Ai*, your reward."

Chapter Twenty-Eight

Dressed in a simple cotton dress and with her hair drawn back and secured by combs behind her ears, Lee-lee looked innocent enough and hoped to capture Richard's fullest attention by approaching him in this way.

Walking up the six flights of stairs beside Timothy, on their way to Richard's private office, Lee-lee's fingers went to the locket that lay splendidly exhibited against her chest. Surely this was proof enough! If not, she would explain to Richard just what lay inside the closed locket. Oh, how she wished to be able to withdraw the lock of her mother's hair from inside it and proudly show it off in front of Richard. He had seen her place it there all those many years ago. He had laughed at her childish gesture then. Would he now, when she explained to him that the locket still held their beloved mother's lock of hair inside it? No, she doubted that he would.

Glancing over at Timothy in his impeccably pressed frock coat of brown wool and snugly fitted, matching trousers, with a diamond stickpin placed in the folds of his tan, silk cravat, Lee-lee knew he looked the epitome of a man of wealth. No one could accuse him of helping her in hopes of eventually procuring some of her fortune. *Nay*. It was evident that Timothy helped her because he loved her. It showed in the way he looked at her, touched her, and treated her. No man could be as thoughtful or as gentle.

Then Lee-lee's thoughts went to Tak-Ming. He was as thoughtful and as gentle. But he was these things toward her for different reasons. His behavior had been only that shown by a brother. *Ai*, if only Richard could be as kind . . . as lovable.

Stepping up onto the sixth floor landing, Lee-lee placed a hand gently on Timothy's arm, encouraging him to stop. She swallowed back a growing lump in her throat, the first sign of her dread of the moments ahead.

"Wait, Timothy," she whispered. "I need to catch my breath."

Timothy placed a forefinger beneath her chin and lifted it, forcing her eyes to meet his. "Afraid, darling?" he asked thickly.

She searched his face, letting him and his handsomeness give her inner strength. *"Nay.* I'm not afraid," she murmured, reaching a hand to his cheek. "Not while I have you with me. It's just that I see this thing as so offensive—something almost too intolerable to bear— this thing that my brother is requiring of me."

"Yes, darling, I can understand."

"But, we're only moments away from showing him, aren't we, Timothy?"

"Let's do it now." He gestured with a hand toward the

closed door. "Let's do it and get it over with."

"What if he isn't there? What if we have to return another time?"

"We will do what we must when we must."

"*Ai*. Then let's see if he is there now. I would like to put this behind me as quickly as possible."

Timothy placed his hands on her shoulders and drew her to him, kissing her softly. "You are being very strong about this," he said. "I'm proud of you."

"Some things are easier than others to be strong about."

"It's good that you've chosen this to be the strongest about."

"It's not for me to choose which of the times I am strong. It's my heart that does the choosing."

Timothy smiled warmly down at her, winked, then placed an arm about her waist. He walked with her by his side into the outer office were Richard's secretary sat staring up at Timothy and Lee-lee in disbelief as they approached her desk.

"Not you two again," she said, rising quickly from behind her desk. "What do you want this time?"

"It's no concern of yours," Timothy growled. "And you don't need to announce our arrival to Richard. We're quite capable of taking care of that little chore ourselves."

"But you can't," she gasped.

"We can and we will," Timothy said, encouraging Lee-lee to go with him into Richard's office.

Richard met their entrance with an annoyed grimace. He rose quickly from behind his desk, dressed smartly in his dark suit and shirt of ruffles, and began nervously twisting an end of his mustache as he looked from Lee-lee to Timothy. Then he spoke in a voice that was not only cold but this time drawn and with an occasional quiver to it, as if he were no longer so sure of himself.

"You don't give up easily," Richard said, giving Lee-lee a more lingering look, this day seeing so much of their mother in the way she wore her brilliant red hair and the way her eyes looked at him, as though looking into his soul. It would be harder to deny her this day.

"No sense in beating around the bush," Timothy suddenly said, reaching inside his frock coat to his hidden pocket for some folded legal papers. "I've had my lawyer draw up these papers. Your signature is all that is required for us to leave you to your business at hand."

"Papers?" Richard said, watching as Timothy slowly unfolded them to place them opened on Richard's desk. "What sorts of papers? I don't intend to place my name on anything that you or your lawyer has drawn up. Do you think me daft?"

"Well, I can't deny that I feel that possibly you are a bit crazy, but that's not the real issue here. Lee-lee. Your sister, Letitia, is my true purpose for being here, and I'm offering you an easy way out. If you don't comply, I won't be responsible for what I'll do to you."

Richard stiffened with hate. His right hand moved toward a desk drawer. "I don't take to being threatened," he snarled.

Timothy grew cold inside when he watched Richard's hand slip inside the drawer. Surely he wouldn't go that far! Not . . . a . . . gun!

With speed, Timothy rushed toward Richard and began trying to get the derringer from Richard as Richard pulled it from the drawer.

Lee-lee's heart skipped a beat as she watched the threat of the gun that both Timothy and Richard fought over. "Timothy! Richard!" she cried. "Please stop!"

Timothy wrestled Richard to the floor. They began rolling over and over, grunting, cursing, and when the derringer flipped away from them and scooted across the floor to Lee-lee's feet, she quickly stooped and grabbed it. Her fingers trembled as she cradled it in her hands, yet she knew that at least in her possession it wouldn't be misused.

Timothy finally succeeded at getting Richard beneath him. He grabbed his wrists and held them powerfully to the floor. "Now, damn it. I think it's time for you to get a few things straight," he growled. "Lee-lee had thought my approach was wrong—that I should present you with the papers *after* she showed you her necklace."

"Necklace?" Richard panted, perspiration blurring his vision. "First papers and now a necklace. What's next?"

"Lee-lee, show him," Timothy said, gesturing with a nod of his head.

Lee-lee placed the derringer on the desk then slowly walked toward Timothy and Richard. With a pounding heart, she bent to her knees, all the while watching Richard. Then she unclasped her necklace from around her neck. Dangling it down before his eyes, she saw no recognition in them.

"Richard, don't you recognize the locket you gave me on my seventh birthday?" she asked weakly, feeling a tormented sadness troubling her as she fought the frustration building up inside her, still finding Richard's attitude so hard to believe.

Richard's mouth dropped open and his eyes wavered. "I see only a necklace," he said hoarsely. "Nothing more . . . nothing less. There are thousands of those types of necklaces in the world."

Lee-lee almost choked on her words. "None but mine have your initials engraved on the back, Richard," she murmured, turning the locket and pointing out his initials to him.

Richard's vision cleared and there was no denying what he saw.

"Richard, do you remember the day I found a lock of mother's hair on the floor after she had trimmed her hair? Do you remember that I placed this lock of hair inside this locket? You thought me childish and silly for wanting to save it. Don't you remember, Richard? Surely you do."

"Letitia . . ." Richard said, the word catching awkwardly in his throat. "Oh God, Letitia, I'm sorry. . . ."

Sighing heavily with relief, Timothy released his hold on Richard and rose slowly to his feet, giving Lee-lee a look of reassurance combined with a smug look of victory.

"Then you do accept me as your sister?" Lee-lee asked, nearing tears.

She had fought and she had won—yet had she? She could never feel anything for her brother but loathing, for she knew that he had known her all along.

Richard leaned up on an elbow and reached a hand

toward Lee-lee. "Yes. There is not a trace . . . of . . . doubt in my mind," he said. "Can you ever forgive me, Letitia?"

"My name is now Lee-lee," she said coolly, flinching as his hand touched hers. She quickly recoiled from him, the sisterly feelings she once had had for him now suspended somewhere in space, a part of the past, as was her childhood name, Letitia.

Timothy went to the desk, thrust the derringer inside his rear trousers pocket, then gathered up the papers and showed them to Richard. "Now you'll sign or, damn it, I'll break your neck," he growled.

Richard curled the hand that had tried to touch Lee-lee into a tight fist, knowing that he could never expect respect from her, and knowing that he deserved it even less for the dastardly act of betrayal that he had perpetrated upon her. But he would not let himself be affected by this one way or another. It would be no different than when he thought her to be dead, except that now he would be only half as rich.

He rose to his feet, brushed his pants off, and straightened his jacket. Then his hands combed through his rusty mane of hair as he stared down at the papers once more being forced upon him.

"What does signing those papers have to do with any of this?" he grumbled.

"They are legally drawn papers stating that you recognize Lee-lee as your sister *and* half owner of all you possess," Timothy said, now holding a pen toward Richard. "One might call it a contract of sorts. Very binding, once signed. But that point shouldn't concern

431

you. It is your sister who will be getting what has been legally hers, anyway, all those years that only you benefited from the Taylor fortune."

"I can't agree to give Letitia half."

"Lee-lee, Richard," she coldly corrected. "My name is Lee-lee. You will even find that name on the papers."

Richard glowered at her. "I can't agree to give you half," he said. "For the past ten years I have worked hard to make this company what it is today. Surely you can't expect me—"

"Richard, father built this business from the ground up. Do not fool yourself by thinking you could have come this far without the wealth he had already accumulated before his untimely death. It is with my knowledge of this that I know what is due me."

"But . . . half?" Richard said, twisting an end of his mustache nervously between two fingers.

"At least that," Timothy growled, slamming the papers and pen down on the desk. "Now sign. You've had your proof that Lee-lee is your sister. Now we must have assurances that you won't try to back out and deny that you ever said that she was. The papers will reassure Lee-lee . . . enable her to enter the mansion on Washington Square without her having to be scrutinized and questioned for doing so."

"What's in this for you?" Richard snarled, leaning down over the desk, scanning his eyes over the printed words.

"Satisfaction."

Richard's gaze lifted to meet the challenge in

Timothy's eyes. "Satisfaction? What sort of satisfaction?"

"To see justice done. A bastard such as you usually wins. Well, this time good wins over evil."

Richard laughed sarcastically. "You don't fool me for one minute," he said. "The Taylor fortune is what you're after. When is the wedding? Surely there will be a wedding after I sign half I possess over to my sister."

Timothy's face twisted in silent rage. "Are you suggesting—"

"Exactly."

Lee-lee went to Timothy and locked an arm through his. "Timothy has already told you who he is," she said in defense of him as well as herself. "He is a wealthy man in his own right. He has no need for further riches, Richard."

Richard straightened his back, laughing hoarsely. "No man who has tasted the pleasures of wealth ever passes up the opportunity to possess more."

"Yes, to some it is a sort of sickness," Timothy said, trying to contain his temper. "You are in that category, Richard."

"And you are not? You are among the select few who are satisfied with what you have in life?" Richard scoffed.

"I am not the one in question here," Timothy growled.

"As far as I am concerned, you are," Richard argued. "I do not want to see you the winner here."

Lee-lee stepped away from Timothy, feeling drained from the emotional impact of the past several days. She placed the necklace around her neck, clasped it, then went to Richard's side. She let her gaze move slowly over him, swallowed up in memories, almost drowning in them.

Richard looked down at her, giving her a nervous half glance. "What are you doing?" he asked thickly.

"Studying you, Richard."

"You're studying me?"

"*Ai.* I'm trying to see something of Mother and Father in you, or perhaps some resemblance to myself."

"Why are you doing this?"

"Because it is I who am now doubting that you could ever have been my brother."

Timothy paled. He went to her and lifted her chin with a forefinger. "Lee-lee, what on earth do you think you're doing?" he whispered harshly.

She placed a finger to his lips. "Shh," she whispered. "Trust me."

"But, Lee-lee, you will lose—"

"*Nay.* I won't."

She gave Richard a sad look. "But, no matter, Richard," she said, shrugging. "You are my brother just as I am your sister."

She lifted the pen from the desk and placed it in Richard's hand. "Now, Richard, sign the papers. Mother and Father would want it this way. Please, in their memory and for love they gave you as a child, do what is right. Your nights will be nightmare-free if only you do what is right."

"I really don't have to, you know," he said. "There's no way anyone can force me to do this thing."

"There are many reasons why you should," Timothy growled.

"Like what?" Richard argued. "Is it blackmail you're once more considering?"

"Perhaps."

"I could have you arrested."

"I doubt that."

Richard went silent as he read the papers. He dipped his pen into his inkwell then gave Timothy a pensive stare. "All right," he said. "I'm ready to sign, but only under one condition."

"Name it," Timothy grumbled.

"That you will accept my challenge to a duel," Richard snarled, smiling darkly.

Lee-lee's insides splashed cold and her knees went suddenly weak. "A duel?" she gasped. "Surely you don't mean—"

"I believe he does," Timothy said. "But I seem to be having difficulty understanding his reason why."

"It is my only way to be sure that none of the Taylor wealth will ever fall into your hands," Richard said flatly.

"You are so sure that in fighting a duel, you would be the victor?" Timothy scoffed.

"I'm skilled in all weapons. You may choose which will be used."

Lee-lee ran to Timothy and grabbed onto his arm. "*Nay*," she cried. "This is foolishness! You cannot accept the challenge, Timothy."

"I never back away from any challenge," Timothy growled. Then his tone softened. "And, darling, it is a way to get him to sign the papers."

"Nothing matters to me but you, Timothy," she begged. "Let's leave now. Let's put all this behind us."

Timothy clasped his fingers to Lee-lee's shoulders and looked sternly down at her. "The papers will be signed and there will be a duel," he said flatly. "You'd best accept that, Lee-lee. There's no backing down now."

"Then the challenge is met?" Richard asked, placing his pen to the paper. "You will agree to meet with me at daybreak tomorrow?"

"Sign the damn papers. You name the place. I'll be there."

"Battery Park," Richard said. "You name the weapons."

"Pistols, of course," Timothy said dryly. "I've a set that I purchased while in France. I will have them with me when we meet in the morning."

Lee-lee placed her hands to her mouth as Richard wrote his signature on the papers. She was filled with dread. In gaining her right to the Taylor fortune, would she lose something even more precious? Would she lose Timothy?

The nightmare of the sound of gunfire was already there, forming inside her brain.

Chapter Twenty-Nine

Fog swirled up from the bay, resembling storm clouds approaching. With a hooded, black velveteen cape protecting her from the morning chill, Lee-lee was one among three casting shadows in the early dawn.

"Well? Where is he?" Calvin Hoots asked, nervously pacing. Though he was Timothy's equal in business affairs as Timothy's partner, he was not the same in appearance. Calvin was Timothy's opposite with his half-balding blond hair and faded blue eyes. The black cape that covered his expensive suit flipped around his legs as he made another turn on the dew-dampened grasses of Battery Park which stretched out to the bay where foghorns blared eerily.

Timothy placed a firm hand on Calvin's arm to stop him. "It's easy to tell that you've never been a second in a scheduled duel before. You're obviously nervous as hell."

"Yeah, I am," Calvin grumbled. "I guess you're thinking I'm a poor choice for one who is supposed to assist . . . to give you support."

"Well, now that you've said it, yes, perhaps so," Timothy said, then laughed.

With his free hand, Timothy patted Calvin fondly on the back and with his other, he supported the leather-bound case, inside which lay two fancy dueling pistols. "Now, Calvin. I am only jesting. You know that I have all the faith in the world in you, my very trusted best friend."

Lee-lee stepped between them, the tips of her hair exposed at the hood of her cape curled tightly with dampness. She looked from Timothy to Calvin, her thick lashes heavy over her eyes, revealing the intense worry that she was suffering.

"Timothy, let's leave now while we have the chance," she said with a soft, trembling voice. "I implore you again not to do this thing. No amount of family fortune is worth the risk being taken here. I wish now that I hadn't confided in you about my problems. Perhaps it would have been best if I had stayed in China."

Her gaze traveled over him, wanting to absorb every inch of his handsomeness in case this was her last chance to do so. She would always remember him as impressive in appearance, dressed smartly as he was now in his dark frock coat and snugly fitted trousers which displayed his tall, lithe form—broad shouldered and thin flanked.

And, oh, those sculpted features—his long, straight nose, sensually full lips, and hauntingly dark eyes displayed on his weather-tanned face. His silk top hat only hid a portion of his dark hair, and what was revealed lay snugly against his neck, carefully styled even on this occasion.

Calvin stepped around Lee-lee and sidled up next to Timothy. "She speaks wisely," he encouraged. "If you don't get killed, then you could be arrested for doing the killing. You know that duels are no longer legally accepted as a means of settling personal quarrels between two men. You know that you could be tried for murder or manslaughter."

"Only if the authorities are able to discover who did the killing," Timothy growled. "This is why I've chosen this secluded spot. Richard spoke the name Battery Park, but I have chosen the corner of the grounds in which to do the shooting. We'll get the ugliness over quickly and leave."

"Hah! But you forget the one Richard chooses to bring with him," Calvin warned. "He will scream to the authorities that it was you who did the killing."

"Then he would, by doing so, be getting himself into the entanglements of the law by admitting to having been a part of such a plan."

Lee-lee placed her hands over her ears, frantically shaking her head. "No!" she cried. "Stop this! You are forgetting, Timothy. You could be the loser here!"

Realizing the stress that Lee-lee must be under, Timothy handed the leather case to Calvin, then his arms circled about Lee-lee, drawing her into his embrace.

"Darling, I'm sorry," he murmured. "I have simply blocked your feelings from my thoughts. Your mind must be a turmoil of worry about what is about to happen here. Either you will lose a brother or—"

Lee-lee placed a hand over his lips, sealing his further words. "Don't say it," she cried softly. "I don't want to

439

hear the words. Nothing can happen to you. I wouldn't be able to bear it."

"What can I do to convince you that you have nothing to fear?" he argued as she dropped her hand to her side.

"The only thing that will truly reassure me is if we leave now before this thing goes any further," she argued back.

"I can't do that," Timothy grumbled. "I've told you over and over again. I meet my challenges. Never would I back away."

"But, Timothy—"

Timothy brushed his lips softly against hers. "Shh, darling," he encouraged. "I now realize that it was wrong to bring you here with me. I should have known how you would react to the waiting. I don't know what I was thinking when I agreed to your coming. And when your brother is shot, what then will your reaction be? You will suddenly realize the loss, I am sure."

Lee-lee lowered her eyes and shook her head. "I had to be here with you," she murmured. "No matter what. I couldn't have stayed behind, wondering and haunted by doubts."

"And your brother? What are your feelings for him?"

Without a blink of the eye, she said, "None. I have no feelings for Richard whatsoever. It is only you that I am concerned about."

"I could see to your return to your hotel suite now, before this goes any further."

"*Nay*, I shall stay here . . . with . . . you," she said, now looking imploringly into his eyes. "I'm sorry I have been difficult this morning, Timothy. I shall remain

440

quiet now."

She stood on tiptoes and kissed him on the brow. "And God be with you, my love," she softly whispered.

Stepping back away from him, Lee-lee glanced up through the fog, seeing slivers of sunshine trying to break through the haze as the sun rose slowly in the sky. The faint chirpings of the birds could be heard in the trees and a rooster crowed somewhere far away in the hills that rose from the bay. Only a few houses dotted the horizon, unknowingly witnesses to possible tragedy on this early October morning.

Timothy withdrew his watch from his frock coat pocket and checked the time. An eyebrow rose, seeing the late hour. He glanced over at Calvin as he placed the watch back inside his pocket. "It's late, Calvin," he said.

Timothy then took a cigar from his pocket, chomped its tip off and spat it onto the ground. He scraped a fingernail against the tip of a match, lighting it, then set the flame against the end of his cigar and patiently puffed until the cigar was well lighted.

Flipping the match away from him, he placed his hands into his front trousers pockets, watching in all directions for any signs of movement but seeing none except those of the horses reined to his carriage as they pawed nervously against the ground.

Calvin resumed his pacing, moving the leather case from one arm to the other. "It's getting too light. The fog is lifting much too quickly from the bay. Anyone passing by on a ship could get direct view of anything that transpires here, Timothy. I think it best that we postpone this until another time."

"Where the devil is he?" Timothy growled, puffing angrily on his cigar. "How well do you know him, Calvin? You're the one who has done all the dealings with him. Through transacting business with him, you should know something about his character."

"I would never have guessed he would be the type to challenge someone to a duel." Calvin laughed sarcastically. "Coward is what I'd call him. Perhaps this day will prove just that, do you think?"

"Who can say," Timothy grumbled, now drumming the fingers of his right hand on the stiff brim of his top hat. "Anyone who is capable of what he was about could be called many things. A brother who mistreats a sister so! A coward? Yes, perhaps, that too would properly fit him."

"Shall we wait longer?" Calvin asked, nervously kneading his chin.

"Yes. I will not be the one called coward in case we leave too soon and he arrives and finds us gone."

Lee-lee clasped and unclasped her hands, watching in the distance, praying that Richard *was* the coward he was now suspected of being. There would be no killings. Both Richard and Timothy would remain alive. To her, it was all that was important now. That lives would be spared. For anyone to die now, because of her—ah, what a life of misery she would live, plagued by guilt both day and night.

Ai, if Richard did not show up, how much easier it would be for her to live out the remainder of her life.

As the sun became stronger and the fog dissipated to nothing, the hood of Lee-lee's cape became unbearably hot. She tossed her head, ridding herself of the hood, then unfastened the bow to her cape and let the cape ease a bit from her shoulders. She watched as Timothy's face grew red with growing anger and frustration. She looked toward Calvin who was now waiting at the carriage, having already given up on Richard's arrival.

Lee-lee went to Timothy and placed a hand gently on his arm. "Darling, he isn't going to come," she murmured. "Let's leave. Don't you see that it is no longer early morning? The sky is brilliantly blue. The sun is high. No duel could take place now even if he did arrive. It would be too dangerous."

She looked out over the waters of the bay, seeing the influx of arriving and departing ships with their snowy white sails separating the blue of the sky from the blue of the water.

"There would be many witnesses now should anyone fire a shot from these shores," she further encouraged.

She reached a hand to Timothy's cheek. "Come on, darling. Let's not wait any longer. Don't you see? My brother has proved that he is a coward. He didn't show up. And he won't, now that it is totally daylight."

"I wonder what his excuse will be," Timothy said, dropping his cigar to the ground. He stomped it out, into the thickness of the grass at his feet.

"Does it matter?"

"Doesn't it to you?"

"I'm thankful that he didn't come, Timothy."

"Yes. I can understand why."

Draping his arm about her waist, they walked together to the carriage.

"And can we now put this behind us, Timothy?"

"I can only answer that once I've questioned Richard," he growled. He placed his hands on Lee-lee's waist and helped her up into the carriage.

"Do you mean to . . . to pursue this further?" she asked, grabbing his hands.

"I must, Lee-lee. I have no choice. Please remember that it was Richard who offered the challenge."

With shoulders heavy and heart aching, Lee-lee settled her back against the plushly cushioned seat. She was tired of arguing. She was now completely drained.

Timothy leaned over to kiss her lips. "I must ride up front with Calvin in case we pass Richard on his way here," he said. "Calvin will direct the horses. I will keep my eye on the road and who travels it."

"*Ai*," Lee-lee said. "Whatever."

She watched the door close her in with her total sadness. She held onto the seat as the carriage lurched forward. She moved closer to the window and watched as the world rolled peacefully by beside her. Many fragrances were carried to her by the sea breeze blowing in from the bay and from wild flowers dotting the landscape in pale orchid colors. In the distance the autumn colors were already a pleasurable sight to see. It seemed as though the trees had been embroidered by deft fingers intermingling threads of rusts and golds throughout them.

But none of this tranquillity rubbed off on Lee-lee. There was still too much left unsettled in her life.

The carriage rambled on, first on a dirt road and then on cobblestones. Houses became thick at the sides of the road and then other buildings were there, massive, tall, and impressive, and once more Lee-lee was a part of the city of New York's hectic thoroughfares.

She recognized Fifth Avenue and then her posh hotel. It was evident that Timothy's further plans for the day did not include her. He was going to insist on questioning Richard without her. He would be surprised when she didn't argue this point with him. She was quite tired of it all and cared less about Richard's reasons for changing his mind. It was just a blessing that he had.

When she felt the carriage come to a halt, she waited for Timothy to open the door, and when he did, she gladly let him assist her to the sidewalk.

"After I see you to your room, I must be on my way," Timothy said, already guiding her by the elbow to the hotel's front door. "But I shall return sometime this afternoon."

A newsboy in a battered cap with filth-laden breeches and shirt came toward them, holding papers in the air, shouting.

"Get yer *Herald* here!" he yelled. "The most up-to-date news! Yessir! Strictly up-to-date news!"

Timothy whisked Lee-lee out of the boy's way, frowning toward him.

The boy began to shout: "Read this mornin's headlines! Murder! Murder on Fifth Avenue! Successful businessman, Richard Taylor, dead! Shot and robbed last night on Fifth Avenue!"

Lee-lee heard and felt a sudden spinning of her head. She felt Timothy's arm tighten about her, drawing her to a quick halt.

He looked down at her, searching her face. "You heard?"

"*Ai.*"

"Are you all right?"

"*Ai . . .*"

"I must have one of those newspapers to read the details. Will you be all right?"

"Timothy, what we just heard is a shock, but, *ai*, I'm all right."

He stepped cautiously away from her, keeping his eyes on her as he hurried toward the newsboy. He paid for a newspaper then hurried back to Lee-lee and ushered her into the hotel and up to her suite.

Lee-lee tossed her cape aside and settled down into a chair, exhausted. She felt as though in a daze, so hard was it to comprehend these quick changes in her life.

"I'll pour you a glass of wine," Timothy said, tucking the paper beneath his left arm. "You need it to steady your nerves. I know what a shock this latest news must be for you."

"All along . . . while we were waiting for Richard, he was already dead," Lee-lee whispered. "How ironic, Timothy, that he would die now and in such a way."

"Fate," Timothy said, carrying a glass of wine to her. "Drink up, darling. You need it."

Lee-lee took the glass with one hand and with the other pushed some fallen hair back away from her shoulders. Her velveteen dress was cut low with lace gathered at her bodice and at the cuffs of her long sleeves, and her petticoats rustled as she crossed her legs.

"*Ai*, fate . . ." she murmured.

Staring down into the rosy liquid, she suddenly felt misplaced in life. She hadn't belonged in China and she wondered if she wanted to belong in America. Both places, it seemed, were ruled by violence, hatred, and mistrust. All she ever wanted in life was a small corner of the world where she could have peace and love.

Timothy began reading the acount of Richard's death aloud. "Prominent businessman Richard Taylor was walking along Fifth Avenue, alone, at sunset when a gunman approached—"

Lee-lee rose quickly from the chair, spilling wine down the front of her dress. "Stop it, Timothy," she cried. "I don't want to hear it."

Timothy blanched and tossed the newspaper to the floor. He went to Lee-lee and took the empty glass from her. "I didn't realize you were so distraught," he said thickly. He placed the glass on a table and drew her into his arms, hugging her tightly to him. "I'm sorry, darling. How thoughtless of me to read that out loud."

"He was my brother," she sobbed. "Though he was cold hearted and was unfair to me, he *was* my brother. I did love him at one time. I did."

"I'm sure you did," Timothy crooned. "And it is only natural for you to be upset about his death."

"I feel so guilty, Timothy.'" Lee-lee sobbed louder.

"Why should you?"

"I'm no better than he was."

Timothy held her away from him, looking down into her eyes filled with tears. "Why would you think that?"

"Because I forced those . . . those papers on him to sign."

Timothy grabbed Lee-lee's shoulders. "Darling, you had better feel grateful that we did that when we did. Don't you see? Had we waited one more day, it would have been too late."

"What do you mean, Timothy?"

"Lee-lee, had Richard not signed those papers when he did, admitting to the world that you were his sister, there would have been no way to prove that you are, now that he is dead."

Lee-lee felt a weakness in her stomach. "I never thought about that," she gasped. "Timothy, you are right. I would never have been able to claim what is mine."

"But now you can. And now not only half of the Taylor fortune is yours, but all of it, Lee-lee. The shipbuilding business . . . the mansion . . . the money. . . ."

Lee-lee's head began to spin. She swallowed hard. It was all too much at once for her to handle. She grabbed her cape and purse and rushed toward the door.

Timothy followed after her. "Where are you going?" he gasped, puzzled.

Lee-lee turned on a heel and faced him, her cheeks flushed crimson. "I need to get away from all of this," she said dryly. "And I must do it now."

"I don't understand, Lee-lee," Timothy said. "The world is suddenly yours. Can't you see that? You are now a very wealthy woman."

"I know," she murmured softly. "This is why I need to get away for a few days."

"Where will you go?"

"To Tak-Ming's."

Timothy's gut twisted and his face paled. To hide his humiliation . . . his hurt . . . his frustration, he turned his face away from her. He wouldn't reveal to her just how wronged he felt at this moment. He had battled for her and had handed the world to her on a silver platter, and who did she run to for God knows why—Tak-Ming!

"Please try to understand, Timothy," Lee-lee said then fled from the room without a backward glance.

Timothy gritted his teeth and hit the wall with a doubled fist. "The sea," he growled. "I've waited too long. I must once more drown my sorrows at sea."

Chapter Thirty

The wind howled down the streets of New York, but inside Tak-Ming's restaurant, which was being readied for its grand opening, all was cheerful and cozily warm with the aroma of chicken and pork simmering on the stoves, temptingly tantalizing to the palate.

Lee-lee stepped from the kitchen into the main dining hall, proud for Tak-Ming. Everywhere she looked, she saw the bright color of lacquered red and embroidered hangings gracing the walls with their splendid backgrounds of silk and satin.

Lanterns of every conceivable type and color in the shapes of flowers and human and animal figures hung low over tables that were covered with expensive, red linen tablecloths, and smoking teapots with matching cups sat ready to be used by the restaurant's first customers.

Lee-lee's and Tak-Ming's lives had been changed due to Lee-lee's sudden wealth, and she was glad to have been given the opportunity to thank Tak-Ming in this special way for all that he had done for her. She had proudly shared her money with him and the deed to the property handed to him had been one of the first acts that she had performed after it had become a known fact that she was, indeed, the surviving legal heir to the Taylor fortune.

Fate had been on her side when she had discovered that Dennis McCaffree, the lawyer who had served her father, was Richard's lawyer as well. And since Dennis had been one of her favorite people in her childhood, because he had always given her a peppermint stick when he had seen her, it had been easy enough to convince him that she was who she professed to be. And there had also been the papers signed by Richard.

Glancing down at the way she was dressed, Lee-lee was reminded of business that needed her attention before she could return to her mansion on Washington Square to change for the evening's celebration at Tak-Ming's restaurant.

She smiled, thinking she did pass well enough for an executive-type business lady, attired in her black taffeta skirt with scalloped silk trim at its hem. Her plain white, long-sleeved shirtwaist blouse was set off by a neat, black bowtie at its buttoned collar, and her hair was pulled severely back from her face and tied into a ponytail with a black velvet ribbon.

Ai, she was a lady of business in what was usually a man's world, and she was beginning to love it. Thanks to Dennis McCaffree, she was quickly learning the ship-building trade and commanded respect from all of her employees as she ran the business from behind the grand old oak desk which had been first her father's, and then Richard's.

It seemed that she had it all. But the one ingredient was missing in her life that could make her feel completely happy and whole. Timothy. She hadn't seen him now for two full months. Again he had gone to sea in his *New Yorker* without a word of good-bye to her. And again, she didn't understand.

"And did you invest wisely, Lee-lee?" Tak-Ming said suddenly from behind her.

Wrenched so quickly from her thoughts, Lee-lee jumped, startled. Then she swung around and smiled at Tak-Ming, seeing the excitement of this blossoming day in his dark, almond-shaped eyes.

He never seemed as tall as now, displaying his strong Manchu physique in his silk embroidered robe which clung to his muscled shoulders and chest. His black hair was sleek and glistening from the application of perfumed oils and hung in a long queue down his back, completing the handsome, Chinese appearance of which he was so proud.

"*Ai*, I did," Lee-lee said. "The money was spent very wisely, Tak-Ming. Your restaurant is gorgeous. And, ah, what aromas are floating from your kitchen. No one will be able to resist the Yeung Chinese Palace once they discover its doors unlocked and ready for customers to enter."

She went to him, wrapped her arms about him, and lay her cheek against his powerful chest. Her thoughts drifted back to that first time, when the touch of cool silk against her burning, sun-scorched flesh had been so welcome. Since that time, so much had been shared between them. It had been a bond that no one could break. And it still remained so.

She relished the feel of his arms as they slipped around her, returning her affectionate hug.

"Are you as happy as I am, Lee-lee?" he asked hoarsely. These moments with her were now rare, since their worlds had become separated by culture. *Ai*, he missed her nearness, but Koo-See had become more than a favorable substitute. Soon she would hopefully bear him a son! But he didn't care at this stage in her pregnancy even if it was a girl. It would be a blessing just to have her through her misery and to have a child to fuss over. If this first born wasn't a son, there would be a next time.

A slow ache circled Lee-lee's heart, as once more she thought of Timothy. "*Ai*," she lied. "Immensely, Tak-Ming."

"Then our voyage from Foochow has finally become one of success for both of us," he said, easing her out of his arms. "You and I are now both owners of fine establishments. Fate has been good to us, Lee-lee."

Lee-lee's gaze moved slowly about the dining hall. "Then you are pleased enough with what you've been able to do here, transforming what was once a cleaning establishment into a restaurant?"

"It is more than adequate," Tak-Ming said, walking from table to table, straightening silverware. "And my venture will be a success. Don't you recognize that I've chosen red as the prominent color for decoration? As both you and I were taught in China, the color red stands for good fortune."

Strolling to the front window, pulling a red velvet

drape aside, Lee-lee looked up into the sky and at its dark gray clouds which seemed to be shrouds hanging low over the city. "I hope the threat of snow doesn't discourage customers from venturing out on your first day of business," she said. "The month of December in New York has thus far been a cold and dreary one. Snow would make everything beautiful but dangerously so."

"New York isn't China," Tak-Ming growled. "In Foochow, the morning after a blizzard was one of sadness. I've witnessed firsthand the carts going from street to street picking up the frozen dead for pauper burial. The beggars did not have fur-lined garments for which to keep them warm."

"*Ai*, the poor *unfortunates*," Lee-lee sighed. She then swung around, facing Tak-Ming with a broad smile. "But when thinking of the happy times in the snow, I remember so much, Tak-Ming," she said. "I shall never forget the fun we shared while riding across the snow on *pizas*, those open sleds with raised seats for passengers. How fast the felt-shod coolies could push them along the snow-covered earth! And when they got up enough speed, they would jump on the back and ride too."

"*Ai*. Snuggled warmly in our fur-lined garments, sitting side by side, it was a time of pleasure for me," Tak-Ming sighed.

"I favored the open *pizas* over the private, closed Imperial *pizas*," Lee-lee scoffed. "Though I sometimes traveled in those elaborate little rooms covered by yellow brocade and equipped with all the trappings of royalty, it was the freedom of the open *pizas*—the ones usually traveled on by common people—that gave me the most pleasure, Tak-Ming."

Tak-Ming went and looked out the window, studying the sky, then let his gaze move to Lee-lee. "And speaking of royalty, the belated news that has just reached us from China of the death of the Son of Heaven does not surprise me all that much and saddens me little," he said. "How do you feel to realize that you would have been a concubine for the now reigning Emperor Hsien Feng, instead of Tao Kuang, now that Tao Kuang has ascended on the dragon throne to be a guest on high?"

A cold shiver raced across Lee-lee's flesh with the thought. "One would not have been better than the other," she said dryly. "Though Tao Kuang's official name meant 'brilliant reason,' it did not fit him well. And his ill-fated son, Hsien Feng, is not one I wish even to think about."

"*Nay*. I would think not," Tak-Ming grumbled. He looked toward a narrow staircase at the far end of the room, mostly hidden behind a curtain of bamboo. "Lee-lee, I must go and check on Koo-See. She was behaving most peculiarly this morning. Perhaps this day will grant me two rewards—many customers for my restaurant and a son! I'd best go upstairs and see how Koo-See is feeling."

"Are you and Koo-See pleased with your upstairs apartment?' Lee-lee asked, having wondered how Tak-Ming could be after being used to the spaciousness and magnificence of the House of Yeung.

"It is not what I would wish to raise my children in," he said softly. "It isn't quite large enough to raise many sons. And there is the lack of land ownership that prevents me from planting my personal groves of *lanmu* trees, and that displeases me. It is the excellent, fine-whorled wood that I need from the *lanmu* for coffins in which to bury my loved ones in the future. The body does not rot in such a coffin and with that my heirs could be well provided for—from birth to beyond death."

Understanding the Chinese customs, Lee-lee went to Tak-Ming and draped her arms about his neck. "*Ai*, and maybe one day we can go in search of such land for you," she whispered. "I want to see to it that you are completely happy while so far from your homeland. You did the same for me while I was in China."

Koo-See's faint, sweet voice calling for Tak-Ming drew his eyes back to the staircase. "My duty to my wife comes before everything else," he said hoarsely. "I must go to her now and see to her comfort."

Lee-lee stepped away from Tak-Ming and took her black velveteen cape from the back of the chair on which she had draped it. "Give Koo-See my love, Tak-Ming," she murmured. "Tell her my thoughts are with her."

"*Ai*, that I will," he said, bowing humbly.

Lee-lee slipped her cape around her shoulders then gave Tak-Ming a quick kiss on a cheek as he straightened his back and smiled toward her. "And good luck today, Tak-Ming," she called softly. "I'll be back this evening. I hope we will have many reasons to share a bottle of champagne."

She turned on a heel, tying the cape securely at her neck, and after its hood was in place she stepped out into the cold, brisk breeze of mid-morning.

The air had a definite smell of snow to it and somehow

this made Lee-lee realize just how lonely she was, knowing that those days with Tak-Ming in the snow were in the past and that now everything he shared would be with his wife, Koo-See. It made Lee-lee all the more alone in the world, this absence of sharing. It didn't matter that she was now continuously surrounded by beautiful things that were all her own to enjoy in whatever manner that she pleased. "Things" were not a good remedy for loneliness.

She boarded her private carriage and traveled the streets to her office, surrounded by a strange aura of dejection she attributed to her loss of Timothy. What was it about her that always sent Timothy away from her? He had seemed sincere in his love for her, yet he always left her without . . . even . . . a . . . good-bye.

Relieved to reach her place of business, Lee-lee hurried up the six flights of stairs and into her office, hoping that paper work would be her escape. Dennis McCaffree had taught her well enough how to enter the correct figures into the ledgers.

But once settled in her office, hearing the extreme silence all about her, the loneliness became overwhelming. She didn't even have a secretary with whom to have private, womanly chats. Soon she would have to find a replacement for Richard's secretary who Lee-lee had fired the first day she had taken on her duties as the owner of Taylor Shipbuilders.

Tossing her cape over the back of a chair, Lee-lee took up her usual morning vigil by the window to study the moored ships at the quay. Two months had passed without her seeing the black hull with the name *New*

Yorker painted boldly in white on its side. She had to wonder what adventure Timothy was enjoying without her.

Slowly scanning the ships, having trouble focusing because of the gloomy gray of the day, she once more earnestly searched for the *New Yorker*, yet felt it a hopeless gesture on her part. But then something grabbed at her insides. She stepped closer to the window and leaned against its sill, breathless, to take a better look.

"Oh, heart be still," she whispered, placing a hand over her nervously pounding heart. "I cannot care this much that I see his ship moored at the quay this day. He does not care for me. How can my love for him still be so strong?"

A noise behind Lee-lee—the sound of her door opening—drew her quickly around. Her eyes grew wide, her pulse raced, and her knees took on a strange weakness when she saw Timothy standing in the doorway with his one hand still firmly gripping the doorknob.

"Lee-lee?" Timothy said hoarsely, a thick, dark eyebrow cocked, showing his obvious surprise.

Seeing his surprise made Lee-lee stiffen and her jaw firmly set. If he hadn't known she would be there, he hadn't come purposely to see her. Well, she would show him that she didn't care. She had her pride to protect, though all the while she would be aching to run into his arms and be kissed a thousand times by him.

Trying her best to make herself businesslike and aloof, she went to her desk and settled down behind it in her thickly cushioned leather chair. She opened a ledger and began to thumb through its pages. "And what can I do for you, sir?" she said icily, refusing to look up at him. Her eyes would betray her as her heart continually did. She would not fall into another trap which would give him the opportunity to love her then leave her again!

Lee-lee heard his heavy footsteps approaching her, and then she saw his hands on the desk and knew that he was leaning down close to her. There was no denying the familiar scent of him—cigars and expensive male cologne. She could even hear the harshness of his breath and wondered if his annoyance was because she was ignoring him or because he cared that she was. No matter. She forced herself to continue to ignore him.

"Lee-lee, what are you doing here?" Timothy asked, her nearness, her loveliness almost swallowing him whole in feelings that were invading his senses. He did not want to love her. Yet while away from her, he had only been half a person.

Lee-lee sighed exasperatedly. "Timothy, what does it look like? I am busy at work," she said, now trying to look as though she were studying a page of figures yet seeing nothing but his shadow darkening them. Her gaze hungrily followed the outline of him, seeing in it his powerful build, his handsome tallness. To be kissed by him again would surely be the same as placing her feet inside heaven's golden gates. Yet she couldn't afford such a fantasy, because she wouldn't allow it to happen.

"Work?" he gasped. "Are you trying to tell me that you now run the company? That you've taken your brother's place?"

"*Ai.*"

"Calvin didn't tell me this," he growled.

"I'm sure Calvin Hoots doesn't know," she said dryly. "We have not yet had the opportunity to meet to discuss business."

Timothy laughed. "I'm sure he knows," he said. "My dear, I think we've been set up."

Lee-lee moved her eyes slowly upward. "Set up? What do you mean?" she asked softly, now wishing she hadn't looked into his eyes, for she was slowly becoming lost again. There was no stopping the sensuous melting of her insides or the passion that was crowding out her need to ignore him.

Timothy straightened his back and walked to the window to stare from it, to escape the honey-brown of her eyes . . . eyes which haunted his every breathing moment. "Calvin pretended to be too ill to come here today to transact business for a much-needed new ship," he said thickly, clasping his hands tightly behind him. "He sent me here in his place."

Lee-lee swiveled her chair around to look toward him. "Why would he do that, Timothy?" she asked, fearing the answer. She couldn't allow him to play games with her heart again, and his attitude had all the signs of the beginning of a plan to do so.

Timothy couldn't hold back his feelings any longer. All the while he was at sea this last time, he had felt a fool for having given her up to the Chinaman so easily. One other time he had decided to fight for her and had walked away from her when the going had become rough. But now . . . now that he was with her again, thanks to the maneuvering of Calvin, he knew that he'd be damned if he'd walk away from such a fight again. He would . . . he could not allow anyone else to have her.

He turned on a heel and boldly faced her. "Why? Because he knew that you were here and would be the one I would talk business with," he said huskily.

Lee-lee knew that she was outwardly trembling and hated herself for such weakness. "And why would that mean anything to you or Calvin?" she asked icily. "Was it because Calvin did not wish to deal with a lady? Did he not think me capable of knowing how? Did he believe that our relationship—yours and mine, Timothy— would make it possible for you not to have to pay so much for a new ship?"

Timothy went to Lee-lee and bent over her, placing a forefinger beneath her chin. "You know that isn't the reason," he said. "Calvin recognized my dark mood and suspected the cause right away. You see, he's a very alert friend as well as an adept business partner. He knew my deep feelings for you that first time he saw us together."

Lee-lee swallowed hard, not wanting to be his loving prisoner again. She very casually brushed his hand aside and rose from her chair. She walked across the room, needing to put space between them.

"I still don't understand," she said. "Feelings should not enter into a business transaction."

She turned to face him, needing to show authority in her office. "What type of ship are you in need of, Timothy? All in my employ can build you a ship that can match the strength of your *New Yorker*."

"It is the *New Yorker* that needs replacing," Timothy said, lowering his eyes. "She was not performing correctly on this latest voyage of mine. Seems the last trip around the Horn inflicted more serious damage than I had thought."

Placing her hands to her throat, Lee-lee softly gasped. "The *New Yorker*?" she said. "You are taking it out of commission? Timothy, that is your favorite ship."

Timothy took quick, wide steps toward her and clasped her shoulders. "I do not wish to discuss ships," he said thickly. "I wish only to speak of my feelings for you."

Lee-lee's knees became rubbery and the sweet pain between her thighs was certainly due to his closeness. "Timothy, your initial reason for coming here was to discuss business matters. You had no thoughts of me until you saw me here. Please unhand me. We've ships to discuss. Nothing else."

"By God, you're going to listen to what I have to say and it has nothing to do with ships," he growled.

"So, it is love . . . your feelings for me, you wish to discuss?" Lee-lee said bitterly, squirming away from him.

"Yes. I have such a need to do that, Lee-lee."

"And the reason you left me again, Timothy? You plan also to explain that to me?"

"Yes."

"And you do not plan to discuss business matters at all while here in my office?"

"No. Not at all."

Lee-lee went and drew her cape up from where she had laid it. "Then since you do not wish to speak of business matters, I will bring this meeting to a close," she said, flinging the cape around her shoulders.

"What?" Timothy gasped.

Without blinking her eyes, though quite heavy in heart, Lee-lee stared blankly up at him. "How many times do you expect me to fall back into your arms after you leave me with a confused, broken heart?" she hissed. "Timothy, it is I who now leaves *you*."

Running from the room, numb with despair, Lee-lee stifled a sob, knowing that she was right to do this thing. She was not one to be used as a pawn, whether in business or matters of the heart.

Rushing out of the building toward her waiting carriage, she became aware of the soft crystals of snow falling and melting on her face. Oh, the loneliness! It was unbearable now.

Chapter Thirty-One

The news of the birth of Tak-Ming's and Koo-See's daughter had helped to raise Lee-lee out of the depression caused by her clash with Timothy earlier in the day. She had taken refuge in her many-roomed mansion after so abruptly leaving Timothy standing in her office, and now her hurt was deeper, as she puzzled over why he hadn't followed her to question her about her refusal to listen to him.

It hadn't been in her plan for him to come after her, but the fact that he didn't was enough proof that his feelings for her were not sincere.

But why, oh, why did he persist in telling her these untruths? Did he enjoy toying with her emotions? Did he do this often, to other women?

Perhaps it was a game he enjoyed playing, inflicting wounds in a woman's delicate heart.

"I must hurry," she said aloud, glancing toward the window of her bedroom, seeing the monstrous flakes of snow bouncing from it. "The snow cannot stop me from seeing my adoptive niece. Ah, I do feel like a true aunt!"

"Aunt . . . Lee-lee," she whispered, mouthing the words slowly, testing and liking the way they sounded.

It hadn't seemed to matter to Tak-Ming that his first born had been a daughter. To have his child born and healthy had been all that was important to him. And Koo-See! Surely she would be radiant with happiness!

Smiling, Lee-lee posed before a mirror, admiring her new woolen suit in its beige twill design. On such a cold, blustery evening, the warmth of the wool suit would be welcome, and it didn't look all that bad either.

She placed her hands on her hips, slowly turning, admiring her image in the mirror. The smart cut of the suit accentuated the smallness of her waist, nipping in narrowly, even helping to show the sensuous flare of her hips. The curve of her breasts was more in evidence because of the double-breasted, pointed front of the suit jacket, and the long taper of its sleeves was set off by a soft cuff of dark brown velvet which matched the collar fitted snugly to her neck.

Lee-lee flipped her hair back from her shoulders, to let it hang long and free down her back. It seemed like red satin, perfumed with only a trace of oil that had been applied to make its luster breathtakingly unique.

"I learned much from the Chinese of ways to be more beautiful," she murmured. "The shine and smell of the hair is one that I choose to use, even though I am in America. Perhaps I will begin a new trend among the American ladies."

Her mind slowly drifted to Timothy and how he had seemed to enjoy burrowing his nose into her hair, usually immediately before or after they had made love. She could even now feel the warmth of his breath on her neck . . . she could feel the pounding of his heart against her bare flesh . . . and she could smell his manliness.

All these things remembered so vividly were pure torture to her. She simply had to busy herself, to place him totally from her mind!

"The baby. Tak-Ming. In their presence I can forget," she said.

She wriggled into her cape, carefully covering her hair with its hood, and fled from her bedroom down two flights of steps until she was walking past a wall lined with family portraits. It hurt her to look at them, for Richard's had been added to the grouping just prior to his death.

She hoped that one day she could forget their last troubled meeting. It had not been one of affection as it should have been between a brother and sister reunited after ten years of separation.

She also hoped that somehow he knew that she hadn't wanted him to die, that she hadn't wanted all of the family fortune. She had truly been satisfied with half.

Shaking her head, troubled by too many things at once this evening, she rushed on beneath the cut-glass chandelier that hung overhead, huge and glistening. On all sides of her the rooms leaped with light from gas fixtures and candles in holders, and the very dark mahogany furnishings shimmered enticingly.

Fires burned in fireplaces in each room, and an aroma of fresh wallpaper and enameled wall trim hung heavy in the air due to her remodeling. Brightly covered upholstered divans and chairs had been her choice to erase all of Richard's decor, which had mainly consisted of drab blacks.

Walking silently over the thickly carpeted floor, Lee-lee went outside where the coachman in his top hat sat patiently waiting for her on the outside carriage seat. She glanced up and saw the fine trimming of snow on his hat and shoulders and felt somewhat guilty for having taken so long. She had sent word to him at least thirty minutes before that he was to ready the carriage for her. But her thoughts had slowed her, and there was no way to explain that to a man who was only hired to transport her from place to place.

"Thomas, take me to Tak-Ming's," she said, holding her hood down over her eyes to protect them from the persistent, falling snow. "*Nay*. I should have said take me to Tak-Ming's Yeung Chinese Palace. That has a better ring to it, don't you think?"

Lee-lee's eyebrows lifted when she heard what sounded like a grunt from Thomas, which was strangely unlike him. But she had to believe that it was because he was annoyed at having to wait in the cold longer than he would have liked.

She shrugged and climbed into the carriage, shaking snow from her cape as she eased down onto the seat. And when the carriage lurched and began moving away from Washington Square, Lee-lee pushed the hood from her head then settled herself as comfortably in the carriage as was possible with the coldness of the air seeping in around the door and window sending chills across her flesh.

Looking from the window, Lee-lee saw the snow-covered streets and walks and how it beautifully laced the trees.

Lee-lee's eyes widened. "Trees?" she gasped. "I shouldn't be seeing trees. By now, I should be seeing buildings. Where on earth is Thomas taking me? He knows where Tak-Ming's restaurant is."

More confused than annoyed, Lee-lee opened a window and hung her head from it, battling the snow falling on her lashes and in her mouth. "Thomas, where are you going?" she shouted. "Has the snow caused you to lose your way? Thomas, you are more skilled than that!"

When he didn't answer her and instead yelled harshly to the horses and raised a whip to their backs, Lee-lee became angry. She clung to the door and once more shouted at him.

"Stop this carriage at once! Do you hear me, Thomas? If you don't, you shall be finding employment elsewhere!"

She felt the wheels of the carriage dangerously slipping and sliding over the snow, causing her anger to change to fear. Had Thomas suddenly gone mad? This was not at all like him!

After closing the window, she eased back on her seat and clung desperately to it, fearing the carriage would soon overturn in its fast speed on the snow. Her heart pounded and her mouth went dry as the carriage began traveling alongside the waters of the bay. This was a secluded spot, hardly traveled by anyone. What did Thomas have on his mind? She had thought him an upright enough citizen to keep in her employ after Richard's death. But perhaps his devotion to Richard was causing this crazed moment of his. Perhaps he thought her responsible for Richard's death and now he was going to do away with her, to avenge that death!

Such a thought caused fear to completely engulf her and it seemed to be strangling her, for her throat had now gone totally dry and her pulse was racing out of control.

Then suddenly the carriage lunged sideways in an effort to stop. Lee-lee closed her eyes tightly as she felt the carriage sliding, almost toppling over, then coming to a shuddering halt.

Letting out a quivering sigh, she slowly opened her eyes as she heard the carriage door being thrown widely open. She had no idea what to expect next. It would be so simple for Thomas to jerk her from the carriage and throw her into the bay. Or would . . . he . . . rape her first?

The aroma of cigars and expensive male cologne entered the carriage before the man. Lee-lee's insides splashed warm, knowing these smells. Somehow Timothy was there to save her from whatever harm Thomas had planned for her. But how?

Timothy climbed quickly into the carriage with Lee-lee, closing the door behind him.

Lee-lee was only barely breathing, understanding none of what was happening, but relieved to at least feel that her life was in no danger of being taken from her.

"Timothy, I don't understand," she said, now recognizing that the clothes he was wearing were the same as those she had seen on Thomas. The snow-trimmed top hat . . . the dark suit, with dots of snow along its shoulders . . .

She scooted to the edge of the seat, looking around Timothy. "Thomas. Where is he?" she asked, eyes wide.

"He was easily bribed," Timothy chuckled, removing the top hat. He tapped it against a knee, spraying snow to the carriage floor.

Lee-lee blanched. "Bribed? What do you mean, bribed?"

"I paid him well to take his place this evening," Timothy said matter-of-factly. "It was easily enough done when I arrived in your drive and saw him sitting there waiting for you in the snow."

"You? In my drive?"

"The snow muffled my arrival."

"Timothy, why did you come?" she asked dryly, scooting away from him, remembering so much from earlier in the day. She couldn't make a mistake with him again. It was too hard to forget his kisses . . . his embraces.

"So much was left unsaid this morning," he said, placing Thomas's hat on the seat beside him.

"I've nothing more to say to you," she stubbornly argued. "Unless, of course, your reason for further conversation is for purchasing a ship from my company."

"Money? Is that all that's important to you?" he growled. "Was your interest in me from the beginning because of the wealth I represented as well as for securing passage to America for both you and Tak-Ming on my *New Yorker*?"

Lee-lee blinked her eyes nervously, not believing what she was hearing. "What on earth are you implying?" she gasped. "Is this why you have further need to talk with me? To . . . to . . . insult me? I am not one who schemes or uses. How dare you, Timothy Hendricks!"

She opened the carriage door at her side, jumped to the ground, and began running through the snow, tears stinging her cheeks as they rushed from her eyes, turning instantly cold against her flesh. From the beginning had he thought her capable of such loathsome tactics? Why, she had kept hidden from him her true desire to flee to America, because of her lack of trust in *him*.

When had he begun to doubt her then, if not from the beginning? Then she had her answer. Each time he had left her without a good-bye, she had most surely, unknowingly given him a reason.

"Lee-lee, stop!" Timothy yelled, now following her in the snow. "Surely we've misunderstood each other all along! Darling, please stop. Let's talk it all out. I can't live without you. Lee-lee! You . . . must . . . marry me! Tonight! Tomorrow! Whenever you choose! Just say that you will!"

Hearing his pleas and his renewed proposal of marriage made Lee-lee's heart skip several beats. She stopped to turn, but as she did her feet gave way beneath her in the slippery surface and she lunged, face forward, into the snow. Screaming, she threw her arms up to protect her face from the fall then felt the impact as she clumsily sprawled into the soft cushion of the snow.

Embarrassed and aching, she pushed herself up to a sitting position just as Timothy arrived to assist her. But as he placed his hands at her waist, he also lost his footing and he fell clumsily over her, pinning her to the ground beneath him.

"Ouch!" Lee-lee screamed, pushing at his chest. "Timothy, you're mashing me!"

Never having felt so awkward in his life, Timothy fell away from her and stretched out on his back in the snow, laughing fitfully at himself.

Lee-lee rose on an elbow to look down at him, bewildered. "Timothy, why do you continue to lie there in the snow? And what do you find so funny? I surely don't feel like laughing!"

With his chin quivering and his eyes watering, his laughter died, yet he continued to smile up at Lee-lee with a sudden mischievous glint in his eyes. He lunged up after her and grabbed her, throwing her back into the snow and kissing her ardently as he stretched out atop her.

His hand searched under her cape and found the swell of her breast that lay carefully guarded beneath the heavy woolen fabric, yet just touching it in any way was enough to set his loins afire.

With Lee-lee's nerve endings screaming for his touch, she closed her eyes, twined her arms about his neck, and drew his lips even harder against hers. Her head was beginning to spin and her heart to pound fiercely. And when his tongue probed between her teeth, she welcomed it and sighed in passion as his free hand crept up the inside of her skirt and underthings and found her open and ready for his fingers to enter her between her thighs.

A foghorn from somewhere in the distance broke through the silence. Lee-lee's eyes flew widely open. She became quickly aware of the cold, wet snow in which her hair was spread like a brilliant red halo and of the coldness where the wet snow had seeped through to her skin.

She loosened her arms from about Timothy's neck and once more began shoving at his chest. When his lips set hers free and his hands crept away from her, she felt a bit foolish for having given in to his romantic whims so easily.

"Timothy, please get up," she pleaded softly. "This is very crazy. I'm becoming quite soaked and I'm freezing."

"It is because our passion is so heated we've melted the very snow around us," he chuckled, helping her up from the ground, yet still holding her, drawing her into his arms to look lovingly down into her honey-brown eyes. "I do love you, Lee-lee, and I mean to fight for you if that's what is required of me. I should have done this long ago instead of giving you up to Tak-Ming so easily."

"Tak-Ming?" Lee-lee said, shocked. "What on earth are you talking about, Timothy?"

"Your devotion to Tak-Ming. I saw that it ran deeper than you admitted. I only hoped—"

Rage overcame Lee-lee. She jerked free of his arms, glowering at him. "Are you saying that you had thought that Tak-Ming and I were . . . were . . . lovers?" she screamed. "Do you think me capable of going from your bed to his as a whore might? Timothy, you don't know me at all!"

She swung around and began walking quickly away from him, kicking angrily at the snow at her feet, hurt and humiliation eating away at her heart.

Timothy ran after her. He grabbed her by a wrist and

forced her back around to face him. "Always! Always Tak-Ming was uppermost in your mind," he growled, leaning down into her face. "What else was I to think?"

"Not that I would go to bed with two men," she cried softly. "Surely you knew that I wouldn't."

"No. I didn't want to think that," he said. "But your devotion was so strong. It cut me deep to know you cared so much for him."

"But I've always only thought of him as my brother," she whispered, lowering her eyes. "Nothing more, Timothy. You shame me so with your thoughts."

"Can you deny that he doesn't think of you in ways stronger than that of a sister?" he said, lessening his grip on her wrist. "Have you been so blind that you could not see how he truly felt about you? Didn't he even once approach you to declare such feelings to you? Didn't you see how he looked at you?"

"*Nay*," she murmured. "Never! He has treated me quite honorably. You are wrong, Timothy. He has never thought of me other than as a sister."

A thought suddenly struck Lee-lee. "Timothy, all those times you left me? Was it because of your suspicions of Tak-Ming?"

"I was wrong. I am sorry," he said. He framed her face between his hands and placed a soft kiss on her lips. "Am I forgiven? More than once my jealousy blinded me from the truth."

"How do I know that you truly understand my feelings toward Tak-Ming now? Have you, indeed, been able to separate sisterly devotion and love in your mind, as far as Tak-Ming and I are concerned?"

"I hope that I have."

"Until I know that you have, I could not relax in our love, Timothy. I would always wonder what you were thinking when Tak-Ming and I shared a friendly embrace."

Just the thought of this happening caused renewed jealousy to tear at his heart, and he doubted that he could learn to live with the picture of them together, even if only for a moment. Though Lee-lee hadn't known of Tak-Ming's deeper feelings for her, Timothy had. It had only taken seeing them together once to see the desire for her in Tak-Ming's eyes.

"Time, Lee-lee. You would have to give me time," he murmured.

"I can be patient," she sighed. "Just as long as I can be sure you'd never leave me again."

Seeing the layer of snow on her hair and shoulders and even lacing her long, thick lashes, Timothy chuckled and scooped her up into his arms and carried her to the carriage. Once inside and with her huddled snugly into his arms, he asked the question that had been plaguing him.

"I can only promise you that I will never leave you again if you say that you love me, truly and fully love me," he said hoarsely, cupping her chin in his hands, directing her eyes upward to his.

"*Ai*, I do," she whispered, placing a hand to his flushed cheek, feeling the heat of his flesh beneath the outer layer of cold. "I've always loved you. I don't see how you didn't know this. Didn't I always show you in a thousand ways when we were together?"

"Yes. And that made it all the harder to leave you each time that I did."

"Kiss me now, darling," Lee-lee said, placing a hand behind his head to weave her fingers through his hair. She drew his lips to hers, giggling as she felt their utter coldness.

Then she warmed up against him as his hands crept beneath her cape and sensuously circled a breast through the woolen fabric of her suit. She moaned as he urged her downward onto the seat.

"Not here . . ." she was finally able to whisper as his lips became only butterfly touches, first on her lashes, then her cheeks, and the lobes of her ears. "Darling, I need you with a passion, but no matter how much you set me aglow inside, it's hard to forget just how cold it is in this carriage."

"Then we shall return the carriage to your coachman and then, my love, you can show me to your bedroom," Timothy said, helping her up from the seat.

"I must do something else first," she said, straightening the lines of her suit and then her hair.

"What could be more important than being alone together, making love? It's been too long, Lee-lee."

Lee-lee's eyes wavered, hating to tell him where she was expected, yet wouldn't telling him be a true test of his understanding of her and Tak-Ming's relationship? *Wei!* To even think that Timothy suspected that Tak-Ming loved her in that way! How utterly ridiculous and wrong Timothy had been!

"Tak-Ming is expecting me," she said in a rush of words, flinching when she saw his jaw suddenly set and

476

his face take on a somber appearance.

"Tak-Ming?"

"*Ai.*"

"Ah, yes, I do remember you instructing me to take you there when you mistook me for your coachman. Didn't you make mention of a . . . uh . . . Tak-Ming's Yeung Chinese Palace?"

"*Ai.* He now is the proud owner of a Chinese restaurant in Chinatown."

"Oh, I see," Timothy said coolly. "And does he . . . eh . . . make residence, also, in Chinatown?"

Lee-lee couldn't suppress a giggle. If Timothy suspected that Tak-Ming lived with her, oh, how much he had to learn! "*Ai,* he does," she said.

She wouldn't tell him of Koo-See and the baby just yet. She had other plans! She would *show* him!

"Come," she encouraged, taking him by the hand. She opened the carriage door and stepped out into the snow. "You must go with me to Tak-Ming's."

"Why should I?" Timothy grumbled, following her from the carriage.

"Darling, I want to show you, once and for all, that your jealousies are unfounded."

He studied her expression, seeing a mischievous gleam in her eyes. "I don't guess it could hurt to see what you are referring to," he said. "All right. I'll go with you. Just tell me where, then you get back inside the carriage, out of the weather."

"*Nay,*" she said, tilting her chin stubbornly. "I want to ride alongside you. I want to let everyone see my future husband of whom I am so proud."

"You'll freeze . . ."

"No more than you," she argued softly.

Timothy laughed. "Yes. You're right, darling. How could I ever forget that your fiery spirit makes you different from most women. You? You are, indeed, a survivor!"

He climbed up on the seat beside her, accepting how she snuggled up against his right side. He took up the reins and shouted to the horses, yet all the while dreading seeing Tak-Ming again, for fear of being swallowed whole by his jealousy.

Lee-lee clung to him, smiling coyly. She could hardly wait to see Timothy's expression when he was introduced to Tak-Ming's wife and shown their newborn daughter.

Chapter Thirty=Two

The click of chopsticks and the low drone of voices were left behind them as Lee-lee and Timothy began climbing the staircase at the far end of Tak-Ming's restaurant's main dining hall. Lee-lee held her cape draped over an arm and Timothy was nervously turning his top hat round and round in his hands.

"I wish you would explain why you insist that we do this," Timothy whispered harshly, barely able to see Lee-lee in the dark shadows of the staircase. The aromas of fried foods were overwhelming in these closer quarters, and they seemed to cling to his every pore.

"Just be patient," Lee-lee whispered back to him. "We're just about there."

She glanced over at Timothy, only able to see his outline, but that was enough to see his powerful build, and, oh, wasn't it one that she adored? She could hardly believe that they had finally ironed out their differences. And to imagine that Timothy had thought that she and Tak-Ming . . . !

Nay. She wouldn't think about his wrong accusations.

479

She wouldn't let anything spoil an evening so filled with the promise of a beautiful future together.

Yet, what Timothy had said about Tak-Ming having more than brotherly feelings for her was deeply puzzling. Was there a fraction of truth in what Timothy had pointed out . . . ? Shaking her head, she made herself believe that even in that assumption, surely Timothy also had to be wrong.

Timothy placed his arm about Lee-lee's waist as they reached the upstairs landing where only a small foyer led to three opened doors. A brightly colored lantern was burning softly overhead, casting a shadowed red glow from its shade along the walls and doorways, and, hearing a soft, sweet, voice Lee-lee guided Timothy into the room from which it had come.

Stepping into a softer light where candles flickered faintly from beside a low bed where Koo-See lay covered with a pale blue *beiwu* and with a small bundle tucked snugly next to her, Lee-lee's heart warmed, and she was glad that she had chosen to bring Timothy here to also witness the serene sight of mother, father, and child. Tak-Ming was kneeling down beside the bed, smiling, even more handsome in his pride as he gently stroked Koo-See's pale cheek.

Lee-lee smiled coyly as she looked up to see the surprise in Timothy's eyes.

Timothy was in a state of semi-shock, seeing Tak-Ming with what surely had to be his wife and child! The Chinaman was married!

Timothy gave Lee-lee a quizzical look.

"*Ai*," she whispered. "I have brought you to show you

how wrong you were about Tak-Ming. You see he is happily wed, and he is now a new father.''

"Why didn't you tell me, Lee-lee?"

"Earlier, I didn't know that it mattered to you that he had a wife—a wife whom he took even while we were in San Francisco," she said. "And only tonight when I discovered that it did matter, I wanted you to see . . ."

Timothy wanted to say that seeing wasn't always believing, for he still felt that even though Tak-Ming had taken a wife, it didn't mean that he didn't love Lee-lee. Instead, he kept his feelings to himself.

Tak-Ming's eyes shifted upward when he heard footsteps enter the room. His smile slowly faded when he turned and saw the American businessman standing there with Lee-lee, so possessive as he held her close to him with an arm about her waist. Not only was this confusing to Tak-Ming, but also the fact that the American was with her at all! She hadn't spoken of him in months. It was hard to accept that they were now together, obviously happy in one another's presence.

Then Tak-Ming was overcome by guilt. He had all a man could want! He had a wife. He had a newborn daughter. And perhaps a son would be the next born of his union with his wife. *Ai*, he had wanted a son first, but that truly did not matter now that he had looked upon the face of his tiny daughter, his Mei-King.

Slowly rising to his feet, Tak-Ming moved quietly toward Lee-lee. He ignored Timothy's presence by talking only to Lee-lee. "You have come," he murmured, humbly bowing. "*Hao. Ai*, that is good, adopted sister Lee-lee."

"I hope you don't mind that I have brought Timothy with me, Tak-Ming," Lee-lee said, having noticed how Tak-Ming was purposely avoiding looking toward Timothy.

Then she stiffened, glancing from Timothy to Tak-Ming. Had Timothy been right after all? Was this coolness toward Timothy because Tak-Ming was . . . jealous?

Then she looked toward the bed where Koo-See smiled softly back at her. There was full proof that Timothy had to be wrong. Tak-Ming's wife . . . Tak-Ming's child.

"Why have you brought him here at such a private time which should be shared only by family?" Tak-Ming growled, casting Timothy a sour glance.

Lee-lee's eyes wavered, hearing the bitterness in his words. "Tak-Ming, do you remember this morning when we were talking about sharing champagne, looking forward to the many things we would celebrate?" she asked, watching his eyes for any more signs of jealousy and desperately hoping that Timothy was wrong. But now, in Tak-Ming's presence, wasn't she recalling the many times Tak-Ming had been too possessive of her?

"*Ai*," Tak-Ming said, nodding. "I do." He turned his eyes toward the bed. "And as you can see, we have true reason to celebrate."

Lee-lee was dying to see the child, yet she knew she must first untangle this resentment between the two men she loved most in the world.

She reached her free hand to cover Timothy's, which rested on her hip. "Well, Tak-Ming, we have something else of importance to celebrate," she said, laughing softly.

Tak-Ming's eyebrows lifted. "*Ai*? And that is?"

"Tak-Ming, you are soon to have an adopted *brother-in-law*," Lee-lee giggled, looking adoringly up into Timothy's eyes. Her happiness lessened when she saw that Timothy wasn't any more pleased with this situation than Tak-Ming. Between the two of them, there seemed to be much mistrust and possibly even hate. But that couldn't be. She wanted them to be friends, to have respect for each other.

Tak-Ming paled. He took a quick step backward. "*Nay*," he insisted. "You are not telling me that you are going to marry this . . . this . . . American businessman."

Lee-lee felt her heart skip a beat. "*Ai*, I am," she murmured. "And why should I not?"

"It has been such a short time that you have enjoyed your freedom from China. Why would you want to imprison yourself, in yet another way so soon, Lee-lee?" Tak-Ming growled, his eyes dark, his face shadowed with anger.

Lee-lee stepped away from Timothy, her shoulders squared determinedly. "Tak-Ming, you also have only recently gained freedom by coming to America, and you have chosen not to live alone for the same reason I have," she said stubbornly. "Do you not have a wife? Do you not have a child? Do you wish that I remain alone, not to be able to enjoy such companionship?"

Shame entered Tak-Ming's heart, fueled by guilt. "I

was not thinking," he confessed, lowering his eyes. "*Ai*. You would want these things. How could I be so selfish in not wanting you to have them?"

"Then, Tak-Ming, you do understand?"

"*Ai* . . ."

"Can you and Timothy be friends?" she asked, her heart pounding hard, seeing so much that she hadn't wanted to see in Tak-Ming's eyes. There was a deep hurt. And she knew that she had been the one responsible for its infliction.

Ai, Timothy had been right. Why hadn't she seen it? Felt it? Oh, how she loved Tak-Ming, but only as a brother.

Tak-Ming's dark, almond-shaped eyes moved to absorb Timothy's presence. "You will be good to my adopted sister?" he growled.

Timothy saw Lee-lee's expression and knew that she finally understood about Tak-Ming, and he was glad. That would make it easier now to accept Tak-Ming, for Lee-lee didn't show signs of loving him back in the way a woman shows love for a man.

He stepped to Lee-lee's side and once more draped an arm about her waist. "Tak-Ming, there is not a thing to worry about as far as your adopted sister is concerned," he said thickly. "I will make her happy as well as see to it that she doesn't feel imprisoned while living with me, as my wife."

He looked down at Lee-lee, whose honey-brown eyes were brimming with tears. "I promise you that, Lee-lee," he whispered.

"And you love this man with all of your heart, Lee-

lee?" Tak-Ming asked, moving his eyes to capture her full attention.

Lee-lee couldn't help but beam with her answer. "*Ai*, Tak-Ming," she said proudly. "More than life itself, it seems."

Tak-Ming looked boldly back at Timothy. "And you do promise to make her happy? Only by hearing that you will, can I approve of such a marriage for my adopted sister."

"I will see to it that she is happy in every way," Timothy said hoarsely.

Lee-lee watched as Tak-Ming went to Koo-See to kneel down beside her, take her hand in his and softly kiss it. The hurt was no longer in his eyes. There was only love and affection for his wife. It seemed to Lee-lee that her confession of love for Timothy had somehow broken Tak-Ming loose from his ties with her—ties that somehow had been tangled along the way when love had entered into his heart in the guise of romantic feelings for her. In a way, it had set *her* free as well.

"How could I ever be as happy as at this moment?" she finally said, sighing. Then she grabbed Timothy by the hand. "And, Timothy, let's see my niece! Surely she is as beautiful as both her mother and father!"

Chapter Thirty-Three

The champagne bottle sat open on the nightstand. Lee-lee let the last of her clothes flutter to the floor, watching Timothy as he stepped from his trousers. "And, Timothy, what do you think of my Washington Square mansion now that I've given you the grand tour?" she asked, giddy from the many glasses of champagne she and Timothy had shared with Tak-Ming before saying their good-byes at his restaurant, and from the one glass she had emptied only moments ago here in her bedroom.

"I would say between the two of us, with both our houses, we have enough room to raise many children," he said, going to Lee-lee to pull the curve of her body against his.

Lee-lee's eyes widened. "Children, Timothy?" she murmured. "Never before have you spoken of children."

"Don't you want children, Lee-lee?"

"*Ai*. But why speak of them now?"

"*Mei-King*," he sighed. "Isn't she a darling? I've never seen such a tiny baby before. And she is perfect in every way."

Lee-lee giggled. "She affected me in the same way,"

she said. "I just didn't think you would want to think of children for ourselves so soon."

"Tak-Ming is very lucky, Lee-lee."

"And also Koo-See."

"And also myself," Timothy said, scooping her up and into his arms. "My darling, how can we even think of children, when we are using this bedroom only for talk?"

Lee-lee clung to his neck. "I'm sure you have the solution to that," she said, already drifting on her cloud of rapture, with him so definitely hers now, for forever. . . .

His eyes swept over her in a silent answer as he placed her ever so gently on the bed. Her every pleasure point became his as he pressed his lips against the sweetness of her flesh.

Lee-lee's eyes hazed over with passion, as she reached to run her fingers over the expanse of his sleekly muscled shoulders.

As his lips moved over hers possessively, she surrendered to him fully. She moaned as with one hand he kneaded a breast, causing the golden flames of desire to rise higher inside her, while his other hand ran from her thigh to her hip and then to her other breast.

His lips slipped down to a breast and fastened gently over it, sucking sensuously on her hardened nipple, teasingly nipping it with his teeth.

Sweeping her hands over Timothy's cheek in a gentle caress, she watched as his eyes rose to meet hers.

"Timothy, I want you," she whispered. "Fill me, darling."

"My little vixen," Timothy chuckled, placing his strong thighs against her legs as he positioned himself over her.

He traced the line of her jaw with his thumb. "I hope you are always this warm blooded. I will always hurry home to be with you."

"Timothy, how can you if you will be traveling the high seas?" she pouted softly.

"My love for you is much stronger than my love for the sea," he said huskily. "I'm sure something can be arranged so that I can spend most of my time on land."

"But is that really your wish, Timothy? You have always confessed to such a profound love for the sea."

"My wish is to be with you. Now why argue that? Unless . . ."

"Unless what, Timothy?"

"Unless you'd rather I still be the man I was—totally a seaman."

Lee-lee rose up on an elbow. "Why would I?" she murmured. Then her face shadowed with concern. For a while she had thought he had understood about Tak-Ming. Was there still more doubt troubling him?

"Perhaps you enjoy being a lady with corporate decisions facing you each day. Do you fear that I will stand in the way of this new life you've found at Taylor Shipbuilders?"

Lee-lee's shoulders relaxed, relieved that Tak-Ming's name had not entered into this conversation. "*Nay*," she laughed softly. "Taking on the responsibilities of my company was only a means to put you from my mind."

"Oh? Was that required? Did you have me on your mind all that much?"

"*Ai*," she murmured. "From the moment I first set

eyes on you, darling."

"You were such an amusing sight dressed as a coolie," he chuckled.

"Timothy! I thought that you had been taken with *me*, not my disguise!"

He framed her face between his hands. "My darling, it was your eyes," he whispered, kissing one eye closed and then the other. "Those gorgeous . . . honey . . . brown eyes."

With a passion he crushed his lips against hers and swiftly entered her, experiencing a delicious shiver of desire as he felt her warm moistness wrap itself around his throbbing hardness.

Lee-lee could feel his animal heat and lifted her hips to meet him in silent answer to his demands. She twined her arms about his neck, breathing hard as his lips set her free, so that he could burrow his nose into the thickness of her hair.

"Oh, how I love you," she whispered, clinging.

Her lips quivered with intense feelings . . . her eyes closed, and she felt herself being carried away on a cloud of ecstasy. When their release came, it was a quiet explosion, fusing them together as one.

Afterward, sighing, Lee-lee raised her fingers to her hair—now damp from her efforts to give and take pleasure—and lifted it from beneath her. As she watched Timothy roll gently from her to rise from the bed and pour two glasses of champagne, she looked on past him, at the soft yellows of her room. She saw the wallpaper with the delicate yellow roses on a white background, the yellow satin drapes at the two windows, and the white lace trim on the yellow satin canopy of her magnificent four-poster bed. This was her room, just as it had been those many years ago, and it was amusing to her to have had a man in the bed that she had slept in as a child. *Ai.* Amusing . . . but wonderful!

Then a different sort of thought occurred to her. She crept from the bed and drew on a sheer, white silk robe then accepted a glass of champagne from Timothy.

Eying him with a tilt to her head, she asked, "Darling, what shall we do with two houses once we're married?"

"We shall live in one one week and the other, the next," he teased, settling down into a chair, slowly sipping his champagne.

"Timothy," Lee-lee scolded. "I'm serious. We don't need two houses. We should make a choice."

Then her eyes grew wide with the answer. She set her glass down on a table then eased to the floor, onto the plush, yellow carpet at Timothy's feet. Placing her hands on his knees, she said, "Would you mind terribly if we lived in your house?"

Timothy lifted an eyebrow. "Is that what you want?"

"*Ai.*"

"But I would have thought you would prefer to live in your own house. You were denied it for so long."

"I have other plans for my house if you will agree."

"What sorts of plans?"

"Tak-Ming," Lee-lee said quickly. "I will give it to him as a gift. You saw how he now lives—in rooms hardly large enough to turn around in."

A low gasp rose from deep inside Timothy. He very gently moved Lee-lee's hands from his knees and rose from his chair, silent.

A cold fear entered Lee-lee's heart as she watched him,

hearing his silence. He was still jealous though he knew such feelings were unfounded.

Lee-lee rose to her feet, went to him, and placed a hand on his cheek, forcing him to look down at her.

"Tell me I'm wrong," she murmured. "Tell me that your silence is not because of . . . of . . . jealousy."

"Lee-lee, that is a feeling not so easily cast aside," he grumbled. "Even now, only moments after making love, that damn Chinaman is on your mind!"

A slow anger began to rise inside Lee-lee. "I will admit that he is on my mind quite frequently," she said hotly. "But not in that way, Timothy, and you have to know that now. Why must you ruin our time together because of your lack of trust?"

"Why must you have the need to give him such an outlandish gift as a *house*?" he stormed, throwing his glass across the room where it shattered into a million pieces against the wall.

Lee-lee covered her mouth with a hand, never having witnessed Timothy in such an angry state before. If ever she had doubted his sincere love for her, she knew never to do so again. Though jealousy was ugly, it did have its lighter side when it sparked Timothy to a physical display of just how much he loved her.

Timothy turned on a heel, his face pale. He rushed to Lee-lee, drew her into his arms, and hugged her tightly to him. "I'm sorry, Lee-lee," he murmured. "I shouldn't have done that."

"Timothy, let me explain why I—"

"No. You don't need to. Do what you wish with your house. My house will become our house."

"But, Timothy, I do want to explain—"

"Please? Just forget that I made an ass of myself again?" he pleaded, raining kisses across her face.

Lee-lee was becoming passionately breathless. "But, Timothy," she argued softly. "There is more than one reason why I want to give Tak-Ming my house. It is because he needs land ownership to have acreage in which to plant his *lanmu* trees. I know my yard isn't all that large, but it will be enough for the planting of a few trees. And then he needs the many rooms to raise many children. He and Koo-See—"

Timothy stepped back away from Lee-lee with a twinkle quite visible in his eyes. "Now, wait a minute," he said. "What's this about *lanmu* trees?"

"It is a Chinese custom for all Chinese families to have a grove of such trees."

"Why?"

Lee-lee lowered her eyes and giggled softly. "You really don't wish to know."

"Yes, I do."

"For coffins, Timothy," Lee-lee blurted, watching him as his face reflected a blank look.

"Coffins?" he gasped.

"See? You didn't really want to know, did you?" She laughed, going to her wardrobe and searching inside until her fingers made contact with the sleek silk material of a dress. Talking about China and its customs had made her recall a conversation between Timothy and her not long ago. He had requested something special of her and she was now ready to comply.

She heard his intake of breath when she held her Chinese dress up before her. She laid it across the bed long enough to remove her thin gown, then watched out of the corner of her eye as Timothy slowly sank into a chair, absorbing her each and every movement.

Lee-lee slipped the silk Chinese dress over her head. It was a brilliant red with multicolored embroidered swirls across its front. She girdled the dress at the waist with a length of darker red silk, until it clung to her voluptuous figure, revealing all of her curves, especially the swell of her breasts as the silk lay so splendidly against them.

Lifting a brush, Lee-lee stroked her hair until it lay in a gorgeous red sheen across her shoulders and down her back, and all the while she continued to look seductively at Timothy with her lips slightly parted and her lashes heavy with building desire for him.

Timothy rose from his chair, went to her, and took the brush from her to give it a quick toss over his shoulder. "You're beautiful," he said huskily, placing his hands on her breasts.

"Then you prefer me without a breast binder?" she teased.

"It was a crime for you to have been forced to wear such a garment," he grumbled.

Then he chuckled as his eyes brightened. "But it did keep all other men's eyes from seeing what you possessed."

"*Ai*, it did," she giggled.

She turned the palm of her right hand up and held it out before her, to look at the scar. "And your brand, Timothy? Have you forgotten it? Wearing it surely makes me truly yours."

"To hell with the scar," he growled. "Tomorrow we will go and buy you the largest ring in New York. That is what you will display to show that you are mine."

Lee-lee laughed softly. "You will buy me two rings? One for each hand?" she teased.

"Two?" Timothy asked, lifting an eyebrow quizzically.

"*Ai.* Two," she persisted. "While in China, my serving woman, Soonya, taught me that jewelry must be worn in pairs to carry out the fundamental rule of Ying and Yang."

Timothy chuckled. "Then two rings it shall be," he said. "We musn't disappoint Ying or Yang."

Lee-lee splayed her fingers across his chest, crushing his chest hairs beneath them. She looked up into his eyes passionately. "Do you remember how I once told you my meaning of love?"

"You didn't think that I would forget?" he said, moving his hands to the curve of her hips, pulling her into the rising swell of his sex.

"Please tell me, my love," she whispered, feeling his hardness against her through the softness of her dress. "I want to hear you say it."

Timothy's eyes darkened and he quietly mouthed the words while slowly lowering his lips to hers. "Love," he murmured. "It is for . . . the . . . losing of self . . . in . . . another."

Twining his fingers through her hair, he drew her lips even harder against his, kissing her with a new intensity. For Timothy there were no more torturous thoughts of Cathalina Unser. There was no more dread of the handsome Chinaman. Now and forever, there was only Lee-lee. . . .

THE BEST IN HISTORICAL ROMANCE
by Penelope Neri

MORE RAPTUROUS READING